I0665825

THE MARRIAGE MAKER

RULES OF REFINEMENT

One Good Gentleman
Shameless
Redemption of a Marquess
A Marriage of Necessity

Scarsdale Voices

This is a Scarsdale Voices romance collection and is part of *The Marriage Maker* series written by Tarah Scott and Sue-Ellen Welfonder.

Rules of Refinement © 2018 by Scarsdale Publishing. All rights reserved. No part of this publication may be reproduced, stored in a retrieval system, or transmitted, in any form or by any means without the prior written permission of the author, nor be otherwise circulated in any form of binding or cover other than that in which it is published and without a similar condition being imposed on the subsequent purchaser.

This is a work of fiction. Names, characters, places, and incidents are either the product of the author's imagination or are used fictitiously, and any resemblance to actual persons living or dead, business establishments, events, or locales, is entirely coincidental.

One Good Gentleman The Marriage Maker Book Five: Rules of Refinement
Copyright © 2017 by Summer Hanford
All rights reserved

Shameless The Marriage Maker Book Six: Rules of Refinement
Copyright © 2017 Tarah Scott and Jennifer Elaine McCollum
All rights reserved

Redemption of a Marquess The Marriage Maker Book Seven: Rules of Refinement
Copyright © 2017 by Tarah Scott
All rights reserve

A Marriage of Necessity The Marriage Maker Book Eight: Rules of Refinement
Copyright © 2017 by Tarah Scott
All rights reserved

ISBN: 10: 0-9980815-1-5
ISBN-13: 978-0-9980815-1-9

www.scarsdalepublishing.com

Cover design by dreams2media
Editor Casey Yager

First Trade Paperback Printing by Scarsdale Publishing 2018

10 9 8 7 6 5 4 3 2

If you purchased this book without a cover, you should be aware that this book is stolen property. It was reposted as "unsold and destroyed" to the publisher, and neither the author nor the publisher has received any payment for

this "stripped book."

RULES OF REFINEMENT

Noblemen aren't always honorable... but a rake is always charming

In a narrow lane off Edinburgh's illustrious Charlotte Square, stands a town house that is not quite as impressive as nearby residences, but remains a place of distinction. An air of quiet dignity is maintained by the courtyard that fronts the street, while privacy is assured by a wrought-iron gateway. This house is Lady Peddington's School for Young Ladies and is owned and run by Lady Honoria Peddington.

Girls fortunate enough to attend the academy are instructed in all aspects of proper comportment with emphasis on the importance of a pleasing demeanor and appearance, grace and good manners, the skills a lady needs to run a large, well-to-do household, and – of course - the necessity and advantages of an impeccable reputation. Scandal, the girls are warned, must be avoided at all costs.

Lady Peddington's own reputation is the finest, and all Edinburgh considers her above reproach. She is especially well-loved by the affluent merchants and lesser gentry who live on the fringes of the city's New Town where she operates her school. These clients appreciate her knack at finding affluent husbands for their daughters. No one suspects that her knowledge of men comes from the long-ago days when she wasn't Lady Honoria Peddington, but simply Honey Pedding who ran a well-doing Glasgow brothel.

Those skills, though secret, still serve her well, for when her school's famed graduation balls fail to secure suitable husbands for some of her more high-spirited girls, other gentlemen come to the fore, eager to accept these gems as pampered mistresses. So, however a girl's heart might lean, Lady Peddington's School for Young Ladies guarantees happiness for all.

ONE GOOD GENTLEMAN

THE MARRIAGE MAKER BOOK FIVE
RULES OF REFINEMENT

SUMMER HANFORD

CHAPTER ONE

AT THE END OF each season, Lady Peddington's School for Young Ladies threw not one, or even two, but four balls over the course of four weeks. If a young woman couldn't meet the man of her dreams in that length of time, well, she'd best hope a man awaited her at home because four was the schools' more than generous limit. To Miss Emilia Glasbarr's dismay, the first of these balls was stuttering to an end, and she still lacked a suitor.

Emilia huddled near the refreshments table and tried to untangle the scene before her. Many of the girls, certainly the ones already spoken for, had retired for the evening. Those who remained, behaved with a lack of propriety that Emilia found moderately shocking. Gloves were removed. Laughter, not polite titters, sounded. Footmen had appeared to snuff out most of the candles, leaving the vast ballroom enshrouded in flickering half-light. Most disconcerting, the few instructors who still chaperone turned a blind eye. Only Emilia's desperation not to live out the remainder of her days as a country Miss kept her there. Normally, she would retreat from such a scene.

A waltz began and Emilia stifled a gasp. No respectable young woman danced the waltz. They'd been taught as much at the very school in which she stood. Gentlemen reached out, clasped ladies close. Distressed by the bedlam before her, Emilia turned away from the whirling figures. She swallowed, her throat dry, and reached for a glass of punch.

The gulp she took burned the whole way down, laced with some strong spirit. She raised incredulous eyes to the woman who oversaw the punch table, their etiquette instructor, and received a wink. Disconcerted, Emilia set out around the edge of the room, unsure what to do with the glass she held. Putting the punch down now would be ill-mannered, but she dared not drink more. The one gulp already left her dizzy.

A gentleman strode toward her. Emilia dropped her gaze demurely. She knew who he was, for the school kept miniatures of all the local nobility, and she knew he wasn't there to find a wife. He was already wed. She could only assume he came to support the school, to help Lady Peddington's students practice the art of dancing at a real social engagement, not under the eyes of an instructor.

She suppressed a sigh of disappointment that an eligible gentleman refused to appear, for well-bred ladies didn't sigh, and angled toward the wall to give him room to pass without interfering with the dancers. She stopped in surprise when he stepped in front of her. His too-strong cologne assailed her nostrils. Punch sloshed onto her gloved fingers. Her face heated at her clumsiness.

His eyes dipped toward the glass for a moment. "Partaking of Lady Peddington's famous midnight punch, I see." His accent was urbane. Dark eyes looked down at her from under oiled brown hair.

"Midnight punch?" she repeated, confused.

"No need to play coy. I love Lady Peddington's special midnight brew, and a girl who drinks it." He leaned forward as he spoke and used his six inches of superior height to look down the front of her white muslin gown.

Emilia's blush deepened. "I've only taken one sip." She almost choked on her own inanity, but what was one to say to that statement, or that look? He wasn't behaving the way they'd been taught men should behave, let alone married members of the peerage.

"You should drink up then, dear girl." He wrapped a hand around hers and lifted the glass to her lips.

Emilia was too shocked by his hand on hers to protest. She gagged as the heavily laced punch tumbled into her mouth. She choked it down, for one could hardly spit up on a viscount.

"That's better," he said when the glass was empty. He dabbed at the corners of her mouth with a glove-encased thumb.

Emilia watched him through eyes as wide as saucers. "My lord," she managed to gasp out.

His smile was pleased. "So, you know who I am?"

"Indeed, I do, Lord Ailbeart, but I'm sure we've never met, and certainly do no' know each other well enough for you to put your hands on me."

He raised thick eyebrows. "Don't we? Perhaps you would care for a bit more punch?"

"I most certainly would not." Already the room had begun a gentle spin. Emilia rarely tasted wine, and had eaten lightly, nervous for the dance. Whatever was in the punch, and she suspected scotch, had gone straight to her head.

Far from appearing offended by her rejoinder, the viscount grinned. His fingers grazed her cheek as he tugged on one of her yellow curls before letting it spring back into place. "Spirited, aren't you? I want a spirited mistress this time. The last one was too well trained. A lady can be too polished."

Emilia was doubly upset she'd consumed the punch, for she had nothing to throw in his face. "Did I hear you suggest I be your mistress, my lord?" she gritted out. She hadn't spent her entire dowry on finishing school to become this man's plaything.

"I knew I'd picked a good one in you." His grin was smug.

Emilia glared through narrowed hazel eyes. "Picked?"

"Aye. I told the other fellows, stay clear of that golden-haired beauty. She's mine." He spoke in a warm, almost sweet tone, as if praising a favored pet. His gaze roamed over her.

Emilia drew in a harsh breath, too offended to be embarrassed. "I do not believe that is for you to say, my lord."

"But it is, and since I have, no one else will dare dance with you." He closed the distance between them, his voice low and suddenly edged with malice. "And when you find yourself all alone at the end of the fourth ball, with the choice of a fine house in the heart of Edinburgh or slogging back to whatever obscure corner of the countryside you crawled in from, you'll realize that being my most prized possession is more desirable."

He grabbed the back of her neck, yanked her forward and kissed her. It was a brief, rough kiss that left her reeling as he sauntered away. Emilia was aghast. She jerked her gaze around the room, but no one seemed to have noticed. Mortified, breath ragged, she fled the ballroom.

Emilia clutched her skirt in both hands to keep the hem off the floor and ran through the dim halls of Lady Peddington's School. The stench of Viscount Dunreid's cologne clung to her. She didn't know where she went until she burst through the door to the drawing classroom, the room where she always felt happiest. To her relief, Missus Millview, the drawing instructor, was there.

"Miss Glasbarr?" Missus Millview rose from her chair. "Whatever is the matter? What are you doing here? It's well after midnight."

She stumbled across the room toward her instructor. "Lord Ailbeart, that is, Viscount Dunreid kissed me," she blurted. "I didnae want him to, but he did." She burst into tears.

Missus Millview reached her side and wrapped Emilia in a warm embrace. "There, there, my dear child," she murmured. "You shouldn't be up after midnight. You aren't the sort. There's been an error."

Emilia sniffed. "An error?" Did midnight signify in some way? "I don't understand."

Missus Millview shook her head, eyes sympathetic in her long face. "It's nothing, child, nothing at all. Only that you should retire earlier at the next ball, to avoid this sort of thing. Gentlemen tend to get out of hand in the later hours."

"They do?" Emilia pulled away. She wiped at her cheeks with the heels of her hands.

"Of course." Missus Millview gave her a gentle smile. "You dance the early dances from now on and retire before midnight, and forget this incident with Lord Ailbeart ever occurred."

"But I can't," Emilia cried. "No one will dance with me. Not one gentleman asked. Lord Ailbeart said he warned them away because I'm to be...to be..." She couldn't say it aloud, what he'd propositioned. "What am I to do? I convinced my parents to let me use the money they set aside for my dowry to come here. I told them a man would prefer a cultured bride over one with a small sum. I don't want to go back to the country. I want to stay here where there is music and art."

Missus Millview's brow creased, her look one of compassion. Emilia glanced around the nearly dark room. Why was Missus Ailbeart in her classroom at that hour? She took in the desk. The scattered candle stubs illuminated receipts and pages filled with rows of numbers.

Missus Millview followed her gaze. She let out a sigh, and passed a hand over tired eyes. "Yes, we must all worry about our funds, child."

Concern of another sort stole through Emilia. Missus Millview was a good person, and her favorite instructor. "Is there anything I can do?"

"Do?" Missus Millview shook her head. "No. I'll be well enough, so long as I keep my place here." She pressed her lips into a tight frown and dragged her gaze from her desk, back to Emilia. "I should like to help you, child. You aren't one who should have been brought to Lord Ailbeart's attention. I suspect it's your beauty that's the trouble, not that you can help that."

Emilia blinked. Beauty? She knew she had no obvious flaws in appearance, but she hardly thought she had sufficient beauty to garner attention, especially from a viscount. "You can help me?" Her voice caught at the hope that surged within her.

Missus Millview looked to her pages of numbers again. She gave a sharp nod. "I can, but you must promise not to tell any of the other girls. I can't lose my place here. I'm not young or beautiful enough to make my way if I do."

"I promise," Emilia said eagerly. "Please, what can I do? I simply want to marry a kind man. I do no' need a title, or wealth, or much of anything, really. Just a gentleman who lives in the city."

"You won't tell those three friends of yours?" Missus Millview eyed her shrewdly. "I know how inseparable you four are, and I suspect they may be in the same boat. You must promise not to tell them what I'll reveal to you, child. I've come to care for you, but a woman alone in this world must look out for herself."

Emilia bit back a hasty acceptance. Her friends had all retired earlier as, apparently, proper young women did. They'd been discouraged as they'd also lacked admirers. Could she consign any of them to men like Lord Ailbeart?

She drew in a breath. She couldn't, but she would find a way to help without breaking Missus Millview's confidence. "I promise I won't tell the other girls, even my friends."

Missus Millview offered a relieved smile. "Well then, this should help you." She crossed to the desk, then pulled free a clean page and began to write.

Emilia followed her. She looked over Missus Millview's shoulder to take in the elegantly penned address and a name. "Sir Stirling James," she read aloud.

Missus Millview turned to offer the page. "Yes. They call him The Marriage Maker. If anyone can help you, he can." Her face went stern, as it did when Emilia attempted anything less than her best work. "But don't forget your promise."

"I won't, Missus Millview." Emilia folded the page in half. "Thank you."

"You're a good child," Missus Millview said. "Too good for the likes of Viscount Dunreid. Can you reach your chamber well enough?"

Emilia thought about the empty halls. No one had stopped her on her way to the classroom. She nodded. "I can." She gave Missus Millview a quick hug. "Thank you. You've saved me, and I won't tell the others."

Missus Millview sighed and shook her head. "I hope not, child, I truly do."

Emilia left with a lighter heart than she'd had in hours. She took the back way to her room, thankful the halls and stairs were as blissfully empty as she'd hoped. As she walked, she formulated a plan. She would write this Sir Stirling James now, before bed. She would tell him of her plight, and include a small portrait she'd done of herself, on the chance she really was as pretty as Missus Millview said.

In fact, she would include portraits of her three friends as well, and beg him to help them all. Missus Millview had made her swear not to tell any of the other girls about Sir Stirling James. That didn't mean Emilia couldn't tell him about them. She smiled as she reached the safety of her room and lit a candle, pleased with her plan.

CHAPTER TWO

ROBERT BANBROOK SAT ALONE at a table in his club, staring into a half-empty glass of scotch. The only good thing about Scotland, as far as he was concerned. One up, then, on England. The Irish had Irish Whiskey, the Scots had Scottish Whisky. What did England offer a man to drown his sorrows? Gin. Robert shuddered at the thought. He swallowed the rest of the glass to dispel the memory of the revolting stuff.

"You look a bit peaked there, Banbrook," a jovial voice said. A large hand clasped his shoulder briefly.

Robert looked up from his empty tumbler and squinted to bring Sir Stirling James into focus. Stirling pulled out a chair and seated himself at the table.

"I'm as fine as a fiddle, Stirling, I can assure you." Robert reached for the nearly empty decanter before him. He missed once, but claimed it on the second try. He flashed Stirling a grin, proud of his success. "You see? Fine as a fiddle," Robert repeated.

Liquid sloshed onto his fingers and he looked down. Whisky tumbled from the mouth of the crystal decanter and over the hand clasping the tumbler. Furrowing his brow in concentration, he angled the bottle to get more into the glass.

"I'm glad to hear it, Banbrook, because I was worried you'd spent the past three days in this club drinking yourself to death." Stirling lifted an arm and waved. A footman hurried over with a cloth to sop up the spilled liquor.

"Oh, I have. I am." Robert offered a grin, though he could hardly feel his face.

"I take it this ill-conceived effort has to do with a certain young lady?" Stirling asked as the footman mopped the spill.

"You, Geoffrey, bring me another bottle," Robert said to the footman. He turned back to Stirling. "You use the word *lady* loosely."

"I find that doubtful." Stirling nodded toward the footman. "John will ignore your request." Stirling emphasized the man's name. "The entire staff will. I've had you cut off."

Robert let out a mumbled curse. The footman departed without looking at him. A glance showed no others near.

"Can't you leave me to drink myself to death in peace?" Robert asked. He squinted at the older gentleman. "You used to be fun." He knocked back his drink and realized very little whisky had made its way into his glass.

"Oh, I have something fun planned, never fear." Stirling stood and gestured again.

Footsteps sounded behind Robert. He craned his neck in an effort to see who approached. Two of the burlier footmen, their faces set, marched toward him. Or was there one and he was seeing the man twice? He blinked several times, but neither of the two disappeared.

Large hands clasped his arms and lifted him from the chair. At least four hands, so at least two of the fellows, then. Or was that three? The empty tumbler slipped free of his grasp to hit the table with a thunk.

The sound drew his attention as the men got him to his feet. Sad empty tumbler. All it wanted was to do its duty by him. So loyal. Not like women.

Stirling appeared at his side, swaying like a storm-tossed schooner. "What do you think, Banbrook, can you walk?"

Robert shook off the hands and straightened. "I most certainly can. What do you take me for?" He raised his chin, endeavoring to stare Stirling down, but his chin wouldn't stop. It went up and up. Robert's head tilted back. He'd never taken time to properly contemplate the ceiling of his club before. One always overlooked the details.

Four hands gripped him and stood him upright again when he started to topple backward. Stirling, still swaying, appeared greatly amused. He gestured and the hands began to half walk, half carry Robert.

The faces of other gentlemen at the club moved in a slow spiral around him as they crossed the room. Most were turned his way. Expressions ranged from sympathetic to disgusted. Robert would have taken careful note of who owned the latter, but the names of his peers were strangely absent from his brain. Maybe they were all named Geoffrey. The idea inclined him to laugh, but he didn't want to amuse Stirling any further.

The hands didn't toss him from the club as he half-expected, but instead took him up the steps and into one of the private rooms, furnished with a bed, desk, chairs and table. Inside stood a large, full washtub, as well. He had just enough sense to wonder why no steam rose from the tub before he was picked up and plunked, fully clothed, into the chilly water.

In shock, he slid under the surface. He came up gasping for air. Rapid blinking brought Stirling into view beside the tub. Robert unleashed a stream of invectives. Stirling gestured. A large hand settled on Robert's head and pushed him back under, then let him up immediately.

"Feeling better yet?" Stirling asked as Robert's head cleared the surface once more.

"You bloody, rat-faced, son-of-a—" A gesture from Stirling. Robert went down into the water again. He flailed at the hand, but it didn't remain on his head long enough to strike. He pushed himself to the surface, spitting water. "Do you mean to kill me?"

Stirling looked down at him, arms crossed, expression contemplative. "I thought death was your goal."

"You bloody well know it's not, you madman. This water is damned cold."

"Here in Scotland, we call it refreshing."

"Well I'm a bloody Englishman and I don't appreciate being dunked in a trough." Robert pushed a hand over his face, skimming away water. "What are you playing at, Stirling?"

"Playing?" Stirling shook his head. "No. I've a favor to ask, actually."

"A favor?" Robert gaped. He stood. Water streamed from his hair, coat, flattened cravat, everywhere. "This is you asking for a favor?"

"I need you clear-headed enough to comprehend my words." Stirling's tone was reasonable, but amusement lurked in his features.

Robert muttered a few choice curses as he stepped over the edge of the tub. Water sloshed across the floor. One of the footmen immediately began to wipe it up. The other offered Robert a towel, his expression neutral.

Robert took the proffered cloth and mopped at his face. "Look what you've done to my jacket. My vest." He let out another curse. "My boots, man. Look what you've done to my boots."

"Put them by the fire. John will take your clothes and see them made right."

Robert turned to take in the cheery blaze. Now that his vision was clearer, he also noticed a set of clothes laid out, as well as a nightshirt and robe. His clothes. His nightshirt and robe.

He cast Stirling an incredulous look. "You've been to my residence?"

"Yes. Your staff are rather worried about you. They haven't seen you in three days."

Robert shook his head, bemused. He crossed to the fire, then began stripping his lean frame. Stirling ordered the tub removed and the floor mopped. Robert shucked his sodden attire.

After toweling dry, he took up his robe. His original intention had been to dress, but weariness had settled. What was the point in dressing, after all? Once he heard Stirling out and sent him on his way, Robert could return to drinking just as easily in a private room in his robe as he could in the public room, dressed.

He belted his robe closed, plopped into an armchair and propped his feet on the nearby stool. He watched with little interest as servants gathered his wet garments, sopped up the last of the water and disappeared. The chair was near the fire, the warmth lulling. His eyes closed.

"Now, about that favor."

Robert forced his lids open to find Stirling seated on the other side of the fireplace. "The answer is no," Robert muttered.

"All I require is for you to attend three balls."

"Balls? With dancing?" Robert scowled. "With ladies?"

"That is generally the way of balls." Stirling rested his elbows on the arms of the chair and steepled his fingers before him.

"Can't. I've sworn off women. For good. No more." Robert shook his head, then regretted the movement as the room bounced. "I will not be jilted a third time, and certainly not again in Scotland. I'm leaving."

"Oh?" Stirling raised an eyebrow. "Headed back to London, are you?"

Robert looked away from those perceptive eyes. He could never go back to London. Every inch of the city reminded him of Cinthia. "Maybe the Continent. Perhaps even France."

"France? Do you intend to get yourself shot?"

Robert shrugged. "At least in France, when a man is jilted, he can drown his sorrow in cognac."

Stirling watched him over his steepled fingers.

Robert resisted an urge to squirm under that gaze. "Or I could hang about Edinburgh for a time. I've nothing against Scotland, just women."

With a sigh, Stirling brought his hands to the chair arms. "Miss Thomas did the right thing, breaking it off with you."

Robert went rigid. "What did you say?"

"Kitty Thomas did the right thing when she broke your engagement."

Anger coiled inside Robert.

"Anyone can see you're still in love with Cinthia."

Robert's anger disappeared like summer rain. Cinthia. The real reason he'd come to Scotland. For two years, they'd been engaged. In London, they were the toast of the *Ton*. Every dance, the theater, the park. Always together. Blissfully happy as they waited for her father to return from his government appointment in India so they could wed.

Then Lord Ailbeart had come along, with Scottish title. He enticed her with his lineage. Whispering that she was meant to be a member of the peerage, Lady Cinthia, Viscountess Dunreid. Not simply Missus Banbrook.

Fool that he was, Robert hadn't been worried. He'd believed in her. Believed in their love. Not until the morning he'd called round and learned she'd left for Scotland did he have any idea Viscount Dunreid had succeeded in his conquest.

He passed a hand over his eyes, weary. "What are you after, Stirling? I've heard rumors of your new game, matchmaking." He eyed the other man. "I'm not looking for another woman to propose to. Twice was enough."

Stirling leaned back in his chair, his expression too innocent to be so. "The last thing I want to do is get some poor girl's hopes up with an introduction to you. Until you get over Viscountess Dunreid, you aren't fit for any woman." He shook his head. "No, I simply need you to help a certain young Miss stave off an aggressive gentleman long enough to find herself a good husband."

Robert frowned. "Stave off? She doesn't want to marry this gentleman? At least she's smart enough to realize as much."

"Aye, she seems an intelligent sort, but I believe the key issue is the offer of the gentleman in question. He wants her, but he has no intention of making her his wife."

So, a cad up to no good and apt to tarnish a young lady's reputation. "I see. She's in need of protection, then, not one of your quick weddings." He scrutinized Stirling. "Why don't you do help the girl?"

"I could, I suppose, but I wouldn't want to deprive you of the honor, or the amusement. Anyone can see you're in need of a bit of distraction."

Robert supposed there was some truth in that. Still, "Escorting some young Miss to dances doesn't sound particularly amusing." It sounded painful.

A sly grin formed on Stirling's face. "Oh, I daresay escorting this young Miss is just what you need. That, and a bit of revenge." He leaned forward in his chair. "You see, Banbrook, Dunreid wants the young lady for his mistress. You, my friend, are going to save her."

CHAPTER THREE

EMILIA STOOD TO ONE side of the candlelight-bathed foyer of Lady Peddington's School. She studied the carved wood panels and endeavored to project serene confidence. She knew it was improper, perhaps even brazen, to lurk in the foyer in wait of a man, but she dared not enter the ballroom without her protector.

That he would arrive, she had no doubt. That afternoon, one of the school's maids, Mary, had delivered a bouquet of pink gillyflowers to Emilia's room. With the flowers was a note that read, *Wear these in your hair tonight - SS*. As she'd sent a sketch of herself, the flowers were an insult to her artistic skills, but one she would willingly swallow to have someone by her side to fend off another kiss from Viscount Dunreid.

Each time the school's stone-faced butler opened the ornate front door to admit more gentlemen, hope coursed through her. Any one of them could be her savior, Sir Stirling James. Each time said gentleman walked past without slowing, her heart fell.

Had she missed him? Earlier, Emilia had glimpsed Viscount Dunreid as he ascended the steps and she ducked into the cloakroom once, much to the shock of the footmen. She hadn't dared come out for several long moments, until multiple cloaks, hats and greatcoats had been stowed. Perhaps Sir Stirling had entered on the viscount's heels?

Emilia patted the gillyflowers artfully arranged among her blond ringlets and suppressed a sigh. The influx of gentlemen had waned, and none had approached her yet. If she'd missed Sir Stirling, she would have to enter the ballroom to seek him. That risked Dunreid finding her first.

The butler stepped back from the small window he peered out and pulled open the door with a bow. In sauntered four more gentlemen. They handed coats, walking canes and hats to the footman, who handed them to another, to be placed in the cloakroom behind the artfully hidden door built into the paneling.

Hope sprang to life within her as the men turned to cross the foyer. Emilia dropped her gaze demurely to the inlaid floor in an attempt to be noticeable but not noticed. She didn't want to attract the wrong sort of attention, after all.

She kept her gaze downcast as four pairs of polished shoes passed by. None slowed. None turned toward her. The gentlemen chatted amiable, obviously friends. Laughter drifted down the hall in their wake, followed by strands of music. The dancing had begun. Somewhere in the ballroom, her three dearest friends likely clustered together, wondering at her odd behavior of late and her absence.

A twinge of guilt stabbed at the thought of them, clad in their finest gowns, clustered near a wall in hopes a gentleman would ask them to dance. Her three friends hadn't received flowers, and to inquire if they'd received some other assistance risked breaking her promise to Missus Mill-view. Unsure she could witness her friends' despair at their lack of partners without confessing, she avoided them.

"Hiding from me, Miss Glasbarr?" a silken masculine voice said behind her.

Emilia stiffened. Dunreid. He'd found her. She remained facing the door. Perhaps her stiff posture and refusal to turn would discourage him.

He stepped up behind her, too close. His overly-musky cologne seared her nostrils. Heat from his body caused her skin to crawl, as if spiders tiptoed across her shoulders. She looked to the servants, but they'd gone still, gazes locked ahead. With a heartsick sensation, she realized they couldn't stop the viscount, no matter how he elected to torment her.

"You've already given me far more sport than my last mistress." He exhaled the words against the back of her neck with hot, sticky breath.

Emilia suppressed a shudder.

A gloved finger slid along her skin. "Such an elegant neck shouldn't go unadorned, and won't once you're mine. My pockets are deep and I'm not stingy. I know how to reward a woman who pleases me."

She stepped away to gain much needed space, then faced him. She tilted up her chin. "I shall never please ye, my lord."

His smile was warped with condescension. "You already do."

"No, some idea you have of me does, but *I* never shall." She bit off the honorific he clearly didn't deserve.

His gaze narrowed. He reached for her arm. Emilia stepped back. Dunreid's expression went flat with displeasure. A long stride brought him to her, her wrist captured before she had time to retreat farther.

Behind her, the servants moved, but not to come to her aid. Rather, toward the foyer door, which she could hear the butler open. She prayed Sir Stirling would enter. She tugged against Dunreid. Her efforts only tightened his grip.

A look of condescension on his face, he yanked her toward him. "Don't forget what I told you." His voice was low, touched with vitriol. "No one else will have you. They won't dare dance with you. You have no choice. It's me, or no man."

"Then I'll die an old maid," she hissed.

"Now, that would be a shame," a man's voice said.

Dunreid's gaze snapped toward a spot over Emilia's left shoulder. Dislike flickered in his eyes. He released her with a shove. Emilia stumbled back. Strong hands caught her by the waist and kept her upright. They dropped away as a man stepped up beside her.

Heart pounding, Emilia glanced at her savior askance, almost afraid to take her eyes from Dunreid, lest he put his hands on her again. Was this finally Sir Stirling James, come to save her? She certainly hoped so.

He was taller than Dunreid by several inches, and lean. Even out of the corner of her eye, she noticed his sculpted features, the impression of stone made stronger by the rigid set of his jaw. The cut of his dark hair, shorter than was fashionable, suited him. In every other way, from the gleaming diamond pin in his cravat to his perfectly tailored black tailcoat, he was impeccably modish.

Dunreid pulled his lips into the semblance of a smile. "Banbrook, how good to see you. Come to find a young lady to jilt you? Again."

Banbrook? Jilt him again? Not Sir Stirling, then.

"Not this time, Dunreid." Mister Banbrook's voice was as hard as his countenance. "I've simply come to thwart you."

He spoke in a cultured English accent. Not from Edinburgh, then, Emilia realized, as she would have when he first spoke, had she not been fixated on Dunreid. She didn't have much experience with Englishmen, but he displayed more temper than one expected of them.

"Thwart me?" Dunreid snorted. "As if you could. Put us before a hundred women, and I'll be chosen over you a hundred times. Why do you set yourself a challenge you will surely lose?"

Emilia could hear the Englishman grind his teeth. "I will not win or lose, merely safeguard this young woman from your advances."

Dunreid raised his thick brows. "We shall see about that." He held out a hand to Emilia. "Miss Glasbarr, come dance with me."

She shook her head. "I will not. Not now, not ever."

Though she expected anger, Dunreid appeared amused. "So you say, but you'll soon realize that a man with my class and title can offer you so much more than the likes of Mister Banbrook here. More than you ever dreamed of while whiling away nights in your maidenly bower." He dropped his gaze to her décolletage.

Emilia brought a hand to her chest and suddenly wished her gown had a higher neckline. Her face burned hot, but she kept her chin up. "I said never, my lord, and I mean never."

Dunreid shrugged. He dropped his hand and turned his amused look back on Mister Banbrook. "Good luck with this one. She's got even more fire than Cinthia. Too much spirit for the likes of you." His grin turned malicious. "Be a good chap and keep her entertained until I'm ready for her—just as you did Cinthia. You're practiced at that." He turned and strolled away.

Emilia stared after him. What did his vicious words mean? If she recalled properly, Lady Cinthia was the viscount's wife. Did this Mister Banbrook know her?

Emilia turned to her savior to ask him, but one glimpse stopped her words. He stood taut as a bowstring, hands balled into fists. His expression was murderous as he watched Dunreid's retreating form. Though rather handsome, Mister Banbrook was also more than a touch frightening.

She looked around. With the viscount's exit, they were alone in the ornately paneled foyer, save for the inscrutable servants. Maybe Sir Stirling would still come. Maybe she needed to be saved from two men, for Mister Banbrook looked near violence.

"Shall we consider that a formal introduction, then?" Mister Banbrook asked in a neutral tone.

Emilia shifted her attention back to him. Candlelight flickered across a strong jaw. The eyes regarding her were deep grey, and calm. She blinked, almost convinced she'd imagined his rage of moments ago.

He offered a rueful smile. "I apologize for letting Dunreid aggravate me. I don't suppose unbridled hatred makes for the best first impression." He bowed, movements smoothly elegant. "I'm Banbrook. A mutual friend sent me to look after you at this dance, and the next two, if you'll still have me."

"Sir—" She broke off and cast a quick look around. The servants hadn't stood up for her against Dunreid, but that didn't mean they hadn't heart, and wouldn't gossip. "That is, he is no' coming? He sent you?" Though she'd never met Sir Stirling, she felt oddly bereft.

Mister Banbrook gestured in the direction of the ballroom. "A schoolgirl dance isn't the sort of place you're likely to find him."

"Is it the sort of place I'm likely to find you, Mister Banbrook?"

A startled look crossed his face. He chuckled and the final vestiges of coldness melted from his features. "No, not especially, Miss Glasbarr, but I'm here now, and I would be honored to take a turn about the room with you and introduce you to any gentlemen here I know. That is, the respectable ones." He offered his arm.

As she had no better option, Emilia lightly rested her hand on his coat sleeve, aware of the hard strength beneath the soft fabric. Sir Stirling hadn't come, or even sent her a man to marry. Instead, he'd sent Mister Banbrook, who seemed to have his own, quite antagonistic, relationship with Viscount Dunreid. Was Mister Banbrook even there to help her, or had he arrived with his own agenda?

As they walked together down the short corridor, she tried to stifle her unease. Though the expression felt a bit strained, she maintained a polite smile when they entered the ballroom. Heads turned. Men and women alike whispered behind gloved hands and lace fans. Emilia had no notion if the murmurs were directed at her or Mister Banbrook. He showed no concerned, and angled them toward the center of the vast chamber, where a dance had just ended. Couples left the dancefloor, the women a bouquet of pastels, the men a montage from gaudy to drab. New couples surged forward to fill the space.

"Perhaps, to set the example, I should dance with you before we take a turn about the room?" Mister Banbrook asked with casual politeness.

"I should enjoy that," Emilia replied, her stomach a nervousness knot.

He gave a sharp nod and escorted her to her place in line, then took up the position opposite her. The musicians struck the first notes to an adapted country reel. Emilia's smile widened into real happiness. The dance was one she knew well, and enjoyed. Much livelier than most choices, the variation was also considerably more fun, and offered no time for chatter. Given the tall, foreboding form across from her, Emilia felt not talking might be a good circumstance.

When the musicians struck the proper note, she skipped forward in time to the beat. She and Mister Banbrook met in the center and clasped hands. They executed a turn, giving her just enough time to notice his strong grip, not limpid like some gentlemen's, and returned to their corners to permit the next couple to pass. Emilia linked arms with the man to her left. He spun her about slightly out of time, the over-long tails of his mustard-colored coat trailing along behind him.

The next gentleman who took her arm wore a more somber green, and a slightly leering expression, though his step was surer. She was relieved the dance took her back to Mister Banbrook for another turn in the center, between the rows of dancers. His smile was cheerful. His gaze never once dropped below her face.

Several more turns switched up the roles, so she met the leering green-clad gentleman in the center, and linked arms with Mister Banbrook in the line. He swung her about with such vigor she would have laughed had she not just completed finishing school. Ladies did not laugh in public.

She wished she might, though. She thoroughly enjoyed the delightful partner Mister Banbrook made. As the dance progressed, Emilia couldn't help but admire the fine form he cut. Tall, upright and lean, his superbly tailored black a sharp contrast to other men's popinjay ensembles. He was a skilled dancer, and even seemed to be enjoying himself, if his expression could be believed.

Too soon, the obligations of the set freed them. Emilia took Mister Banbrook's proffered arm and permitted him to escorted her to the fringes of the crowd. With a sharp turn, he began their circuit about the crowded ballroom. Emilia glanced at him askance, and found his expression once again serious. She couldn't help but miss the joy the dance had called forth.

"It will help, I believe, if you tell me what you desire in a gentleman," Mister Banbrook murmured in a low tone. "That is, assuming you know?"

"Oh, aye. I know quite well." But to tell him, a man and a new acquaintance, seemed odd. Still, long-held dreams of the perfect gentleman filled

21

her thoughts, and his request was reasonable under the circumstances. "I shouldn't care overly about his looks, or his income, really." She offered an apologetic look. "I realize that does little to narrow the field."

"You mean, you'll settle for any toad with pockets to let?" He didn't sound convinced.

Emilia's face heated. "Well, no. I mean, he needn't be terribly well put together, like you, or very wealthy, like the viscount, but I would be lying if I said I want a ghastly husband or one who's too below hatches. I should like very much to live in the city, you see, and realize that takes funds." She locked her gaze on the inlaid floor. Had she just called Mister Banbrook handsome?

"Ah, so you wish to be a socialite, to put your training to good use? I suppose a title is preferable?" His tone was light, yet somehow edged.

Emilia darted another glance his way, but his face was a mask in the wash of candlelight. Unsure how to construe his expression, she could only answer without prevarication. "Oh no, I shouldn't like a title, or anyone too wealthy. It seems to me being at the center of things would be a great deal of work, and would not permit time for anything truly enjoyable."

"For most women, being at the center of things is what's truly enjoyable," he countered in that same tone.

Here she was on surer footing. "Well then, most women are wrong. What's truly enjoyable is art, and music, and theater. I should like to listen to concerts and go to exhibits, and travel to London to visit the British Museum. Perhaps go even farther someday, to the Continent."

"In the pursuit of music and art?" Another glance showed his brow creased in surprise.

"Is that so difficult to believe?" she asked. Worry touched her. "Or is it so difficult to find a man who will want those things? At home, they say Edinburgh is a place of great culture. When I came here from the country-side, I thought I would find gentlemen who appreciate that."

"There's very little gentlemen appreciate outside of horseflesh, gambling and—" He grimaced. "Let's leave it at horseflesh and gambling." He turned his head and scanned the room. "Well, Miss Glasbarr, you ask much, but I'll see what I can do."

CHAPTER FOUR

AS THEY STRODE ABOUT the ballroom, Robert stole glances at the young woman by his side. He shouldn't have danced with her. He'd told Stirling he was through with dancing, and he'd meant few words more sincerely. Dancing was where the trouble started, and Miss Glasbarr was trouble if ever he'd seen it. Mercurial hazel eyes. Hair a shade of burnished gold he'd never encountered before, even in Scotland. A beguiling innocence he thought might actually be unfeigned.

So, he'd given in to temptation and danced with her. One set. What could be the harm?

If she'd been tempting in the soft candlelight of the foyer, she was triply so while dancing. No longer nervous, or shaking with some mixture of anger and terror evoked by Dunreid, she was all enthusiasm, vivacity and joy. Watching her dance was enough to make a man call for a priest.

Call for a priest? He was clearly mad. He'd sworn never to fall in love again after Cinthia.

Robert nearly tripped, startled by his thoughts. In his musing, he'd glossed over Kitty Thomas, the young woman who'd jilted him not a week ago. What sort of a monster was he to so quickly forget a girl he'd wanted to marry, his mind and heart already back on Cinthia?

He frowned. Stirling was right. He had never loved Kitty. What he'd loved was the idea of being over Cinthia. Well, he wouldn't permit himself to imagine his way into love again. Not at the expense of a sweet soul like Miss Glasbarr.

That decided, he doubled his efforts. He would find her a worthy young man. Someone not jilted, jaded and temperamental. A quick scan of the revelers before them revealed several acceptable candidates. He brought her to a halt before the nearest.

"Campbell," Robert greeted. "May I introduce Miss Glasbarr?"

"Miss Glasbarr." Campbell shot Robert a surprised look as he bowed over her hand.

"Mister Campbell." Miss Glasbarr offered a pretty smile. "I'm very pleased to make your acquaintance."

"Miss Glasbarr would like to dance, Campbell. Be a good fellow and escort her in the next set, will you?" That earned Robert two startled looks. Well, what did they expect? He wasn't her mother. He had no practice making subtle introductions.

Campbell leaned in. "I would, Banbrook, but Dunreid…" He trailed off and nodded his head toward the other side of the room with a roll of his eyes.

Robert didn't need to look to know Dunreid lurked there, like some sort of many-armed sea slug, his tendrils of malice snaking about the glittering room. "Leave Dunreid to me, Campbell. Take the lass for a set. She's a delightful partner."

Miss Glasbarr blushed. She turned her hazel eyes on him in what was likely as near a glare as her lovely features could manage. "Mister Banbrook, really, I'm not a mare at market. If Mister Campbell finds himself too much pressured, I need not dance."

"You hear that, Campbell? Miss Glasbarr thinks you're afraid of Dunreid." Robert added a grin to his words.

Campbell stood up straighter. "I am most certainly not." He scowled at Robert, then bowed to Miss Glasbarr again. "I would be honored if you would dance with me, Miss Glasbarr."

"Thank you, Mister Campbell," she said. "It would be my pleasure."

She gave Robert a grateful smile. Campbell held out his arm. Miss Glasbarr left Robert's side to place her hand on Campbell's ridiculous

25

crimson coat sleeve. Robert suddenly wondered if Campbell truly was worthy. Didn't the man gamble himself into debt every other Thursday?

As they walked off, Miss Glasbarr's polite chatter about the weather drifted back to him. She hadn't chatted with Robert inanely. Did that mean she didn't care for him?

Robert watched them line up with the other dancers. Miss Glasbarr was vibrant with eagerness. While they waited for the musicians to begin, Campbell looked her up and down, not hiding his appreciation. Robert clenched his teeth. What had possessed him to consider Campbell worthy? A gambler in a gaudy coat was not what Miss Glasbarr needed.

Robert looked about. There had to be someone worthier. His gaze landed on Mister Paterson. Paterson didn't drink, gamble, dally, or even race. He was the most boring man in Edinburgh. He also couldn't string three words together in the presence of a pretty female. He was perfect.

With one eye on the dance for Campbell's leering glances, Robert strode toward Paterson. Dressed in rumpled light grey, which was a sight better than popinjay-red, he stood beside one of the tall windows. Robert agreed with Paterson's choice of location. He drank in the cool air coming from the courtyard as he approached.

"Paterson," he greeted.

"Banbrook," Paterson said cheerfully.

"You aren't dancing."

Paterson winced. "I, ah, haven't made the acquaintance of any of the young ladies present."

"You're in luck." Robert offered a pleasant smile. "See that lovely creature dancing with Campbell? I'm introducing her around. She would be pleased to dance with you."

"With me?" Paterson appeared startled. His eyes narrowed. "Wait, isn't that Miss Glasbarr?" He shot Robert a worried look. "I can't dance with her. Dunreid sai—"

"Dunreid doesn't own the girl and she wants nothing to do with him. I danced with her. Campbell is dancing with her." He offered a frown. "I've always taken you for shy, not cowardly."

Paterson made a sputtering sound. He straightened, shoulders thrown back. "Now, see here, I am not a coward and I won't stand for being called one."

Robert slapped Paterson on the back, hard enough to rock him forward onto his toes. "Wonderful. I knew I could count on you. Come along, then. We'll go stand near the dance floor." Where he could keep an eye on Campbell. "So she won't miss us when they're done with their set."

He led the still sputtering Paterson back to where he'd introduced Miss Glasbarr to Campbell. They spoke idly while they waited for the set to conclude. Paterson was every bit as boring as Robert recalled.

After an interminable length of time, during which Robert concluded the musicians had seen fit to play lengthier pieces than usual, her set with Campbell ended. He proffered his arm with a familiarity Robert couldn't approve of and escorted her back. They chatted brightly as they approached. As far as he could ascertain, their conversation was, of all things, about horse breeds.

"Miss Glasbarr," Robert said as soon as they drew near. "This is Mister Paterson. He's requested the next set."

"M-Miss…G-Glas…" Paterson concluded his stuttering with a bow.

Miss Glasbarr gave no reaction to Paterson's inability to properly address her, and she curtsied. "That would be lovely, Mister Paterson. Thank you."

He offered his arm. Miss Glasbarr cast Robert a quick smile before permitting Paterson to lead her back toward the other dancers.

"Well put together little piece, isn't she?" Campbell said as he watched her go.

Robert shrugged. He tried to tamp down the anger sparked by Campbell's too-familiar scrutiny of Miss Glasbarr's retreating form.

"I can see why Dunreid claimed her," Campbell continued. "And why she doesn't want him. She's got an active mind, too, does that one."

"You expect me to believe you assessed the quality of her mind while dancing and staring down the front of her dress?"

Campbell grinned. "If God didn't want gentlemen to look down ladies' fronts, he wouldn't have made us the taller sex." He gave Robert a slap on the back and chuckled at his own joke.

Robert made no reply, attention on the dancers. The set was a collection of slow, careful dances. As impossible as it seemed, Miss Glasbarr appeared to speak with Paterson quite amiably throughout. This strange circumstance was confirmed when the third dance in the set ended and he escorted her back. Robert could hear them conversing on the British Museum as they returned. Even worse than Paterson's newfound ability to put more than three words together was the besotted look he leveled on Miss Glasbarr.

The situation only grew worse after that. Apparently other men thought that if Paterson could ignore Dunreid's claim and dance with Miss Glasbarr, any gentleman could, the cretins flocked to her. Robert was soon relegated to the fringe of the group of men that engulfed her. Campbell, immune to Robert's glower, took up his role and introduce her to newcomers.

Finally, near midnight, Robert decided Miss Glasbarr had met enough gentlemen for one evening. He was sick near to death of watching so-called men, who'd been too fearful before, dance with her now. Even after so brief an acquaintance, he was certain she deserved better than a coward. Worse, the majority of the men who'd approached her were complete oafs. If she couldn't have brave men, she should at least have the pleasure of skilled partners.

He resisted to urge to escort her out a second time, to show the lot of them how to properly dance with a lovely young woman. He wouldn't do her any good by partnering with her twice in one night. Not if she wanted to find a husband among the assembled gentlemen, though not a one of the louts deserved her. Of course, who she settled on wasn't truly his concern, so long as she didn't settle on Dunreid.

The next time she was escorted from the dance floor, Robert circled the waiting group of men and met her before she reached them. He offered his arm. With a quick farewell to her partner, she placed elegant fingers on his sleeve. Robert steered them away from her admirers.

"It's nearly midnight," he observed in a low voice.

"So soon?" She glanced about, a slight frown marring her features.

"Shall I escort you to the front hall?" Robert nodded in the direction many of the other young women were headed. Pastel ruffles swishing about them, they resembled nothing so much as one of Mary Moser's acclaimed paintings.

"That would be very kind of you."

Relieved at her ready acquiescence, he angled them toward the front of the ballroom. "Did you enjoy your evening?"

"I did, and thank you for your assistance." Her dispirited tone belied her words.

"But?" Her obvious displeasure reassured him. He was pleased she realized the unsuitability of the flock of gentleman, rather than being buoyed by their unworthy attentions.

She shrugged delicate shoulders. "They danced with me, which really was delightful, but I don't believe a single one will pursue me. They're still afraid of him."

Robert nodded. She was likely correct, which only proved their lack of worth, but he was there to find her a gentleman. He meant to meet that obligation. He wouldn't consign her to choose between Dunreid or no man. What more could he do to thwart the viscount? "A carriage ride." The offer was out before he could restrain the words. He hadn't taken a carriage ride in the park since Cinthia's betrayal.

"I beg your pardon?"

He contained a grimace. Apparently, he enjoyed making himself miserable. "Let me take you for a carriage ride tomorrow afternoon. A few turns about the park. You can meet a greater variety of gentlemen. He can't have cowed every man in Edinburgh."

She smiled up at him, too sweet and too young for any man he knew. Why, with her only just completing finishing school, he must have seven or so years on her.

"Well, he hasn't cowed you," she said. "So certainly, he can't have intimidated every man in the city, and yes, a carriage ride would be lovely, thank you."

Robert nodded. Her cheerful smile and innocent compliments lightened his mood. She was right. A carriage ride would be lovely. Because he and Cinthia used to take them almost daily didn't mean he could never enjoy one again.

He parted ways with Miss Glasbarr in the front hall. She fell in with a stream of young women headed above stairs. Once she was out of sight, Robert exited into the Edinburgh evening to await his carriage. Miss Glasbarr's smile lingered in his mind and evoked one of his own.

Robert paced the curb in the cool night air, in no mood to speak with the other gentlemen waiting for their carriages. He'd had enough of the lot of them for one evening. Watching Miss Glasbarr dance with so many eligible, yet wholly unworthy, men had soured the sociable side of his nature.

He would not misconstrue his protectiveness as affection, however. She was beautiful, kind and sweet, but that didn't mean he was drawn to her. He had to exorcise Cinthia from heart and mind before he flung himself impulsively at another girl. He wouldn't repeat the mistake he'd made with Kitty.

His carriage pulled up, the stately, four-horse one he generally used when he attended society events, not the open curricle he would use tomorrow to take Miss Glasbarr around the park. Robert frowned. Every stray thought shouldn't lead back to her.

"Where to, sir?" his coachman asked.

"My club." Robert climbed in.

The carriage moved slowly until they finally broke free of the crush of traffic leaving Lady Peddington's School. When the vehicle lurched into a faster pace, he leaned back against the cushion and watched the bright square of light that entered, crossed and left his carriage at each passing streetlamp. Each time the lamplight glinted off the gold threaded cord that tied back the window curtains, he was reminded of Miss Glasbarr's curls. When they reached his club, he disembarked, annoyed by a journey that had only emphasized his inability to put her from his mind. He stomped up the four steps and entered the elegant, three-story structure with a frown.

Once at his usual table, he sent for a glass of whisky. He awaited the solace the smooth liquor offered with impatience but somehow, when the glass arrived, the dark liquor didn't seem worth drinking. Idly, he turned the tumbler in his hand and stared into the russet depths. If he angled the cut crystal the right way, the surface of the whisky caught the candlelight and gleamed the color of her hair.

"Very well, Banbrook, what will it take to make you go away?"

Robert looked up as Dunreid pulled out the chair across from him and settled into the cushioned seat.

"Your presence is enough." Robert set his glass down and stood.

"For God's sake, sit down," Dunreid said, tone friendly. "You're making a spectacle of yourself."

"You're the one who posed the question." Robert didn't bother to conceal his animosity as he looked down at Dunreid. "I'm simply giving an honest answer."

The viscount scowled, neck craned backward to look up. He stood, and placed his stocky form between Robert and the rest of the room. "I want that girl, Banbrook. You don't."

"I might."

Dunreid snorted. "What happened to your honesty? The world knows you're still pining for my wife."

Robert's hands balled at his sides. The muscles in his arm twitched. He longed for the satisfaction of burying his fist in Dunreid's fleshy face.

"I'll ask again, nicely, for old times' sake." Dunreid's voice was low, but still convivial. "What will it take for you to go away? You should accept something, because I'll have her in the end, either way."

"I'm not a horse trader and she is not a mare at market," Robert said, echoing Miss Glasbarr's words.

Dunreid shrugged. "She may as well be."

Robert answered that with a glower.

Face bright with an evil glee, Dunreid leaned closer. "You can't be bought, I know. You're even wealthier than I am, but I have one thing you want. What about a trade? One night with Cinthia for a go at the lass. I'll give her back when I'm done. I'm sure you're used to other men's—"

Robert swung. Dunreid dodged the punch. Hi fist plunged into Robert's middle. The air drove from his lungs. Pain doubled him over. Dunreid's rasping breath penetrated the blood surging in his ears. Robert straightened and loosed a wild punch. His fist connected with something solid.

"Bloody hell." Dunreid fell back several paces.

Men closed in around them. Voices rose. Hands fastened on Robert's shoulders, though he made no move to pursue the viscount. He blinked tears of fury from his vision and yanked against the men's hold.

Dunreid collapsed into a chair, one hand clutched to his left eye. With the right, he glared at Robert. "You bastard. This will blacken. What am I supposed to tell Cinthia?"

"That's not my concern," Robert bit out. "Use whatever lies you normally tell your wife."

He shook off the hands and tugged his jacket straight. He turned and cast a glare around the room, lest anyone decide to avenge Dunreid. Most of the assembled gentlemen had adopted neutral expressions, though some looked amused.

Several large footmen crowded the far doorway, eyeing him. The club's proprietor kept them on hand, for there was no fighting permitted. Robert offered the footmen a grimace of apology and strode toward the exit.

CHAPTER FIVE

AT THE APPROACH OF footsteps, Emilia looked up from the sketch on which she worked. Seated in the inner courtyard of the school, she sought to capture the soaring oak that grew in the center. She'd done so many times, but never failed to see something new in the arching branches. She hoped, should she be fortunate enough to find a husband, he would have a garden even half as lovely as the school's.

Quick steps brought the approaching maid, Mary, to stand before her. The girl bobbed a curtsey. She proffered a wrapped package. "Miss, this arrived for you. There's no note saying who from, so we thought it best to accept it." She darted a glance about the courtyard, but they were alone. "I was told to remind you, though, that accepting letters or gifts from gentlemen to whom you are not related, engaged or wed is against school policy."

Emilia took the package with a twinge of trepidation. "I am very much aware of that, thank you. I wish I could say I'm not violating that policy, but I haven't any notion who this is from."

Mary shrugged. A grin dimpled her cheeks, giving her an innocence Emilia didn't quite trust. Mary was Lady Peddington's favorite and a consummate spy for the headmistress. "What's wrapped in there doesn't matter really, Miss. So long as you don't make a scandal for the school, no one cares much."

Emilia smiled, for Mary likely meant well. Emilia cared, though. She didn't want to accept packages from men. Especially from a certain man. The small wrapped parcel was there now, though, so she hadn't much choice. "Thank you."

Mary offered the package a lingering look, obviously disappointed at being dismissed before the paper was removed. Emilia kept a bland, pleasant expression until the maid turned and walked away. She was never comfortable with dismissing servants, and couldn't bring herself to order them to leave. At home, they'd only two footmen, two maids, a cook and a house keeper. The six lived with them and had for as long as Emilia could recall. They were more family than staff.

Once alone, she drew off the paper. A note lay tucked beside a small box embossed with a jeweler's mark she didn't recognize, not that she knew many. The placement was clever, for a note on top may very well have been opened by the zealous staff, but they wouldn't unwrap the package. Unease making her fingers clumsy, Emilia unfolded the message.

Consider this but a glimpse of my generosity, and a thank you for services you shall one day render. That slender neck of yours shouldn't go unadorned. - VD

Emilia grimaced. She looked down at the box in distaste. Did she even wish to open it?

An inspection of the note revealed no address, no way to send the gift back. She stared at the box, this present which, if discovered, would tarnish her reputation, perhaps beyond repair. Open or not, whatever was inside was in her keeping until she could figure out a way to rid herself of it. She lifted the lid.

A pendant lay on black velvet. The accompanying chain looked too delicate to bear the weight of the monstrosity. Gold, diamonds, sapphires and rubies winked at her. The stones themselves were lovely, but the conglomeration overdone to the point of distastefulness. She snapped the lid closed, wishing she dared curse like some of the other country bred girls she knew.

With quick hands, she gathered her work, then tucked the note and box in with her drawing tools. The message she could burn. The despicable pendant she would have to hide. Perhaps she could make an excuse to visit the more expensive shopping districts. If she could glimpse the jeweler's marks in a shop, she could determine where to divest herself of the monstrosity.

She was halfway across the yard when Mary reappeared. The girl hurried toward Emilia, leaving little doubt she was the goal. Mary curtsied when they met near the entrance to the school. Nervous fingers smoothed her uniform.

"Miss, you've a caller." Mary's tone held an odd note.

"At this time of day?" Emilia squinted upward. "The hour cannae be much past noon." When Mister Banbrook said afternoon, she assumed a time much later.

"The visitor is a viscountess, Lady Cinthia."

Emilia recognized the note in Mary's voice now, mingled worry and awe. She didn't share the maid's reverence, but did appreciate her apprehension. The name twisted a knot in Emilia's gut. Viscount Dunreid's wife coming to call could not be good.

She pursed her lips. To carry her sketchbook and satchel of drawing tools into an audience with the viscountess would be unseemly. She could hardly ask Mary to take them to her room, though. The satchel contained the necklace, and servants snooped, especially Lady Peddington's Mary. The girl would report the necklace within moments of its discovery.

"I'll be only a moment. I must return to my quarters."

"If you don't mind me saying, Miss, her ladyship seemed agitated, and specifically said she wished to see you immediately."

Emilia winced. Well, if Lady Cinthia wished to see her in a hurried fashion, she would bear the disrespect of Emilia's encumbrance. She nodded and gestured for Mary to lead the way.

The walk to the front parlor wasn't long. Though not the largest receiving room, the space was the most opulent the school boasted. Emilia knew the servants had standing orders to place anyone of noble birth or considerable wealth there. She squared her shoulders as Mary knocked once on the open door.

"Miss Glasbarr, as you requested, my lady," Mary said, then bowed and stepped inside. She moved to stand to the right of the doorway, gaze ahead and unfocused, awaiting any further orders.

Emilia's steps faltered as she entered. Straight backed, Lady Cinthia sat perched on the edge of a red velvet, gold fringed settee. White-blonde curls, china-fine skin and graceful limbs, all arranged in stiff perfection. Light blue eyes, not hazel ones of an undefinable color like Emilia had, regarded her above high cheek bones. With a woman as beautiful as Lady Cinthia in his home, how could the viscount possibly care to stray?

Emilia managed a somewhat graceful curtsey, which Lady Cinthia acknowledged with a nod. When Emilia straightened, she took up a study of the opulent red and gold carpet, aware the viscountess scrutinized her. Emilia glanced up in time to see those ice blue eyes look past her to the maid.

"We do not care for refreshments, or to be disturbed," Lady Cinthia said in perfect English tones, rarely heard in Edinburgh. "Close the door when you leave."

Emilia's face heated. To offer refreshments and dismiss the maid was her role. She hadn't, though. She'd stood there like the country dolt she was.

The door closed with a thud. Silence stole over the room. Emilia felt like a child called before her mother to answer for her crimes.

"Well, come here, girl." Lady Cinthia's words snapped with impatience.

With careful steps, Emilia crossed as far as the end of the settee. Lady Cinthia's cloying perfume filled her nostrils. Emilia didn't know where to look. Though she felt it impossible the other woman knew of Viscount Dunreid's kiss, his determination to make her his mistress, and the very expensive gift in the satchel she clutched to her side, guilt and shame prevented her from meeting Lady Cinthia's eyes. Emilia couldn't very well stare anywhere lower, though. After a few glances, she settled on a spot over the woman's left shoulder.

A sigh escaped the viscountess. "You're a buxom little thing, aren't you?"

Was she supposed to reply to that?

"Not what I imagined at all," Lady Cinthia continued. "Although I suppose some men find a lack of sophistication attractive, in a tawdry sort of way."

Emilia's face grew hot. How much of her husband's plans did the viscountess know? "I beg your pardon, my lady?"

"Why? Have you done something that requires my pardon?"

Emilia yanked her gaze to meet the woman's stare. "Oh no. Of course not. I wouldn't."

"Wouldn't you?" Blue eyes narrowed. "Tell me, then, what am I to think when my husband comes to breakfast with a black eye? Then, when I have him followed, as any good wife would, he goes to the most expensive jeweler in town, picks out a costly trinket, and has the shop owner send the bauble here, to you. A gift like that is only given for unpardonable things."

"Oh, but I didn't do anything," Emilia cried. She dropped to the settee, satchel clutched before her. "I really didn't. Viscount Dunreid tried...that is, he may have asked...but maybe I misconstrued. I must have, of course." Shut your mouth, Emilia, she railed in her head. You don't tell a woman that her husband is trying to have an affair with you, especially not a powerful socialite who could see you run out of town.

"What did my husband ask?" Lady Cinthia's tone was icy.

Emilia shook her head. "Nothing."

"And you refused him this nothing?"

Hesitantly, Emilia nodded.

Lady Cinthia snapped to her feet. Back straight, she paced away, then spun to face Emilia. "You fool girl, that's the worst thing you could have done. Ailbeart loves the hunt. How do you think I ended up with such a wealthy, titled, self-proclaimed bachelor? All of London told him I was the one woman he would never win." She aimed another glare at Emilia. "If you'd simply given in to him, he would have moved on and I would be the one receiving gifts, by way of apology, as it should be."

So, she was to blame, for not permitting Viscount Dunreid to have his way with her? The unfairness of Lady Cinthia's logic stung. Emilia wrenched open her satchel and pulled out the box. She proffered the unwanted gift. "You take this, then. It should be yours. I want nothing to do with the viscount, or his gifts."

Lady Cinthia eyed the box. Quick strides brought her back to the settee. She snatched the box from Emilia's hand and open the lid.

"It's hideous." Lady Cinthia grimaced down at the pendant. "But I could have the stones reset into separate pieces." She shoved the lid closed and leveled a contemplative look on Emilia. "I will take this."

Emilia vented her relief in a long exhale. At least that was one trouble solved. "Please, my lady, I don't want anything that's yours. How can I... extricate myself from this?"

Derision shone in Lady Cinthia's eyes. "I find that statement difficult to believe, Miss Glasbarr. Everyone wants something of mine, be it wealth, social advantage or a matter of the flesh."

Emilia fended off a grimace at the woman's vulgar words. "I assure you, I do not. I only want a husband and a small home, and I've made arrangements to seek those things. Why, this afternoon, I'm going for a ride in the park with Mister Banbrook to—"

"A ride in the park with Mister Banbrook?" Lady Cinthia snapped.

Too late, Emilia recalled there was some greater connection between the two than both being English. Lady Cinthia glowered at her for a moment, then threw her head back and laughed, to Emilia's astonishment. When she lowered her chin, she leveled a hard, pity-filled look on Emilia.

"You'll have no luck with Banbrook, my dear. He's one who will never wed." Her lips pulled into a smile, but her blue eyes were devoid of kindness. "You know Miss Kitty Thomas jilted him only last week?

She was a smart girl, to see he was only leading her on." She lowered her voice, conspiratorial. "He likes to engage himself to a girl so he can, shall we say, sample the wares, but he doesn't mean to see the engagement through."

Emilia gaped. Could that be true? Mister Banbrook hadn't struck her that way at all. She shook her head in disbelief.

"Trust me. We were engaged for two years, back in London. Ask anyone." Lady Cinthia's parody of a smile was patronizing now.

Unsure what to make of such an accusation, Emilia blurted, "I thought you left him." Hadn't the viscount said something about Mister Banbrook being jilted yet again?

Lady Cinthia nodded. "I did. How long would you wait for a man to reach the altar?" She tapped the pendant box against her thigh in an agitated rhythm.

"I do no' know," Emilia murmured, thoroughly confused. She did know one thing, though, lady or no, wronged party or not, the viscountess seemed increasingly like a terrible person. One Emilia didn't wish to spend further time with.

"Such an innocent." Lady Cinthia shook her head. "It's a shame you'll have to grow out of that. I daresay your naivete is the sum of your appeal." She looked Emilia up and down again, her expression one of distaste. "Certainly, your allure doesn't stem from your overly-plump curves or straw-yellow hair."

Emilia clutched her satchel close and hunched her shoulders in an effort to hide at least some of her distasteful curves. The viscountess's words were ones she'd heard since the age of sixteen, but Emilia had no ready reply. She knew she was a plump little country mouse. That's why she'd come to finishing school, to try to become suitable for city life.

Lady Cinthia shrugged, the gesture dismissing Emilia's lack of worthiness as beneath her notice. "I can see myself out. Take my advice, return to wherever you came from before you become embroiled in a world you're too simple to understand." She strode to the door and stopped, back to Emilia. "I trust this is the last I'll have to see or hear of you."

Lady Cinthia swung open the door and swept gracefully from the room. Emilia remained hunched on the settee. Could the viscountess be right?

CHAPTER SIX

ROBERT WHISTLED AS HE tied his cravat in readiness for his ride with Miss Glasbarr. A ride in the park used to be one of his favorite activities. Fine weather. Expertly guiding his team. Light banter with his acquaintances. An exquisite woman by his side.

He hadn't taken Kitty Thomas to the park. The idea of doing so brought Cinthia too much to mind. Today, his thoughts held no room for the willowy socialite he'd worshiped for years. Instead, his imagination dwelled on a petite, slightly buxom, golden haired girl whose Scottish burr was made lovely by traces of a soft country lilt.

He wondered if Miss Glasbarr had an appreciation for fine horseflesh. Most women did not, but she was from the countryside, and he'd overheard the tail end of her discussion with Campbell. Had she been humoring the unworthy fop, or genuinely interest? It would be a marvelous thing to travel the park's lanes with someone he could converse with on one of his favorite topics. So many splendid teams would be on display during the afternoon promenade.

His hands stilled halfway through the final knot. And there would be many eligible gentlemen, and introductions to be made. That was the main goal of the outing, after all. He must not lose sight of the point of their ride. Robert gave his reflection a firm nod and finished the knot.

He permitted his valet to help him shrug into his coat and left the room. The plush carpets in his chamber gave way to equally luxurious weaves in the hall. What would Miss Glasbarr think of his Edinburgh home? She dreamed of something a bit shabbier for herself, he would wager, but surely opulence would be a pleasant surprise? A man couldn't help if he was wealthy, after all. Not that Robert was the wealthiest man in Edinburgh, but after a certain point, greater wealth couldn't add additional ease—or joy—to life. Robert was well past the point where more money could increase his happiness.

He accepted hat and gloves from his butler, Edwards, and left his townhouse. As he descended the steps, a large black lacquered carriage pulled away from the curb down the street and rolled to a halt behind his curricle. He eyed the crest on the side with distaste. Dunreid. Robert turned his back and headed toward his own conveyance.

"Mister Banbrook."

The familiar honeyed tone halted Robert midstride. He turned slowly. His name, uttered in that voice, was the first words Cinthia had addressed to him since she ran off with Dunreid, over a year ago.

The dark red curtains of the carriage were pulled back to frame her alabaster skin and pale locks. She was a painting, or a vision, neither of which were real. Robert stayed where he was, touched with an odd unease. He'd only just begun to shake off the clinging tendrils of her web. He didn't know if he would survive another entanglement.

"Mister Banbrook, will you not approach?" She dipped her lashes. Ice blue eyes gazed up through them. "I should like to have words with you. Quiet words."

He looked up and down the street. Seeking aid, distraction? He knew not. Which he sought didn't matter, for the only other people were their stone-still, expressionless servants. Against his will, Robert walked nearer. Why was she there, now, finally, when he'd pursued her fruitlessly for so long?

"Will you sit in the carriage with me?" she asked when he came to a halt beside the vehicle.

"I think not, my lady. I have someplace to be." He'd punched her husband the evening before. Did she know he was the one who'd blackened Dunreid's eye? Was her warmth a lure, so she could issue a complaint?

She craned her head out the window, offering a generous view of long white neck and cleavage. Her eyes narrowed as she took in his curricle. "Going for a ride in the park?"

"I am."

She turned back and employed her long lashes once more. "Time was, you only rode in the park with me."

"Time was, we were engaged. Now, my lady, we are not, and you are wed to another man." He was aware his words were clipped, but what politeness could she truly expect from him?

Her lips flattened into a hard line. He knew her well enough to see the effort she exerted to plump them back into a smile. A white gloved hand snaked through the window and closed on his cravat. She gave a tug and drew him closer. "There are things I should like to speak with you on. Will you not come in off the street? Someone may overhear."

Though movement was a bit awkward with her clinging to his cravat, Robert looked up and down the street again. The quiet roadway remained empty. The homes were all quite large, with sizable gardens. Few houses led to little traffic. "We seem alone enough, my lady."

"And why do you insist on *my lady*, when you once called me your Cinthia?" she asked in a throaty whisper.

"Because you are Dunreid's Cinthia now, my lady." It would take a better man than Robert to keep bitterness from his tone.

"But I could be your Cinthia again." Her hand smoothed his cravat and came to rest against his jacket front, over his heart. "That's what I've come to speak with you about. It's a very…delicate matter, you understand." She lowered her voice even more. "You see, I have yet to produce an heir."

A bolt of pain went through him at her choice of topic. Children, as he'd once envisioned for them. "You've been wed little more than a year. I wouldn't let the lack of a babe worry you." What was this new torment? Was this her underhanded way of getting back at him for striking Dunreid?

"But I am worried. More importantly, Dunreid is worried. I can tell by the way he looks at me. He means to send me into the country while he does as he pleases and hopes for a by-blow to carry on his line." Her whispered words held a frantic edge. "Only, I don't believe I am the trouble. Even with a string of lovers and mistresses, he's never once sired a child. Once I'm sequestered, I'll be helpless, but if I can get myself with child now, while Dunreid and I still share a bed, he'll never know—"

"Enough," Robert ground the word out.

"But Robert, who else can I go to? You're the only man I trust." A sheen of tears formed in her eyes. "You're the only man I've ever loved."

He backed away from her, a bitter laugh wrenched free. "How easily you employ the word, my lady." He shook, but knew not if in rage or with some other, more desperate emotion. "Once, I would have believed the claim of love from your lips."

"Robert," she hissed. Her eyes darted about, taking in her servants. Dunreid's servants.

He returned to her carriage window. She was correct, their exchange was not one he would wish overheard. "You cannot ask it of me, Cinthia. I can't do it." Though his words were whispered, they grated between lips nearly numb with rage, a throat that felt raw, as if the refusal had torn from him.

Twin lines appeared on her brow. "Can't? Of course, you can. I shall make aiding me in this easy for you." A smile curved her lips. "And enjoyable."

He stared at her, horrified he'd once loved the creature before him. "Leave me out of your mad scheme. Find someone else."

Her lips flattened again. This time, she didn't force a gentler expression. "I won't take no for an answer, Robert." She raised a staying hand when he opened his mouth. "Think on my request. That's all I ask. We'll speak again. Soon."

Robert backed away, shaking his head. Perhaps she truly was mad, and bent on dragging him into insanity alongside her. "Let me answer you another way, my lady, for you are correct, I could." He scoured her with his gaze, took in every perfect feature. "But I won't. I don't want to. Not anymore."

She jerked back. Her features pinched into sourness. "We'll see, Robert."

He shook his head again. "If you'll excuse me, my lady, as I said, I have somewhere to be."

"I do excuse you, for now." A new smile reached her lips, but stole even more beauty from her face than her sour expression had. "By the by, you should know that your new little amusement accepted a rather expensive pendant from Dunreid this morning. I'm sure she'll look lovely wearing his gift."

Robert retreated another step. She may as well have struck him.

"When will you learn, Robert?" she asked, her look pitying. She yanked the curtains closed. Dunreid's coachman flicked the reins and the carriage eased around his vehicle.

Robert stood, unable to force movement into his limbs, and watched until the coach turned down the side street out of view. The sun no longer appeared bright. The sky was not blue, but a dull grey. In fact, he was sure the heavens would spew forth rain at any moment. He pivoted on his heels and jogged up the steps. His butler opened the door.

"Tell them to put the curricle away, Edwards," Robert said as the door closed behind him. "Send for my carriage. I'll be in my study." He yanked off his gloves and hat, and proffered them.

His butler excepted the items with the slightest frown. "Your carriage, sir?"

"Yes, my carriage."

"Not going to the park, then, sir?"

Robert didn't miss the regret in the man's tone. He passed a hand over his eyes. He was aware his staff had been worried about him for quite some time. "No. I'm going to my club. Send word to that finishing school, Lady Peddington's. Tell one of the maids to inform Miss Glasbarr I shall not arrive. Something came up. Perhaps tomorrow." Robert was struck with the unexpected—and unwelcome—thought that she would be disappointed. "Rather, tell her definitely tomorrow."

"Yes, sir. I'll see to it."

"Thank you. Let me know when my carriage is ready." Robert accepted his butler's nod and headed toward his study. He was sure he had at least one decanter of whisky there.

CHAPTER SEVEN

THE DAY AFTER LADY Cinthia's disturbing visit to the school, Emilia sat in the courtyard once more, as she often did. Her drawing tools lay in their usual arrangement. The page before her, however, remained blank. She would study the row of blossoms she wished to capture, focus on the page, and then her mind would wander.

She let out a sigh. Truth be told, the only thing she wished to sketch was Mister Banbrook's countenance. His strong jaw, his fathomless grey eyes. She wondered if she could capture his fleeting look of amusement. He was even more handsome when he permitted himself to be cheerful.

She shook her head to dispel his face from her mind, and narrowed her gaze on the flowers. The pink blooms where what she wished to draw. Flowers. Not a man who had no wish to wed, had failed in his promise to take her for a ride in the park and who, she suspected, loved Lady Cinthia. Emilia poised her hand over the page.

Could she count on Mister Banbrook? Even if he wasn't for her, she still required his protection from Viscount Dunreid, and his aid. True, she'd danced at the second dance, a fine improvement over the first, but she hadn't snared a suitor. Mister Banbrook had promised to help her find one.

Should she write Sir Stirling again? Ask for a new savior? But if she did that, would she ever see Mister Banbrook again? Not seeing him again seemed quite unacceptable. The thought hurt more than his failure to appear the previous afternoon.

Light footfalls broke into her awareness. She swiveled to find Mary approaching. Emilia wondered what new torment the girl was there to announce.

"Miss, there's a gentleman asking if you're in. A Mister Banbrook. He says he's here to collect you for a ride in the park."

Emilia stood, unable to suppress a sudden smile. "He's in the large parlor? Please tell him I won't be long." She began stowing her drawing tools.

"I will, Miss. He's in the small parlor, Miss."

The small parlor. Emilia frowned. He wasn't titled.

"Will you require one of us girls to accompany you, Miss?" Mary asked.

Emilia's hands stilled. She didn't want to be accompanied by one of Lady Peddington's spying servants, even if Mary always seemed kind. "Did he arrive in an open vehicle, or closed?"

"A curricle, Miss. A very fine one."

Emilia raised her eyebrows at that observation. How fine was very fine? Mister Banbrook dressed impeccably, but then the English always did, even if they ended up in debtor's prison to do so. Yet Mary said he waited in the small parlor. Was he wealthy?

"Given he's arrived in a curricle, I feel I shall be well enough chaperoned by the community at large, but thank you for the offer."

"It's my duty, Miss."

"Thank you," Emilia repeated.

The maid left and Emilia finished stowing her drawing tools. She tried not to appear in an unseemly hurry as she carried them to her room, where she would collect gloves, shawl and bonnet. Her feet, however, seemed to wish for a happy pace. Her heart beat easier knowing Mister Banbrook hadn't abandoned her.

Once properly attired for a ride in the park, Emilia went to the small parlor to find Mr. Banbrook seated on the same settee Lady Cinthia had used. He made the delicate piece look small, almost child-sized. In one flowing movement, he stood and executed a graceful bow.

"Miss Glasbarr. I have come for our agreed upon outing to the park."

The perfect neutrality of his tone halted her in the doorway. She hadn't expected warmth, of course, but he seemed almost as if he contained ire. With the English, a cool façade could mean so many things, but his grey eyes were intent on her and not overly convivial in cast. His gaze moved to her throat. She touched her neck, worried something was there.

"Thank you?" She winced at the question in her voice.

"It is my pleasure," he said in those same cool, clipped tones.

Is it? She wondered. She would more believe the opposite. "I do realize ye must be busy, Mister Banbrook. I mean, you must have other things to do with your day than escort young misses about. If you don't have the time to take me, I—"

He held up a staying hand. "I do have the time." Some of the tension left his features. "I was looking forward to a ride in the park with you, Miss Glasbarr."

Was? Did that mean he wasn't any longer? How could his attitude toward her have cooled so when she hadn't set eyes on him since the second ball? "Thank you," she repeated.

His gaze returned to her neck. She wished for a mirror. Had she broken out in hives? She felt nervous enough to have.

"Shall we?" He raised his eyebrows.

Emilia realized she blocked the doorway. Her face heated as she turned and led the way to the foyer. She mumbled thanks to the butler who opened the door to permit her escape into the cooler air of the street. Her attention fell on a magnificent matched pair of Cleveland Bays.

Their coats gleamed with health, and their deep chestnut tone and glossy black manes mimicked to perfection the lacquered wood and dark trim of the curricle they drew. She could see why even a city-bred girl like Mary would be impressed, though the maid likely saw the vehicle rather than the superb equine specimens.

Mister Banbrook halted beside her. Emilia schooled her awed expression. She made certain her mouth was closed and headed down the steps. She wished she could introduce herself to the bays but, if she'd learned anything at Lady Peddington's School, it was that gentlemen didn't care to have their realms invaded by females unless they led the conversation there, and horseflesh was a man's business.

Mister Banbrook handed her up, palm warm through his glove. When he climbed in beside her, the curricle dipped, but evened back out. She hid a smile, thinking the team would be better pleased if their master could sit in the center of the bench seat. With his tall frame, he must weigh twice what she did, even if she was too plumply curved, as Lady Cinthia had noted.

Emilia held her breath when Mister Banbrook took up the reins, for it would be a travesty if he couldn't handle the pair as well as they deserved. She expelled the air she held, relieved when he guided the curricle into traffic with the offhanded surety of skill. He navigated the mild chaos of Charlotte Square with ease.

By the time they reached the park, Emilia's mood had lightened. The day was fine, even brighter than the one before and possessed of a light, warm breeze. She rode in the most elegant vehicle she'd ever set eyes on, pulled by a peerless team, with a tall, handsome Englishman beside her. She would not dwell on the fact that he was not to be her tall and handsome Englishman, but rather would enjoy the beauty of the ride.

Mister Banbrook merged his curricle into the parade of vehicles circling within the park, the gentry in each on display for one another. She wore her best day dress, but Emilia realized she appeared a bit shabby for the occasion. Other women wore hats piled high with adornments, held lace parasols offering flattering, dappled shade, and sported glittering jewels. She hoped Mister Banbrook wasn't embarrassed by her appearance. Certainly, she wasn't fine enough to occupy his curricle.

She couldn't suppress a small sigh. How would she ever attract a husband? She had no dowry, no willowy grace like Lady Cinthia, and not enough funds to purchase clothing that would conceal either condition.

"Sighing, Miss Glasbarr?" Mister Banbrook's tone was still neutral, though no longer as cool.

Emilia put a hand to her mouth. To sigh was bad manners. In truth, she hadn't needed finishing school to know that.

"I am not engaging you in proper conversation, I know," Mister Banbrook continued. "Please forgive me."

She dropped her hand. "Oh, no, the error is mine. I am meant to begin conversation, I believe. On the weather, or perhaps the classics. Being a bit overwhelmed by the display before me, I forgot."

"The display?" He turned his head, and took in the other carriages. "Edinburgh needs a larger park."

"I think the park is lovely." Did he think his English cities so much grander? "Not every place is London, or wants to be." Her hand went back to her mouth as her aggrieved tone reached her ears. She needed to learn to shut her mouth and keep it closed.

Mister Banbrook looked at her askance. "Which is fortunate. The world would be a boring place were every city the same."

Emilia nodded, not trusting herself to speak. They rode on in silence. Her mood well dampened once more, she cast about for a safe topic.

"You meant the other ladies, I take it?" Mister Banbrook said. "Your sigh was of the envious sort?"

So, he'd noticed her unmodish attire. Not surprising, since there was no hiding her drab garb. Emilia shrugged. "They look awfully fine, but my sigh wasn't envy. More, well, despair. How can I attract a husband, any husband, with such a display? No man will notice me."

"If you look about you, I think you'll find many men noticing you."

"They're noticing you, Mister Banbrook, and your curricle and team. If they look at me, they glance only to wonder why you would possibly keep company with someone so shabby."

"If any suggest as much, I'll put them in their place," he replied.

Emilia felt a blush threaten, for his words seemed oddly sincere.

"You're the most beguiling creature in this park," he continued. "Men don't care about bonnets heaped with bows and lace, or dresses trimmed out in the latest fashion. We often don't even notice such things. Or the lack of jewelry."

Her hand went to her throat again. Did he know Viscount Dunreid had given her a necklace? Was that why he was cool, why he kept looking at her neck? But so few people knew. He wouldn't have learned such a detail from the viscount.

No, if Mister Banbrook knew, the knowledge could only have come from the viscountess. So, he was keeping company with Lady Cinthia. Emilia suppressed another sigh. The thought was like someone draping her in a sopping wet cloak. The knowledge stole all potential joy from the day.

High above, a fluffy cloud slid across the sun. Emilia squinted heaven-ward, finding the sudden dimness fit her mood. Across the open expanse they rode, she could see sunshine in other areas of the park. The light made the ladies' jewels sparkle.

"Now you truly are letting the conversation lapse, Miss Glasbarr," Mister Banbrook said. He watched her from the corner of his eye. "I mentioned your lack of jewelry."

"I own no jewelry, Mister Banbrook. Though I can't think my lack of adornment a fitting topic to discuss after so short an acquaintance, I will say that if anyone observed I do not wear, say, a necklace, and attempted to rectify the absence, I would certainly return such an item." She sought to press the disappointment of his involvement with Lady Cinthia from her mind so she could glean why he was so dogged about the pendant.

"Would you, now?"

"I would," she said firmly. He must wish to know if he was wasting his time, she concluded. If she had accepted a present from Dunreid, Mister Banbrook had no reason to help her. "To keep such a gift, let alone wear it, would be tantamount to accepting a proposal from a gentleman. I would no' do so lightly."

"Even if the object in question was quite valuable? Something you could sell at a later date?"

"Especially then," she said, a touch exasperated. Must the English always be so convoluted?

"That's good to know, and I apologize for my unfitting topic."

She resisted the urge to roll her eyes. Mister Banbrook was so very English. Couched in impeccable manners, they did as they pleased, then apologized with the same stiff aplomb. A Scot would have asked if she'd accepted the gift, taken her no as a yes, and gone off to challenge Viscount Dunreid.

Some of her exasperation fled. No, not challenge him, for Mister Banbrook was not her suitor. He was only there to find her one.

CHAPTER EIGHT

ROBERT COULDN'T SHAKE HIS dark mood. He was being a poor companion, but how could he be otherwise? The knowledge of Dunreid's gift to Miss Glasbarr, and seeing the way she ogled his expensive curricle, had put him in a terrible frame of mind. He'd thought her better, that she would not be so easily swayed by a show of wealth.

Then, they'd reached the park and he could read her envy. She wished for gowns, hats and jewels, just as any other young Miss did. Her sigh belied her talk of art and music. Her avarice soured him. She wasn't the woman he'd thought.

She spoke not of envy, but of fear she fell short compared to the ladies about them, but that was absurd. Surely, closeted in a school of young women, she had ample opportunity to compare herself and realize her beauty. Dressed to the height of fashion or in a secondhand frock, not a one of them could equal Miss Glasbarr. For her to be unaware of that was impossible.

Robert worked to ease the tension in his jaw. She also denied keeping Dunreid's present, more a payment for future sins than a gift, as she must know. Could he believe her? He would not see another woman plucked from him by Dunreid.

He flicked the reins to increase their pace.

Plucked not from *him*. From his *care*. He wasn't courting her, he was her chaperone. Why had he permitted Stirling to talk him into such a ridiculous task? Robert knew nothing about finding a match for a young woman. He couldn't even find a match for himself.

"You wish to take the turn at a faster pace?" Miss Glasbarr asked. "I feel that's contrary to what most do."

On top of fortune hunting, she would criticize how he handled his team? "Would you care to drive?"

She turned wide eyes on him, bright with surprise and...eagerness? "You would permit me? Only, they're such a fine team. I've never had the opportunity to handle Cleveland Bays."

By God, she did wish to drive. Eyebrows raised, he proffered the reins. Hopefully, doing so wasn't the most foolish decision of his life.

Her happy smile as she accepted the reins was an instant reward, and sapped some of his ire. Her hazel eyes, which reflected the colors of park and sky, were utterly guileless. Hands sure, she guided his bays. In moments, he garnered her competence.

Free of the duty of manning his spirited team, he studied the young woman beside him. Golden curls bounced in concert with the movement of the curricle. Straight backed, she perched on the edge of the seat, excitement at being permitted to drive clear, though she kept her hands soft on the reins. She looked like a child who'd just been handed a longed-for kitten. Eager, but gentle.

Robert rubbed the back of his neck, in attempt to ease the tension there. He was being a fool. He'd let Cinthia and her wiles snake into his thoughts and make him see treachery and avarice where none existed. Miss Glasbarr, in her obviously second-hand gown, stitched over to resemble city fashion, was quite young. He knew enough about women and their insecurities to believe she feared being overlooked.

Rather than dwell in that dark place where Cinthia's conniving heart lived, he should attempt to improve Miss Glasbarr's confidence. Convince her that she would never be out shown. Only a fool wouldn't recognize her sweetness and beauty. Of course, most young men qualified as fools.

Reminded of his duty, Robert looked about him at the other gentlemen in the park. Quite a few eyed Miss Glasbarr in appreciation, while others were obviously incredulous to see her with the reins. A glance showed her oblivious. Expression cheerful, she guided his team along the park avenues nearly as well as he would.

"There's Mister Campbell," Robert said. "You danced with him. Perhaps we should say hello?"

Miss Glasbarr turned her head toward Campbell and frowned. Robert wondered if she wasn't as sure with his team as she seemed. To bring the bays around and then merge back into the parade, coming up alongside Campbell's gilded cabriolet, would be tricky.

"I think I should rather keep going the way we are," she said. "Would that be ungrateful of me, after you went to the trouble of introducing us?"

"I can bring the curricle around, if that's your worry," Robert offered.

She shot him a surprised look. "Oh, no, that isn't the trouble. It's his horse."

"You don't care for him?" She definitely hadn't ogled his team if she couldn't see how fine Campbell's horseflesh was.

"He's splendid, but a Thoroughbred stallion hitched to a cabriolet for a ride in the park? That's criminal. That horse was born to race and jump. I can't possibly become engaged to a man who would hook him to a glorified, gold-encrusted cart."

Robert laughed. She cast him a wide-eyed glance. Her cheeks reddened, but still he laughed. She was so clearly offended. Twin lines appeared on her brow. Her outrage was adorable. His desire to contain his amusement was difficult as her words mirrored his opinion.

"It isnae funny," Miss Glasbarr said. "If he could handle the creature, hooking that stallion to a cart might be somewhat excused, but he's obviously a danger to everyone around him."

Robert laughed harder. Tears blurred his vision. He was aware of scandalized looks from anyone near enough to hear, but he couldn't stop. How long since he'd laughed? Barring the occasional chuckle, years, he was certain.

"I'm glad you find the impending rampage of a Thoroughbred through Edinburgh's gentry amusing." Her tone was light. She offered him a tentative smile.

Robert replied with one of his own, still chuckling. "Drive on then, dear lady, and we'll see if we meet a gentleman whose team, gig and skills meet with your approval."

"Very well, then." She flicked the reins lightly. His bays picked up their pace.

The remainder of their afternoon proceeded in a more cheerful vein. Robert found the country-bred Miss Glasbarr did know her horseflesh, and was more than willing to discuss the teams of their peers. First, she offered the information that her etiquette instructor had forbade them from conversing on such topics with gentlemen unless greatly pressed, but Robert brushed that aside. He was enjoying himself too much to worry over silly proprieties.

When he retook the reins to drive them to Lady Peddington's, Robert was surprised to realize how low the sun was. He brought his somewhat spent team to a halt before the elegant stone school for young ladies, but didn't move to assist Miss Glasbarr down. He was aware of her expectant eyes on him. He had too fine an afternoon to permit the ride to end.

"Well, Miss Glasbarr, did you discover the gentleman of your dreams this in the park today?" He kept his tone light, though a heaviness settled on him as he awaited her reply. None of the men they'd spoken with were worthy of her.

She turned her face toward the glove encased hands in her lap. "I'm not certain." A blush brightened her cheeks.

Though her reply meant he had failed in his duty to her, the heaviness left him. He didn't want to see her settle for an unworthy gentleman. Cheerful again, he secured the reins and vaulted down, then went around to offer his hand.

Blue-green eyes gazed down at him from a still-blushing face. Robert held out his hand. One hand gathering her skirt, Miss Glasbarr placed the other in his. Even in gloves, they were fine, delicate fingers. He would be very careful who he gave them over to, assuming he could find a single man in Edinburgh worthy.

"Thank you for a wonderful afternoon, Mister Banbrook."

"You are most welcome," he said, and helped her down.

She didn't turn away when she reached the street. Her hand tightened on his. "I will see you again?"

"At the next ball," he agreed.

Miss Glasbarr offered a pretty smile. "Thank you." She slipped her hand free.

He closed his fingers over the warmth left by her hand and watched her walk away. Both hands holding up her skirt ever so slightly, she gracefully ascended the steps. The door to the school opened. She looked back, still smiling, and disappeared inside.

Robert let out a slow breath. Finding a gentleman was a more formidable task than he'd excepted. The city was awash in fools, cowards and scoundrels. Not a single gentleman held the proper mix of intelligence, kindness and liveliness for Miss Glasbarr.

Trying to shake off the disquiet that settled in her absence, Robert climbed back into his curricle and took himself to his club. As the place refused to soothe him, he stayed only for a meal, forgoing his usual scotch. Soon enough, he was in his curricle again. As he maneuvered his team through streets crowded by evening festivity seekers, he turned his thoughts to his day in the park, and his beguiling companion, and finally achieved a semblance of peace.

Upon his arrival at his townhouse, he left curricle and team with his servants, then jogged up the steps. As usual, the door opened before he reached the top step. Unlike usual, his butler wore a worried frown.

"Sir."

"What's the trouble, Edwards?" Robert asked as he stripped off hat and gloves.

"I'm not certain there is trouble, sir."

"Yes, you are, or you wouldn't wear that dour expression." Whatever the problem, Robert was resolved to deal with the issue quickly. He would not return to his earlier dark mood. To fend off his malaise, he conjured the memory of Emilia as she accepted the reins.

"A lady arrived while you were out. She insisted she be allowed in. Once inside, she ignored all protests and entered your private chambers, sir. We haven't been able to draw her out." Edwards's features pulled down in mingled disapproval and worry. "We weren't sure how firm to be, sir. She insists she's expected and welcome, and has been making demands on the staff."

Anger hardened in Robert's chest and robbed him of his brief joy. "A lady? I assume you mean Cinthia."

"I do, sir. Viscountess Dunreid, sir," Edwards said, in a not too subtle reminder of Cinthia's status. "I do not mean to intrude, sir, but is she expected and welcome?"

There was no mistaking the despair in his butler's tone. The question would be impertinent, if the entire staff hadn't been uprooted and dragged to Edinburgh in Robert's pursuit of Cinthia, then forced to endure months of him bring misery on himself. He could only imagine how distressed the household was to have her there.

"She is neither expected nor welcome," Robert said. "I will take care of this, and you have my future permission to bar her from the premises."

"Thank you, sir." Edwards almost smiled. "Shall I have a carriage brought to take the lady home? She arrived in a hired hackney."

"Yes, immediately."

Robert turned and took the steps two at a time. What was she thinking, coming alone to his home? Going to his rooms? Had she lost her wits? He didn't bother to tame his angry stride, dissatisfied that the thick carpet muted his footfalls. Not slowing when he reached his chamber door, he flung it open and strode inside.

He stopped. Candles filled the room with wavering light. A heavy scent wafted through the shadows, a nearly visible miasma of honey-laden tendrils. Reclined in the middle of his bed, atop the bedclothes, clad in a confection of silk and lace that displayed more than concealed, lay Cinthia, a book in hand.

Eyes round with surprise dropped closed. They opened on a seductive look. A smile curled her lips. "Robert. I didn't expect you so soon." She closed the book and dropped it over the side of the bed to land on the carpet with a soft thud. "But I'm pleased you're here."

"What the devil are you doing in my bed, Cinthia?" He locked his gaze on her face. Damn, if he would satisfy her with even a glance south of her chin.

She stretched, her smile widening. "Waiting for you."

"Get out."

A startled jerk of her head turned into a shrug. Her coy expression wavered. "I know you don't mean that, Robert."

"On the contrary, I very much do." He had to grit the words out through clenched teeth. "I want you dressed and out of my bed."

"Oh? Want to remove my clothes yourself?" She came up on her knees in the middle of his mattress, silk and lace a puddle around her. "I'm still wearing enough for you to have the pleasure."

Robert closed his eyes. His pulse pounded. His whole body leaned toward the siren on his bed. His body, but not his mind, and never again his heart. "I won't do it, Cinthia. You're Dunreid's now."

"Am I?" The harsh edge to her tone brought his eyes open. "I'm a piece of property, then? A man's possession? No longer my own?"

"That's not what I mean." His words came out too soft. She was so beautiful in the candlelight. How many years had he waited to have her? "You're his wife."

"Yet, he can take his pleasure where he will." She brought her hands to the coverlet and crawled toward him across the bed, eyes on his. "Why can't I? Why can't we, Robert?"

He couldn't help but watch the way she moved. Why couldn't they? He shook his head to clear the spell she wove. "Maybe that's how you and Dunreid want to live, but I don't."

"You mean me to believe that once you wed, you'll never stray?" Her silken voice was soft again, teasing. She reached the edge of the bed and rose to her knees. "Not even a little?"

"I will wed for love, and I will never stray." He could barely make out his own words.

She opened her arms wide. Pale-blonde hair cascaded down her back. "I'm offering you everything you always wanted. What we always wanted."

Robert took a step back. "No," he croaked, throat dry as ashes. He gave a more vigorous shake of his head. "This isn't what I wanted. I wanted breakfast every morning. I wanted to watch our children grow." He took another step back. "I wanted a life together."

"We can still have a child, and he'll be a viscount someday." She smoothed her hands down her frame and angled her face to look up at him through thick lashes. "You can't tell me you don't dream of this."

"Of bedding the woman I once loved so she can raise my child as another man's heir?" The sound that wrenched from his throat bore little resemblance to laughter. "That is not my dream."

Her lips turned downward, muting their bowlike perfection. Blue eyes narrowed. "It's that Scottish chit, isn't it? You're both enamored of her. My husband because he thinks she'll be a fertile little whore and you...I thought you simply wanted to take something from him, but now I see you fancy yourself in love."

Robert blinked. In love? An image of Emilia's open, smiling face, blotted out the treacherous beauty before him. Framed in sun-kissed tresses, that face was all things good.

"You think she's better than I am, don't you? That she's sweet, innocent." Cinthia's tone was harsh now, ugly. "Well, you'll come around once she betrays you. She's no match for Dunreid's persistence. He's like a fox hound with the scent. You'll never best him, Robert. You aren't man enough to take what you want before he can. Once she's his, you'll come crawling to me, brokenhearted and alone, and I'll have what I need from you."

Her hard voice stole through him, cooled him, settled his hammering pulse. "Is that the way of it, Cinthia? I wasn't man enough to keep you?"

"You weren't, and now you aren't man enough to take me," she snapped.

He crossed to the bed, anger alive inside him. "I mourned our future, Cinthia. I wept for it, like a dead lover, but I am not the one who killed it." He raked his eyes up and down her frame, and saw not beauty, but a desperate, vulgar display. "I'm glad Dunreid came along. He stopped me from making the greatest mistake of my life."

She gasped, white-faced.

Robert turned away, a bit surprised to find he'd left the door open. He shrugged, for his servants may as well hear. Perhaps his response to her would reassure them.

"Robert." Cinthia's tone pleaded.

He didn't turn back. As he strode from the room he said, "I'll send a maid to help you dress. I already have carriage ready."

A string of invectives followed him down the hall. Cinthia's shrillness faded as he jogged down the steps. He found Edwards in the foyer.

"Send someone to assist Lady Cinthia back into her garments," Robert said. "I'll be in my study. Let me know when she's gone."

"In your study, sir?" Edwards' face pulled down with worry. "Will you need a new decanter of scotch, then, sir?"

Robert frowned. Would he? Emilia's smile flittered through his mind. "No, Edwards, I think not."

CHAPTER NINE

EMILIA WOKE THE MORNING of the third ball with mixed emotions. She wished to find a husband, and remain in Edinburgh, but the second ball and her ride in the park had produced no suitable candidate. This was partly because none of the available men seemed interested in her, or rather interested enough to defy Viscount Dunreid, but also because, to her despair, she'd come to realize that only one man would suit...Mister Banbrook.

Robert, as she now called him in the privacy of her thoughts, was everything she'd hoped for in a husband, and more. He was also things she never imagined she wanted, but now did. He suppressed his passions. Drawing out a man was a pleasure she'd never before experienced. In the park, when he'd laughed so hard and free, she'd given up any hope of keeping her heart.

Yet two obstacles prevented pursuit of him. He might still love Lady Cinthia, and he wasn't in the market for a wife. Emilia sighed.

These obstacles occupied her thoughts as she went through her morning. No matter how she twisted and turned them, they couldn't be set aside. She could find no way over, through or around those two truths. A sinking despair began to fill her. How could she wed any other man now that she knew Robert? If she couldn't wed, she would return to the country and die an old maid, a burden on her family forever. She almost rued the day she wrote to Sir Stirling and brought Robert into her life.

In need of solace, she went into the garden to draw. Not the flowers that bloomed before her, but to give in to the impulse to sketch *his* fine features. Once down on the page, she gazed at his likeness in misery until she could no longer bear the pain, then forced herself to turn to a clean sheet. Resolutely, she began a sketch of his Cleveland Bays.

She had a fair rendering, one she felt Missus Millview would approve of, before the familiar patter of a maid's footfalls drew her attention. Emilia looked up to find she was, once again, Mary's goal. She felt a surge of hope, for perhaps Robert had come to call, to give some indication he esteemed her as she did him.

Mary proffered a box. "Another package for you, Miss."

"Thank you," Emilia said. She took the package, and waited for Mary's departure, which was almost immediate. Emilia turned the paper wrapped box over in her hands. This time, the message was affixed to the outside, and showed signs of having been opened. More than likely, Lady Peddington already knew what the note said. With a shrug for what couldn't be changed, Emilia opened the page.

To wear tonight.

Yours, with the greatest affection,

RB

With hands that shook, Emilia peeled back the paper. The box inside came from the same jeweler Viscount Dunreid had used, which wasn't surprising. Lady Cinthia had said they were the best in Edinburgh, which meant the jeweler on High Street. Likely, someone more experienced that Emilia would have recognized their box when given the first gift. Carefully, she opened the lid.

Inside gleamed a pendant. The single sapphire, accented by several small diamonds, hung from a delicate chain. The stone was the same size as the largest on the necklace Dunreid had sent, but the similarity ended there. This piece was beautiful. Elegant. Perfectly lovely.

Emilia put a hand to her mouth. Her vision blurred with tears. Robert hadn't asked about jewelry because he'd learned of the necklace. He wasn't keeping company with Lady Cinthia. He'd simply noticed the lack, and attempted to ascertain her feelings, and she'd said...

She clutched the box to her chest. She said that if a gentleman sent such a gift, and she accepted, it would be as if she accepted a proposal. Surely, there was no ambiguity in her words. He'd taken them in, and the pendant was his response.

She jumped to her feet, drawing tools flying. She must ready for the ball. She had a gown selected, but the pink muslin would not do. She must try on every suitable dress, few that there were, and see which best displayed the pendant. Her hair would need to be perfect, as well, a frame for the piece.

Her hands trembled as she opened the box once more. The sapphire glittered in the dappled sunlight beneath the oak. Almost dizzy with joy, she closed the box and dropped to her knees to collect her scattered tools.

Emilia spent the remainder of the afternoon in a happy haze. She stepped in and out of gowns, trying each at least three times. She brushed her hair until it shown, and curled the silken locks, then arranged and rearranged them to perfectly frame her face. Finally, when she felt she'd come as near to faultlessness as she could with her unstylish curves and yellow tresses, she clasped the pendant about her neck.

The hour for the ball rang out from the church bells of Edinburgh, the whole city singing along with her heart. Trembling with excitement, Emilia perched on the edge of her bed to don her slippers. She didn't stand once they were on, but rather stayed where she was, and drew in deep breaths. She didn't know what she'd done to deserve Robert's regard, but she was endlessly thankful. Her hand went to the pendant, to ensure the gift was real. She inhaled in another long, steadying breath.

Finally composed enough to venture out, she stood, crossed to the door and slipped from her room. The hallway was deserted. Her slipper-clad feet made no sound on the thin carpet, though the faint rustle of her skirt filled the silence. Steps light, she flew down the stairs to the foyer.

She wished to meet him alone, there, where they'd first met. Somehow, she knew he would arrive late, as he had then. He would do so in the hope he would find her waiting. Emilia smiled. If she was wrong, no harm would be done. She could seek him in the ballroom, and tell him of her foolishness. Perhaps he would laugh. She loved his laugh.

Emilia took up a position under the great candelabra that hung in the center of the vaulted space, so the pendant would sparkle, and tried to wait calmly. She was aware the butler and footmen darted covert glances her way, but ignored them. If they'd ignored her when Dunreid had foisted his unwanted attention on her at the start of the second ball, they could ignore her now, when she waited full of joy.

She held her hands at her sides, then clasped before her, then behind. She'd decided they should be at her sides again when heavy footfalls sounded in the corridor that led to the ballroom. She tensed. In their few short encounters, she'd come to recognize that aggressive tread. Viscount Dunreid would ruin her meeting with Robert.

Emilia's gaze snapped onto the servants' door hidden in the paneling, closed now while the footmen stood to the side, awaiting more guests. The small room had saved her before, and would again.

She tiptoed to the door. Refusing to look at the footmen and butler, she pulled open the panel. She glimpsed greatcoats and top hats in the instant before she closed the door and found herself smothered by wool and felt. Something soft bounced off her head and hit the floor. A hat, she realized.

Light streamed through the keyhole, disguised in the scrollwork on the outside paneling, and illuminated a single patch of some gentleman's greatcoat. She hardly dared move for fear of toppling the pile of top hats. Carefully, she turned, then inched into a crouch until she was eye-level with the knob. She placed her eye to the keyhole, then jerked back.

True to her fear, Viscount Dunreid paced the foyer. Her heart took up a quick beat. In her eagerness to meet Robert, she'd ignored that the viscount had also found her in the foyer at the start of the last ball. Why, oh why, hadn't it occurred to her that Dunreid might seek her there again?

She mustered her courage and returned her eye to the keyhole. He walked along the wall opposite her. When he reached one end and turned, his gaze caught in her direction. She straightened. Oh dear, had he seen the glint of her eye through the keyhole?

Though muted by the paneling, she discerned approaching footfalls. She squeezed her eyes closed, though how that might help, she didn't know. He came ever nearer. She tried to breath quietly.

More footsteps sounded, near the front of the foyer. She realized the butler must have seen a coach arrive and opened the door in anticipation of new guests... which meant soon the cloakroom door would open as well. She cast about, frantic. Could she push back among the coats and remain unseen?

She eased deeper into the forest of greatcoats. The cloakroom door opened. Light filtered through tiny spaces between the fabric. Heavy fabric was pushed about. The door closed. She could hear the footman hurry away, but Dunreid and the newcomer didn't move.

"Lurking in foyers again, Dunreid?" Robert's voice was so devoid of warmth her happiness dimmed, though his ire wasn't directed toward her.

"I was looking for a certain Miss, but I'll take you." Viscount Dunreid sounded equally hostile. "We need to have words, Banbrook. If you're fortunate, I won't issue a challenge."

Emilia pushed back forward through the coats, eager to see Robert, even if he was angry with Dunreid.

Robert gave a derisive snort. "Challenge me? You're the one trying to ruin an innocent young woman."

"But I'm not the one trying to cuckold a viscount."

Emilia pressed her hands to her mouth to hold in her gasp.

"Nor am I." Robert's words were clipped.

"Then explain to me how it happened that, not four days past, my wife arrived at my townhouse in your carriage, in the evening, thoroughly disheveled."

Palms crushed to her mouth, Emilia bent once more to the keyhole. She needed to see Robert's face, to know if Dunreid's accusation was true.

The view out the keyhole was the back of Dunreid's coat.

"You'll have to ask Lady Cinthia for the details," Robert said. "It's a matter best kept between man and wife."

Why didn't he deny the affair? Emilia's head spun. She leaned her forehead to the door.

"Bloody right it is," Dunreid snarled. "I know you probably think I deserve you taking Cinthia as you please, but for God's sake, man, it isn't as if I kidnapped her. She wanted my title as much as I wanted to give it to her."

"I'm aware of the circumstances of your courtship, thank you," Robert gritted out. "Don't play righteous with me. You saw something that wasn't yours, and you set out to have her."

"She wasn't yours either, or I wouldn't have been able to." The viscount's voice was harsh. "I intended to step aside, you know. Let you have the little Glasbarr chit. But you've crossed a line. You brought this on yourself, and her. Don't forget that."

"Try your best. Miss Glasbarr is too good to give in to you."

Emilia's heart constricted. Too good, was she? But not good enough to keep Robert, rather Mister Banbrook, from having relations with Lady Cinthia. Not good enough to win his heart from his first love.

"Oh, I'm sure she's good, and I mean to find out how good."

Dunreid's lascivious tone brought bile to Emilia's throat. She squeezed her lids closed as tears spilled down her cheeks.

"Watch yourself, Dunreid." Robert's voice was low. Anger curled around the edges of his words.

"Don't worry, when I'm done with her you can have her back."

A loud smacking sounded. The door ricocheted as something crashed into the paneling. Emilia sprawled backward with a squeak and landed in a heap on the floor. Top hats rained down on her. She threw a hand over her head and buried her face in the fallen coats.

The door shook. A final hat hit her shoulder. She yanked her head up.

"I'll have you jailed," Dunreid shouted. "You think we won't hang an Englishman?"

Footsteps sounded. The door rattled. Emilia crawled to the keyhole and jammed her eye against it. Some of Lady Peddington's burlier footmen had arrived. Two restrained Robert as he tried to shake them off.

Wiping at the tears on her cheeks, Emilia struggled to her feet among the toppled hats and greatcoats. There was no point in Robert hanging for her. She wouldn't go to Dunreid, but she didn't have any use for a man who was in love with someone else's wife, either. Even life as a spinster in the country was preferable.

She flung open the door. Viscount Dunreid and another footman turned to her, as did the butler beyond. Robert strained against the grasp of Lady Peddington's footmen. His gaze fell on the pendant she wore and he stilled.

"There's no need for anyone to hang." Emilia tried to make her voice strong, but the words wavered. "No one need fight over me."

"What are you wearing?" Robert whispered.

Emilia cast him a beseeching look. She would return the pendant immediately, but that would associate them in a way she now knew she could not bear. She wouldn't declare herself all but engaged to a man whose heart would never be hers, especially before Viscount Dunreid.

"You wish this man spared?" Viscount Dunreid asked, his tone officious.

Though she knew Robert wouldn't hang on the viscount's word alone, and likely had resources at his disposal, she also knew many among the Scottish peerage bore no great love for their English cousins, so she turned to the viscount and nodded. "I would. He was defending my honor, mistakenly thinking it is his place to do so."

The viscount's smile was slow, almost stunned, but ended as a smirk. "Very well. For you, Miss Glasbarr, I shall drop my complaint against him." He tugged at his jacket, pulling the brocade fabric straight.

"What does this mean?" Robert asked, his voice barely audible, his gaze locked on the pendant.

"It means, my dear chap, that you lose. Again."

Emilia wished she could punch the viscount, as well. She raised beseeching hands to Robert. "It means...it..." She shook her head, unable to find the words. She sucked in a shuddering breath, turned on her heels, and ran.

CHAPTER TEN

SITTING ALONG IN HIS club, the drone of cheerful male voices a backdrop to his misery, Robert stared into his scotch. In his vision stood an image of Emilia, beautiful in a pale blue gown, golden tresses tumbling about, and Dunreid's sapphire at her throat.

His grip tightened. Damn Dunreid and his sapphire, and damn... no, he couldn't bring himself to damn Emilia. If anyone else should be consigned to hell, Robert should be. He wouldn't even have to leave his club. Hell was the world in which he lived.

He eased his grip on the tumbler. He'd already squeezed one into fragments that week. He had the cuts to prove it. His eyes drifted to the decanter in the center of the table, only drained when he poured a new glass each afternoon. A glass he stared at but didn't drink. Not even scotch could numb the pain of Emilia's betrayal.

Even dreams of the Continent held no draw. Nor did dreams of seductive French women, or vivacious Italians. The smooth lull of cognac, the vivid bite of grappa. No amount of exotic beauty or expensive liquor would make a difference. The usual pleasures didn't matter. If Cinthia had broken his heart, Emilia had mended the tortured organ, made it whole. Then she'd taken a blade to it and shave it into little pieces. He set down his tumbler, rested his elbows on the table, and dropped his face to his palms.

The chair across from him scraped out. Fabric rustled as someone settled into the seat. The tumbler at his elbow made a low grating sound as the heavy crystal was dragged across the table. The thick scent of Dunreid's cologne clogged Robert's nose, and threatened to gag him. He heard the viscount swallow. The glass clunked back to the tabletop.

"Don't see what you're so dismal about," Dunreid said. "Good scotch."

Robert lifted his head. So many curses clamored at his lips, he couldn't get one out. "You unmitigated ass," he finally managed.

Dunreid raised his eyebrows. "Look, I only came over to find out if you know who won the Glasbarr chit. Been driving me mad, not knowing. I even went to that jeweler, the one on High Street. They admitted to making the piece she wore, but won't tell me more."

Robert stared. He tried to make sense of Dunreid's words. "Bribed?"

"Don't act as if you've never bribed anyone." He narrowed his eyes. "Don't judge me, Banbrook. Least you can do after I didn't press charges when you bedded my wife."

"I didn't bed anyone," Robert mumbled, his thoughts as muddled as if he'd been drinking the scotch Dunreid now sipped. "You're talking about the necklace you sent?"

"You heard about that?" Dunreid frowned, then shrugged and took another sip. "Suppose she told you? Gorgeous piece. Diamonds, rubies, emeralds, and a great big sapphire. Don't know how a girl could resist an expensive bauble like that, but she returned the damn thing. Jeweler even refunded the fee. Who'd think a single sapphire would win out over all that?" Dunreid's expression turned rueful. "Then again, Cinthia has most everything I give her reset, so maybe my taste doesn't appeal to women."

"You didn't send the sapphire?" Robert gave his head a hard shake to clear his thoughts.

"That one she wore at the ball? I wouldn't insult a girl by buying her with so little." He eyed Robert for a long moment. "You're telling me you don't know who sent that paltry pendant? Whose favor she accepted when she wouldn't have me?"

"When she wouldn't have you?"

"That's what I said. Gads, man, is that your second decanter?"

"But you said, you lost," Robert blurted, confused. "In the foyer, you said I'd lost."

"So you had, and me along with you. You saw that pendant she wore clear as I. A girl like that wouldn't wear a man's gift in public for all to see unless she was in love with the fellow." Dunreid shook his head. "You can't compete with love. I'm smart enough to know when I'm beat."

"But you pursued Cinthia."

Dunreid gave him a pitying look. "I did, and I stand by my words. Can't win over a girl in love." Dunreid downed the rest of the scotch and stood. He set the glass on the table and leaned over to peer at Robert. "You look like hell, Banbrook. Shave, get your valet to dress you for evening, and go find yourself a sweet little piece to take your mind off things. Lord knows that's what I'm going to do."

Robert watched the viscount stomp away, his mind swirling. Not Dunreid's sapphire? Who, then? Someone must have sent the pendant, but not Dunreid. Emilia hadn't agreed to be the viscount's mistress after all. He hadn't bought her, offered her something she thought she couldn't live without, like he had with Cinthia.

But someone had. Robert leaned back in his chair and stared at the far wall. Was the necklace a payment, or a proposal? He thought back through the men Emilia had danced with, and those they'd seen in the park. She hadn't seemed inclined toward any of them.

He rarely agreed with Dunreid on anything, but the viscount was right, the truth must be known, and the jeweler on High Street could reveal who'd sent the necklace. Perhaps charm would win where demands and bribery had not, for Robert was sure those were Dunreid's only tactics.

He pushed to his feet and waved a footman over. "Send for my carriage."

"Yes, sir." The man, John, hurried away.

Long strides carried Robert from the club. He paced outside until his carriage appeared. Not waiting for the conveyance to fully halt, he yanked open the door. He paused only long enough to say, "The jeweler on High Street, now," before he jumped in.

The carriage ride to High Street had never seemed longer. He shifted in his seat, pulled back the curtain a dozen times. Teeth gritted, all he could do was wait for his carriage to arrive.

Robert was familiar with the shop, used by the wealthiest in Edinburgh, and the proprietor. He'd purchased several small, but expensive, items for Kitty there. He hadn't thought on the baubles until that moment, but she obviously hadn't felt the need to return them after calling their wedding off. Not that he begrudged her mementoes of their doomed courtship.

When they finally arrived, Robert leapt from the carriage before his footman could descend to open the door. A rosy-cheeked shop girl met him at the jeweler's door, which she opened from within, offering Robert a dimpled smile. He entered the exceedingly clean, almost sparse space in a mingled state of curiosity and desperation, both of which he concealed behind a properly bored expression. All around him, against the austere backdrop of white walls and dark flooring, gems glittered.

"Mister Banbrook," the proprietor greeted, his smile making a tangle of wrinkles under his spectacles and hairless scalp. "A fine afternoon to you, sir. How can we assist you today? We've acquired some lovely new stones since your last visit."

"I'm more in the market for information today, Stevens." Robert strolled to the counter.

"Ah, well, that we're in shorter supply of, sir, as you know."

Robert did know. Often, part of what the man was paid for was secrecy. "Yes, but it's a matter of the heart, you see," Robert said. "My heart."

The jeweler frowned. "I am not an expert in such matters, I'm afraid, sir, but whatever the trouble is, it will go better for you with the gift of jewels."

"You're wise as always, but that remains to be seen," Robert studied the expensive set stones and loose gems on display before him. How he could bring the conversation round to what he wished to know? Suddenly, he could sympathize with Dunreid's urge to bully. Robert tamped down the desire and tried another avenue. "I'm sure you know, as all Edinburgh seems to, why I came to your fine city?"

That elicited a cough and a pitying look reminiscent of Dunreid's. "As you say, sir, the entire city is familiar with your story. A wealthy Englishman, thrown over for a Scottish title. Many is the time I've heard the tale repeated." His expression turned sheepish under bushy white eyebrows. "Generally, with enthusiasm, by Scots. Then there was Miss Kitty Thomas, soon to be Missus Cathryn McMullin."

Robert grimaced. "I hadn't heard she was engaged again so soon."

"Childhood sweetheart, and a good Scotsman."

"I'm pleased to hear Miss Thomas has found happiness." Robert cleared his throat. "It's not about her I've come, as you can undoubtedly guess."

"You've come about the sapphire pendant I had sent up to Lady Peddington's."

Robert nodded, surprised to gain a foothold so easily.

"You aren't the first to ask about it."

"So I've heard. It was Dunreid who told me you were the source of the item."

Stevens raised his eyebrows. "I didn't realize you were on friendly terms. Rumor has it, you're the source of his blackened eye, not many days ago."

"Friendly isn't the exact word." Robert shrugged. "As for his eye, I admit I may have failed to keep my temper."

Stevens pressed his lips into a thin line and scrutinized Robert. "I didn't advise Viscount Dunreid on the origin of the pendant sent up to the school," Stevens finally said. His face crinkled into a look of apology. "You know it's our policy not to speak of our customers."

"I do, and I respect that." Robert leaned forward. Could he appeal to the old man's heart? "Is there anything you can tell me, though? Even the littlest thing."

Stevens looked about the room. The girl busied herself on the far side, lighting candles. Soon, the shop would be aglow for late afternoon traffic. Robert was familiar with the glittering display. Stevens attempted to provide as much light as possible. He likely spent a fortune in candles, but obviously made up for the cost in sales.

"The circumstances did give me pause," Stevens said in a low voice. "May I ask, Mister Banbrook, why you wish to know?"

Dark eyes, buried deep within crinkled lids, regarded him. Robert paused to think on the question. Why did he? What would he do if Miss Glasbarr had agreed to become some man's toy? Demand she wed him instead?

Definitely. Instantly.

But what if she'd discovered love with another man? Would he walk away, or would he try to win her back, steal her? Do to someone else what Dunreid had done to him?

He shook his head. "I want to see that Miss Glasbarr is happy and cared for. If…if I deem she's contemplating a less than honorable proposal, I shall offer marriage to me instead." He swallowed, clearing the way to force out his next words. "If she's happy, I will bow out."

Stevens studied him for another long moment. He nodded. "You're a good sort, for an Englishman." He let out a gusty sigh. "Truth is, I worry the girl is being used abominably. First the viscount sent her a gift he ought not have sent a sweet country lass. Next, a certain lady enters my shop with the very same gift, pays me to refund the viscount and reset the gems. I wouldn't have minded that. The lady in question was the one he should be giving jewelry to."

Apprehension flickered to life in Robert's gut, writhing outward to tense every limb. Cinthia. How had she ended up with the first necklace?

"What I minded was having the largest sapphire of the lot sent back up to the school, and the card she made me write to accompany the package." Another shake of Stevens' head, slower. "I knew writing that card wasn't right, sir, and I feel I've wronged both you and Miss Glasbarr, which is the only reason I'm speaking about a client. I oughtn't have agreed to do as the lady asked. I wouldn't have, but she was quite insistent, and shrill and, well, threatened my business and even my person. The truth is, Mister Banbrook, I'm ashamed, but she had me send that pendant and sign the note with your initials."

The world might be moving, but Robert was not. He stared at the jeweler as the truth settled over him. His anger dissolved like a morning fog. Emilia thought the necklace came from him, and wore his gift. For him.

Then why had she appeared so stricken? He'd thought, at the time, her horrified look was due to his discovery of her betrayal.

Robert thought back. Shock slammed into his burgeoning joy. Dunreid's words, his accusation. Emilia had heard Dunreid's accusation.

"Here, sir." Stevens pulled out a ring of keys. He turned to one of many locked cabinets behind him and retrieved a box with a note. He pushed them across the counter to Robert. "She returned this, as well. Came in herself. Been wracked with guilt, I have. Sweet girl, and lovely as they come."

Robert opened the box. The sapphire pendant rested inside, still strung on the chain he'd seen about Emilia's neck. He shut the lid and opened the note.

To wear tonight.
Yours, with the greatest affection,
RB

He read the lines several times, equally elated and despairing. She thought the necklace a declaration of his love, and she'd worn it.

But her expression, when she burst from the cloakroom to defend him... Obviously, she had believed Dunreid. Emilia thought he was still set on Cinthia, a woman who knew him so well. Well enough to judge his reaction upon seeing Emilia wearing a jewel he hadn't sent.

Anger twisted his belly. Damn Cinthia, and damn his quick temper. He took a breath. "Thank you, Stevens. I believe you've done the right thing. You're correct, Miss Glasbarr has been treated abominably."

"You won't let out I told you, sir?" Stevens cast another glance about the shop. "The lady was quite explicit about what would happen to me and my livelihood."

"I'll only tell one person, and I can assure you, she wants nothing to do with Viscountess Dunreid." Robert folded the note and pushed the page across the counter with the box.

"Thank you, Mister Banbrook." A gleam, bright like the gems he sold, appeared in Stevens' eyes. "If everything works out, sir, please think of us for future gifts for the young lady."

Robert nodded, for Stevens had done the right thing in the end. In a lighter mood, he would even have been amused by the suggestion. "Until then." He left as hurriedly as he'd come. He wasn't exactly dressed for evening, but he didn't care. He had a ball to attend.

CHAPTER ELEVEN

EMILIA DIDN'T PREPARE FOR the final ball. Instead, she looked over her belongings to judge what should be packed first. Tomorrow, she would write to her father and ask him to bring her home. Her dreams of living in Edinburgh, of a life of theater, music and art, seemed silly now. She didn't belong in the city, with the complex, fickle folk who dwelled there. She belonged in a small home with a garden, and only chickens and a goat for company. Perhaps the occasional goose. They made more sense than men like Robert Banbrook.

She settled onto the foot of her narrow bed with a sigh. Robert. Tall, handsome, with the most fascinating grey eyes she'd ever seen. So often, he seemed withdrawn, even cold, but when he was happy, laughing, he made her happy, his joy, a rare gift. Everything she'd dreamed of.

Emilia shook her head. No, not everything. She didn't dream of a man who was hopelessly in love with Viscountess Dunreid. Only a fool would dream of that.

She reached for her sketchpad and flipped through the thick pages to his face. Heaven help her, she was a fool, for she could think only of him. Her heart beat quicker at the sight of his face, even on a page.

She snapped the book closed. Packing for her journey home, that was her chore. Not woolgathering over Robert.

A knock brought her to the door. The maid, Mary, waited on the other side. Unlike any other time Emilia had seen her, Mary appeared unhappy. Emilia frowned.

"There's someone to see you, Miss, in the small parlor."

The small parlor? A titled someone, or wealthy. Not Robert. Somehow, she was certain of that. Robert wouldn't bring such worry to Mary's face, even in one of his darker moods.

Dunreid, then. Would he ever take no for an answer? Frustration bloomed in Emilia. She firmed her lips into a hard line. This time, he would.

"Thank you, Mary. I'll be right down." She made to close the door, but Mary's foot blocked the way.

"Miss, I know it isn't my place to say, but I don't think you should."

"I beg your pardon?" Mary never voiced suggestions. She was Lady Peddington's creature, there to see all, report all, and not develop attachments.

"The lady waiting for you, Viscountess Dunreid, she can't have anything to say you'll want to hear, Miss."

Not Dunreid, but his wife, Lady Cinthia, who hadn't been shy in her desire never to set eyes on Emilia again. What could possibly bring her? "Be that as it may, I can't simply ignore her."

"I could say I couldn't find you, if you like."

Emilia studied Mary's worried expression. Worried for her? For the school, should Lady Cinthia be angered? Emilia was tempted to take the offer. "No, but I do thank you. I will speak with her. Perhaps I can end the fiasco my life has become."

"Yes, Miss." Mary, expression neutral once more, nodded and backed away.

Emilia closed the door and went to her mirror. She wore her plainest gown. Her hair was pinned up in a severe fashion, no curls to hide the roundness of her face. She had not a single adornment. No mark of sophistication about her.

What did her appearance matter? Lady Cinthia wouldn't care. Her judgement had long since been passed. Likely, Emilia looked like the artless country girl she was. That would please the viscountess. She offered her reflection a shrug and headed for the small parlor. She would look even less grand surrounded by the opulence there.

Lady Cinthia stood framed in the window, gazing out over Charlotte Square. Emilia closed the door quietly behind her, more as a kindness to Mary than to keep the conversation secret. The maid's eavesdropping would be made easier if she could press her ear to the door.

"You asked to see me, my lady?"

Lady Cinthia turned, grace in every limb. Emilia curtsied. She received a nod as regal as any queen's, followed by a disdainful perusal of her person.

"I did," Lady Cinthia said in her cultured, clipped English accent. "I've come to make sure things are clear between us, Miss Glasbarr."

"I'm afraid I didn't realize there was anything between us, my lady. I rate myself less than a passing acquaintance in your eyes."

"You are a clever girl, then, aren't you?"

"I wouldn't know, my lady."

"Hm." Lady Cinthia made an airy gesture. "I heard Robert gifted you a necklace, but that you ran from the ball before speaking with him." She leaned forward, the eagerness in her face repulsive. "May I ask why? Was he inexplicably angry with you? He has high emotions for an Englishman."

"I don't know what he was, my lady. I was in a distraught state myself. Something I overheard upset me, and I left." What could the creature possibly want? Emilia had refused Dunreid, lost...rather, never possessed Robert. Perhaps the viscountess wanted her to leave Edinburgh, altogether? Well, she would have that as well. "But I'm afraid my acuity is not what you think, if you deem me clever. In fact, I'm so out of my depth here, I plan to return home at my father's earliest convenience."

Blue eyes brightened—sparkled like Robert's sapphire and its false promise of his affection. "You plan to leave? I'm pleased for you, child. You'll be much happier back with your own kind."

Anger flickered in Emilia, but died under the weight of despair. The viscountess was correct. Emilia didn't belong in Edinburgh. For all her dedication to finishing school, she'd won only a broken heart, and that hurt more than any of this woman's cruelties. She dropped her gaze to Lady Cinthia's silken slippers, cobalt to match her gown.

Rich fabric rustled as those slippers brought the viscountess near. "You seem sad, child. It pains me that you've been abused so."

Emilia didn't believe Lady Cinthia's sympathy, but she did feel rather abused. An ache filled her throat. She shrugged, for words forced past that ache would come out thick with tears. She would not give her pain to this woman.

"It would be better for you, I think, if you could leave soon." False compassion slithered through Lady Cinthia's voice. "Why suffer while you await your father? A gentleman farmer, I assume?"

Emilia nodded.

"He'll be doubly busy this time of year," Lady Cinthia said. "I don't want you to have to linger in this state for days, perhaps weeks, even."

A gloved hand settled on Emilia's shoulder. She tried not to cringe from the feather-light touch.

"To make up for the poor treatment the men in my life have given you, allow me to provide transport. I'll hire a carriage to take you home."

Emilia looked up. She flinched to find those blue eyes so near her own, the slender viscountess looking down at her from beneath white-blonde locks.

"Thank you." She would accept help from this woman, if only to never have to see her again.

"How about tomorrow morning, then, dear?" Lady Cinthia's smile was smug.

"That would be wonderful. Thank you, my lady."

"Good. You'll want to pack. No time for the final ball."

"Oh, no, definitely not. I wasn't going to attend, actually. I don't feel very...festive."

"Splendid."

How could the woman smile with absolutely no warmth? Was the ability to completely falsify emotions a particular skill of the English? Whereas before she had longed to visit London, now Emilia resolved never to travel there.

"I'm glad we had this talk, Miss Glasbarr, and that I'm able to help return you home with all alacrity."

"I am as well, my lady." She was. The sooner she left Edinburgh, the sooner she could forget Robert. It would be a momentous task not to dwell on memories of his laughter, his grey eyes. But a change of scenery must surely help.

"Well, run along and pack, child." Lady Cinthia's clipped accent scattered Emilia's thoughts.

"Thank you, my lady," she said for what seemed the tenth time. She curtsied and left. As she traversed the nearly empty halls, she hoped the viscountess was behind her forever.

Once in her room, Emilia sent for her trunk from storage and laid out her wardrobe. The drab dress she wore would do well enough for travel. She hadn't brought much, or gained much while in Edinburgh. Once she was gone, her life would be almost the same as if she'd never attended Lady Peddington's school.

By the time the ball began, Emilia was packed. She stood in the middle of the room, empty now of signs of her occupancy. Tomorrow, she would bid Lady Peddington's farewell. This room, the school, even her friends, would become buried in the past with her dreams. If only she could shed thoughts of Robert as easily.

She looked down at her dress. She didn't wish to go to the ball, and couldn't, dressed as she was, but remaining in her room seemed unbearable. Almost unbidden, her feet set out, the rest of her accompanying them by necessity.

Careful to stay clear of the front wing foyer, candlelit halls and ballroom, she wandered the building, silently saying goodbye. When she reached Missus Millview's classroom, directly across the courtyard from the ballroom, she slipped inside to find the space dark. Emilia turned in a slow circle. She wasn't sure if she was disappointed or relieved. She would like to say farewell to her favorite instructor, but didn't wish to admit her failure. Missus Millview had aided her, at risk to her position, and Emilia had squandered that assistance. A man was sent to help her find a good husband, just as she'd hoped. Instead of falling in love with one of the perfectly acceptable gentlemen Robert introduced her to, she'd fallen in love with him.

By moonlight, she paced the room, and trailed her fingers over the long tables. She made a full circuit. Memories of friends and laughter bubbled in her mind. They were overcast now, colored darker, sadder, by this way-stop in her journey. As was the room, muted in the pale glow of moonlight.

Her steps brought her back around to the long windows. The oak slept without. Across the lawn, light spilled from the ballroom, windows thrown wide to permit fresh air to enter. She pushed open one of the long panes before her and let in soft strains of music. Unwanted tears seeped from the corners of her eyes.

Behind her, the door slid open. Emilia tensed. If Dunreid or his wife entered, she would climb out the window and run.

"One of the maids, Mary, said I would find you here."

Her breath hitched. *Robert.* Her heart leapt, but couldn't take flight, sent crashing back to earth in pain. "Why should you wish to find me?"

His footfalls drew nearer. "Are you crying? Will you look at me?"

"I am, and I will not."

"Emilia." His voice was rough, anguished. "I have things to explain."

Music swirled through the courtyard, carried across on a light breeze. The leaves of the oak danced to the rhythm.

"That you still love Lady Cinthia?" She couldn't keep the bitterness from her tone. "There's nothing to explain. She's perfect." On the outside. "What man wouldn't want her?"

"I don't want her."

Now he would lie to her? She looked down at her hands, gripping the sill. "Oh? Not since the last time you had her, when she was at your home, returned in your carriage in…how did Viscount Dunreid describe her state? Disheveled?"

"Dunreid doesn't know of what he speaks." Two more steps, and she could feel the heat of him behind her. "She was at my home. She wanted…"

His tone was tentative. She could hear how he searched for the right words. Pain filled her at the hope he would find them.

"She wanted what you suspect she wanted," he finally said. "I won't lie, a month ago, I would have said yes, engaged to Miss Thomas or not, but the viscountess was too late. My answer was no."

Emilia closed her eyes. Tears slid down her cheeks. He sounded sincere. How could she know? She wanted so much to believe. Could she trust herself?

"I was so happy when you sent that necklace."

"I didn't."

Her eyes flew open. She risked a glance over her shoulder. Serious grey eyes. Dark hair not as neat as usual. Unshaven. He looked miserable, and seeing him that way filled her heart with new pain.

"You didn't?"

"Lady Cinthia did." How cold his voice went as her name left his lips. "She, rightly, suspected I would see the necklace and believe you'd given in to Dunreid. She is the one who told me he sent one."

"When she was with you, at one of your not-longed-for, not-scandalous meetings?" Emilia asked, the pain of imagining them together too sharp to relinquish with ease.

He came around her, to stand beside her at the window. A thumb, skin slightly rough, smoothed tears from her cheek. "I do not love her, or want her, or have even the smallest, remotest desire to set eyes on her again. Ever."

"Ever?" Emilia's voice sounded small. Could he be telling the truth?

He cocked his head. Across the courtyard, strains of a waltz drifted toward them. The hour was later than she thought. She should be locked safely in her room.

"Dance with me."

Emilia nodded, unable to resist. A strong hand gripped hers, no gloves to mute the mingled warmth of their skin. Another hand slid along her waist. Holding her near, but with care, as something fragile, Robert turned her away from the window in time with the distant notes. With her gaze, she traced the folds of his wrinkled cravat, unsure where to look.

The arms about her were strong, a barricade against all that was evil in the world, something to brace her against a storm. She longed to believe they were the arms of a man who loved her.

But if she believed his words tonight, that he didn't love Lady Cinthia, that she sent the necklace to sow strife between them, that also meant he hadn't sent the gift. Robert had never declared his affection for her. A new despair unfurled in her.

"Emilia." His voice was soft, oddly rough. "Look at me."

She hesitated. Could she resist him once she looked into those grey eyes? Did she wish to resist Robert?

Emilia raised her gaze to his face. He smiled. Her attention shifted to his mouth, to the way his lips curved, to the scruff shadowing his chin. Was this how he appeared when he woke in the morning? She lifted her hand from his shoulder, touched his cheek. He leaned into her caress. Her face heated. She dropped her hand back onto his shoulder, breathless.

"I didn't send the necklace, but I should have," he said. "I had a hundred chances, which makes me a hundred times a fool for not telling you sooner." He gave a gentle smile. "I love you."

Her gaze snapped up to meet his. They stilled, though music still drifted in.

"You love me?"

He slid downward, dropped to one knee before her. He raised the hand he still held to his lips. His kiss, the press of his lips to the back of her hand in a fleeting warmth, made her dizzy. When he looked back up, his grey eyes shone in the moonlight.

"Marry me, Emilia Glasbarr. Love me. Grow old with me while our children run in the yard and we pick out fabulous carriage horses together and visit every museum, attend every recital. Let me be yours forever."

New tears threatened. She dropped to her knees before him, pulled his face down to hers. Her heart, freed, took flight as their lips met.

EPILOGUE

ROBERT, WITHOUT A CARE for his fine clothes or the gaping onlookers, clambered down from the tree he'd climbed to free his young son's kite. Emilia sat on a nearby rise, sketching furiously, pad of paper resting on her very round middle. Many women would deem themselves too far along to appear in public, but Emilia loved the sunshine and trees of the park, and their son loved his kite.

If he had to guess, Robert suspected she was capturing the moment he slid out along the limb. He'd been just able to reach the kite as the branch began to dip precariously under his weight. She wouldn't look up until she was done; likely, hadn't even waited to see him return to the ground, perfectly confident in his ability to manage the climb. He smiled.

He turned to his son, and knelt to proffer the bright red kite. "Take this to your mama. When she looks up from her sketch, ask her to untangle the string."

"Yes, Papa," the boy said.

Robert ruffled his blond curls, then turned him toward her with a gentle push. He was young, not even in full sentences, and easily distracted. Robert watched to make sure he reached Emilia. The lad settled down on the blanket beside her to wait with surprising patience for a child.

"You could have sent a footman up that tree."

He turned to find Sir Stirling James standing against the backdrop of the dispersing onlookers. "Stirling," Robert greeted, genuinely pleased. "I never pictured you as one for the park."

"I came to see what the crowd was about." Stirling gestured toward the dwindling throng. "Apparently, everyone wanted to watch the mad, wealthy Englishman climb a tree, to see if he could go up, and down, without cracking open his head."

"Any mad Englishman worthy of being known as such can climb a tree successfully." Robert shrugged. "Besides, once we reach the park, I give the staff a few hours off. With a picnic basket, a toddler and Scotland's most beautiful woman, what could a servant possibly need to bring me?"

"What indeed?" Stirling's eyes glinted with amusement.

Robert frowned. "You didn't come to the wedding. In fact, I haven't seen you since…" Since the day Stirling dunked his whisky-sodden self in a tub of ice cold water.

"I was rather busy."

"Well, we missed you. You should join us. We were about to start our picnic, as soon as my lovely wife puts down her sketchbook. She's quite skilled. I'm sure drawing me sprawled along a tree limb won't take long."

"You're happy, then, Banbrook?" Stirling asked.

"Thoroughly."

"Glad to hear it. I thought you would be."

Robert took in Stirling's smug expression, and the truth hit him like another dousing. "By God, you never meant me to find anyone for Emilia. You meant for me to wed her."

Stirling's smile turned sly. "Some questions are better unanswered."

Robert turned back to his wife. She absently patted their son on the head, still sketching with her free hand. "You set me up."

"Someone had to put you on the right track."

Robert proffered his hand. "Thank you."

Stirling clasped hands in a brief shake. "My pleasure." He squinted up at the sky. "Too bad about Viscountess Dunreid."

Robert shrugged. He hadn't thought of Lady Cinthia in ages. He gestured up the hill, indicating his family. "I have to confess, I haven't had the time, or inclination, to keep abreast of the viscount and his wife."

"He caught her in the arms of another man. Retired her to the country."

"Probably won't help." Dunreid was smart enough to know that. More likely, he felt boredom a fitting punishment. Robert hoped she didn't spend her time there destroying other people's lives. "Where in the country?"

"So you can visit?"

"So I can stay away, and warn anyone there I care about to do likewise."

Stirling gave a satisfied nod. "That pretty much tells me all I wanted to know." He started to turn away. "Enjoy your picnic, Banbrook."

"You aren't joining us, then?" Robert wasn't sure why, but he had the oddest sense he would never see Sir Stirling James again.

"Next time. Busy day ahead. You did well, Banbrook." This last was said over his shoulder as he joined the remnants of the onlookers.

Robert blinked. Somehow, commanding figure that he was, thin as the crowd had grown, Stirling had already disappeared. With a shake of his head, feeling almost as if he'd imagined the encounter, Robert headed up the hill to picnic with his golden-haired son and his beautiful wife.

SHAMELESS

THE MARRIAGE MAKER
BOOK SIX RULES OF REFINEMENT

TARAH SCOTT AND ERIN RYE

CHAPTER ONE

WHAT MORE COULD A GIRL ASK FOR?

JULIET SQUINTED AGAINST THE late morning sun that streamed through the open window behind Lady Honoria Peddington's study desk. Girlish laughter wafted up from the modest courtyard as Honoria rose then skirted the large, claw-footed mahogany desk to where Juliet stood on the dark green, paisley-patterned carpet. For a woman nearing fifty, Honoria was remarkably beautiful, with only the barest hint of gray in her red hair.

She pinned Juliet with a critical stare. "Curl your locks into *proper* ringlets for tonight."

"Tonight—" Juliet broke off when Honoria brushed one of the locks with her fingers.

"I want to see candlelight dance off those gold streaks." Honoria began a slow walk around Juliet, as if inspecting a horse she wished to purchase.

With the real Lady Peddington making her circuit, Juliet stared at the large oil portrait of Lady Peddington that graced the mantle. At her back, hung a collection of small portraits of the local nobles of Edinburgh. She imagined the lords' collective 'tsk, tsks' as Honoria reached Juliet's face and grasped Juliet's chin, tilting her head sideways. "Stain your lips a darker shade of red. Your pout will drive him wild."

Him?

Her heartbeat accelerated.

Honoria released her. "And line your lower eyelashes. Your blue eyes are one of your best features." She stepped back and crossed her arms. "You will meet the Duke of Hamilton tonight at the Midnight Ball."

"Midnight Ball—the Duke of Hamilton?" Anger twisted through her, followed by fear. Of all things the headmistress and founder of Lady Peddington's School for Young Ladies could have thrown at her, Juliet hadn't imagined this.

"So, the notorious Duke of Hamilton intends to make me his mistress?" Juliet forced a smile and added with a double dose of sarcasm, "Why, Auntie Honoria, what more could a woman want?"

"Little, indeed," she said, ignoring Juliet's derision.

"Surely, you remember that I am returning to London in the morning," Juliet said. "I have no time for balls—or dukes."

Honoria pinned her with a stare. "I did not insist you attend the first ball, but I must insist you attend this one."

"Only gentlemen looking for less-than-honorable associations attend your Midnight Balls. You know that isn't what I want."

"There is nothing dishonorable about an agreement between adults," Honoria replied unruffled. "The duke will expect you at midnight. He is not a man who likes to be kept waiting."

Her heart sank. The Duke of Hamilton. His portrait did not hang on the wall alongside the illustrious nobility of Edinburgh. Still, Juliet had heard of the man. Who hadn't? His reputation preceded him. He was daring, handsome, scandalously rich and, "He's never stayed with a woman longer than six months," Juliet finished her thought out loud.

"There is a first time for everything," Lady Peddington said.

Lady Honoria Peddington wasn't truly her aunt, but she was the closest thing Juliet had to a relative. Auntie started her career in the same brothel as Juliet's mother, where they'd formed a sisterly bond. As the years passed, both women had fulfilled their dreams. Honoria Peddington—born Honey Pedding—relocated to Edinburgh and opened Lady Peddington's School for Young Ladies. Juliet's mother moved to London and opened Lady Aphrodite's House of Pleasure—Juliet's childhood home.

Honoria smiled gently. "There is no harm in meeting the man."

"I'm no fool," Juliet snapped. She nodded at the open window where her fellow students giggled in the small courtyard below. "*They* might not know the dangers of a Midnight Ball, but they don't have a madam for a mother, now, do they?"

"My *dearest* child," Lady Peddington rapped her knuckles sharply on the desk at her side, "lower your voice. We cannot have such words overheard."

Juliet huffed another breath, but replied in hushed tones, "I am not staying in Edinburgh, Auntie. I leave early for London."

Honoria gave her a shrewd look. "You are no more anxious to return home now than you were yesterday."

Juliet's heart constricted. Her aunt spoke the truth. She felt more at home here than anywhere else she'd ever lived. The year had passed too quickly. Juliet tossed a wistful glance at the bookshelves filled with leather-bound volumes of deportment and etiquette. She'd read them all—or tried to. Truth be told, they'd put her to sleep better than any posset ever had.

She had a plan to avoid the fate awaiting her in her mother's house. She'd spent the school year fostering relationships with young ladies who would soon head households of their own. They would need a dressmaker. She intended to convince her mother to let her attempt to become a dressmaker before being forced into life as a courtesan.

Juliet met her aunt's gaze. "Why meet this gentleman just as I'm leaving, Auntie Honey—Honoria?" After a year, she still slipped. "Have you sold my virginity to the highest bidder?"

Her mother had attempted just that the year before. She'd auctioned Juliet off to a middle-aged banker, a man with a stomach the size of a bull's, who smelled like one, too. She'd narrowly avoided the man's bed by convincing her mother a year at Lady Peddington's school would allow her to charge twice the amount from better-paying clientele.

Juliet realized Lady Peddington was talking.

"...caught Sir Stirling's eye, Juliet. He specifically requested that you attend tonight's ball and meet the duke."

Juliet frowned. "Sir Stirling James?" She'd seen the man only once, and from a great distance. One of the instructors had pointed him out during a sanctioned holiday outing in Edinburgh as he'd dashed past in a brightly polished carriage. "Where might he have seen me? When? How? I've followed the rules, Auntie Honoria. I've told no one *anything*." How could she? Classmates would faint from shock should they discover she'd been raised in a brothel. A new thought struck and she dropped her voice into an even lower whisper, "He isn't one of Mother's patrons, is he?"

"Heavens, no." She shook her head vigorously. "Nothing like that."

"Then why would he wish to make me a duke's *mistress?*" Juliet hissed.

"I'm not at all certain, child," Lady Peddington whispered. She nodded at the open window and waited for more giggles to drift through before adding, "Sir Stirling is an old friend—not that kind of old friend," she quickly added when Juliet opened her mouth to ask that very question. Her aunt gave her a knowing look. "You have behaved yourself here in Edinburgh, but what of London?"

Juliet winced inwardly. Oh. *London.* "I've been the picture of propriety, Auntie, I swear it," she lied.

After all, what did the pesky word 'propriety' actually *mean?* Everyone she'd met held a slightly different opinion on the matter. And really, who was to say that sneaking into London parties uninvited in order to frequent the card tables was truly improper? She'd been careful to wear a Venetian mask to protect her identity. After all, she'd met more than one gambler in the brothel while growing up. They'd taught her a good many card tricks over the years. Why *shouldn't* she put such knowledge to use? She'd been quite the mysterious and popular figure in London that summer, and she'd won a tidy sum—almost enough money to open her own dress shop. Almost.

"What have you done, child?" her aunt pressed.

"Nothing," she lied again.

Honoria's stare seemed to penetrate clear to her soul. "Did you, by chance, fall in love in London or—"

Juliet rolled her eyes. "Really, how can you ask? *Love* is a word thrown about too easily. I'm of no mind to lift my skirts for any man. Ever."

Her aunt chuckled as if relieved.

Juliet lifted a suspicious brow. "I still feel as if I've been sold as your prized cow."

"Nonsense. Sir Stirling is a matchmaker."

"Let him make a match elsewhere." Juliet tossed her head and turned to go.

"Juliet, listen to me."

Juliet paused, then faced Honoria.

Her aunt stepped forward. "Your blood runs hot, *too* hot for just any man. Mind you, I know. You should embrace that passion. Indeed, you'll blossom under the right man's touch. If the rumors about Duke Hamilton are true—"

"No, thank you," Juliet snapped.

"Think of it," her aunt whispered, eyes alight with anticipation. "A duke's mistress. A man of the duke's wealth would provide you not only a private house, but a yearly allowance, as well. Even your mother never dreamt *that* high for you."

Alarm coursed through Juliet. "You haven't told Ma, have you?" the words shot out before she could stop them.

Too late, Juliet realized her mistake. A calculating gleam entered Lady Peddington's eye. Juliet's heart sank. She'd just handed her aunt victory on a silver platter. There was no recovering now. Honoria knew Juliet would do anything to prevent her mother from gaining knowledge of the duke's interest.

"Let's strike a bargain," Juliet surrendered.

A smile twitched the older woman's mouth. "Have I taught you so little this year? A lady never bargains like a fishwife."

Juliet tossed her aunt a pleading look. "I'll do as you ask. I'll attend this Midnight Ball and dance with this duke. I'll entertain him, just as you wish—outside of bedding him. But mother can't know. *Please*, Auntie Honoria."

Lady Peddington primly took her seat. "Sir Stirling specifically requested that you play a game of commerce with the duke, and that you must win."

Cards? Juliet blinked. So, Sir Stirling *had* seen her at the London parties…but how had he recognized her? She'd always worn a mask. Heavens, had he had her followed? Horror washed over her.

"You should know," her aunt continued, "the Duke of Hamilton never loses."

Juliet took a deep fortifying breath and pushed her worries aside. "Until now," she replied. She hadn't lost a game in years—not with the tools she had at her disposal.

Lady Peddington smiled. "Keep the man happy. It's only one night. Do that, and your meeting with the duke shall remain our secret."

"Bless you." Juliet heaved a sigh of relief.

She left the study quickly. Oh, Honey Pedding was a wily one. She had manipulated the conversation in order to get her way. Juliet grimaced. She'd been raised by such women. How had she fallen so neatly into the net?

At the bottom of the stairs, she paused and peered out the window at the young ladies who still chatted in the courtyard. In the past week, most had found suitors, honorable men offering marriage—not dukes looking for mistresses. As a fresh bout of giggles erupted from the girls, Juliet shook her head. They knew little of men. She'd seen enough men in her mother's brothel to know them for the creatures they truly were: simple-minded fools focused solely on carnal pleasure.

The Duke of Hamilton would prove no different. She would play that lust to her advantage. She would wear her finest gown. She'd flirt, lick her lips, heave her breasts, and flash her ankles. Expose a little flesh and she could make the duke's blood boil. In a blink, she'd have him thinking with his cock. Then, she'd trounce him at cards, take his money and vanish.

CHAPTER TWO

A MOST INTERESTING WAGER

THERE'S NO WOMAN ALIVE who can keep my interest long enough for me to want to marry her, Stirling."

Carrick Hamilton, Duke of Hamilton and Lord of Lennoxlove House, stood on the edge of the lawn, nocked an arrow to his longbow and took aim. The bowstring thrummed, and the arrow buried itself in the center of the target over a hundred yards away.

Sir Stirling James, Marquess of Roxburgh, who lounged under an ancient oak, let out a low whistle. "Impressive."

Carrick set his bow onto a nearby table, beside a collection of daggers, bows, and arrows—anything he could throw at a target. The sun was warm, the sky blue, the wind, nonexistent. All in all, a perfect day for target practice at Crenshaw House. So, why was he struggling with a dark mood? Perhaps, he should cut his Edinburgh visit short and return home. He stretched the kinks from his neck, then raked his dark hair back off his forehead.

"What were you saying? Ah, yes. Women." Carrick frowned. "Why are we speaking of women?"

"I said, you simply haven't met the right one." An amused twinkle lit Stirling's eyes.

Carrick snorted a laugh. "I'd wager my prize stallion there is no 'right' woman for the likes of me."

"I'll take that wager." Stirling grinned. "I'll back it with that red roan you've been lusting after."

Carrick shot his friend a startled look. "You're not jesting."

"Indeed, I am not," Stirling replied. "I've already found *her*."

Carrick lifted a brow. He'd been after Stirling to sell him that red roan for two years. He leaned a hip against the weaponry table and crossed his arms. "Who is she?"

Stirling left the shade of the tree and joined him. "Marrying her will be rather tricky."

Carrick straightened. "Marry? Och, this is a jest, after all."

"Believe me, this is one you'll want to marry," Stirling assured. "Never have I seen a more perfect match."

Carrick grimaced. "Marriage?" He reclaimed his longbow and selected another arrow. "Duty dictates that I someday marry, but I don't see that happening anytime soon." He nocked the arrow and aimed.

Stirling laughed. "What you need is a woman who will bring you to your knees."

Carrick's shot went wild.

Stirling grinned and clapped him on the back. "I look forward to seeing your stallion in my stables." He spun on his heel and headed toward the house.

Carrick frowned. "When shall I meet this harridan?"

"Tonight," Stirling called over his shoulder. "At Lady Peddington's Midnight Ball."

A *Midnight Ball?* Carrick considered. Stirling had saved the most delightful surprise for last. He grinned. Aye, he was in the mood to spend the evening with a woman—especially one who attended midnight balls.

CHAPTER THREE

A GAME OF CARDS LIKE NO OTHER

THE CLOCK ON THE bedchamber mantle chimed the midnight hour.

Juliet yanked her gaze from the book she'd been reading onto the clock. The Midnight Ball had begun. She set the book on the settee and rose. A tingle of anxiety climbed her spine. If even one of her friends lingered in the ballroom after the regular ball ended, the illusion she'd worked so hard to create this last year would shatter into a thousand pieces. Word would spread like wildfire and no one would hire the woman in the low-cut blue silk gown and Venetian mask as their dressmaker.

One way or another, this would be the last time she stood in this room. Juliet turned in a slow circle and inspected at the room, now empty of all signs that she had lived here for a year. Her gaze caught on a sliver of dark blue velvet at the foot of her bed. She crossed the room and scooped up the fabric. A scrap that had fallen to the floor when she'd packed the remnants she'd collected from the sewing they'd done at the school. Most pieces were only large enough to use as samples, but a few very nice pieces would suffice to make gloves or even reticules. Every little bit counted.

The money she'd saved would pay for just enough fabric and supplies to get started as a dressmaker. She didn't have a penny for room and board, but one didn't worry about such small details. Juliet grimaced. All she had to do was talk her mother into letting her live at the brothel until she could afford a modest home of her own. Until then, she had arranged to pay a small portion of her earnings to a shop owner in the fabric district for a place to meet with her clients. But her plans and future depended on her having a safe place to do her sewing.

Juliet released a sigh. The year really had passed too quickly. She loved her mother, but she wasn't looking forward to the battle that lay ahead. Her trunk awaited her atop the hired carriage that would take her to the coach headed for London. The day dress she would wear for the carriage ride home lay tucked in the satchel by the door. Once she escaped the duke, she dared not risk even a change of clothes in her room. The transformation from courtesan to dull dressmaker would take place in the carriage ride between Lady Peddington's and the depot.

Two girls at the school were already engaged to moderately successful London merchants and had begged Juliet to sew each of them full wardrobes. She would earn slave wages, but the girls would tell everyone that Miss Juliet Thatcher, graduate of Lady Peddington's School for Young Ladies, had sewn their dresses. Then her mother would have no good arguments to prevent her from becoming a dressmaker instead of a courtesan.

Juliet crossed to the full-length mirror near the door and inspected her appearance. The blue silk cradled her ample breasts to perfection and accentuated her thin waist. She tilted her head. Per Aunt Honoria's instructions, she'd darkened her lashes and lined her eyes. The dramatic effect made her blue eyes stand out under the mass of curls she'd swept back from her face and fastened in place with two large tortoiseshell combs—all but one seductive tendril, of course. She let it coil gracefully down the back of her neck like a careless afterthought. Men liked that kind of thing. It made them itch to entwine it around their finger.

Her gaze caught on her bodice as she started to turn, and she paused. She should lower the bodice another half inch. The dress was scandalous enough as it was—which meant she had nothing to lose. She tugged the bodice down

She couldn't help a humorless laugh. She looked like a pale ghost asleep on her feet. *That* wouldn't do. A mental image of herself snoring at the card tables made her grimace. If only she had the courage to defy Lady Peddington and her mother. She nibbled on her lip. Not bloody likely. The force of their personalities alone was daunting. But that wasn't the real reason. In truth, she knew they only sought to give her an easier life than they'd had. She suppressed a sigh and pinched her cheeks to bring out the roses.

The distant strains of a waltz filtered into the room.

She could delay no longer.

Juliet reached for the deck of cards she'd set on the mantle. She'd filched them from the card rooms earlier in the day. She removed the aces along with the face cards and tucked them into a small pouch hanging from a garter on her thigh.

Next, she picked up the Venetian mask, a dainty white satin oval trimmed with white feathers and gold piping just large enough to cover her nose and brows. She wasn't attending a masked ball, but she knew how to tease a man. Juliet fluffed the feathers, tied the ribbons behind her head, and twirled in front of the mirror one last time. The gloves had to go. It was Lady Peddington's Midnight Ball, after all. That meant bare flesh. She stripped off the gloves and draped them over the back of the settee.

At last, she was ready—as ready as she would ever be.

"Prepare to be stunned, Duke of Hamilton." She gave a lofty wave of her hand, gathered her skirts, swept out the door and down the stairs. She paused in the downstairs foyer, outside the ballroom.

Juliet had witnessed years of scandalously grand entrances at the brothel. A tantalizing amount of skin, a seductive sway of the hips, and a devil-may-care attitude were the main requirements of a successful entrance. With one final downward tug at her bodice, she lifted her head and swooped through the door.

Few candles burned, leaving the corners of the ballroom shrouded in intentional darkness. The girls who waltzed were cradled closely in their partners' arms. She recognized a few of the men from the portraits that hung on the wall of her aunt's study. The Duke of Hamilton's ancestral lands lay north of Edinburgh, which is why his portrait didn't hang on the wall. What had brought him to Edinburgh? Her ill luck, is what. Her gaze drifted to the refreshment table hugging the wall to the right. Bouquets of spring flowers tastefully encircled silver bowls of Aunt Honoria's special midnight punch.

No one approached her. There could be only one reason for that: the duke had warned all others off. That he made her wait at the door spoke volumes. He was obviously a man of command, accustomed to getting his way. No doubt, women tripped over their feet and drooled after him. Their mistake. A man of his power lived for the thrill of the chase.

Well, it was time to see him run.

With a proud toss of her head, Juliet turned on her heel and quit the room. She'd gone three steps when strong fingers closed around her arm. She suppressed a smile. So easily snared. Juliet paused and, brow arched, slowly faced the man.

By God, he was handsome. Devastatingly so. He wore his dark chestnut hair longer than current fashion dictated, but it suited him. The fabric of his expensively-tailored, velvet cutaway coat stretched across the defined muscles of his chest. She dropped a slow gaze, mimicking the best of Lady Aphrodite's girls in a bold inspection of his lean hips and the tight breeches that hugged muscled thighs. Juliet deliberately lingered on his groin before lifting her gaze to the details of his expertly tied cravat, smoothly shaven chin, and the regal curve of his lips. Her pulse quickened. She hadn't realized how heated the 'Lady Aphrodite Inspection' could make the originator. She shook the feeling aside and concentrated on her prey. Small wonder women found him attractive. He was quite the specimen.

Finally, she lifted her lashes and looked into a pair of piercing gray—and vastly amused—eyes.

"You must be the ravishing Juliet," the duke said in a deep baritone. "Please allow me to introduce myself. I am Carrick Hamilton."

"Carrick," she repeated his name in low, sultry tones, and graced him with a slight nod. He'd hear no 'my lords' or 'sirs' escape her lips.

"Shall we dance?" Slowly, he slid his fingers down her elbow and over her bare forearm before dropping his hand away.

The simple gesture left a trail of fire in its wake. No matter. She had a trap of her own to set; a man to keep intrigued and off balance.

As he offered his arm and nodded toward the ballroom door, she boldly stepped into his arms—much closer than propriety allowed—and murmured, "I would much prefer to waltz here."

Delight danced in his eyes. He crushed her so close, the buttons on his waistcoat pressed into the soft mounds of her breasts as he began to twirl her in the dimly lit hallway. The flex of hard muscle against her softness startled her. His fingers drifted lower to the swell of her hip. Heat radiated off his broad chest. Juliet shoved aside the distraction. She had a game to play.

"I do love a waltz," Juliet said *sotto voce* as she peered up at him through her Venetian mask.

"By Jove, Stirling was right." His chest vibrated with a deep chuckle. "You're quite beautiful."

It was an easy opening. She'd witnessed her mother's girls spar in provocative wordplay countless times and summoned a mischievous smile. "Beautiful? Beauty is merely the cover of the book, is it not? Is not what lies underneath more...interesting?" She punctuated the question by mimicking Lady Aphrodite's most popular girl's signature move: a flutter of the lashes combined with a slow, undulating arch of the back.

The rub of her breasts against the solid wall of his muscled chest hardened her nipples. A shock of sensation rippled straight to her core. She drew a startled breath.

The man studied her through hooded eyes. "I believe you would be a book worth reading, my dear." He executed an expert turn. "Perhaps, even more than once."

Perhaps? That smacked of an insult.

"I fear I may be written in a language you cannot understand." She flashed her eyes.

With a devious quirk of his lip, he trailed a slow finger up her spine. She couldn't halt the shiver of response. He felt it. He couldn't miss it. Not with how tightly he held her.

He lowered his head and whispered in her ear, "There's only one language between a man and a woman, my dear. And yes, I read it astonishingly well, in all its forms."

The situation wasn't proceeding as planned. The man obviously knew a few tricks of his own. She'd been taught that suggestive innuendo drove men mad with desire—she hadn't realized it worked the other way, as well. As he twirled her again, she decided it was time to play a different game, and gracefully slipped free of his arms.

"Where are you going?" He fell into step beside her as she glided toward the ballroom.

Juliet lifted her chin and fixed him with a cool stare. "Perhaps, this book doesn't wish to be read, Carrick."

Their gazes locked. She couldn't deny the strong tug of attraction this time. He obviously felt it, too.

He looked away first, then performed a lazy assessment of her slender form. "On the contrary, my dear, this book is simply begging to be explored."

The lust on his face sent her pulse soaring. She couldn't allow him to get the upper hand. This was a game. Nothing more. She curved her lips in an ambiguous smile and turned away.

The musicians struck the opening notes of another waltz as she stepped through the ballroom door and paused inside.

A balding man immediately emerged from the nearby shadows and bowed low. "May I have this—"

"No, you may not." Carrick clamped a possessive hand around her waist.

She hid a smile. As expected, like a puppet on *her* string, he'd followed her.

The man scurried away like a frightened rabbit.

This time, Carrick didn't ask permission. With smooth, elegant grace, he caught her close and spun her onto the ballroom floor, locking her against his powerful body with a hand placed low on the small of her back.

For several long moments, she surrendered to the foreign desire to mold herself against him. They whirled in the glittering candlelight, easily weaving through the remaining couples on the dance floor. As they spun into a darkened corner, Carrick's hand slid across her buttocks until they emerged into the light once again.

Juliet had expected as much, but instead of feeling affronted, she wondered what his lips would feel like on her naked skin. Somehow, the thought didn't evoke the same disgust it did when observing the clientele in her mother's establishment.

"A penny for your thoughts," the whispered words bathed her ear with warm breath.

Her heart beat fast. Might he nuzzle her ear? He didn't—of course. The man was clearly a master of seduction and, much to her chagrin, he'd won the game—so far. But all was not lost.

Juliet lowered her lashes and, with a naughty little smile, slid the tip of her tongue along the upper seam. "Perhaps, I wished that I danced with the other gentleman."

Was it her imagination or did his muscular arm flinch? It was difficult to tell. The gray eyes looking down at her only held a wry amusement.

"No doubt, if you wished to dance with the fellow, you would be do-ing so."

Again, he whirled her into a darkened corner and, this time, stopped and slid his hands lower until he cupped her buttocks. Excitement thrilled through her as he gently undulated his hard length against her.

"Tell me what you wish, Juliet." He nuzzled the sensitive skin under her ear.

His body fascinated her. She liked how her name sounded like a song when he said it.

What she wished? His question suddenly roused her from the haze of lust. She knew what she wanted. She'd thought of nothing else the past three years. She wished to become a dressmaker—though one wouldn't guess it who watched her in the ballroom's shadows with a man's hardened cock pressed against her abdomen.

That realization evoked a perverse grin even as shock twisted through her. She'd come close to proving her aunt right. She *was* too hot-blooded for her own good. But then…her passionate blood had served her well. She had the man right where she wanted him: thinking with his cock.

Now, it was time to play cards, and, judging by his thick erection, she might not need to cheat.

Juliet slipped free of his embrace. He groaned, and her smile widened. He reached for her, but she avoided his grasp with a quick sideways step. She tossed her head, adjusted the ribbons of her mask, and started toward the card room, which opened off the far end of the ballroom.

She didn't wonder if Carrick followed. She knew he did.

The card room's gaming tables boasted half a dozen gentlemen sipping brandy and lounging on plush green chairs with their legs splayed wide. The men sat up straighter as she entered, but she ignored them and angled toward a table in the darkest corner of the room. The shadows would aid her if cheating proved necessary.

Juliet took the seat with the wall at her back and the door facing. Carrick entered and paused. Her heart beat wildly as he scanned the room. She deftly adjusted her skirts, withdrew the cards she'd tucked in the garter's hidden pouch, and slipped them under her seat cushion as his gaze settled on her.

Eyes locked on her face, he strode across the room.

"Join me," she invited in a low voice when he arrived, and she picked up the deck of cards resting on the table. "A game of commerce, shall we? Three rounds."

"What shall we wager?" He sat down sideways in his seat and stretched out his long legs.

Her throat went dry. Dear God, the man knew what he was about. The blatant lust in his eyes held her mesmerized. For the first time in her life, her pulse raced at the thought of a man touching her most intimate places and suckling her tender flesh. Wet heat pooled between her thighs.

It took a moment to recall he'd asked a question. Juliet frowned. How had she succumbed to his designs yet again? Irritation flared. She inhaled a mind-clearing breath and dropped her gaze to the cards. It was time to turn the tables on the man and his seductive ways.

With deliberate focus, she leaned forward to provide him an unimped-ed view of cleavage as she fanned the cards in a line and ran her finger-tips sensuously over the patterned, gold-painted backs. Juliet repressed a grimace. She'd tugged her bodice so low, she could only hope her breasts didn't escape the confines of her gown.

"What should we wager?" she asked with a little aching pant, mim-icking the sound her mother's girls used to drive men wild. She followed with the standard sucking in of her bottom lip. Slowly, she let her lip drag against her teeth, then released it, and added, "Gentlemen first."

He watched her. "I would see you...uncovered." His piercing gray eyes flicked to her mask before sliding down to her breasts.

Her heart skipped a salacious beat and she flirted with the idea of los-ing—but only for a moment. She gathered the cards and cut the deck with a one-handed pivot cut.

His eyes lit with appreciation. "And your bet?"

It was time to stack the deck. For that, she needed a distraction. She dropped her eyes to his necktie and murmured, "Your cravat. I...would...claim it."

"Are you in the habit of collecting men's cravats?" he queried softly.

She offered a mysterious smile, then dealt the hand. She set the deck to her right then reached for her cards. He grasped her wrist. She glanced up, surprised.

"One round," he demanded in a rough voice.

One round? She would definitely have to cheat.

"Very well," she agreed.

Juliet slid her palm over her cards in a lover's caress and, as his gaze tracked her fingers, she dropped her other hand to retrieve the aces from under the cushion.

His gaze lifted from the fingers skimming the cards to her face. Her breath hitched when the fire in his eyes intensified. She took another stuttered breath and her bodice felt as if it would burst. He shifted in his seat and her nipples pebbled. He couldn't possibly *see* her nipples through her corset. Still, she had to will her trembling fingers into submission when she quickly brushed one palm over the other, skillfully exchanging the cards.

"Shall we?" This time, she only half-feigned her shallow breathing as she tapped the table with her knuckles, signaling time to display their cards.

Carrick's gray eyes caught and held hers as he slowly placed his cards face-up on the table. Four kings. She blinked, her long lashes brushing her mask. He had cheated! She hadn't noticed a thing. Well, that would teach her to watch the man. With a private smile, she rose.

He lifted a curious brow.

"Do not move," she ordered in low, throaty tones. "I would fetch my prize."

Curiosity crossed his face as she walked around the table, trailing a finger along the linen-covered table. She stopped behind him. He smelled of sandalwood and pure masculinity and, damn him, the way his coat stretched over his broad shoulders captured her attention too easily. Heart pounding, Juliet placed the heels of her palms on his broad shoulders and let the cards slide from her hands and down his chest. Two of the aces landed face up on his thighs. The other two landed in his crotch. God help her.

His muscled chest rose and fell.

Slowly, she slipped her fingers around his neck. He tilted his head back against the pillow of her breasts and closed his eyes. Juliet shivered. He inhaled a deep breath. It took longer than she'd expected to untie his cravat—Lady Aphrodite's girls had made it seem so easy—but at last, the deed was done.

With a sensuous twist of her wrist, she slid the silk free and stepped back. "Thank you, Carrick, for a most pleasant evening."

She turned away and heard the harsh intake of his breath followed by the scrape of his chair. She quickened pace when his bootfalls followed, but she eluded him by slipping into the shadows, then made a quick righthand turn out a side door and up the Servant stairs. She was glad to go. Midnight balls were far too dangerous—especially for girls like her.

CHAPTER FOUR

SMITTEN

CARRICK TOOK THE STAIRS two at a time, then sucked in a sharp breath as Juliet vanished into the darkness as if she'd been a ghost. He slowed. He'd break his fool neck if he wasn't careful. He reached the next floor, where meager hallway candlelight gave way to total darkness. His heart thudded. By God, he wanted to kiss her. Never had he played a more sensuous game of cards. The way she'd caressed the deck made him need to feel those slim fingers wrapped around his cock. And the way she'd teased him with her delicate, pink tongue? He was determined to taste those gorgeous lips and ravish them. His body tightened at the thought.

She'd obviously cheated with those four aces. It only made him want her more. He needed her—no, he needed to conquer her.

He stormed back down the stairs and made a thorough search of every darkened corner of the ballroom, demanding every candle and lamp be lit until the place stood bathed in light as bright as day.

As he feared, she had truly disappeared.

Finally, he thundered at a waiter, "Find Lady Peddington. Rouse her from her bed, if necessary. I must speak with her at once."

Lady Peddington told Carrick nothing save that Juliet had left for London. He left the school headed for Stirling's home, then got halfway and realized it was nearly three in the morning. With a curse, he ordered his driver to take him home.

At noon, he knocked on Stirling's townhouse and was shown into the parlor. While he paced, a maid brought tea and, minutes later, Stirling entered the room.

"This is a pleasant surprise, Carrick." He shook Carrick's hand. "Tea?" Stirling seated himself on the divan.

"Nae," Carrick said.

Stirling frowned. "You look harried. Is something wrong?"

"I suspect you know full well what is wrong," Carrick said in frustration.

Stirling filled a teacup, then sat back and took a sip.

The smirk Stirling didn't quite hide told Carrick he was right. "Where can I find her?"

"By 'her,' I assume you mean Miss Thatcher?"

"Thatcher." He threw himself into a nearby chair. "Juliet Thatcher." He pinned Stirling with a stare. "What do you know of her?"

"I received her portrait a week ago and recognized her, at once. I saw her at a London house party last year."

"What do you mean, 'received her portrait'?" Carrick demanded.

"A young lady at Lady Peddington's school asked for my help. She mentioned that three other friends were in the same predicament she was, that is, they hadn't found respectable gentlemen for husbands."

Carrick stared. "Surely, you don't think I'm respectable?"

"What is more respectable than a duke?" Stirling chuckled. "The lass is adept at card cheating, don't you agree?"

Carrick laughed. "She is a vixen."

Stirling grinned. "Sounds like a perfect match."

"Not if she's looking for a husband," he said. "Though, she certainly didn't act like a husband hunting lass. I took her for a courtesan."

"That's probably because her mother owns a very popular gentleman's establishment in London."

Carrick blinked. "You don't mean…"

Stirling nodded. "Aye, she owns an upscale brothel, Lady Aphrodite's House of Pleasure.

"How in God's name did Juliet end up at Lady Peddington's?" Carrick asked.

"She aspires to be a dressmaker."

Carrick stared. "You jest."

Stirling laughed. "Nae. Her mother has other ideas, however."

Carrick studied his friend. "You seem to know a great deal about her."

Stirling nodded and took another sip of tea, then set the cup on the table. "Lady Peddington and I are old friends. Miss Thatcher's mother intends to auction her off to the highest bidder."

"Bloody hell," Carrick cursed. "You aren't serious. You said she wanted to become a dressmaker."

"I also said her mother has other ideas."

Carrick shoved to his feet and started for the door.

"London is a long journey to make for just any woman," Stirling commented as Carrick headed for the door.

"Juliet Thatcher isn't just any woman." He reached the door and paused to look back at his old friend. "Be warned, I still plan to collect that roan from you." With that, he quit the room.

* * *

Three days later, Carrick reined his horse to a stop on a busy London street and hailed a man with prematurely thinning hair, a bulbous nose, and close-set eyes. "Can you direct me to Lady Aphrodite's House of Pleasure?" he asked.

The man grinned. "Aye, m'lord. About two miles down the main road." He pointed the way. "Turn onto the road with a brick townhouse and short, wrought iron gate. Then take the second alley to the right, mate. You can't miss it. There's a tall wrought iron gate in front of the house and a painting of the love goddess in the window." He hesitated, then added, "If I may say so, ask for Lucy. She's a wonder, that one is."

Carrick thanked the man and, half an hour later, he reached the narrow lane. A row of gray limestone houses hugged the street, each house looking very much like the one before, but as the man had said, only one domicile had a small but garish painting of Aphrodite propped in the window.

Carrick drew an exhilarating breath of crisp morning air. He'd found her. Anticipation coiled in his belly as he dismounted. The day he'd taken to wrap up his business in Edinburgh, along with the two-day ride to London, hadn't cooled his ardor. If anything, he wanted Juliet even more than he had. He would double any bids offered from other gentlemen—even if she'd already signed a contract.

He dismounted, tied his horse to the post, and went through the wrought iron gate and up the walk. He'd just stepped onto the porch and lifted his knuckles to rap on the door when it opened to reveal a long-haired, burly gentleman in gaily colored clothing.

"My lord, how may I be of service?"

"I've come to speak with the owner of this house," Carrick informed him coolly.

"Who shall I say is calling?"

"The Duke of Hamilton."

The door yanked wide and he locked gazes with a middle-aged matron with bright green eyes and ginger hair. Her body had been squeezed into a red, low-cut gown that artfully emphasized her curves.

"Come in, Your Grace." She offered a sweeping gesture followed by a low curtsey that offered a bird's eye view of her ample cleavage. "I'm Lady Aphrodite, the owner of this fine establishment."

Carrick ducked under the lintel and entered.

She turned to the butler and directed in a low voice, "Bring refreshments at once," then smiled up at Carrick. "Come, my lord. This way."

He followed her down a hall, where more paintings of Aphrodite adorned the walls, and past a large room where one beribboned, satin-clad young lady lounged on a settee. As he passed, the woman lazily lifted her fan and coquettishly dropped her lashes. Finally, they entered a small parlor. A large portrait of Aphrodite, painted in golds and crimson, matched the upholstery of the low couch and chaise lounge.

"Please, have a seat, my lord." She closed the door. "You look as if you've had a long journey. Would you care for brandy?"

He shook his head and sat down. "I'm looking for a Juliet Thatcher."

Surprise flickered in her eyes, but she quickly recovered and said, "May I ask why you are looking for our lovely Juliet?"

Why? She'd cast a net over him, that was why. For the first time in his life, he struggled to voice the words raging through his mind. "I have business to discuss with her."

"Our Juliet's not here," she said.

Relief flooded through him. It had been unlikely she would have arrived ahead of him and signed a contract with another man so quickly, but the worry had niggled. "Even better," he said. "She will soon arrive, however. I seem to have outpaced the coach from Edinburgh."

"I see," she murmured. "Perhaps I could better help you if I understood the nature of your…business with Juliet."

Lust stormed through him. "Come, madam, we are neither of us naïve. Why else would a man ride from Edinburgh to London for a woman like Juliet?"

A calculated look appeared in her eyes. "You're interested in our Juliet?"

"I am—exclusively," he said, and wondered for the hundredth time what madness had seized him. He'd never set such a restriction on any other woman. "Draw up whatever contract you please," he said. "Price is of no concern. Make it for a month—maybe more."

She tilted her head. "Juliet is much more than a simple lady of Aphrodite, Your Grace." After a pregnant pause, she added, "She's my daughter."

He pinned her with an icy stare. "A mother who intended to auction her daughter off."

Most men squirmed under his stare. Juliet's mother stared back, unabashed. "My lord, surely, you do not condemn a woman for doing the very thing you are paying her to do?"

"Juliet is not *my* daughter," he replied.

"True." Her gaze sharpened. "Therefore, it is my place to ensure that she lives a comfortable life and has security as she ages. If you know a better way for a woman to accomplish that, I am ready to entertain your ideas."

Embarrassment flushed over him. "Forgive me, I overstepped my bounds."

She smiled, and Carrick saw where Juliet got her keen mind. "You're clearly a man with a healthy appetite," she said. "Just the sort of man my daughter needs. I'll see her treated fairly. And while Juliet is my daughter, she's also a lady of this house—or will be, after she's known a man's touch."

After she's known a man's touch? It took a moment for the meaning to sink through his haze of exhaustion and lust. Juliet was a virgin? *How?* She'd appeared well-versed in the arts of tantalizing a man. A wave of disappointment coursed through him. He'd thought to find an experienced lady of pleasure, one trained to slake his need. He didn't deflower virgins. Yet even as the thought swirled in his head, a primal hunger stirred his soul. Juliet, with her sultry voice, her mysterious blue eyes and long wave of gold-streaked hair...Juliet could be his and his alone.

"As the most sought-after lady in this house, the honor of taking her virginity has reached a princely sum," the woman was saying.

Carrick snapped from his thoughts. The most sought-after woman? "Nae," the word ripped from his mouth. "There will be no other."

A triumphant smile curved one corner of her mouth.

He locked gazes with her. "Nicely done, madam."

She angled her head in acknowledgement. "We are agreed then. A woman of her quality requires a house and a yearly allowance. I will not consider anything less than a year."

"Draw up a contract with your demands and have done," he said.

She rose. "Let me fetch the pen and parchment."

She sailed out the door and he leaned back to stretch his arms along the back of the couch. He needed a bath and a good night's sleep. Carrick released a breath. A virgin. God help him.

Movement near the door caught his attention and he glanced over as a woman entered. The winsome lass had long blonde curls and wore a beribboned shift thin enough to provide an enticing glimpse of her dark areolas and the patch of hair tucked at the apex of her thighs.

"Can I offer you anything while you wait, my lord?" She swayed her hips as she approached. "I'm Lucy."

Ah, the fair Lucy. He opened his mouth to send her away, then changed his mind. She *did* have something he needed. Desperately. He tapped his fingers along the back of the couch. "Join me."

She smiled, then settled by his side and reached for his crotch.

He caught her wrist. "Nae, lass, not that." He placed her hand firmly on her knee. "I simply wish to talk, my dear." He reached into his waistcoat, withdrew several pound notes and pressed them into her hand. He had a mistress to seduce, "I need you to tell me everything you know about Juliet."

CHAPTER FIVE

HOME AGAIN

JULIET YAWNED AND OPENED her eyes. She sat in the coach, sandwiched between a large man who smelled like cheese and a frazzled woman travelling with four children—creatures, Juliet now suspected, that had been spawned in hell. Never had she seen a more unruly bunch. Through the coach window, she glimpsed the city of London spread over the horizon. At last. She was almost home.

There had been nothing else to do in the coach but think and, for the most part, she'd thought of little else but the Midnight Ball. She couldn't forget the tingle of Carrick's fingers as they'd trailed over her skin, a tantalizing touch she'd relived again and again the entire journey. Truth be told, she'd imagined much, much more, but with London only minutes away, she could no longer indulge in fantasies of those smoky gray eyes. More pressing matters awaited her. The most important being a mother to outwit before the woman again auctioned off her virginity.

Soon enough, the coach rolled over London's cobblestoned streets and stopped at the King's Head Inn. Juliet alighted into her mother's waiting and welcoming arms.

"It's so good to see you, love." Her mother hugged her close before holding her at arm's length. "You have lost weight."

"I'm fine, Ma," Juliet laughed, inspecting her mother in turn.

It had only been a year since they'd parted. Her mother looked very much the same as she always had, buxom and pleasing, with a pert nose, green eyes and red hair. Juliet with her dark locks and blue eyes had clearly taken after her father—whoever that might have been. Even her mother wasn't sure. They interrupted their greetings and stepped aside as an arrogant lady swept past, her maid in tow.

"Hoity-toity." Her mother rolled her eyes as the young woman swept out of sight. "I'd pity the man wed to that poor soul—if I didn't know he'd turn up at my door as a good-paying customer." She laughed.

Juliet offered a wry smile as one of her mother's hired men shoved her trunk onto the bed of a cart.

"Take the cart on up to the house," her mother ordered the man. "Juliet and I will walk. We must chat."

Chat? Juliet thinned her lips. "Ma, must we talk business so soon?"

Her mother's eyes narrowed into shrewd, calculating slits. "It's always time to talk business, Juliet. Especially now. I moved the ball up a week. It's tonight. I feared you wouldn't make it in time."

"*Tonight?*" Juliet repeated in dismay. She was sore, stiff, and tired from the journey, and she desperately needed a bath.

"You have a few hours, yet," her mother assured with a smile and a fond pat on the cheek. "You're young. You'll feel spry enough in no time. I set up your card table in the sitting room and you mustn't forget to wear your mask."

Cards. That was a relief. At least her mother hadn't auctioned her off—yet. "Well, as long as it's just playing cards, Ma," she gave in, but, unable to resist, added, "But we really need to talk about my career. Much has transpired since—"

"Come, come, we'll chat later," her mother interrupted with a smile.

The smile made Juliet stop in her tracks. Her mother invariably responded to all dressmaking overtures with theatrics—certainly never with a kindly, 'we'll chat later.'

"What have you done?" Juliet demanded.

"What have I done?" Her mother snorted, looped her arm through Juliet's, and pulled her down the street. "I've simply welcomed my daughter home. That's all. Now don't spare the bath oils, and wear your finest. We have a ball tonight: Lady Aphrodite's Night of Wonders."

The last thing Juliet wanted was to attend another ball, but at least she had one consolation. This time, she didn't have to deal with the disconcerting Duke of Hamilton. With a long, loud sigh, she followed her mother, wondering why that thought didn't conjure as much relief as it should.

* * *

Juliet gathered her silvery, gossamer silk skirts in one hand and proceeded out her room and down the stairs. Cut in the French fashion of forty years before, the voluminous skirts floated around her ankles, preventing her from seeing where she stepped. She nearly missed the bottom riser before she reached the floor and entered the crowded ballroom.

"Careful now," her mother called as she arrived.

Lady Aphrodite's Night of Wonders was well underway. Swirls of colorful silk and glittering glass jewelry met Juliet's eyes everywhere she looked as Lady Aphrodite's girls, their assets on full display, mingled with the clientele.

Brenda swooped over, grabbed Juliet's arm, and pointed toward the sitting room. "Your card table is ready." She giggled and dropped her gaze to Juliet's bosom. "But *you're* clearly not, love. Pull that gown lower and show more flesh." Brenda yanked Juliet's bodice. The edge of the fabric slid dangerously low over her nipples. "There." The girl nodded in satisfaction as Juliet fitted her mask over her face. "Your first customers have arrived." She escorted Juliet to the sitting room and urged her inside.

Juliet heaved a sigh. She really wasn't in the mood to play cards with a gaggle of pawing men. She glanced around the sitting room. Someone had decorated the mantle and tables with elaborate ivy and thistle garlands, elegantly tied in gold ribbon. Cheap, imitation Grecian pedestals bearing baskets of fruit and cheese lined the walls. A fire crackled in the grate behind a card table draped in white velvet. A man already lounged there, and several more waited nearby. Juliet scarcely gave them notice as she woodenly approached her chair and, after fluffing her cushion, took her seat with an unceremonious plop.

"A game of commerce for the gentleman?" she asked. She glanced up—and froze.

Carrick Hamilton's smoldering gray eyes stared back at her.

CHAPTER SIX

WHAT LIES BENEATH

CARRICK WATCHED JULIET. SHE wore the same white-feathered Venetian mask she'd worn three nights ago, and her breasts nearly spilled over the bodice of her deliciously enticing silver gown. His cock hardened in approval.

"Fancy meeting you again, Juliet," he drawled.

Her lips—such luscious lips—parted in shock.

Another man strolled across the room.

Carrick jolted from the spell. He rose and faced the other men. Merchants and laborers, for the most part. He knew how to deal with men of their ilk. "Gentlemen, I would like some privacy with the lady. Take your pick of the other women here, at my expense."

"I beg your pardon," Juliet said behind him.

"I beg your pardon?" one man echoed.

Two men came to their feet.

Another snorted and opened his mouth to object.

He nodded at the door. "Tell the lady of the house to send your bill to the Duke of Hamilton."

"Duke of Hamilton?" one man said. He looked at Juliet. "Is this man who he says he is?"

She remained mute.

Carrick imagined she wanted to condemn him to the darker parts of hell, but he kept his attention on the men. They exchanged glances with one another, then shrugged and filed from the room.

As the door clicked shut behind them, Carrick faced Juliet once more. His gaze caught on the hint of pink nipples peeking out of her gown. A flush of heat tightened his groin. He had to maintain his dignity. It was one thing to desire a prospective mistress, quite another to ogle her like a common doxy. He returned his gaze to her face. The blue eyes staring back at him through the mask had narrowed.

"I am pleased to see you again," he said.

She remained silent.

"Surely, you can't be surprised to see me after what transpired between us at the Midnight Ball, Juliet."

Something flickered in her eyes, but he couldn't read her expression through the damn mask. He'd had quite enough of the thing. He rounded the table in two strides and grasped the ribbon holding the mask in place. Juliet jerked, but he grasped her shoulder with one hand and tugged the tie free with the other. The white satin mask fell to the floor.

Juliet stiffened.

Carrick's breath caught. He'd known she was beautiful—after all, the silk creation hadn't hidden everything—but unmasked... Almond-shaped blue eyes held his gaze with an intensity that started his heart to hammer. Dark hair framed high cheekbones and flawless skin. He well understood how her mother had named the establishment after the goddess Aphrodite. He was powerless to look away.

"You're beautiful," he whispered.

Juliet blinked, her thick lashes fanning her cheeks. She shifted, as if to stand, but he whirled and returned to his chair.

"A game of commerce, shall we?" he murmured.

"I am not for sale, Carrick," she said in a fierce whisper. "You cannot just take my body."

"I'm not trying to, lass," he said.

Juliet snorted. "How did you find me? No doubt my aunt sold me out. Honoria doesn't know how to keep quiet."

Aunt? Lady Peddington? Interesting. "Your aunt told me nothing save that you had returned to your London home."

Her mouth thinned. "Why are you here?"

He pulled the contract from his inner vest pocket. Alarm crossed Juliet's face as her gaze fell to the parchment. With a grim twist of her mouth, she snatched it from his grasp and stared at the words.

Finally, she laid the paper on the table and rose. "I must speak with my mother."

He pushed to his feet and stepped into her path. "I won't force you, Juliet. I'm not that kind of a man."

"Won't force me? Then what is that?" She jabbed a finger at the contract.

"That is protection."

The eyes staring up at him were rife with suspicion. "Protection? From?"

They stood close, her breasts inches from his chest. The perfume of her hair swirled around him. "From me," he said. "This contract ensures you'll never do anything you do not wish to do."

Interest lit her eyes. "That includes bedding you?" At his nod, she added, "Of what possible advantage is such a contract to you when I've no intentions of letting you in my bed?"

"Time," he answered truthfully. "The contract buys me time to seduce my mistress."

Juliet laughed, a silvery sound filled with wry amusement. "I've seen it all in the brothel, Carrick. There isn't a trick I don't know."

He grinned. "Then you have nothing to lose, and everything to gain. I'll send my carriage around for you in the morning to take you to Lennoxlove House. My mother and sister are in sore need of a dressmaker."

She went ramrod stiff.

"Should you, indeed, prove impervious to my charms" –he flashed a smile— "sewing the gowns of the Dowager Duchess and her daughter will go far in establishing your reputation, will it not?"

She blinked. "Is this some sort of trick?"

He shook his head. "My mother and sister are in need of new dresses."

"They will be there?" she said, then added as if speaking more to herself than him, "That is very good," and he realized he'd erred. He hadn't intended on his mother and sister being at Lennoxlove House.

"The dowager duchess will not be pleased that her son has installed his mistress as her dressmaker," Juliet said.

"She will not be staying permanently."

"Neither will I," Juliet said. "I see the contract allows for a cottage of my choosing."

He angled his head in agreement. "Even here in London, if you choose."

Juliet pinned him with a stare. "You will tire of me before the year stipulated in the contract—especially when I keep turning you away."

He bent his head until his lips almost touched her ear. She stiffened, but didn't step away. "Shall we say I have until summer's end to…woo you?" Carrick drew back enough to see her face.

A calculating gleam –with a hint of amusement—lit her blue eyes. "If I *manage* to resist your charms until the end of summer, you honor the contract for the year—the money and a cottage."

He nodded.

The gleam darkened. "I sew your sister's and mother's gowns?"

"Aye," he said.

"Done."

"Done," he agreed before she could recant.

"What if I lose?" she said.

His heart began to thud. "If you lose, my dear, I will have you."

Juliet laughed. "Shall we seal the agreement with a handshake?" She extended a hand.

Carrick locked gazes with her and clasped her smaller hand in his larger one. He took a step closer and looked down at her. "Have you the courage to seal the deal properly?"

Understanding flickered across her face and her eyes narrowed. She pulled her hand free of his and for one horrible instant he feared he'd miscalculated. Then she seized his lapel and dragged his mouth down to hers.

The instant their lips met, need rammed through him. She stiffened, and Carrick realized he'd crushed her to him. He loosened his hold and cupped her face with his right hand. Hope surged through him when he detected a tremor in her body. His heart soared. She wasn't as impervious to him as she thought. God help him, he wanted her badly.

She wasn't a doxy off the streets and this cardroom was no place to prove he could please her. Damn, she hadn't even signed the contract yet. He flicked her mouth with this tongue. His heart thundered. Would she allow him entrance? Juliet opened on a soft gasp and he plunged his tongue inside. He'd never tasted anything so sweet.

Desire muddied his thoughts. If he miscalculated without a signed contract, she could send him on his way with no chance to redeem himself. When was the last time he'd miscalculated with a woman? When had he known a woman like Juliet Thatcher?

Carrick broke the kiss and pressed her cheek against his chest. To his satisfaction, her heart beat just as fast as his. She would resist him through the summer, eh? It was just as he thought; the men she'd been surrounded with had treated her like one of her mother's whores.

With a final deep breath, he gave her a gentle hug then forced himself to release her. "I shall send a carriage for you in the morning." He nodded at the contract resting next to the deck of cards. "Sign it and join me in Lennoxlove House." He brought her hand to his lips and murmured, "Until we meet again."

Carrick left her there, standing by the table.

CHAPTER SEVEN

LENNOXLOVE HOUSE

THE FOLLOWING MORNING, CARRICK'S carriage arrived, an extraordinarily large conveyance with elaborate, gilded cherubs and oiled-oak spoke wheels. Liveried footmen tied Juliet's trunk to the back before she stepped inside, the satchel containing the signed contract, clutched close to her breast, and sat down on the plush velvet seat. The carriage jolted, and her heart did a flip as they rolled into motion.

Juliet stared out the window at her mother's townhouse. They'd exchanged farewells the night before, but she glimpsed her mother in the front window. Her mother lifted a hand that clutched a hanky. An expected lump formed in Juliet's throat and she waved in the instant before the carriage left her mother behind. Juliet collapsed back against the cushion. She was being silly. She would see her mother at summer's end, maybe before, if rumors of the duke were true.

A man like him would tire quickly of a woman who didn't swoon every time he entered a room. Blast it all, she nearly had swooned when she'd kissed him yesterday. What had gotten into her? The devil, that's what. She grimaced. Was Honoria right, did her blood run hot? Nae. It was much worse than that. As much as she wanted to deny it, the man fascinated her.

The days marched by. After six days of travel, the carriage rolled through the market town of Haddington and pulled off the main road onto the long carriageway of the Duke of Hamilton's Scottish estate.

With a growing sense of unease, Juliet eyed the towering pines until they parted and a magnificent castle built of honey-and-pink colored stone slowly came into view. The Hamilton banner snapped in the wind above one stone tower. Picturesque gardens and landscaped lawns rolled past the carriage windows.

The carriage stopped, then tilted to the side. When the footman opened the door, Juliet clasped her satchel and allowed him to hand her out. She descended onto a graveled drive and took a deep breath of the crisp, pine-scented air. The wind soughed through the treetops, reminding her of the dull, distant roar of the ocean.

"Miss Juliet?" a female voice called.

Juliet turned toward the castle's front door where a freckle-faced maid bobbed on the step, urging her forward with a wave of her hand.

"Do hurry, miss." The maid grinned. "The dowager duchess has asked to see you at once."

The dowager duchess?

Juliet hurried to the door and followed the maid through the flag-stone entrance and up the wide stairs with their ornate, walnut banisters. Heaven help her, she wasn't sure if she should be relieved or worried that Carrick's mother wanted to see her immediately. The dowager's presence at Lennoxlove would ensure Carrick behaved—she hoped. She'd asked herself a hundred times why he would invite her into the same home he shared with his mother and sister. Did he care that little for convention? He said he would woo her. A tremor rippled through her as it did every time she remembered his words. A man didn't 'woo' his mistress.

She broke from her thoughts when the maid turned into a room to the right.

The sitting room was painted a soft, cheerful yellow and a red-and-gold carpet covered the floor. Afternoon sun flooded the room through large windows that spanned the wall. A young, blonde-haired girl sat in a gold brocade wingback chair, squinting at a book. She glanced up.

"You must be Juliet," a woman's friendly greeting came from the left-hand side of the room.

Juliet whirled as the dowager duchess entered through a second door she hadn't noticed. She was a tall woman in her late fifties with pale blue eyes and blonde hair pulled back in fashionable ringlets only lightly streaked with gray.

"My lady." Juliet dipped into a low curtsey.

"Carrick has been singing your praises, my dear," the woman greeted her kindly as she swept across the room. "My daughter and I are quite excited over the prospect of new gowns. I must say, the dress you're wearing is simply stunning. Is it one of your own?"

Juliet dropped her gaze to her morning dress, a simple enough gown she'd decorated with tastefully elaborate stitching above the waistline. "Why, yes, my lady." She smiled.

"It is gorgeous," the dowager duchess exclaimed. "If your other creations are anything like it, I suspect we will set the pace of fashion. Carrick tells me you just graduated from Lady Peddington's School for Young Ladies."

"That is correct, ma'am," Juliet said.

The dowager gave a business-like nod. "It's heartening to hear that some of the young ladies of today still value a good education."

Relief surged through Juliet. As she'd hoped, attending Aunt Honey's school had been a wise decision.

"But you can tell us more about that later. You must be tired from your journey." The dowager turned to her daughter and clapped her hands. "Catherine, please show Juliet to her room."

The girl jumped to her feet, obviously delighted to leave her book behind. "Please, follow me." She shot Juliet a wide grin over her shoulder and darted into the hallway.

After bobbing another curtsey, Juliet followed the girl. They walked down the hall and up another flight of stairs.

"This is one of my most favorite rooms," Catherine said as she stopped before an oak-paneled door and opened it.

Juliet entered the bedroom. A fine, gold carpet nearly covered the entire floor. An ornate chest of drawers sat on one wall with a red velvet curtained, four-poster bed on the wall opposite. The room was stunning, but Juliet had eyes only for the view beyond the balcony, visible through the open French doors. With a smile, she dropped her satchel on the bed and hurried to the balcony.

"It's so beautiful." Juliet leaned against the wrought iron rail and drank in the beauty of the gardens, the rolling green woodlands, and the hills beyond. She'd never dreamt she could sleep in so fine a place.

"Aye, beautiful," Carrick's deep voice startled her.

Juliet whirled.

He stood, tall and lean in a white shirt with dark breeches and black leather riding boots. Saints help her, she'd forgotten how handsome he was. Her heart beat a little faster.

"I see you've made the journey safely and in good time." He cocked a brow at his young sister and added, "Catherine, fetch Juliet refreshments, please."

As his sister obligingly skipped through the door, he faced Juliet again.

"I believe you have something for me." His gray eyes twinkled with amusement. "A contract, perhaps?"

The contract. She'd signed and amended the agreement, adding their wager at the bottom. Juliet crossed to her satchel and rummaged through it. Her fingers caught on the soft folds his cravat, the one he'd worn at the Midnight Ball. She smothered a snort and pushed it aside to pull out the folded parchment beneath.

"Only until summer's end," she said, extending the paper toward him.

He strode to her side and took the contract from her. He stood close.

Too close. Juliet frowned. The infernal man practically towered over her as he unfolded the paper, scanned its contents and tucked it into his jacket pocket. The corner of his mouth quirked upward.

His smug expression caused her frown to deepen and she crooked a finger to beckon him closer. He angled his head so close that for a moment his heat distracted her, but only for a moment. "I'll never be your mistress."

He tossed his head back and laughed, then dropped a kiss to the top of her ear.

Damn, but his hot breath on her ear made her heart pound.

With a wink, he bowed. "I have pressing business. If you'll excuse me."

Juliet watched his lean hips as he left. She rolled her eyes and picked up her satchel, then pulled out the cravat. Strange how much the little strip of silk had changed her life.

The footmen entered with her trunk and set it where she directed. As soon as they left, she set about unpacking. She'd just pulled out her sewing basket when Catherine returned with a tray of toast, tea, and fruit.

"Why, is that a cravat?" the girl asked after setting the tray down on a small table near the bed.

Juliet glanced over and snagged it from under the girl's outstretched hand. "It's nothing," she quickly assured. "Nothing at all."

Her cheeks heated as she turned and stuffed the cravat into the sewing basket.

Nothing? If it was nothing, then why was she blushing like a fool?

CHAPTER EIGHT

UNFORGETTABLE

NEVER BEFORE HAD A woman gotten so deep under Carrick's skin. That was odd enough, but even stranger, never before had he remembered the details of a woman's face after being away from her for days. But Juliet's? Her features burned in his mind in full, glorious detail, from her dark lashes to the slight worry line between her brows, to the curve of her lips. He couldn't forget her. He had merely to close his eyes and a vision of her gold-streaked hair and laughing blue eyes danced across his mind. At last, she was here, and soon, she'd be his. He strode down the stairs to his mother's sitting room.

"My dear boy." She looked up from a book as he entered. "Sit." She nodded to the chair beside her sofa. "It's time we discussed your marriage."

Marriage? Carrick sat in the indicated chair.

"It's *high* time you wed." She carefully marked the page of the book she'd been reading and set it aside. "I must remind you that you have a duty to the estate."

Carrick stretched out his long legs. He'd heard this so many times before. A maid entered with tea and they remained silent as she set the tray on the table before them, then filled two cups and left.

"I've taken matters into my own hands." His mother lifted her tea cup and sipped.

He tensed. Taken matters into her own hands?

"I've invited a selection of young ladies to a series of dinners this month," she said.

Carrick pushed to his feet. "You are mistaken if you think I will be ambushed by a mob of vapid, title-hungry women." He headed for the door.

"Carrick, wait!" She set her teacup onto its saucer with a clatter.

"There's no need for concern, madam. You will have your grandchild soon enough," he snapped, and left the room.

He paused halfway down the hall. Grandchild? Where had that come from? Damn, his mother picked a fine time to parade women through Lennoxlove House. He didn't have time to concern himself with prospective wives. He had a mistress to seduce.

CHAPTER NINE

MADE FOR PLEASURE

THE FOLLOWING EVENING, WHEN Juliet observed, from the sewing room window, the fifth carriage pull up to Lennoxlove House and a beautiful young woman emerge, accompanied by a doting mamma or perhaps an aunt, Juliet realized the Duke of Hamilton was on the hunt for a wife. The question as to why he would contract a mistress while actively seeking a wife arose with the answer hard on its heels: he was a man.

The next morning, the bustle in the kitchen told Juliet that the evening promised more of the same. She steeled herself against the ridiculous disappointment that hovered just below the surface, turned on her heel and headed toward another long day in the sewing room. She slipped down the hallway, reached the Servant stairs, took four steps, then halted. The male laughter coming down the hall was already too familiar: *Carrick*.

She hurried back toward the kitchen, crossed to the larder, and reached the side door seconds later.

"Good morning, ladies."

She froze upon hearing Carrick's voice in the kitchen.

"Has anyone seen Juliet?"

She didn't wait for the staff to inform on her, but hurried out the door and alongside the wall. Her heart pounded. She could go around to the front stairs and enter, then return to her room. Nae, Carrick would find her there in an instant. What could he possibly want with her when he had so many beautiful women vying for his attention?

He's a man, came the answer, yet again.

Juliet glanced at the sky. Grayish clouds skittered across the light blue expanse. It might rain, but not for a bit. She set off east, toward the stables. A morning ride to clear her head was just what she needed. *And Carrick won't find you*, said a small voice. She sighed. This was going to be a long day...and an even longer summer.

When Carrick's laughter filtered up through the window, Juliet paused in threading her needle and peered out the window. There he was again, for the third day in a row, helping another well-dressed lady from her coach in the drive below. The willowy brunette wore an expensive blue silk with an embroidered bodice cut low enough to expose the creamy white mounds of her breasts. Juliet frowned. No wonder he seemed so pleased. With his superior height, the brunette offered quite the view down her bodice. An unexpected pang of jealousy shot through Juliet and she scowled until Carrick passed from view. With a snort of exasperation, she returned to her sewing.

Three days had passed since her arrival at Lennoxlove House. Her stay hadn't been at all what she'd expected. After his initial interest, Carrick had all but vanished from her life. It shouldn't surprise her. After all, she'd predicted that she wouldn't hold his interest. Then there was the parade of women marching through his estate. Redheads, blondes, brunettes. He didn't lack for variety.

The needle pricked her finger. She jerked and dabbed the blood away with a fragment of cut fabric, astonished at the burst of jealousy.

"To work." She bent her head over the yards of peach-colored taffeta destined to become Catherine's finely-stitched gown.

The day passed slowly. The dinner hour arrived and, as the silvery tinkle of a woman's laughter floated up through her window, Juliet decided she'd had enough for the day. It was time to clear her mind, and she couldn't very well do so when a continual symphony of feminine squealing assaulted her ears.

She set aside her sewing and went down the stairs intent on escaping to the quiet of the gardens. The moment she stepped into the cool early evening air, her mood lifted. She took a deep, calming breath. Twilight streaked in dark blues across the sky and a full moon hung low in the east. Ahead, a stone fountain with an immense statue of the Greek god Apollo stood near an inviting stone bench. She stepped onto the garden path, headed toward the fountain, and reached the tall hedges when bootfalls scraped the gravel behind her. Juliet whirled with a gasp as Carrick grasped her shoulder.

"Forgive me," his murmured words sent a thrill down her spine.

The man looked like a Greek god in dark breeches and, heaven help her, no waistcoat. The top two buttons of his startlingly white shirt were undone, and his dark blue cravat hung untied around his neck. Sight of the tanned flesh visible at the open V of his shirt sent a wave of heat racing through her veins.

Mischief lit his eyes. "It's hot," he explained unabashedly, and she realized she was staring—and he'd caught her. He grinned. "Feel free to slip out of your gown, my dear. You'll find the evening air cool on your skin."

Juliet blinked before realizing he was flirting. So, he hadn't lost interest in her, after all. The knowledge pleased her far more than it should. She peered up at him through lowered lashes, prepared to reply, but she froze when he brushed her bottom lip with his thumb and the witty reply vanished.

"You've been hiding," he accused in a gruff voice before letting his hand fall away.

A shriek of laughter emanated from the open dining room windows at the far end of the lawn.

Juliet's temper flared. "How would you know? You've been busy day and *night* with your *guests*."

Carrick's eyes widened in surprise. His lips curved in dry amusement and she realized her mistake.

"I've blundered with my mistress, haven't I?" he asked.

She narrowed her eyes. "I am not—"

"It's my mother's doing, lass," he blithely interrupted, and chucked her under the chin. "She invited a bevy of beauties here in the hopes one might catch my eye. She's determined to see me wed before summer's end."

He was allowing his mother to find him a wife—while his mistress was in residence? Realization struck. He hadn't bedded her, but that didn't matter. She was his mistress. He'd chased her from Edinburgh to London. She hadn't expected sweet words or love. In fact, if he sent her home with the promised money and the cottage as per their agreement, she would be satisfied. But there was something desperately sad about how little she'd come to mean to him in less than a week. She was a fool. She'd never meant anything to him. Why would she? She wasn't a genteel lady like those he entertained.

Juliet pursed her lips. It was just as well she'd decided to become a dressmaker. She clearly made a terrible mistress.

"Forgive my intrusion." She started to step around him.

He stepped sideways and blocked her path. "Aye, I know I'm an incorrigible rogue, lass, but I haven't touched a one of them. Cold fish, the lot."

Why did that please her? But aloud, she pertly replied, "Fish they may be, but they're pedigreed fish."

"I would not have my children born with fins or tails," he said with a vehemence that startled her. "My mother is right, I should have already wed and secured the succession. But, I confess, I believe I should at least *want* to bed my wife."

"One must suffer for the sake of duty," she said dryly.

He heaved a sigh. "Aye, I can only dream of finding pleasure and duty in the same woman."

It was such an outrageous thought for a man of his position that it made her laugh. "I hadn't thought of you as a dreamer."

He quirked a brow. "So, you've been thinking of me?"

The intensity in his gray eyes made her look away. Movement to the right drew her attention.

Carrick seized her arm and pulled her behind the hedges. "That is my mother," he said.

Juliet blanched. "Heavens," she whispered. Alienating the dowager was the last thing she wanted. She pulled free of him and saw that he was staring through the bushes at the figure standing in the open doorway.

"That would explain why she chose now to wage this campaign," he murmured.

"What?" Juliet said.

His features hardened. "Come with me." He grasped her hand.

"I beg your pardon?" She started to yank free, but he entwined his fingers with hers and pulled her around the hedges.

"Are you mad?" To her relief, his mother no longer stood in the doorway. Still, she said, "Your mother will not be pleased to have her dressmaker join the party she's thrown to find you a wife."

"They are sure to gossip over what we were doing in the garden, unchaperoned for an hour or more," he said with a mischievous grin.

Juliet snorted a hearty laugh.

Carrick halted. "My comment was witty, but not to that extent. What is so amusing?"

"An hour?" She couldn't repress a giggle. "You flatter yourself. From what I know of men, the deed takes only minutes."

He tweaked her nose. "Then you are in for a wonderful surprise, sweet."

Juliet rolled her eyes. "Only the old and *infirmed* take that much time."

"Are you calling me impotent?" he asked in an astonished voice.

"I'm calling you uninformed," she answered cheekily.

"Uninformed?"

Carrick locked eyes with her and Juliet realized her mistake. She retreated a step, but he tugged her back. She shook her head. A tiny smile played on his mouth as he drew her closer, inch by inch. She dug her heels in and his smile reached his eyes by the time she reached him.

"Carrick." She intended a reprimand, but his name drifted out as a bare whisper.

His gaze sharpened. He slid an arm around her waist and skimmed the curve of her buttocks until he cupped her derrière. She couldn't tear her eyes from his as he slowly thrust his hips against her. There was no mistaking his erection. He leaned down and her mouth went dry when his warm lips brushed her cheek. He slid moist kisses down her neck. Juliet shivered when he slid his tongue over her collarbone.

Need pulsed at the apex of her thighs. The hand on her buttocks skimmed up her waist, her shoulder, then her neck. He speared his fingers into the hair bound in a tight chignon. Her heart thundered. He fisted the locks and firmly pulled her head back, baring her neck and—heaven help her—the rise of exposed flesh over her bodice, now warm against evening air that suddenly felt almost cold.

Her pulse quickened in anticipation of his mouth sliding lower. Would he dip his tongue between her bodice and flesh and tease her nipples? God help her, her nipples were so hard they ached.

"I can please you," he murmured against her skin.

Her head reeled. Saints in heaven, if he did nothing more than kiss her breast this instant, she would embarrass herself by screaming his name. She'd never wanted a man like this...never needed his touch. She arched into him.

He gave a low laugh. "Soon, sweet, I promise."

He abruptly stepped back. She stumbled forward. He grasped her arm and steadied her. Juliet looked up at him and frowned.

Carrick lifted a brow. "Uninformed, you say?" With a laugh, he spun and walked away.

✶ ✶ ✶

Juliet knew she should've gone to bed. The dowager didn't expect her to work into the night, but she feared where her thoughts would go with nothing to occupy them. Carrick. She now understood his reputation. She also understood his confidence. The man truly was irresistible… Dangerous. He had kissed her once in the days since her arrival and already her resolve had slipped.

Could she last the summer? What if she didn't resist him? Shame rolled over her. She was a normal woman, she experienced desire. That had been long ago, when she was young, long before she'd seen so many men come and go from her mother's brothel. Some were men who loved their wives, but few of them were faithful. Passion simply wasn't worth the lack of trust. She looked up from the hem she was sewing and sought the mantle clock. 9:30. She would finish this hem, then stop for the night. Tomorrow would be another long day.

Footfalls sounded in the hallway outside her door. Juliet looked up as the door opened and Carrick entered, a large basket in hand.

"I knew I'd find you here still working." He stopped in front of her and lifted the basket. "I come bearing gifts." Juliet frowned, and he added, "Supper."

"I've already eaten," she said.

"Bread and cheese, maybe a bit of tea, no doubt." He lifted a brow.

She narrowed her eyes. "You think yourself clever, don't you?"

He grinned. "Aye, I do." He grasped her hand and she had just enough time to set aside the dress as he pulled her to her feet. "Come." He started toward the balcony.

"Carrick, I really must finish this hem before I go to bed."

"Later," he said. They reached the balcony and he opened the doors, then set the basket down and lifted out a plaid blanket. He stepped onto the balcony, shook out the fabric, then laid it on the ground. "Grab the basket and bring it here," he instructed.

With a sigh, Juliet picked up the basket and carried it onto the balcony. Clouds drifted slowly across a sky littered with stars. She had to admit, it was a beautiful night. Carrick clasped her hand and steadied her as she sank onto the plaid, then he sat beside her and lifted from the basket a bottle of wine, a wrapped cloth, which he opened to reveal blueberry pastries, and a plate with a cloth over it, which held cold chicken. Cheese, of course, along with two plates, two glasses and silverware.

"This is a feast," she said.

"A feast for two," he said.

"What about your guests?" she said.

He shook his head. "They are far too busy admiring each other's dresses and hairstyles to miss me."

She knew that was untrue, but couldn't help a grimace. "You have my sympathies."

He laughed, then filled a plate, which he passed to her. He then poured wine in both glasses before filling his own plate.

Juliet took her first bite. "This chicken is quite good."

"Mrs. Allenby is an excellent cook," he replied, taking a hearty gulp of wine. "What are you sewing?"

"A day dress for your mother. She already had the fabric. A beautiful canary yellow muslin."

"Yellow is her favorite color," he said.

Surprised to find herself so hungry, Juliet set about eating her chicken and washing it down with the wine.

"How did your mother take it when you left?" Carrick asked.

Juliet shot him a dry look. "She was very pleased, as you must know. You paid her a handsome sum."

He gave a small smile. "She is a skilled negotiator."

"It is not the first time she sold me."

He looked sharply at her. "She told me you were..."

Juliet lifted a brow. "A virgin?" Anger stabbed. "I see. You want a virgin to deflower." Why hadn't it occurred to her?

He shook his head. "Nae, I did not—" He paused. "The contract had

143

nothing to do with whether or not you were a virgin. Your mother said you were untouched. I am simply surprised she lied."

"People lie all the time." Juliet regarded him. "If you feel you were cheated, I will return home and ask nothing further from you."

He stared for a moment, then a slow smile spread across his face. "I have until summer's end to seduce you. That's what I intend to do."

"Even if I am *used property*?"

His smile vanished. "You are not *property*. Is that what you believe I think of you?"

He was genuinely offended. "No," she answered softly.

He stared for another heartbeat as if uncertain, then said, "I would have made the same offer to your mother whether I thought you were virgin or not." His gaze intensified. "I want you to know that."

A tiny bit of guilt stabbed, but only a tiny bit. "Well, my mother did not lie."

He blinked. "Then you lied?"

"No. I only said my mother had sold me once before. I never said I got...used."

"You allowed me to believe you had lost your virginity."

She shrugged. "Sometimes people simply leave something out."

He threw his head back and laughed. "I can see, I'm going to have to tread very carefully with you."

Juliet nodded as she finished her chicken. "We dressmakers are a hearty breed."

His eyes lit with mischief. "I shall take great care, then." He reached into the basket, pulled out a small, smooth wooden box and handed it to her.

Juliet looked at him. "What is it?"

He nodded at the box. "Open it and find out."

She hesitated, then took it. Juliet cast a curious glance at him, then lifted the box lid. Inside, on black velvet, rested a silver locket with a silver chain. She frowned. "I don't understand."

"It's a gift."

"But why?"

"Ladies do not ask a gentleman why they give them gifts," he said.

She stiffened. "I see."

"I doubt you do, lass. I have no ulterior motive. I thought you might like it, that's all. Look inside the locket."

She was tempted not to accept it, but setting the box aside, she lifted the locket and opened the clasp. She gasped. An intricate miniature of her mother filled the right side. Juliet snapped her gaze onto Carrick. "I-I don't understand."

"Do you like it?" he asked.

She looked back at the miniature and nodded.

"That's why I did it."

Tears burned the corners of her eyes. She swiped at a teardrop that broke through her resolve and ran a finger over the small portrait. "It's beautiful." She looked at him. "Thank you."

He smiled, the pleasure reaching to his eyes, and her heart tugged. Oh, this man was dangerous, very, very dangerous. Despite the admonition, she leaned across the food and pressed a kiss to his cheek. He went very still.

She withdrew and shook her head. "What made you think of this? It's not as if I will be away from my mother all that long."

He shrugged. "A daughter needn't be separated from her mother very long to miss her."

Juliet's heart pounded. "I had better finish the hem on the dress."

He nodded, pushed to his feet, and extended a hand. As she placed her hand in his, his fingers closed around hers with such gentleness that the tears threatened again. She would never be one of the fine ladies he chose as his wife. He pulled her to her feet and tugged her into his arms and with a slow grin, bent and covered her mouth with his. She should have pushed him away, should have reminded him that she would never become his mistress, but instead, she found herself melting against him, breathing of him deeply as his tongue slipped past her lips. She lost track of time as their tongues sparred, and when he drew back, for an instant, her surroundings seemed to spin.

He steadied her. "Are you all right, lass?"

She nodded, but the satisfied smile she glimpsed in the instant before he turned away told her he was well aware that he'd touched her heart.

* * *

Juliet tossed and turned into the wee hours of the night. Carrick had played her like an instrument. For hours, she'd lain on her bed, aching with need.

As the moon rose high in the sky outside her window, she gave up all pretense of sleep, threw her shawl over her shoulders and slipped from her room. Mrs. Allenby made a very nice lemon water, perhaps it would help.

She'd gone scarcely more than a yard from her door when Carrick's soft voice drifted through the darkness, "Why are you wandering in the night like a wraith, Juliet?"

She spun, then froze at sight of his silhouette leaning against the opposite wall.

"I can't sleep," she whispered.

"Then do not try, lass." He started toward her.

CHAPTER TEN

MISTRESS

CARRICK REACHED JULIET AND caught her close. He had nearly knocked on her bedroom door a dozen times, unsure if she were truly ready for him. But the way she melted against him, he knew beyond a doubt that she wanted him. With a growl, he swept her into his arms and entered her bedchamber, then pushed the door closed with a kick.

Bright moonlight bathed the room in a soft, silvery glow. Carrick set her feet on the carpet and pulled the shawl from her shoulders, letting the moon's light illuminate the outline of her soft curves. Her hair fell over her slim shoulders. She was so beautiful he could scarcely breathe.

He covered her mouth with his. She gasped. He urged her back toward the bed. Without prompting, she parted her lips and he swept inside. Their tongues met in a tingling caress. He sucked her tongue into his mouth. She leaned into him and anticipation thrummed through him.

His knee bumped the bed and she jarred. Carrick lowered her onto the mattress and came down on top of her. She drew a deep breath. Her nipples poked through the thin fabric of her shift. She wanted him. Carrick took one hardened nipple into his mouth and sucked through the cloth of her shift. Juliet grasped his shoulders and arched into his mouth. She slid one hand up his arm, his neck, then threaded her fingers into his hair. He needed her naked. He needed her cool fingers around his shaft. First... He shifted to the other nipple. Her fingers tightened in his hair.

He grunted. "I know, love."

Carrick released the nipple, then shoved to his knees and pulled her upright with him.

She gasped, "Are we finished already?"

He gave a strangled laugh. "Not by half." He grasped the hem of her shift, then pulled it up and over her head.

His breath caught. Moonlight bathed her creamy skin in a glow that gave her an almost ethereal quality. She was a goddess and he planned to worship every inch of her.

He tossed the shift to the floor.

"It's not fair," she said.

He started from the trance. "What?"

"It's not fair."

Carrick frowned. "What isn't fair? I have only just begun—"

"I'm naked. You're not."

His heart thundered. Christ Almighty, she was a brazen lass.

"I cannot argue with a lady," he said.

She tilted her head. "I am no lady, sir."

He gave his head a single shake. "Nae, you are a goddess."

Her mouth quirked. Carrick couldn't believe it. She was amused. He would change that. He jumped to his feet, immensely glad he'd removed his boots earlier. Then, heedless of the buttons, he yanked his shirt open. He sluffed the shirt from his shoulders, yanked open the buttons on his breeches, then shoved them down his hips.

Her audible gasp caused his cock to pulse. No other woman had ever affected him like this. Carrick kicked the breeches aside, then crawled onto the bed and eased her onto her back, then straddled her. She stared up at him, her features in shadow. He glanced at the night table and considered lighting a candle. He wanted to see her. Could he wait the moment it would take to light the damn thing?

She lifted a hand and he froze when she wrapped her arm around his neck and drew him closer. Apparently, *she* couldn't wait.

"You're so beautiful," he whispered in the instant before their lips met.

He settled his body on top of hers. His cock brushed the curve of her abdomen. This time, she sucked his tongue into her mouth. He sparred with her, and covered a breast with one hand. She arched, and her hard nipple pressed his palm. Dare he... Carrick lightly pinched the nipple. She drew a sharp breath. The sound heated his blood.

He broke the kiss, then lowered his mouth to her left breast and flicked the right nipple while he lightly pinched the other nipple again.

She seized his shoulders. Her desperate grip sent a wave of desire through him. Slowly, he thrust his member against her belly. Sweet discomfort tightened his bollocks. He needed to be inside her. But not yet. He had to show her that what existed between them was nothing like the quick encounters that took place in her mother's brothel.

Carrick placed soft kisses on her breasts, then her neck, then her mouth again. She drew in a shuddering breath. When he reached between them and brushed his fingers along the curls between her legs, she tensed. He kissed her again, gently and slipped a finger between her folds. Blood roared through his ears. She was so wet. He forced patience and slowly slid a finger inside her.

Juliet stilled, and he hid a smile. The woman of the world was not quite prepared for the realities of a man stroking her pleasure point. With his thumb, he messaged her swollen nub as he slowly thrust a finger in and out of her channel. To his delight, she began to move her hips in rhythm with his strokes. By God, the woman was hot blooded. He licked her nipple.

"Carrick," she moaned.

Hearing her call his name sent a wave of unexpected satisfaction through him. She began to move faster. He kept his rhythm even. Her fingers dug into his shoulders. Moonlight splashed across her face, bathing her skin in an ethereal glow. His cock strained so hard against his skin he thought the damned member would break free and plunge inside her of its own accord.

Juliet abruptly stiffened and cried out. Her channel milked his finger. Carrick yanked his finger from her channel, closed his mouth over her sex and sucked.

"God have mercy," she cried, and pulsed beneath his tongue as a second climax rolled over her.

She drew a shuddered breath. Carrick pushed upright and quickly fitted his cock to her opening. Her tight opening closed around the sensitive crown. The need to drive into her nearly drove him out of his mind. He slid a hand beneath her buttocks and locked his gaze on her face. He couldn't read her expression.

"Do you trust me?" he asked.

She grasped his arm and said in a barely audible whisper, "Yes."

"This will hurt for only an instant," he said, and thrust into her hilt deep.

She stiffened. Carrick froze until Juliet released a breath and relaxed. He lowered his weight onto her, wrapped his arms around her and buried his face in her hair as he began to move inside her. He was ashamed to admit he wouldn't last long with her magnificent heat wrapped so tightly around him. He tried to think about the accounts he would have to deal with first thing in the morning, but she lifted her hips to meet his thrusts and his climax rolled over him without warning. Intense pleasure ripped through him and, with a startled cry, he spilled his seed inside her.

Heart racing, he continued to drive into her half a dozen times as he milked the last vestiges of pleasure from his member. At last, he collapsed onto her slender form for several heartbeats, then slid off her. He pulled her close.

"I can do better, I promise. Give me ten minutes, and I'll prove myself."

He felt her smile against his chest. She was laughing at him again. He really had to do something about that. He gently pushed her onto her back and looked at her with wonder.

"You were incredible," he whispered.

He kissed her again, tenderly.

The wind rustled through the open window, blowing her hair across his bare chest. He wanted to take her again, but knew her tender flesh needed to rest. He'd have to wait. Instead, he drew her further up into the pillows, and cradled her in his arms. She heaved a sigh and closed her eyes.

His mistress. Aye, she was his mistress. At last.

He lay on his back and closed his eyes, just for a moment.

* * *

Carrick awoke as the first rays of sun filtered through the window, his cock hard with the memory of last night and a new, strange need that coursed through him. He turned on his side, facing the slight form in the bed next to him and his heartbeat quickened. The sheet had slipped down the rise of her breasts and he glimpsed the edges of the soft pink areolas he'd tasted last night. Her hair, a sensuous tangle of thick locks, framed her face and lay across one full breast. His cock pulsed. He grinned. She was truly and fully his mistress.

Juliet arched and stretched. He dropped a kiss to her throat, then added a soft series of kisses under the line of her jaw. She tensed, then relaxed under the ministrations of his tongue and moaned that same husky sound that had driven him wild last night. Shivers raced down his spine.

"I need you." He grasped her hand and wrapped her fingers around his shaft. "Now."

He gently thrust against her loose fist. To his surprise, she pulled away and pushed him flat on his back, his cock jutting up like a pillar of marble. Juliet lowered her lashes, then swung her slim leg over his hips and poised her entrance above his erection.

"Ride me, lass." He grasped her hips and tensed in readiness for her channel to sheath him.

"So demanding," Juliet teased as she took the tip of his throbbing manhood into her slim body.

She tortured him. Horribly. Repeatedly sliding down an inch before lifting herself off until, at last, he could bear it no longer and he shoved her down onto his hard length as he thrust upward. She gasped and tossed her head back in delight. With her heat fully encasing him, he began to rock. They were meant for each other. He couldn't control himself. Not with the way she moved. Within minutes, her lashes fluttered as she shuddered in ecstasy and he came with a loud groan, pumping himself into her until he'd milked his cock to the very last.

When he finished, he lifted her off him and she lay her head on his chest as he traced the length of her spine with a fingertip.

Neither spoke for a time. It wasn't until the distant chime of the grandfather clock announced the breakfast hour that Juliet bolted upright. "Heavens! I'm late to fit your sister's gown."

Amused, he watched her dive from the bed and dart to the armoire.

"Don't bother with the under drawers," he said. "You won't need them."

She snorted and stuffed her arms through her dress sleeves, then shimmied the dress down over lush breasts. His cock twitched. She would be spending an inordinate amount of time on her back with him between her legs.

At the door, she paused and looked over her shoulder.

"We'll continue this later, lass." He rose. Her eyes flicked to his erection before she turned and left.

Carrick caught sight of her drawers on the floor. He grinned. It was going to be a good day.

CHAPTER ELEVEN

BLIND MAN'S BLUFF

NEVER IN HER WILDEST dreams had Juliet thought that bedding a man could be so...consuming. She could still feel the heat of Carrick's body on hers and the warmth of his breath in her hair as he'd groaned her name.

"What made you decide to become a dressmaker?" Catherine asked Juliet.

Juliet started from her thoughts. She pushed the needle through the sky-blue velvet. She sat in the drawing room's bay window as Catherine lounged on a nearby settee, perusing swatches of lace.

"We must all do something. I like creating clothes and I am—I hope—skilled at it."

"Indeed, you are, my dear." The dowager turned a page in the book she was reading.

"I don't like sewing at all," Catherine said. "I know that's a terrible thing to say. Young ladies are supposed to like sewing. But I don't."

"Well, fortunately, you don't need to love it to be skilled at darning a pair of socks or repairing a hem," Juliet said.

"You see there, Catherine, the dowager said, "Juliet understands that sewing is a skill that a lady must have."

"I don't think that's what she said, Mama. She is only saying that just because I don't like it, doesn't mean I can't do it."

Juliet hid a smile.

"What else do you do besides sew?" Catherine said.

"I read, of course. I paint a little, and I speak a little Latin and French."

Catherine made a face. "Surely, you do other things that are much more fun than that?"

"I like to read," Juliet said. "Have you found any lace you like yet?"

She shrugged. "Carrick said you live in London. I adore London. When last we were there, Carrick took me riding in the park every day. Do you go riding in the park as well? Carrick has a wonderful phaeton. I wish that I could drive it, but he says ladies don't do such things."

"He's quite right, of course," Juliet said, and she glimpsed the approving glance the dowager sent her way.

Catherine must've seen it, as well, for she said, "You're only agreeing because Mama is here. But I think you know that a lady is just as capable of driving a phaeton as a man is."

"One must be very skilled to drive any kind of carriage," Juliet said in all seriousness.

"I feel certain I could learn," Catherine said, but Juliet knew better than to say yay or nae.

"Where in London do you live?" Catherine asked. "We will have to visit you when next we are there. Isn't that right, Mama?"

"Indeed, it is," the dowager agreed.

Juliet's pulse quickened, but she had practiced a thousand times what she would say to the first person who asked her address in London, and she rattled off the address of the home of Bonnie Macmillan's milliner shop, which she would rent when she returned to London.

"I'm so glad we were able to come to Lennexlove House to be with you," Catherine said.

Juliet smiled. "I am glad, too."

"It was fortunate we hadn't yet left for London when Carrick told us he was bringing you."

Juliet looked at her sharply. They weren't in Lennexlove House when Carrick said he would bring her here? She had assumed they were already in residence. It had to mean he'd planned on bringing her here alone, and had only brought them later when he'd realized she expected them there.

Suddenly, Juliet felt the dowager's eyes on her. Her fingers trembled. Did the woman suspect what had happened between her and Carrick last night? She would not be pleased. She might even demand Carrick send her away. Strangely, though she'd wanted to be sent away, the idea of leaving now depressed her.

A knock on the door made Juliet jump, and a maid entered and curtsied, but to Juliet's surprise, the maid faced her instead of the dowager.

"His Grace wishes to see you in the library," the maid announced. "At once."

Juliet felt her face flush. "Are you certain?" she asked in a steady voice.

"Aye, Miss," the maid replied. "He came looking for ye in the kitchen. Mrs. Allenby sent me to find you."

Juliet's heart thundered. How could she explain his summons? She didn't dare look at the dowager.

"I imagine he received the bill for the fabrics we ordered," Catherine said with a laugh.

Juliet could have kissed her. She wasn't certain it would be the dressmaker the master of the house would take to task for overspending on fabric, but the excuse was far better than the blank stare she knew she wore.

"Perhaps I overdid it," she murmured as she rose to her feet, keenly aware of the dowager's sharp eyes latching onto her. "Put the swatch you like best here." Juliet patted her sewing basket, smoothed her skirts, then left the room.

She hurried down the hallway. She would have his hide for this. What had gotten into him, summoning her like...like she was his mistress?

Juliet arrived to find the library door ajar and peeked inside. It was an impressive room, painted a warm shade of yellow. Its windows overlooked the sprawling lawn and gardens. Tall, rosewood bookcases lined the walls and the smell of wood polish and leather permeated the air. Juliet eased the door open and caught sight of Carrick at his desk, penning a letter. Her breath caught. His sleeves were rolled up to reveal tanned forearms. A lock of hair had fallen across his forehead. He glanced up and a smile lit his face.

"You sent for me?" Juliet entered and closed the door behind her as he set down his pen and leaned back in his chair.

He lifted an eyebrow and she knew he was wondering why she'd closed the door. Let him wonder. She took three paces to his desk then stopped. "Have you lost your mind, Carrick?"

He blinked.

"I was with your mother and sister when the maid arrived to inform me that you'd summoned me."

His eyes widened slightly, then he gave a lopsided grin that caused her stomach to flip. "I didn't find you in the sewing room or the kitchen and assumed you were avoiding me." He shrugged. "I decided one of the maids would have better luck finding you."

Juliet stared. He looked so contrite and so...so damnably attractive that she suddenly wondered how she was going to escape this—him—unscathed. She wasn't, she realized. She'd already lost the bet. He owned her for the next year. How long could she continue as the dowager's dressmaker before the older woman figured out the truth?

His eyes darkened and suddenly his mother, their bet, nothing else mattered. "Come closer, my dear. You know where you belong."

"Where do I belong?" she whispered.

He smiled. "In my arms."

Her pulse quickened. Juliet stepped around the desk, but stopped beyond reach. He leaned forward, seized her arm, and tugged her into his lap. She shrieked. He laughed and hugged her close while she twisted in a halfhearted attempt at freedom. Her hip bumped his hard length and she froze.

"Good Lord, Carrick. I'm surprised you have any energy left after last night."

He laughed and hugged her tighter. "I told you I would have many wonderful surprises for you."

Her heart began to pound, and she realized she wanted him so badly it hurt. Juliet pushed away from him and he released her as she slid from his lap. With a quick twitch of her skirt, she knelt before him. His gaze sharpened when she reached for the buttons on his breeches and slowly unfastened them. Her fingers brushed the bulge straining against the constraints and he sucked in a startled breath. Embarrassment warmed her cheeks when her fingers trembled slightly as she freed the last button. His erection spring free and his shirt tented. She pushed aside the shirt and heat rushed through her at sight of his rigid manhood. She raised her gown to her thighs and straddled his thighs.

He closed his eyes and took a long, luxurious breath as she slowly slid down onto his hard length. With a sigh of pleasure, she dropped her gown, the silk making a soft swish as it covered them both.

He skimmed his fingers lightly over her arms and tugged her bodice until her breasts spilled over the neckline. Eager to feel his mouth on her flesh, she arched forward and pulled his face toward her. He sucked a nipple into his mouth.

She shivered. "Carrick," she whispered.

Slowly, she lifted off him, then lowered until he filled her. She rose, and he thrust to meet her downward motion. Pain and pleasure spiked. Juliet braced her hands on his shoulders, steadying her torso so that he could continue to suck her breasts as she rode him. He grasped her hips and brought her down hard. Her breath caught. The man knew how to please a woman.

He increased their rhythm and suckled her other breast. Pleasure built inside her core. Her nipple slipped from his mouth and his grasp on her hips tightened as she slammed down on him. His jaw tensed. A wave of gratification rolled over her. She pleased him. Her climax caught her off guard. Juliet threw her head back and arched. He rammed his cock deeper. She cried out and light flashed behind her eyes. It seemed the world spun around her. Her body went weak as a kitten.

Juliet was vaguely aware of his groan as he ground himself against her sex. She'd seen the girls in her mother's brothel backed against walls while their customers pumped into them, had heard more stories than she could remember of the mechanics of the joining of a man and woman. But she'd never heard the girls speak of this sort of…magic. Is that what it was, magic?

Juliet collapsed onto his chest and listened to the powerful thump of his heart until its rhythm slowed.

Carrick buried his face in her hair. "I can't get enough of you." He nuzzled her neck. "Come to my bed. Let's spend the day there."

Juliet snorted and reluctantly straightened. "You know very well I have gowns to sew."

"As if my mother and sister don't have enough of the blasted things." He ran his hands over her breasts and tweaked her nipples.

She shivered.

"Come to my bed," he repeated.

Juliet pulled her sleeves back over her shoulders and slid off his lap. He tucked his shirt back in his pants, then fastened his pants and released a long breath.

"I imagine your mother and sister are still in the drawing room where I left them." A thread of panic wound through her. "Lord, the dowager will wonder why I took so long."

He grasped her hand and his expression sobered. "I will deal with my mother."

The panic intensified. "Carrick, she can't know—"

A knock sounded at the door. "Carrick," his mother called.

Juliet yanked her gaze onto the door. Dear God, if the dowager saw her before she has a chance to smooth every hair back into place.

The door knob started to turn, and Juliet dropped to her knees.

"What the—" Carrick began, but she scurried under his desk as the door opened. She pulled her knees to her chest. He turned, and she was forced sideways against the wood when his knees nearly struck her shoulder. He shifted, and Juliet realized he was looking up from his desk. His arms rested on the desktop. Dear God, she hoped his expression gave away nothing of the fact that his mistress was hiding there.

"I thought I would find Juliet here," the dowager's voice came from the direction of the door.

Juliet jammed her eyes closed and silently prayed, *Please, please, please, do not come in.*

"You missed her," he replied.

The door creaked, and Juliet's heart thundered. Was the dowager entering the room and closing the door behind her or had she left?

"I am busy, Mother," Carrick said, and Juliet's heart fell. The dowager hadn't left

"I have planned another dinner for tonight," she said.

"I believe you told me that." His right arm shifted slightly, and Juliet thought he might be writing as he had been when she arrived.

"Catherine and I will be spending the autumn and winter in Edinburgh."

"That is your habit," he replied distractedly.

"Lady Audrey is very nice, don't you agree?" The dowager's voice was closer. Silk rustled, and Juliet realized she was sitting in the chair opposite Carrick's desk.

"I'm too busy to discuss women, Mother," he said.

"Even Juliet?"

He jerked.

Juliet tensed.

"I beg your pardon?" he said.

"I'm no fool, Carrick," his mother said. "I know —

He shoved his chair back and stood. "I will thank you to keep anything you *know* to yourself, madam."

He turned, and his legs disappeared from sight as he strode around the desk. Juliet could barely hear his bootfalls through the pounding of her heart in her ears. The doorknob rattled, then he said, "I am busy, Mother."

Three heartbeats later, the dowager said, "Lady Audrey will be attending the dinner tonight." Her voice was farther away.

"How kind of you to invite her a second time," Carrick replied in a cold voice.

"I have never known you to act like this," the dowager said.

"You have never gone so far as to choose my bride for me," he said.

A moment of silence passed. "It is time you married, Carrick. Whatever pleasures you might seek—"

"Madam, I have been patient thus far."

The warning in his voice sent a shiver down Juliet's back.

"Then I will see you at dinner," the dowager said.

The door clicked shut and a moment later, Carrick's legs came back into view. He squatted and bent his head so that he could make eye contact. "Come on out, love."

Juliet pulled her dress to her knees and crawled from beneath the desk. He grasped her hand and pulled her to her feet.

"She's right, you know," Juliet said as she brushed imaginary dust off her dress. She gave thanks that her voice remained steady.

He placed a finger beneath her chin and she froze when he tilted her face toward his. "Never mind my mother."

How could she possibly do that? The woman was determined to see her son wed. "She's your mother," Juliet whispered.

"And she has nothing to do with us," he replied.

Juliet stepped away. "I'd better return to the drawing room." She started to turn, but he grabbed her arm.

"Not that way." He tugged her to the bookshelves near the sideboard and pressed on a shelf. It sprang away from the wall.

"What in the world?" she exclaimed.

He grinned. "Lennoxlove is full of surprises." The look in his eyes said that he, too, was full of surprises.

* * *

Juliet spent the afternoon in the sewing room trying her best to ignore thoughts of Carrick. Carrick laughing. Carrick staring down at her. Carrick caressing her breasts. Carrick in another woman's arms. Why did it bother her so? She knew the proper place of a mistress—in practice, anyway. In reality, remembering her place was so much harder.

As evening approached, the crunch of wheels on the graveled drive drew her attention to the window, yet again. Despite the conviction to ignore everything outside her room, she shifted and looked out the window. Her heart wrenched when Carrick stepped into view as a carriage rolled to a stop in front of the house. He opened the carriage door and took the elegant hand that reached toward him. The dark-haired beauty wore an olive-green velvet dress as fine as any Juliet had ever seen. She gave a silvery laugh that reached the window.

The woman slipped her hand into the crook of his arm and Juliet glimpsed his smile as he turned toward the house. Her heart squeezed. He was charming. They disappeared from view and his baritone laugh abruptly cut off when the door shut. The evening was young. Who knew how many more young ladies would arrive?

Juliet reached into her sewing basket to pull out a spool of thread, but her fingers caught on the silky folds of Carrick's cravat. Slowly, she withdrew the narrow length of fabric and pressed it against her cheek. Incredibly, it still carried his scent. Spicy sandalwood.

The young woman's silvery laugh came again in the distance.

Juliet stiffened and suddenly felt rather foolish to be sniffing the cravat like a loyal hound. She stuffed it back into the basket. She wasn't about to sit there, listening to the sounds of their merrymaking, not when she could sit in the quieter solitude of the servant quarters one floor up. Quickly, she gathered her sewing and went upstairs.

The evening dragged. Her thoughts returned too often to the memory of Carrick's lips on her skin—and his smile for the beautiful dark-haired lady. Just *how* did he entertain the debutantes in the drawing room below? When the clock struck ten, her mind still churned with uncomfortable questions. She set her sewing aside and stretched her stiff neck. Her fingers ached. The day was done, but the guests remained. Were they staying for a house party? She nibbled her lip. While she yearned to slip into Carrick's bed, she refused to consider such an action while he entertained other women.

"It's a book for you tonight, Juliet," she muttered. Perhaps for many nights to come—if she were wise. A book was a poor substitute for Carrick's lips, but it was the best—and safest—her evening could offer.

After a quick detour to the kitchen for a simple meal of fresh bread and cheese, she hurried down the hall toward the library. The candles and oil lamps burned low in their sconces and wall holders. In the drawing room, just three doors away, someone played the pianoforte.

At the hum of voices, Juliet quickened her steps to the library then stopped outside its door when feminine laughter drifted toward her. She recognized too well the titter of a woman trying to impress a man. Which one of them was laughing? She crept toward the drawing room. If she was careful, no one would notice if she stole a peek.

Catherine suddenly darted into the hall.

Juliet stopped short and pivoted on her heel.

"Juliet," Catherine called, but Juliet hurried away. An instant later, Catherine reached her side and caught her hand. "Oh, do play with us, Juliet." The young girl giggled. "*Please*, Juliet!"

"I really shouldn't." Juliet tried to shake free.

"Don't be a ninny." Catherine tugged her several paces toward the drawing room. "Come join the fun."

Juliet knew she should break free—for a mistress didn't socialize with ladies invited to respectable parties. Her mother had pounded that into her head long before she truly understood what the words meant.

They reached the drawing room. Juliet took two paces into the room, caught sight of Carrick and stopped. The Duke of Hamilton stood before the fire, dressed in black breeches with a gray brocade waistcoat, white shirt, and a fine red silk, elaborately tied cravat. He smiled as he examined a large sapphire ring against the firelight. Half a dozen guests gathered around him, three of whom were ladies vying for the closest position.

"It's such a beautiful ring, Carrick," a petite redhead in an expensive blue satin evening gown said. "A truly stunning ring any woman would be *pleased* to wear."

"Not just *any* woman." The dowager shifted in the nearby settee. Her voice held a distinct note of pride. "Hamilton brides have worn that ring for the past eighty years."

Brides. Juliet turned to leave.

Catherine shut the door, her back to the wood, and grinned. "Juliet's come to play with us."

All eyes turned onto her.

"Ah, Juliet," the dowager said.

Juliet faced the older woman, careful to keep her gaze from straying to Carrick.

The older woman waved her forward. "Come, join us."

Juliet hesitated. If the woman disapproved of her presence, it was difficult to tell. Juliet needn't glance at the prospective brides to know they didn't approve. She felt their assessing gazes inventory her face, figure and, no doubt, her clothes. A sliver of satisfaction bolstered her. In that regard, they would not find her lacking.

Catherine bounced over to her brother. "We have more than enough players now."

Juliet couldn't halt her gaze from following the girl.

Catherine tugged his sleeve. "Juliet's here for a game of Blind Man's Bluff."

Carrick grinned down at his sister. "Then what are we waiting for?" His attention shifted to Juliet.

Other guests laughed and rose from their seats as Carrick started toward her. She should leave. She knew it. Yet, her feet wouldn't move.

He reached her side. "Good evening, Miss Thatcher." He bowed and peered down at her with a twinkle in his gray eyes.

An answering smile curled her lips and she curtseyed low. "Good evening to you, as well," she murmured, deliberately refusing to utter the expected words 'my lord' or 'your grace'. Indeed, she wouldn't join the gaggle of fawning creatures in the room.

A sharp clapping of hands startled them both and Juliet blinked to find the dowager watching them closely.

"Let the game begin." She clapped her hands a few more times and raised her brow in an obvious reprimand.

Juliet averted her gaze, and wished mightily that she had left. Carrick chuckled, looped his arm through hers and drew her toward the circle of players.

"Allow me to go first," a slim gentleman with thinning brown hair offered.

Catherine obligingly tied the band of cloth over his eyes and spun him around as the countdown began. The players fanned out across the room and began calling his name.

Juliet edged toward the door.

"Edward, this way," the calls began as the man began to bump about the drawing room, arms outstretched.

Juliet retreated another pace and Carrick edged closer. He leaned down, clearly intending to whisper in her ear, when the redheaded woman bumped his arm.

"Forgive me, Your Grace." She giggled and lay her hand on his arm.

Carrick's expression hardened, and Juliet's heart sang.

The blindfolded man stumbled past two women who sidestepped him, and he collided with Carrick. The man seized Carrick's cravat and announced, "It's Hamilton."

Carrick snorted a laugh. "Damn cravat," he said in a low voice, and glanced sideways at Juliet. He faced the thin man. "I'll take this, my dear fellow." Carrick whipped the blindfold off him and began tying it over his eyes.

Catherine appeared at his side and began to spin her brother in circles. The redheaded woman giggled and made no move to fan out and join the others.

Catherine rolled her eyes in disgust. "Let's change up the rules, shall we? The *last* one Carrick catches will earn a kiss."

Above the blindfold, Carrick's brows knit into a frown.

A chorus of 'ohhs' went up amongst the woman and the redhead said, "How delightful," then darted away.

"I say, I don't care for this new rule," the thin gentleman objected.

Carrick cocked his head to the side and teased. "Then, Edwards, here I come."

As he took a step forward, one of the women pushed Juliet into his path. He caught her arm and tensed, then relaxed and slid his fingers down to her wrists to give her a little yank. She stumbled and fell against his chest.

Catherine clapped. "I changed my mind. I say Carrick must kiss the first woman he catches."

Juliet stiffened. The other women protested loudly.

"That isn't fair."

"That will teach you not to push other players, Lady Audrey," Catherine said.

Carrick planted a chaste kiss on Juliet's forehead. "'Tis Miss Thatcher," he said with conviction.

"Bravo!" Edwards laughed.

"Enough of this game." Carrick tore off the blindfold.

"Let us sing, shall we?" Catherine suggested as she skipped to the pianoforte.

"It's getting late, Catherine dear," the dowager objected.

Her daughter ignored her and plopped down at the pianoforte, then began to play. As the room filled with voices—and the women swooped over to commandeer Carrick's attention—Juliet made good her escape. She ducked into the library and turned to close the door when Carrick stepped inside. Juliet cried out when he caught her in his arms.

"Where are you running as if the devil himself were after you?"

"To my room," she said, and silently added, where I belong. "You should return to your guests."

He peered down at her, looking more handsome than a man had a right to, with his lips curled into a lazy smile. "Let them wonder. I've had enough of duty tonight."

The words made her heart thud, but then her attention caught on the word 'duty.' Duty would always stand between them. The thought soured her mood.

He drew his brows into a faint, puzzled line. "What is it?"

"Nothing," she lied.

"I'm no fool, Juliet. What's bothering you?"

"It's nothing, truly." She shook her head. "You shouldn't ignore your guests in favor of your mistress."

Surprise overcame his puzzlement, then the gray eyes staring down at her glittered. "Make no mistake, Juliet, a paper doesn't dictate what lies between us. I would tear it in half this moment, if not for the fact that it secures your wellbeing."

There was truth to that, no matter how hard it was to admit. Already, she'd earned her house and yearly sum. She winced. She'd fallen prey to his charms so fast. Damn her passionate blood.

"My mother will be pleased." She couldn't hide the bitterness in her voice.

He grasped her shoulder. "Forget your mother and that damn contract. What *we* feel is the only thing that matters." He drew her close once again and softly traced the outline her jaw. "You're mine and mine alone," he whispered. "*My* mistress."

My mistress. The way he said the words made her feel like a cherished possession, and the gentleness of his touch sent shivers down her spine. He dropped his head to nuzzle her temple and she melted against him, keenly aware of the rise and fall of his chest as he inhaled deeply before he pressed his forehead against hers.

"I can't get you out of my thoughts." He pulled back enough to look in her eyes. "You're not like any woman I've known."

Juliet searched the depths of his gray eyes. "I most certainly have never met a man like you."

He held her closer. Then kissed her. The passionate ravage of her mouth softened to an intimate nibble. The thud of his heart beat in time with hers. She'd thought him all fire and passion, but this tender, gentle exchange left her weak-kneed with desire. Might she—

A sharp knock on the door caused her to jerk back.

The dowager's muffled voice called from the other side, "Carrick? Are you in there?"

Carrick's head jerked in the direction of the door.

"Carrick?" the dowager repeated.

The door knob rattled and Juliet broke free of his embrace.

"Juliet, wait," Carrick hissed.

He grabbed for her, but she bolted toward the servants' door. She couldn't face the dowager. Juliet winced and dashed up the stairs.

At last, she slipped into her room. She flopped onto her back on the bed and contemplated the plastered ceiling. Why, oh, why had she allowed herself to fall for the man? A mistress. She truly was his mistress now. Why had she fallen into this trap when she knew that she wasn't the kind who wanted to share?

CHAPTER TWELVE

LOCK, STOCK, AND BARREL

CARRICK EYED THE DOOR through which Juliet had vanished. Something clearly bothered the lass.

"Carrick?" His mother knocked louder.

He huffed an impatient breath and reached the door in three long strides, then flung it open.

His mother's lips were pressed into a thin line of disapproval. "Carrick, you must bid you guests farewell. It's the *least* you can do under the circumstances."

"Circumstances?" he repeated.

The dowager's lips parted as if to reply but then, apparently thinking better of it, she turned and swept back down the hall.

Carrick followed in a pensive mood. Juliet was downright skittish. Why? Och, the matter of the contract didn't help matters, but surely, something more bothered her.

They reached the drawing room and he began the long series of farewells, absently participating in the 'oh, let's do this again, soon' conversations to the round of 'thank you's' and a good hearty 'farewell' when he finally herded them to the door. With his thoughts revolving around Juliet, he found the torturous ritual even more tedious than usual.

Finally, the last carriage departed, and his mother headed toward her suite. Carrick turned to the stairs that led to Juliet's room.

"What happened to Juliet?" Catherine said.

He glanced over his shoulder and slowed to allow his sister to catch up with him.

"If I may say so, brother dear, your prospective brides were rather catty tonight, especially Audrey. Did you see the way she shoved Juliet into your arms? Oh, you couldn't have. You were wearing the blindfold. Well, let me assure you, Audrey was trying to be the last…"

Prospective brides. He winced. What mistress would enjoy the company of her lover's prospective brides? He'd been so eager to see her, he hadn't given her perspective thought. What a fool he'd been.

"And Mother said…" Catherine prattled in the background.

Mother. Her determination to see him wed was the root of his problem. It was time to get his mother and her interference out of his life.

An idea flashed across his mind. He reached the stairs and paused. His sister swung around the newel post at the base of the stairs. "What would you say about a trip to London and an allowance to spend?" he interrupted her stream of complaints.

From the sudden shine in her eyes, he knew her answer.

"London?" she breathed.

"And let's add a sea holiday at Brighton as well, shall we?" he suggested. That southern-most tip of England was as far away from Lennoxlove House as he could get without dropping his mother into the sea.

"Mother *loves* the sea," Catherine gasped. "Oh, it will be wonderful, Carrick. I am so weary of the country. Mother was complaining of it herself, just yesterday."

She hurried up the stairs ahead of him, clearly headed for their mother's suite to share the news.

Carrick chuckled. Whatever money they spent would be well worth their absence. He jogged up the remaining stairs and continued up another floor to Juliet's room. Finally, they could be alone. He could hardly wait. He took the hall in long strides, his cock hardening with each step.

He reached her room and hesitated. No light shone under the door. Surely, she wasn't asleep already. He rapped softly on the door. No answer. He grasped the knob and turned. The door was unlocked. Slowly, he opened the door a crack and peeked inside.

In the dim moonlight streaming through the window, he discerned Juliet beneath the blankets on the bed. She didn't stir. Disappointment threaded through him. His cock was so hard it hurt. He stepped inside and padded to the foot of the bed, but when he caught sight of the frown etched on her face, his primal thoughts fled.

Aye, this issue of a wife had and would only worsen matters between them. He'd have to think of an arrangement that would satisfy them both. He couldn't—he *wouldn't*—lose Juliet. Not over something as trifling as a wife.

With a rueful sigh, Carrick unbuttoned his shirt. He should go to his own bed... He pushed his breeches down over his hips, then stepped out of them and slipped under the covers beside Juliet. It felt so right to have her by his side. He couldn't imagine being anywhere else.

He didn't expect to find sleep so easily, but her rhythmic breathing soothed like a lullaby, and his eyes drifted shut.

* * *

Carrick awoke when Juliet stirred, and opened his eyes to the sun cresting the tree line beyond the bedroom window. Juliet's hair fanned across the pillow and the slight frown from the night before still marred her brow. He propped onto an elbow and brushed his lips against that worry crease.

Her eyes fluttered open.

"Good morning, sweeting," he murmured.

Her face relaxed.

Carrick brushed a lock of hair from her cheek. "Shall we spend the day in bed, love?"

She laughed and the warmth in her tone made the blood surge straight to his cock. She abruptly tensed and the frown lines returned.

"There's too much sewing to be done." She sat up. The movement caused her shift to slip over her shoulder and expose her white skin.

"Forget the sewing." He settled back amongst the pillows. "Take off your shift and sit on me, lass." She glanced at the sheet, tented by his cock, and his shaft further thickened.

She sent him a sidelong glance and for a long moment he thought she meant to refuse. Then she got to her knees and ever so slowly pulled the hem of her shift up and over her shoulders.

Eyes locked with his, she tossed the garment on the floor. "I'm already late. Why not a few minutes more?"

"Minutes?" Carrick snorted, recalling her taunt that he'd last only minutes in her bed. Ah, he still had so much to teach her. He tracked his gaze over her breasts. Her nipples protruded in a way that begged to be suckled.

She shook her hair. The mass of silky strands tumbled over her shoulders as she twisted her fingers in the sheets and slowly tugged it off his body. He drew a long, ragged breath as the soft material slid over his flesh.

She didn't immediately mount him, like he wanted. Instead, she traced a finger up his thigh and chest, then back down again. Her feather-light touch along with the wait threatened to drive him mad.

"Sit on me," he demanded again.

A tiny smile played at the corner of her mouth as she swung a slim leg over his hips and straddled him. He cupped her breasts and gently squeezed. She closed her eyes and moaned. Gently, Carrick tweaked her nipples. Still, she didn't slide down onto him. Instead, she leaned into him. The curls between her legs tickled his shaft, then her mons bumped him. Pleasure streaked through him.

"I need you, lass, *please*," he begged.

She wiggled her hips. "How much?"

"Desperately." He fought the temptation to grab her hips and slam her down onto him.

"I see," she murmured, lowering her body with excruciating slowness until the tip of his shaft nudged her wet entrance. "Perhaps I should take pity on you and —"

Carrick seized her hips and shoved her down as he thrust.

She drew a sharp breath. He began to buck beneath her. He drove deeper. She braced her hands on his chest and ground down on his hard length.

Her breath quickened. Worry followed satisfaction. The way her channel closed around his cock, he wouldn't last long. He clenched his jaw and willed his desire to orgasm into submission. He slid his thumb between her wet folds and swirled it over her swollen nub. She rocked against him and he exerted herculean effort to delay his pleasure.

Her muscles abruptly went rigid and her channel tightened around him. Carrick lost control. A moan ripped from his lungs. Blinding pleasure spasmed his body and he emptied his seed deep inside her.

When the last ripple of pleasure faded, she collapsed against his chest and he cradled her close as he ran his fingers through her hair. She was so beautiful. He wanted the moment to last forever.

A sudden knock on the door caused them both to start.

"Miss Thatcher?" a maid called. "Are you awake?"

Carrick smothered a grin as Juliet slid off his body and hopped from the bed.

"Just a moment, please," she called.

He lay back on the pillows, folded his arms behind his head and watched her scramble into her shift.

Juliet hurried to the door and opened it a crack. "It's the dowager," the maid informed. "She wishes to see you in the breakfast parlor, at once."

Carrick tensed.

"She says to hurry."

Juliet promised to come immediately and closed the door. She faced Carrick, her face white. "The dowager," she whispered, and darted to the armoire to select a light green muslin day dress.

Carrick rose and scooped his breeches from the floor, then pulled them on over his hips, one eye on Juliet. She looked terrified. He scowled. Could his mother be tormenting the lass? He retrieved his shirt from the floor and tossed it on the bed before crossing to where Juliet wriggled into her gown.

"Allow me." He tied the ribbons on the back as he studied her face in the armoire's mirror. The frown lines had returned. "Don't fret so, lass. What's between us is not my mother's concern."

She lifted her eyes to his in the mirror. "I know the rules, Carrick—and I know better than to break them."

She pulled free and grabbed the brush from the vanity to give her hair a few quick strokes before turning in the mirror for a final inspection. Satisfied, she hurried back to him, rose on tiptoes, and gave him a quick peck on the check before she dashed out the door.

Carrick drew a thoughtful breath.

She knew better than to break the rules, eh?

He had to do something about that.

CHAPTER THIRTEEN

CRAVATS AND CARDS

THE DOWAGER LOOKED UP from her breakfast of eggs and toast as Juliet entered.

"Your Grace," Juliet croaked through dry lips and curtsied.

"Juliet, dear, please have a seat." The dowager nodded, indicating a chair at the table to her right. "It's time we talk."

Juliet drew a deep, shaking breath. *Time we talk*. There could be nothing good about those words. "Certainly, Your Grace," she murmured as she obediently seated herself in the indicated chair.

"You're from London, aren't you?" the dowager asked as she set her hardboiled egg in its porcelain holder and expertly cracked the shell with a spoon.

"Yes, Your Grace."

"Thatcher," the woman said thoughtfully. "The Sussex Thatchers?"

Juliet blinked. Sussex Thatchers? Puzzled, she shook her head.

"Oh? Then where does your father live?" the dowager asked.

Juliet smiled a little sadly—she'd practiced this response in the mirror a hundred times—and said, "My father…has passed away, Your Grace." It could have been the truth. Who knew?

The woman appeared surprised. "My condolences, child. And your mother?"

Juliet bit her lip, then caught the nervous action. "My mother—"

"Good morning, Mother," Carrick's deep voice interrupted.

Juliet sent him a smile of relief.

The dowager nodded at her son. "Catherine mentioned you're sending us to London." She gave her egg another whack.

"Aye. From the number of trunks I see littering the halls, you plan on taking the entire estate with you." Carrick took his seat opposite the woman.

The dowager pursed her lips, then turned to Juliet and patted her hand. "Run along, dear. We'll chat later."

Juliet blinked, surprised at the friendliness of the gesture, but she didn't have to be asked twice to leave. Studiously ignoring Carrick, she rose and hurried toward the door.

Before she reached the hallway, she caught Carrick words, "I have had enough of you interfering in my affairs," before the door closed.

Fear knotted Juliet's stomach. The dowager knew of her son's affair. She rounded a corner and ran straight into Catherine. The young girl grabbed her arms and swung her around in a dance.

"We're off tomorrow," she said, grinning from ear to ear. "Oh, please say my new gown is ready. I simply *must* wear it on holiday."

"You're leaving?" Juliet asked, surprised.

"Carrick's sending us to London," she bubbled, falling into step as Juliet resumed her walk down the hallway. "And Brighton. Mother loves the sea. But I need my gown. Do say you can finish it before we leave to-morrow, please?"

Juliet smiled as they neared the stairs. "I'll try my best."

"Thank you, thank you a thousand times," Catherine cried. "Now, I must pack." She blew Juliet a kiss and raced up the stairs ahead of her.

Juliet watched her go with a smile and began climbing the stairs. Truth be told, she was relieved to be escaping the dowager's censorious eye—along with the promised awkward chat concerning her parents. Hopefully, the woman would be too busy readying for the trip to continue the chat. Spending the day tucked away in the sewing room hemming Catherine's gown would help ensure that happened.

The day proved busier than expected, not only with finishing Catherine's gown but with mending various day and morning dresses the dowager sent up for repair. Juliet felt sure that both the dowager and her daughter had packed every article of clothing they possessed.

Twice, Carrick dropped by. But the hustle and bustle drove him off with no more than a look—a sultry, seductive one—passing between them. Finally, the clock struck midnight, and Juliet rose stiffly from her chair. Her fingers ached, but she released a sigh of satisfaction from a job well done.

It didn't take long to tidy the room. She tossed the last spool of thread into her sewing basket and reached to shut the lid. A glimpse of silk caught her eye and she smiled as she slipped a finger over Carrick's cravat, still safely tucked away. Hopefully, he'd be waiting in her bed. As tired as she was, she would wake the moment his lips caressed her skin.

To her disappointment, she arrived to find her bed empty.

Perhaps he thought her too tired. Juliet considered seeking him in his room, but with her luck of late, she would run straight into the dowager.

With a sigh, she undressed, pulled her night rail over her shoulders and dropped into bed.

She was nearly asleep before her head touched the pillow.

* * *

Juliet awoke to the noon sun warming her face. She sat bolt upright, heart pounding. She'd overslept. The dowager and her daughter had left for London hours ago. She dressed in a hurry and rushed downstairs on the off chance they hadn't yet departed. The last thing she needed was for the dowager to find a reason to dislike her.

At the bottom step, she encountered one of the maids.

"The duchess? Catherine?" Juliet asked, pausing to catch her breath.

"Lordy, miss, they left at dawn," the maid replied and shuffled off.

Juliet blew out a long breath and bit her lip. Oh well. No doubt, the dowager had noticed her missing from the line of staff biding them a safe journey. She could only hope the woman would forget the matter before she saw her next.

She glanced around, noting how quiet the place seemed, then started back up the stairs. She stopped in the library, hoping to see Carrick, but the room stood empty. With a sigh, she closed the door and headed for the sewing room. The dowager and her daughter might be gone, but she still had plenty of dresses left to sew.

Juliet slowed at sight of the open sewing room door. Had she forgotten to close it last night? She entered the room and frowned. The partially sewn dresses and her sewing basket were missing. She glanced around, noting the chests of fabric missing, as well. As she slowly pivoted, her gaze snagged on her sewing basket sitting on the floor near the inner door that led to an adjoining room.

She hurried to the basket, but to her surprise, discovered it empty. Her gaze caught on a pair of scissors peeking out from the bottom of the door. As she touched the door it swung open slightly. A pincushion sat on the rug in the center of the adjoining room. Six feet farther away lay a spool of thread.

"This is exceedingly odd," she murmured and retrieved her tools, then noticed a second spool of thread near the far door.

She paused, then smiled. This was a breadcrumb trail. Carrick's doing. It had to be. With a heart growing lighter by the step, she followed the trail of pincushions, thimbles and thread spools down the servants' stairs and out a side door leading to the castle's side lawn.

The trail led across the grass. Near where the garden path vanished behind a copse of trees, a length of muslin was artfully draped over a bush. She frowned and hurried to rescue the fabric before it stained.

What was the man thinking? Still, she found herself smiling as she folded the fabric and placed it atop her sewing basket. She saw the playing cards, a line leading down the center of the path and disappearing behind the trees.

She'd missed him the night before. Her smile widened as she followed the trail, collecting the cards along the way until the path gave way to a private garden. A gazebo nestled under an ancient oak, and Carrick practiced archery nearby, wearing only a white shirt and a pair of form-fitting, dark gray breeches.

She paused to admire his muscular buttocks and powerful thighs. Her fingers itched to slide over those firm, warm muscles. She'd never thought of a man's buttocks and thighs as particularly fascinating before.

He bent to remove an arrow from a quiver lying on a table and she watched the shift and flex of his thigh muscle before wrenching her eyes away. A throb pulsed between her thighs.

He lowered his bow and she lifted her gaze to his face. His eyebrow raised in amusement. Heavens, she could only be glad he wasn't privy to her thoughts. He'd be prancing around the estate in smug satisfaction for a week—maybe longer.

A mischievous grin crossed his face as he crooked a finger and motioned for her to join him. When she arrived, he took the sewing basket and set it on the ground as she eyed the target, taking note of the half-dozen arrows clustered around the bullseye.

"You have astonishing marksmanship," she said.

A humorous glint entered his eye. "Aye, my shaft is hard and its aim true."

She jerked her eyes back to his, forcing herself not to look at his crotch. The man was shameless. She couldn't prevent a smile. then recalled that she'd overslept. "I fear I failed in bidding the duchess and Catherine farewell," she confessed.

He chuckled. "Mother insisted you catch up on your rest. She wasn't offended, if that's what concerns you."

That was difficult to believe, but she smiled anyway. "Well, I'm well rested now."

His eyebrow lifted as he reached past her to prop his bow against the gazebo's nearest wall. He murmured, "For now, aye?"

She lowered her lashes.

"I found a most curious item in your sewing basket." He bent and retrieved something from his quiver.

His cravat. She took the fabric, suddenly tongue-tied.

"You kept it," he said.

She lifted her eyes to his. Slowly, he lowered his lips to hers. He smelled of fresh air and the sandalwood spice of his cravat. She closed her eyes and melted into his embrace, a thrilling kiss soft, tender, and sweet.

A kiss that ended far too soon.

He pulled away and she opened her mouth to object, but he surprised her by swinging her up into his arms.

"I'm of a mind to taste your charms, lass." He peered down at her through hooded eyes. "Here. Now."

She shivered. "Here?"

He carried her into the gazebo and lay her on a plaid spread across the weathered wooden floor.

"Carrick," she said with mock sternness.

He shrugged and dropped down by her side. Objections died on her lips as he covered her lips and sucked her tongue into his mouth. A sizzle of heat shot through her inner core and clenched her sex.

He loosened her chignon and threaded his fingers through her curls as he kissed a path from her lips to her neck before pausing to suck the tender flesh beneath her ear. She slid her hands over his arms. Muscle shifted beneath her fingers as his palm skimmed her waist. He covered a breast and kneaded the soft flesh. Heat pooled in her belly. She arched her hips.

"You're more than ready, aren't you?" He chuckled.

"Take me," she whispered.

He rose to his knees, rucked up her dress, then slipped her under drawers down and off.

"Open your legs for me, lass," he murmured as he leaned over and kissed her eyes closed.

She obliged, enjoying the heightened sensations of his lips as he planted another line of kisses along her jawline and down her throat.

She tensed in anticipation of him levering himself over her. A warm hand clasped her thigh. A quiver radiated through her stomach. He clasped her other thigh and Juliet shivered. The man was a magician. She discerned the shift of his weight on her legs, then gasped when warm lips closed over her sex.

Juliet shoved upright, then froze at sight of Carrick's head between her legs. While she'd heard plenty of Aphrodite's ladies speak of taking a man's member into their mouths, she'd never heard of a man doing the same to a woman. His tongue flicked her engorged nub. Pleasure rocketed through her.

"Carrick," she breathed.

He shifted so that he could look at her, but his mouth continued its wicked work. She squirmed when he sucked her. He laughed against her flesh. The sound tickled heightened senses.

"Lay back and close your eyes, lass. Let me please you."

Please her? Close her eyes? He suckled harder. She didn't think she could tear her gaze from his dark head buried between her thighs even if she wanted to. He drew his tongue from the base of her channel, up through her wet folds and circled her sex.

A wordless whimper escaped her lips. Pleasure mounted. He wrapped his arms around her thighs and pulled her tighter against his mouth. Palms flat on the floorboard, she closed her eyes, braced herself and pulsed against him.

Her orgasm exploded through her, stealing her breath as her body spasmed, the force of her pleasure ripping a cry from her. "Carrick. Oh, God, Carrick."

Juliet collapsed back against the wood. He stroked her until the last shudder subsided, leaving her weak-kneed. "I couldn't last long," she whispered, feeling uncharacteristically shy.

He chuckled and straightened. "Your passion is what I love most about you, Juliet."

Love. The word slipped from his tongue so naturally, yet hung in the air between them like lead.

He unbuttoned his breeches. His engorged member sprang free. Her heart pounded. He settled between her legs and buried himself inside her to the hilt. Juliet wrapped her arms around his neck as he thrust with increasing urgency. His breath bathed her flesh where neck met shoulder. Shivers raced across her flesh. His breath hitched. Pleasure rippled through her. He thrust harder and groaned as her channel flooded with his seed.

Her heart thundered. She would never get enough of this man. He stroked slower and a strange sense of need rippled through her. The unexpected need to cry surfaced. Juliet buried her face in his shoulder until, at last, he relaxed. He breathed deep, his chest expanding against hers. Juliet tightened her hold around his neck in the moment before he rose onto his elbows. He caught her chin with his hand and kissed her slow and tender. Finally, he broke the kiss and rolled off her, then propped himself up on an elbow.

Gently, he ran his fingers through her hair before he tucked a curl behind her ear. "Now that we have Lennoxlove House to ourselves, I'll be making love to you in every room and against every tree."

She lifted her eyebrows and laughed. "We're surrounded by a forest, Carrick."

His grin softened into a warm smile. "Then we'll be busy, won't we?"

CHAPTER FOURTEEN

A DECISION

LOVE. **CARRICK HAD NEVER** uttered that word in a woman's presence before. In fact, he'd taken great care to avoid it. With Juliet, the word flowed effortlessly from his lips. At first, he'd thought his mother had planted the fool notion in his head. She'd surprised him that day in the breakfast parlor. He'd opened his mouth to inform her he would no longer entertain her matchmaking attempts, but she'd announced she no longer felt her services were needed on that particular subject now that he'd found love.

Love. He'd thought his mother quite mad, but now, he was no longer so certain.

The more he thought about Juliet, the more he found the word suited her.

"You're not paying attention," Juliet's scold shattered his thoughts.

Carrick lifted an eyebrow. They lay in her bed with the early afternoon sun slanting through her bedroom window. Of late, they'd taken to playing cards and wagering articles of clothing, but he'd yet to win. Today would certainly be no different. He had only his shirt left while Juliet had only lost her under drawers.

He grinned. On the angle in which he lay, he had a fine view of her white thighs.

"Focus, Carrick." Juliet laughed, even as she opened her legs to provide him an even more distracting view.

Indeed, how could he focus on the cards? She had his full attention.

"It's time to show your hand," she said.

He lay his cards face up on the bed. Three jacks and a deuce.

Juliet snorted and tilted the cards in her slim fingers. Queens. Four of them. It was the third time he'd seen them that round.

"You're cheating," he said.

"Am I?"

She said the words with such confidence that he momentarily wondered if he'd erred. "Well, aren't you?"

"You're asking? Then you can't prove a thing." She giggled.

He rolled his eyes. How could a man concentrate on anything save her luscious body? He should have known never to second guess himself.

She dropped the cards on the bed and nodded at his shirt. "Take it off."

Och. As usual, he was the first one naked...but not for long.

As he unfastened his buttons, she rose from the bed and lifted the lid of her sewing basket, which rested on the bedside table. She pulled his cravat from the basket, turned back to him and ordered, "Lay back and close your eyes."

He lifted a brow but obeyed, his cock hardening even more. "As you wish, my love."

There it was again. Love.

Juliet didn't seem to notice. She laughed and hurried around to his side of the bed, then leaned over and tied the cravat like a blindfold.

Her breasts brushed his shoulder. He reached for the soft mounds, but she evaded his grasp. "Now, now, don't move, Carrick. Not yet."

The perfume of her hair floated around him. She smelled like roses. The soft rustle of cloth told him she undressed. The thought only heightened his need.

A delicate finger touched his shoulder then trailed down the center line of his chest and circled the base of his cock before she wrapped her small hands about his cock. He shuddered in anticipation, but then a thought crossed his mind.

"Tell me, lass, did you have this in mind when you claimed my cravat at the Midnight Ball?"

She gave a quiet laugh, then murmured in a low, sultry tone, "No. I intended to win the wager and be rid of you."

Her soft, wet lips closed over the tip of his cock as she drew several inches of his length into her mouth and began to suck.

He groaned. "What a luscious mouth," he gasped.

Slowly, she licked the length of him, before once again arriving at the tip. He drew a sharp breath and fought for control, but to no avail. He pumped faster. Pleasure—need—rushed to the surface. He *needed* her. His breath hitched as his orgasm started to crest. God help him, she was merciless. Carrick yanked his member from her mouth and ripped the blindfold from his face.

She knelt on the bed, naked. With a growl, he flipped her onto the mattress and mounted her. She arched into him and, to his surprise, within half a dozen strokes, she whimpered with pleasure. In seconds, his orgasm shuddered through him.

Carrick threw back his head and filled her to the brim. As the last ripples of pleasure subsided, he slid aside and held her close. They lay, drowsy and sated.

Never in his wildest dreams had he thought to find a woman who could match his passion stride for stride. Just as tantalizing, her mind was sharp.

He had to do something about that damn contract, and soon. A year was not long enough.

He needed Juliet to be his mistress—for a lifetime.

Realization struck with an intensity that took his breath, then settled over him as natural as breathing. There was only one solution: he had to marry her.

That presented a challenge. Not due to her lack of noble birth, but from her madam of a mother. Surely, he could find a way past that world-wise warden.

Sleep blurred the edges of his consciousness. If anyone could help him dance through this mire of the heart, it would be Sir Stirling James.

* * *

Two weeks later, Stirling entered Carrick's library. "My dear fellow," he boomed in a laughing voice as he strode through the door. "I have come to collect my prized stallion."

Carrick closed the book he'd been reading and rose from his desk. "I should have known you would come yourself. You've an uncanny talent for matchmaking. I should never have doubted you."

Both men laughed and clapped each other on the back.

A maid entered carrying a silver tray with a decanter and two full glasses of claret. They settled comfortably in high-backed mahogany wing chairs near the window and the maid set the tray on the small rosewood table between them.

Carrick took a glass and raised it in salute. "Something special I just received from France," he said.

Stirling picked up the remaining glass. He leaned forward and rested his elbows on his knees. "I've found a solution for your problem, Carrick. Well, several solutions, as you have more than one problem."

His friend drained his claret and returned the empty glass to the tray. "France," he said in a tone of finality. "It just so happens that Victor de Balzac, playwright extraordinaire, has had difficulties finding a passionate enough woman to, shall we say, satisfy his needs. I have discovered that Madam Aphrodite has always dreamt of living there as a woman of means..." He let his voice trail off.

Carrick snorted. If Juliet's mother was a tenth as passionate as her daughter, then Victor de Balzac would live the remainder of his life a very happy man. "What does Madam Aphrodite have to say about this?" he queried.

"The deed is already done," Stirling assured with a laugh. "They became besotted the moment they met. One of the best matches I've ever made. She's off to France, though you have agreed to see her girls settled."

"How many dowries am I financing?" he asked dryly.

"A small fortune." Stirling offered a droll smile. "Count yourself lucky there is nothing your money will not buy."

Carrick shrugged. To secure Juliet's hand in marriage, he would sign over his estate. The thought of spending nights carousing and gambling at card tables had lost all appeal.

"When will you ask her?" Stirling asked.

"Soon," Carrick murmured.

A smile played over his lips. The time had come to play another round of cards.

CHAPTER FIFTEEN

QUEEN OF HEARTS

JULIET SMILED AT CATHERINE as the girl spun before the mirror. "You have such talent, Juliet," Catherine cried, obviously thrilled to have returned from London to find yet another creation waiting in the sewing room, this one a blue-sprigged muslin day dress with green satin trim. "It's beautiful. I'm not taking it off. I'm wearing it now. It's beautiful."

Juliet smiled as she removed the pins from her mouth and jammed them one-by-one into the pincushion resting beside her on the carpet.

"I quite agree," Carrick's deep baritone approved from the doorway. "Join us for dinner, my dear."

Juliet glanced over her shoulder. He stood in the doorway, looking as handsome as ever in dark gray breeches.

"Please, do come," Catherine chimed in before skipping to her brother. She placed a kiss on his cheek, then hurried past him and disappeared down the hall.

Carrick crossed to Juliet and extended a hand. She placed her fingers in his and he pulled her to her feet—then yanked her into his arms. "I agree with Catherine," he said, holding her tightly. "Join us."

She suppressed a sigh. Now that the dowager and Catherine had returned, the parade of wife candidates would resume. The thought rankled more than ever.

"I can't, not when I have so much hemming to do." She pulled his head down to hers and gave him a sound kiss, then twisted out of his arms.

Carrick lunged for her, then straightened when his mother's voice sounded in the hall. "Carrick? Carrick, my dear, the guests have arrived."

"Dinner. Please," he whispered, catching her hand and planting a kiss on her fingertips.

She shook her head.

"Join me with the gentlemen at cards after dinner tonight in the study." He pulled her into his arms again. "Afterwards, we shall enjoy more of this. Hmmm? I would see you wearing your mask and nothing else."

"Or your cravat?" She smiled up and fluttered her dark lashes. They had discovered many delightful uses for his cravats.

"Yes."

"Carrick?" The dowager's voice sounded much closer.

"Damn." He released her and hurried from the room.

The day flew. Juliet finished a riding jacket for Catherine, stopping only to enjoy a quick snack of toast slathered with fresh butter and topped with marmalade.

At last, the sun set, and she returned to her room to ready herself for an evening of cards. She often played cards with Carrick in bed, although they rarely finished a game, and while she'd discovered him to be a card cheat in his own right, she still held the edge.

She picked up her white Venetian mask and turned it over in her hands before tying it to the bedpost, imagining the enjoyment it would provide later. Juliet perused the selection of gowns in the armoire, skipping over those with the provocative bodices that Carrick preferred, and selected a peach taffeta with white satin rosettes adorning the scooped neckline. Finally, she paused before the mirror, gave her ringlets one last pat, then headed for the door.

By the time she reached the study, a group of gentlemen lounged about the card table. The gentlemen rose immediately and Carrick invited her to join them.

"Gentlemen, may I introduce Juliet Thatcher," Carrick said, then turning to the two silver-haired gentlemen, continued, "Lord Haynes and Mr. Lamont." Lastly, he nodded at the portly young man who was clearly awestruck by her breasts. "And Mr. Thaddeus Turnby."

Juliet dipped a polite curtsey and took her seat. The men followed suit. "I shall deal," Carrick announced.

While the gentlemen murmured agreement, she smiled and prepared for an enjoyable evening. As they played, she watched her opponents, observing and cataloging their expressions and ticks as the rounds played out.

By the third game, she'd determined that only the elderly Mr. Lamont possessed any sort of skill. She eyed Carrick as he dealt another hand, puzzled as to why he'd asked her to join their card game.

As they picked up their cards, Juliet glanced down at hers. Queens. All four. She blinked in surprise and glanced up into Carrick's amused face. Clearly, he'd dealt her a winning hand. She frowned, wondering why, as the men looked at their cards and placed their chips.

As Mr. Lamont raised a hand to knock on the table, Carrick lifted a finger.

"Wait," he said. "I'd like to add this."

They watched as he drew a parchment torn in half from his breast pocket and laid it down over the bets.

"I say, what's this?" the portly Lord Haynes asked.

"Wait." Carrick locked gazes with Juliet, then withdrew something from his front pocket and dropped it on top of the paper.

Juliet froze.

The hereditary Hamilton engagement ring glinted in the chandelier light. Her eyes snagged on the heading of the paper and she recognized her contract...torn in half. Her heart pounded. Surely, he wasn't foolish enough to propose to her? This was no ordinary card game. Her throat tightened.

She looked up at him.

He leaned back and rested an elbow on one of the armrests, then lifted a brow as if daring her to decline the offer.

"What have we here?" The old gentleman raised his hand to give the table a rap.

Juliet shoved to her feet. "I withdraw from the round."

Carrick slowly arose.

"By Jove, lass," Mr. Lamont chuckled. "That's not how commerce is played."

"Then his grace is fortunate," she said.

"Hardly," Carrick murmured.

Juliet whirled and raced from the room.

"Wait!" he called.

She ran. He caught up with her at the stairs, reaching for her, but she evaded his grasp and ran up them as fast she could.

"Juliet, why? You owe me an answer," he shouted.

He was right. Juliet stopped on the landing and backed toward the wall. He stopped two stairs beneath her and stared straight into her eyes.

"You know quite well I can never accept that ring," she said in a shaky voice.

"Why not?" he demanded.

"Don't be absurd," she snapped. "I'm no lady. I possess no title or money. How can I marry you? The difference in our social standing is far too great." She clenched her hands and fought tears. "I am your mistress, Carrick. A gentleman does not marry his mistress."

He started to reply.

Juliet shook her head. "Please, no more."

She gathered her skirts and fled to her room. After locking the door, she threw herself headlong onto her bed and wailed.

He knocked on her door. Several times. She begged him to leave. He left with the promise that they would speak in the morning.

An hour later, Juliet took a deep breath and sat up, looking down at the cards crumpled in her hand. She knew now what she had to do, before the situation grew worse for the both of them. What made her think she could succeed as a mistress?

She penned a letter, begging him to forget her. Of course, society would never let her marry him, regardless of how he might feel. But now, she knew she couldn't survive him marrying someone else. The thought of him making love to another woman would break her heart. She held nothing back, ending with a last line that conveyed the truth she'd been hiding all along: *I can never share you with another woman, and thus, I can no longer be your mistress.*

With that, she packed a canvas bag with her belongings, including the crumpled cards from the game. After the castle occupants retired, she slipped into the dark hall. She'd purchase fare at the village coaching inn and be gone before anyone thought to look for her.

* * *

Seven days later, Juliet exited the mail coach and trudged up the cobblestone street toward Lady Aphrodite's House of Pleasure. She'd taken the fastest coach to London she could find, but they'd met with more than one setback along the way, which delayed the coach's arrival until after dark on the seventh day. It didn't matter. Her mother didn't expect her. There had been no point in writing a letter that would have arrived at the same day and time she did.

She'd thought of Carrick the entire journey. Her heart twisted, knowing he could never truly be hers. Finally, she turned at the wrought iron fence. Lady Aphrodite's house stood before her, but instead of lights twinkling cheerfully in the windows, all but one stood dark. Where strains of music had floated through the front rooms, silence reigned.

Juliet ran to the door and twisted the brass knob. "Ma? Ma?" She darted inside.

A single taper in a pewter holder rested on the floor, illuminating an empty room—save a single chair upon which her mother sat, chin on her chest.

Her mother jerked awake and jumped to her feet. "There you are, at last, child." She smiled widely and held out her arms.

Juliet frowned. "What happened?" She glanced around the empty room. "Where are the girls? The furnishings? Is there trouble with the law?"

Her mother enveloped her in a hug and chuckled. "The girls have gone and married, and the same for me, as well, love. The duke and I thought it wiser if I left without a fuss." She pinched Juliet's cheeks. "You shouldn't be here. Not after how hard we've worked to whitewash your past. Why, I only came back here tonight because he fetched me. He's distraught, the poor boy. You're lucky you came when you did. Come morning, and I would've sailed with the tide to France."

"France?" Juliet repeated in utter disbelief. "Whatever are you speaking of?"

"Lawks, child, I'm a proper wife now, wed in a church. Sir Stirling and your duke found me a husband. We thought I should stay there for a week. You know, until things are settled and everyone thinks I've always lived in France." She winked.

Juliet frowned, more confused than ever.

"And not only me, the girls as well, every one of them wed with a proper dowry." Her mother waved her hands to indicate the empty room. "All for you, Juliet. When I return from France, no one will think to connect me with this place. They've made us respectable. There's naught to fear." She pulled a folded paper from her bodice and rolled her eyes. "Have I taught you nothing, girl? Gone and torn your contract? Really, now, though it's hard to be angry with you." She clucked her tongue.

Juliet stumbled to the chair and sat down, her mother's words starting to sink in. Whitewash her past? Thousands of pounds in dowries? Her gaze fell on the torn contract in her mother's hands.

"Where did you get that?" The last time she'd seen it, it lay atop a mound of chips on a card table.

"Where else?" Her mother snorted.

"Carrick?" Juliet swallowed. "Here?" Of course, her mother had said that, hadn't she?

"Rode his horse straight here after fetching me to help find you," her mother said. "The boy hasn't slept in days. I put him up in the Swan Room. It's the only one left with a bed—"

Juliet stopped listening.

She raced up the stairs and down the hall to the third door on the right. The door stood open enough to reveal a guttering candle and the shape of a man lying on his back with his arm flung over his face, a booted foot hanging off the bed.

Carrick.

She halted in the doorway and stared at him for a long moment, then turned on her heel and fled back down the stairs to where she'd dropped her canvas bag on the floor.

"Juliet, wait." Her mother grabbed her hand and tilted her face up to meet her eyes. "The man loves you, child. Don't be a fool and throw it away. He's fixed it all so you can marry him. Put good hard coin where his mouth is."

It was the highest compliment her mother could pay.

Juliet took a deep breath, her heart growing lighter by the moment. "I know, Ma." She rummaged through her bag until she finally found what she sought.

"Then you'll marry him?" her mother demanded. "My daughter...a lady—a duchess?"

The pride in her mother's voice was hard to miss. "Not because he's a duke, Ma." No. It had nothing to do with a title. It never had. She couldn't live without him, just as he obviously couldn't live without her. She'd be a fool to throw it away—especially when she felt the same.

"Well, you can love him if you want," her mother called as she ran back up the stairs. "As long as the outcome is the same."

Juliet hurried back up the stairs and down the hallway. She slipped back into the bedroom, softly closing the door behind her.

He still lay asleep on the bed.

Slowly, she unbuttoned his shirt and breeches, keeping an eye on his slow, steady breathing. In the dim light, she could see exhaustion on his face. He'd clearly ridden hard, but then, perhaps the exhaustion on his face had more to do with dealing with her mother. She quickly unpinned her hair, shook it over her shoulders, and then pushed her gown from her shoulders. The fabric pooled to the floor. Slowly, she climbed onto the bed and straddled him.

He awoke with a start and started to straighten, but Juliet pushed him back down.

"Juliet." His gaze dropped to her breasts, the apex at her legs, then lifted back to her face. "Marry me, lass. I beg you."

His manhood stirred and began to harden beneath her sex. With a smile, she guided his shaft into her wet entrance, sinking down on him fully as she revealed the crumpled cards that she'd retrieved from her canvas bag. Queen by queen, she dropped them onto his chest, ending last with the queen of hearts.

"My beautiful duchess." He gave her a tender smile—then flipped her onto her back. She squeaked, then gasped when he drove into her.

She wrapped her legs around his hips and clung to him with all her might.

"You are mine," he growled, and thrust deep.

Yes. She was his.

REDEMPTION OF A MARQUESS

THE MARRIAGE MAKER
BOOK SEVEN RULES OF REFINEMENT

TARAH SCOTT

CHAPTER ONE

VALAN GREY, THE 6TH Earl of Edmonds, the Marquess of Northington, sipped wine and watched the brown-haired beauty waltz with Mr. Evans, a peacock amid a glittering barnyard of hens. Evans had twice stepped on her toes, yet her smile hadn't faltered. Valan slowed his stroll and spared a glance for the other wolf, almost a pup, that prowled near the open balcony doors. A breeze ruffled the young man's styled blond locks. The youth of today relied far too much on well-made coats and coiffured hair in an effort to catch a lady's attention. Any man of worth understood that what lay beneath the coat mattered far more to a lady of taste. He returned his attention to the beauty. Her partner turned to the music. Valan winced. Evans' step was off by half a beat.

Between pale satin dresses, the swirl of the beauty's emerald velvet skirt molded around her firm buttocks before she was lost from view in the sea of dancers. Had Lady Peddington suggested the dress? The beauty certainly stood out amongst the demure pastels that flared on the dance floor. She was older than the others who attended the Midnight Ball. *Perfect*. Tomorrow, he would send a letter of thanks to Honoria for her invitation to the soiree. She had a knack for knowing just the right lady for a gentleman.

Above the music and murmur of guests, a female gasp was followed by a man's curse. Valan glanced left, toward the small commotion, but a half-closed curtain hid the man and woman in the alcove. He shifted his gaze back to the dance floor. A blur in the corner of his eye registered an instant too late, and a woman collided with him. Wine sloshed over the rim of his glass and onto his crisply pressed, ivory silk waistcoat. He seized the lady's wrist to stop her fall.

Valan glanced down at the now ruined waistcoat, then met the young woman's wide-eyed gaze. "I assume you learned enough etiquette at Lady Peddington's to know that it's bad manners to collide with guests. Or is this your way of gaining an introduction?"

Her brown eyes flicked to the wine-stained waistcoat then back to his face. The fear in her gaze flashed into annoyance. "I do not want an introduction."

"Where is that bitch?" A large man lunged past the alcove curtain, half limping.

Valan deftly sidestepped him, pulling the young woman with him. Viscount Hesston stumbled two paces, narrowly missing two ladies. They cast him frowns and hurried past as he whirled.

He came up short when his gaze met Valan's. "What the devil are you doing here, Northington? Didn't think this sort of place was one of your usual haunts." The music ended and the last words were overloud in the absence of the orchestra. The viscount's eyes narrowed on the young woman. "Looking for another victim, little pigeon?" He grabbed for her.

Valan tugged her out of her assailant's reach. "This 'little pigeon' is otherwise engaged."

The man's face contorted in rage. "She is mine. I've spent the evening with her. She *owes* me."

Valan glanced where he'd last seen the beauty on the dance floor. Gone. No doubt, claimed by the young wolf. With a sigh, he returned his attention to Hesston. "Ownership is a matter of perspective. As she has ruined a very expensive waistcoat, I believe she *owes* me."

She tugged in an effort to break free. Valan held tight and nodded at a passing waiter.

"My claim supersedes yours," Hesston said as the waiter stopped beside them.

Valan set his wine glass on the waiter's tray.

"I d-do no' belong to either of y-you," the girl said.

The waiter frowned. Valan ignored him and turned curious eyes on her. "Where are you from, child?"

"That is none of your c-concern," she said.

"Perhaps not," he replied, "but indulge me."

She shook her head.

"Would you rather go with this man?" He nodded at Hesston, whose face reddened.

"She is mine," the viscount growled.

"Patience," Valan said. "She may choose to go with you, in which case I will not interfere."

"You have no right to interfere, at all," Hesston snapped.

Valan turned cold eyes on him. "Even you can wait sixty seconds." He looked at the girl and lifted a brow in question.

She glanced at Hesston, then looked back at him and shook her head. "N-nae."

"There you have it," he said. "Even at Lady Peddington's Midnight Ball, a lady is free to choose her companions."

Hesston cast a disgruntled look at her. "Dumb bitch," he muttered.

She lifted her chin. "I would rather be dumb than cruel."

The remark earned her a disdainful look from a woman strolling by on the arm of a man.

Hesston again lunged for her. Valan stepped between them. "You're drunk, Hesston. Go home before you irritate the wrong person."

"Like you?" he sneered.

Valan shrugged. "I am not the best shot in Edinburgh."

"Damn right, you're not," he growled.

"I am more likely to set a runner on you," he said.

Hesston's eyes widened. "They hunt criminals. I have never committed a crime in my life."

"That is a matter of perspective."

A vicious glint lit Hesston's eyes. "If that is so, then one might contend that you stepped outside the law on at least *one* occasion. Last I heard, marriage to an underage woman is against the law," Hesston said.

Ah, the viscount had heard that Valan's old nemesis had returned to Edinburgh just today. Gossip traveled fast when *Society* smelled blood.

Valan gave a bland smile. "Then I am fortunate not to have committed that crime."

"You tried hard enough," Hesston declared.

"Even I do not always succeed," Valan remarked.

"You succeeded at winning your fortune in a card game," he snarled. "That is highly illegal."

"A friendly game of cards is never illegal," Valan said, then added before he could reply, "The important point to remember, my dear viscount, is that runners give an ear to high-ranking peers."

The man's face twisted into a scowl. "You think well of yourself."

Valan angled his head." I am on excellent terms with Bow Street."

Hesston took a step back. "You pay them well, is what you mean." He sneered at the girl. "A bit of muslin isn't worth this much trouble."

"I am no bit of muslin," she retorted.

Hesston turned, stumbled past a group of men, then hurried away.

Valan looked down at the young lady. "You cost me a great deal tonight."

Her brow furrowed. "The cost of that waistcoat is a pittance for a man like you."

He thought of the brown-haired beauty. "Money is not the only thing of worth in this world, child."

"I am no' a child."

He arched a brow. "Pray tell, how old are you?"

"Nineteen."

"A nineteen-year-old girl who nearly got herself accosted by a rather nasty viscount."

"Release me." She yanked the wrist he still gripped.

He started when something pricked his wrist. Valan drew her hand upward. She yanked harder and nearby guests glanced their way. Valan offered them a chilly smile, then urged the girl back three paces nearer the alcove.

"I beg your pardon," she began, then broke off when he tightened his grip.

He turned her hand over and forced her fingers apart. A modest diamond stick pin balanced halfway across her palm.

Valan looked at her and raised a questioning brow. "That is a gentleman's pin, if I am not mistaken."

Her mouth thinned in a mutinous line.

"Shall I call Viscount Hesston back and ask if he has lost a diamond pin?" he asked.

Her eyes widened. "Nae. D-do not do that. Please."

Valan lifted the pin from her palm then released her. "I assume, then, the good viscount did not give this to you as a token of his, er, undying love?"

"Undying love?" she scoffed. "That man loves only himself."

He repressed a smile. "Forgive me, but I am curious as to how you came to be in possession of his pin. It's unlikely he removed it in order to disrobe. Removal of his cravat would not be necessary to—"

"He did not give it to me," she cut in.

"Then you slipped it from his cravat when he kissed you?"

She lifted her chin. "Ladies do not allow strange men to kiss them."

"How wonderful to know you recognize some conduct befitting a lady. I suggest you remember that when next a man asks you to accompany him to an alcove."

She dropped her gaze. Ah, he had her. She slanted a look up at him through her lashes and it was easy to see why she had captured Hesston's attention. Her innocence was a lure few men could resist. She extended a hand toward him and stepped forward. Then tripped. She cried out and collided with him. His lapel tugged downward when she grabbed him and Valan caught her.

He set her at arm's length. "That is the second time this evening you have landed in my arms." He tugged his cravat back into place, then felt the knot in an effort to assess the damage. "Perhaps we should be formally introduced before a third *encounter*?" Valan paused, then felt along the length of the cravat. His pin— He lowered his hands to his sides and leveled an assessing gaze on her. "My pin, please."

Her eyes sparkled as she opened her left hand. His ruby pin lay on her palm.

Valan took the pin. "It is not often I am shocked, but you have managed to shock me."

The laughter in her eyes vanished and her back went ramrod straight. "A gentleman would give me a head start."

He paused while slipping both pins into the front pocket of his coat. "A head start?"

"Before ye call Bow Street."

A corner of his mouth twitched again, harder. He removed his hand from his pocket. "You are safe, my child. I do not set Bow Street on the scent of young ladies."

She studied him as if uncertain, then her expression cleared, and she flashed a brilliant smile. "You are kind—despite the austere face." Before he could reply, she added, "Admit it, once you discovered the pin missing, you would have assumed you lost it by accident and would no' have suspected me—just as that evil viscount will not."

"Fortune favors you on that score," Valan said. "Hesston would not hesitate to have you arrested—if, that is, you failed to comply with his demands."

She frowned. "Demands? Oh, you mean, he would make me his mistress."

"Nothing so elevated as that, but never mind. Dare I ask how you came to have this, er, talent?"

She shrugged, but a steel determination underlay the nonchalance. "A woman develops skills necessary to survive."

"Aye," he agreed. "Women are very adept at surviving. I take it, then, you need the money."

She frowned. "I do not steal for money. Well, not for myself. By-the-by, please return my pin."

He lifted a brow. "*Your* pin?"

"It certainly isn't yours," she said.

"Neither is it yours," he said.

"Finders keepers."

"Is that what you call your talent, 'finding'?"

She scowled. "You don't need it."

"My dear, if you pawn this pin, you will surely find yourself hunted by Bow Street. Unless—tell me, have you already a relationship with a pawn broker?"

She gave him a haughty stare. "I do not."

"Then we shall not begin now."

She shook her head. "Everyone thinks they know what is best for me. I don't not want—"

Valan grimaced. "Pray, say no more. Surely, Miss Peddington taught you not to use double negatives in a sentence."

She dropped her gaze. "Aye, she did."

"Will you throw away every penny your father spent to send you here by speaking like a common fishwife?"

"M-my mother sent me here."

Valan regarded her. "Do you only stutter when you're afraid?"

Her cheeks reddened even as her chin lifted. "I cannot help it. If you don't like it—" her cheeks pinked more "—then you are no gentleman."

"Your judgment of what constitutes a gentleman is sorely misguided." She opened her mouth to reply, but he lifted a hand, palm out. "Please, we will save that discussion for another time. I happen to agree. You cannot help the stutter. You can, however, choose the words you speak. I suggest you make a habit of choosing them more carefully."

Movement beyond the girl's shoulder drew Valan's attention. He recognized the tall man who approached. "Wedded bliss losing its luster so soon?" Valan asked when Sir Stirling James reached them.

Stirling grinned. "Not at all." He looked pointedly at the young lady.

"I cannot make introductions," Valan said. "I don't know the young lady's name."

"Then allow me." Stirling bowed. "Miss Jeanine Matheson, I am Sir Stirling James, and this is his Lordship, the Marquess of Northington."

She extended her hand and Valan bowed over it. "A marquess?" she said. "You did not tell me you were a peer."

"You did not ask," he said, then looked at Stirling. "Do you know all the young ladies? Never say you come here often."

Stirling shook his head. "I saw ye two together. Honoria told me who she was."

"Ah," Valan intoned. "It is Lady Peddington you came to visit."

"Honoria and I are old friends," Stirling said. "Not *that* kind of old friends," he added when Valan started to reply. "But if we were, the past is the past."

Valan angled his head. "As you say."

"You knew Lady Peddington before she started the school?" Miss Matheson asked.

Stirling smiled. "Indeed, I did."

"I want to have a school like this someday," she said.

"Good God, why?" Valan asked.

"To be an independent woman. Lady Peddington says a lady will do best if she finds a nice gentleman to care for her. But that is not what she did. She started the school. She makes her own money and spends it any way she pleases."

"Much responsibility comes with running a business," Valan said.

THE RULES OF REFINEMENT

She waved her hand dismissively. "Running a gentleman's household is just as big a responsibility."

"When a lady has a gentleman to look after her, she has someone to care for her should something go wrong," he said.

She frowned. "I have known too many ladies whose husbands do not take care of them."

"She has you there, Northington," Stirling said.

"That she does," Valan said. "On that note, I shall say goodnight."

"Leaving so early?" Stirling asked.

"Aye. The hunt is finished for tonight." He looked at the young lady. "Good evening, Miss Matheson."

She took a step toward him. "Must you go?"

He flashed a bland smile. "Old gentlemen need their rest."

She grimaced. "You are not old."

"Old enough."

"The choice of gentlemen to dance with has dwindled," she said. "I hoped perhaps…"

"Perhaps his lordship will dance with you." He nodded at Stirling.

She frowned at Stirling. "Lordship? You introduced yourself as Sir Stirling James."

"He is both," Valan said. "The marquess suffers an unnatural modesty. He seldom admits his title."

"The title is a courtesy, and hardly signifies," Stirling said.

Valan glimpsed Hesston talking with Lady Peddington near the far right wall, not far from a cluster of ladies. Valan returned his attention to Miss Matheson. "The marquess is probably the only gentleman present. If, that is, he's still a gentleman."

Stirling chuckled. "You would have to ask Chastity."

"Chastity?" she asked.

"His wife," Valan said.

"You're married?" The young lady wrinkled her nose. "Then it will not do for me to dance with you."

"You are refreshingly forthright," Stirling said.

"She is naïve," Valan said. "A married man has his uses."

She narrowed her eyes. "Are you married?"

"Nae, and I have no wish to be. Goodnight, Miss Matheson. Sir Stirling." He bowed and left.

CHAPTER TWO

AS SOON AS VALAN arrived at Lady Douglas's ball, he began to think that his steward had erred in suggesting he attend—until he spotted the same dark-haired beauty he'd seen at Lady Peddington's ball two nights ago. He retired to the shadows of one of the ballroom's ridiculous columns and watched the beauty dance a reel with Viscount Chilson. When she began a second dance with the viscount, Valan knew he had made a dishonest woman of her. Chilson was short and stout. A dishonest woman would no doubt prefer a tall, handsome lover—if only for an evening.

The music rose above the murmur of voices as the dancers' steps picked up speed.

Chilson wouldn't last more than two sets. Already, his face was flushed. As was his habit, he would play cards and lose five hundred pounds before the night ended.

"Northington, I thought that was you." The Earl of Davon stopped in front of him. "I thought, perhaps, you were hiding here," he said.

Valan kept his eyes on the dark-haired beauty. "Yet you came to speak with me."

"Well, yes—surely you aren't truly hiding?" the earl said. "I was only joking."

Valan sighed. "Of course, you were."

"Here, now," Davon said. "There's no need to be rude."

The dark-haired beauty disappeared behind a cluster of dancers. The dance would last another three minutes.

Valan looked at the earl. "You are right, of course. Was there something you wanted?"

The man blinked. "Well, no. I was just being friendly."

"Thank you," Valan said. "If you will excuse me, there is a lady in need of my services."

"Your services?" he began, but Valan left him standing beside the column and headed for the opposite side of the room.

He reached the spot where Viscount Chilson had exited the dance floor with the lady on his arm.

"Of course, my dear," Chilson was saying. "You may have all the champagne you like." He tweaked her nose. They reached the refreshments table. The viscount picked up a glass of champagne and handed it to her. "You may rest with the other ladies," he said, and added in a whisper, "Remember, you're my cousin's daughter visiting from Bath."

So that was the excuse he used to explain his mistress's presence at a society ball. He had no wife to complain of his indiscretions. Still, the story wouldn't gain them entrance to more than two or three parties, for no reputable hostess wanted her party sullied by the presence of a man's mistress.

Valan chose a glass of champagne and faced the dancers. From the corner of his eye, he observed Chilson guide his young mistress to a chair near a corner occupied by other ladies. He tweaked her nose again and Valan couldn't help but envision the earl tweaking her nose while he puffed, out of breath, on top of her. Valan half wandered if the earl had yet deflowered her.

Chilson left and no one spoke to the girl. No doubt, many knew *what* she was. Valan finished his champagne, then placed the glass on a nearby table and strode toward her chair. Her head snapped up and she looked at him, her brow furrowed in confusion.

"Would you care to dance?" he asked.

She glanced uncertainly in the direction Chilson had disappeared. "I do not know."

Her voice, low and sultry, matched her dark beauty. He might have to steal her from Chilson. "Have you promised this dance to another?" he asked.

She shook her head.

"You do dance?" he asked.

She nodded.

He lifted a brow. "Do you speak?"

Her cheeks colored. She started to nod, then stopped, and said, "I speak."

"And you dance?" he said.

"And I dance," she replied.

He extended a hand toward her. "The set will soon begin."

She placed her fingers in his, then rose. He led her to the dance floor and they joined a group on the edge. She stood across from him, eyes on his chest instead of his face. Either Chilson hadn't deflowered her or he had been unkind when he did.

The music began and, as he'd already observed, she danced well. That pleased him. A smile twitched the corner of his mouth. Perhaps he would bring her to balls like this one. He would, no doubt, attend at least half a dozen soirées before doors closed to him. Perhaps they wouldn't close at all. Being wealthy had its advantages.

When the dance ended, Valan slipped her hand into the crook of his arm and led her through the open balcony doors. A dozen other guests milled about the balcony. She cast a nervous glance toward the ballroom and slowed. Valan placed his hand over hers, keeping her fingers firmly wrapped around his arm. She was forced to walk alongside him as they descended the steps to the lawn.

"I do not think that I should come out here with you, my lord," she said.

"Why not?"

"Viscount Chilson won't like it."

"Then we shan't tell him. Do you like gardens?"

"Gardens are beautiful, of course. But a lady—"

"Viscount Chilson's cousin's daughter?" he cut in.

She looked sharply at him.

He flashed the smile that had earned him the name *The Morning Star*. "Would you prefer Viscount Chilson's company to mine?"

She regarded him for a long moment as he slowed their steps across the lawn. "May I ask who you are, sir?"

"Valan Grey, the 6th Earl of Edmonds, the Marquess of Northington."

"An earl *and* a marquess?" she said in a breathless voice.

He nodded, slightly disconcerted that it was his title that captured her attention and not his smile. He was getting old.

"You are more handsome that Viscount Chilson," she murmured.

"You are too kind," he said with a sardonic smile.

They left the lights of the mansion and entered a pebbled path lined by flowers. Moonlight illuminated her face. They had gone far enough. Valan slipped an arm around her waist and began lowering his head to hers.

"You are no gentleman!" a woman shrilled.

Valan stilled. Surely that wasn't...

The bushes up ahead rustled violently, and a small form broke through at a rapid walk, headed toward them. The dark-haired beauty stiffened as the woman approached.

"Lydia?" The newcomer reached them and stopped. "Is that you?"

A large figure emerged from the bushes, but turned in the opposite direction and disappeared around a hedge.

"What are you doing here in the garden?" Miss Matheson asked.

"The same thing you are, it seems," Lydia replied.

Miss Matheson looked at him and frowned. "*Y-you.*"

"I see you did not heed my warning about going off alone with a man, Miss Matheson."

"You know her?" The dark-haired beauty stepped from his embrace.

She glanced from Miss Matheson to him.

"Miss Matheson and I met the other night at Lady Peddington's Midnight Ball."

"Met the other night—" Lydia turned to face Miss Matheson. "What are you doing here?"

"I was trying to take a walk—"

"Not that," she cut in. "What are you doing at this party?"

"I was invited, just like you."

"Not like me, I think," Lydia snapped, and looked at Valan. "You invited her?"

"This is not my party."

Lydia slipped her hand into the crook of his arm and addressed Miss Matheson. "Lord Northington and I are going for a stroll. Find your own gentleman."

Miss Matheson laughed. "What a wicked girl you are, Lydia. I saw you in the ballroom with that short, pudgy gentleman. You were not at all proper. Now you are walking in the gardens with a different gentleman."

"How interesting that you notice impropriety in others," Valan said.

"I did not come to the garden with a gentleman," Miss Matheson said. "So, I am not guilty of impropriety."

"How dare you?" Lydia breathed. She tugged his arm. "Are you going to let her speak to me in that manner?"

"You are angry only because it's true," Miss Matheson said.

Lydia stamped her foot. "I can't help it if gentlemen like me better than you."

"It isn't *you* they like, Lydia."

Valan forced back laughter, unable to speak for fear of encouraging the lass. His efforts were in vain, however, for she cocked her head and said, "See, even his lordship agrees with me."

The dark-haired beauty drew in a sharp breath. "A true gentleman would not allow a lady to be spoken to in this manner."

"If I were a gentleman, I wouldn't be here with you in the garden," he replied. "As for you being a lady..."

She yanked her hand free and took a step back. "I have never been treated so shabbily." Without another word, she whirled and marched back toward the mansion.

Valan watched her retreat for two heartbeats, then faced Miss Matheson. "You have a knack for interfering with my plans. Tell me, who invited you to Lady Douglas's ball?"

"Lady Douglas, of course."

"The two of you are acquainted?" he asked in surprise. Perhaps, like Lydia, she had found herself a protector.

"Lady Peddington sometimes obtains invitations for us to attend other balls," she said.

"Does Lady Douglas not chaperone you?" he asked.

"She filled my dance card and sent me off. I have been dancing for two hours. My feet hurt, and I am tired. I came out here for some fresh air. That *gentleman* found me and was not very polite."

"Neither were you, my dear," Valan said.

"What? Should I have let him take liberties?"

"It didn't occur to you that you should not be out here at all, that perhaps it wasn't proper?" he asked.

"A lady shouldn't have to fear being accosted when she takes a walk."

He tsked. "I fear you've wasted the money your poor mother spent to send you to Lady Peddington's school. How do you propose to teach young women to become ladies when you do not act the part?"

"Oh, that. I need no' be a lady to own a school."

"Interesting logic. Where, pray tell, will you get the money for this school?"

She glanced around as if to be certain no one listened, then leaned close and said, "I plan to marry a very old, rich gentleman."

He stared. "Marriage to a rich gentleman. A time-honored tradition among ladies. Come." He grasped her arm and began walking toward the mansion. "For your plan to succeed, you must not be caught in these gardens with the likes of me."

"That is silly," she said. "You have been nothing but a gentleman. No one could accuse you of being improper."

She practically trotted to keep up with him, but he didn't slow. "If we do not reach the ballroom unseen, you may discover how wrong you are."

"This is the first time a gentleman has tried to drag me *back* into a ballroom," she said.

"It is a first for me, as well," he said dryly.

"Then why do it?"

He gave her a thin-lipped look. "You would prefer I drag you into the bushes?"

"Nae," she replied. "I was just curious."

"Surely, you know that curiosity killed the cat," he said. "Did your mother teach you not to trust strange men?"

"Oh, I learned that on my own—and you usually can't trust those you know, either."

"For one so cynical, you are naïve to enter any garden alone."

"I think you are the one who is naïve," she said. "Most men don't need gardens to become forward."

He couldn't help a hearty laugh. "I stand corrected."

They turned a corner in the path and came face-to-face with another couple. Valan cursed before the moonlight revealed the couple as Sir Stirling and his wife.

"Your lordship." He gave a slight bow. "My lady. I understand congratulations are in order."

Lady Chastity smiled. "Yes, thank you. Ella is a hearty baby."

"I see you are hard at work, as always, Northington," Stirling said with laughter in his voice. "Miss Matheson, fancy seeing you here. You and the marquess seem to be getting along well."

"Miss Matheson was lost," Valan said. "I happened upon her and am escorting her back to the mansion."

"Why don't I see her back?" Lady Chastity said.

"That would be best, ma'am." Valan canted his head in gratitude.

"But—" Miss Matheson began.

"Go along," he cut in. "It is far better you are seen returning to the party with Lady Chastity than with me." She shook her head and he added, "Remember your plans."

She pouted prettily, but nodded. "I will go, this once. But don't think you can order me about."

"Heaven forbid," he said, and the two women left.

"You are fortunate it was Chastity and I who happened upon ye," Stirling said as they trailed the ladies at a leisurely pace.

"Far more fortunate for her than I," Valan said.

"That is most assuredly true," he said, making no effort to hide his amusement. "What is she doing here?"

"It seems Honoria secured her an invitation to the ball."

"Interesting," Stirling said. "I had no idea her services extended to securing ladies invitations to private parties. What were you referring to when you told her, 'remember your plans'?"

"She hopes to finance a school by marrying a wealthy gentleman who will promptly die and leave her his money."

Stirling looked sharply at him. "Are you serious?"

"She confessed the plan herself."

"Well, the girl is industrious."

"She is silly," Valan said.

"Perhaps, but there are worse plans. Speaking of which, I hear you intend to visit London for an extended stay."

Valan shook his head. "Nae, I try to have as few plans as possible. Where did you hear that?"

"Chastity told me, if I recall."

Valan cast him a sidelong glance. Sir Stirling James wasn't known for engaging in gossip—though plenty of gossip surrounded the man who more and more people referred to as The Marriage Maker.

They reached the balcony steps, ascended, then entered the ballroom. They stopped just inside the double doors and Sir Stirling scanned the crowd.

"Chastity probably took Miss Matheson to the ladies' retiring room," he said. "We will likely not see them again for some time."

"More likely, I will not see Miss Matheson again," Valan said.

"Unless she finds herself a rich old gentleman," Stirling said.

Valan laughed. "I wish her luck." His gaze caught on a tall man talking with two others. Cold uncoiled in his gut. At last, the evening had gotten interesting.

"I met Lord Gordon yesterday at a luncheon," Stirling said. "He's just returned from England after being away for..." Stirling looked at Valan.

"Eighteen years," Valan finished for him.

The curtain on an alcove a few feet to the left of Lord Gordon parted and Lady Chastity and Miss Matheson stepped out. Gordon turned toward them, said something to his companion, then took three steps to the alcove. He bowed over Lady Chastity's hand. She made introductions to Miss Matheson. Gordon lifted Miss Matheson's hand. Valan noticed the extra seconds Gordon held the girl's hand.

"Lord Gordon is no' an elderly gentleman with only a few years left," Stirling said. "Miss Matheson would do better if a man took her on as his ward."

Valan looked at him. "What man would do such a thing?"

Stirling shrugged. "A man who wanted to ensure she didn't fall prey to Lord Gordon."

"You don't like him," Valan said.

"I know little of him. But his attentions strike me as unwholesome." Stirling frowned. "I seem to remember there is bad blood between you two."

"Between Gordon and I?" Valan recalled Gordon's words that fateful night twenty years ago, *"His father shot himself and left him penniless,"* but smiled politely and said, "Nothing more than boyhood mischief. We haven't seen one another since our university days."

Curiosity flickered across Stirling's face, then he flashed white teeth. "Shall we say hello?"

Valan angled his head in acquiescence. "To do otherwise, would be rude."

Stirling lifted his eyebrows in obvious amusement, the gesture, Valan thought, almost as practiced as his own. Valan followed him to the alcove. They approached Gordon's back, which suited Valan well. When they neared, Lady Chastity looked past Gordon's shoulder and Gordon turned. Valan was rewarded with a glimpse of Gordon's shock—and unguarded anger.

Gordon immediately turned his attention to Sir Stirling and bowed. "Your lordship, it is a pleasure to see you again."

"And you, Lord Gordon," Stirling replied. "You know Lord Northington?"

A corner of Gordon's mouth went grim, but he nodded stiffly in Valan's direction.

"Gordon and I are old friends," Valan murmured. "We attended the University of Edinburgh together."

Frustration flashed in Gordon's eyes and Valan repressed a smile. It seemed some things never changed. When Gordon's brother unexpectedly became Viscount Dryer twenty-two years ago, it became a point of pride for Gordon that he be recognized as 'Lord Gordon.'

"I did not know you attended university in Edinburgh, Lord Gordon," Lady Chastity said.

"My father insisted I study business," he replied.

"What did you study, Lord Northington?" she asked

"Nothing so illustrious as business. Art and poetry."

"I do not believe it," Miss Matheson said.

Everyone looked at her.

"May I ask why?" Valan asked.

"You are not at all romantic."

"She is perceptive for one so young," Sir Stirling murmured with a laugh.

Valan regarded her. "As you do not know me, I wonder what brought you to this conclusion."

"As a woman of sense, Miss Matheson can see that you are not a romantic," Gordon said.

"You say that as if being unromantic is a bad thing," Valan maintained a contemplative voice intended to incite him.

Gordon's mouth thinned. "You wouldn't understand the difference."

"His lordship understands the difference perfectly well," Miss Matheson said.

Once again, everyone looked at her.

"Pray tell, how do you know?" Valan asked.

She offered a smug smile. "As a woman of *sense*, I can see that you are intelligent enough to understand what romance is—even if you aren't romantic."

Valan laughed. "Far be it from me to argue with a woman."

"Woman?" Gordon said. "She is barely out of the schoolroom."

Miss Matheson scowled. "I am nineteen, a full-grown woman. I have two younger sisters. One married at eighteen, the other at seventeen. I am an old maid."

"An old maid?" Valan grimaced. "If you are an old maid, then I am ancient."

She rolled her eyes. "Age is different for men."

"How very fortunate for us," Valan said.

"How fortunate, indeed," Lady Chastity said in a dry tone.

The orchestra began a waltz. Miss Matheson looked at the dancers, longing in her eyes, then shifted her gaze to Valan. "We learned the waltz at Lady Peddington's. Will you dance with me?"

"A lady does not ask a gentleman to dance," he admonished. "She waits for a gentleman to ask her."

"But a lady might wait forever," she said.

He tweaked one of her curls. "You will not wait long, trust me, my dear."

"Be warned, Miss Matheson," Gordon said, "a true gentleman does not touch a lady's hair in public." He bowed. "May I have the honor of this dance?"

She looked to Valan and Gordon's cheeks reddened.

"Trust me," Gordon persisted. "We shall dance and have refreshments, then I will see that you arrive home safely."

"How very entertaining," Valan drawled. "I believe Gordon hopes to become your protector, my dear. Never fear—" Valan flashed Gordon a smile "—she has a protector."

CHAPTER THREE

SATISFACTION RUSHED THROUGH VALAN when understanding registered in Gordon's eyes.

Lady Chastity looked at her husband and Valan glimpsed the tiny shake of Stirling's head an instant before Gordon addressed Valan, "You think yourself so clever."

"Excuse me," Miss Matheson said, "But—"

Gordon swung his gaze onto Sir Stirling. "She is an innocent, my lord. You cannot allow Northington to make her his mistress."

Valan widened his eyes. "Mistress?" he repeated in unison with Miss Matheson.

Her eyes snapped onto him, but he kept his stare on Gordon. "You misunderstand, Gordon. She is not my mistress. She is my ward."

Gordon gaped. "Your ward?"

"Forgive me." Valan gave a tiny bow. "That is a gross misunderstanding and completely my fault. I should have clarified earlier."

"No misunderstanding, I wager," Gordon muttered. "We all know your reputation as *The Morning Star*."

Valan flashed a broad smile. "The Morning Star was considered the most beautiful of all God's creations."

Anger born of thirty years of envy flashed in Gordon's eyes. "Aye, you are arrogant enough to believe that of yourself."

"You give me too much credit," Valan said. "I have never held myself in such high esteem."

"Oh, but you do—and you do not deny the nickname."

"Excuse me, Lord Gordon, but this is not your business." Miss Matheson gave a dismissive wave of her hand. "Go away."

Valan struggled to maintain a neutral expression.

"You will thank me, Miss Matheson," Gordon replied tightly, then said to Sir Stirling, "My lord, I appeal to your sense of duty. Northington cannot be allowed sway in this young woman's life."

"I find this wildly amusing," Valan interjected. "It seems Gordon would like to reinterpret the law."

A group of ladies passed close by. Once they left earshot, Gordon said, "I happen to know, sir, that Miss Matheson is a student of Lady Peddington's School for Young Ladies and she is no relation to you."

"Indeed?" said Valan. "I am all agog. How is it you find yourself in possession of this knowledge and what has it to do with anything?"

"That is none of your concern. All that matters is that your so-called guardianship is a ruse to take advantage of her."

"You are very rude," said Miss Matheson with heat. "His lordship has been a perfect gentleman. Why, when he found me in the garden, he was very adamant that I return to the ballroom before my reputation was ruined."

"Found you in the gardens?" A glint appeared in Gordon's eyes and his gaze shifted to Valan. "I will not allow you to take advantage of *another* unsuspecting woman."

"One might wonder, my dear Gordon, how you propose to stop me were that my plan." Valan lifted a brow. "With a pistol, perhaps?"

"That method worked in the past."

"The inexperience of youth, do you not agree?" Valan laughed. "In truth, you saved me much grief by intervening that night."

Gordon blinked. "I beg your pardon?"

"Victoria and I didn't suit at all. Marriage would have been disastrous." Valan flashed a grin. "The passion of youth." Gordon's eyes sparked. Valan gave him no chance to reply, but turned to Lady Chastity. "Might I impose upon you, my lady, to take Miss Matheson home with you tonight—with your husband's permission, of course? Tomorrow, my ward will have a female companion at Finley Hall."

"I would be pleased to have Miss Matheson stay with us," she replied.

Valan addressed Miss Matheson. "Would you prefer to stay with Lady Chastity rather than return to Lady Peddington's school?"

She beamed. "Oh, indeed, I would, sir."

He smiled. "Good, then go with her, as I ask."

She pinned him with a shrewd look. "Promise that tomorrow you will find a companion for me and I shall come live with you?"

"You must save your penchant for negotiation for business," he said.

"That is not an answer," she said.

He sighed. "I promise, my child."

She wrinkled her nose. "And you will stop calling me 'child.'"

He angled his head with cultured grace. "As you command."

She gave a succinct nod. "Then I shall do as you ask." She looked at Lady Chastity. "I will leave when you are ready."

Lady Chastity exchanged a look with her husband, then said, "We can leave now."

"My lord," Gordon said to Sir Stirling, "surely you see how dangerous this situation is for Miss Matheson?"

Sir Stirling's expression chilled. "In fact, there is nowhere safer for her than in the company of my wife."

Gordon paled. "Of course. That is not what I meant. I only meant that Northington's plans for her are less than honorable."

Miss Matheson snorted. "I am done with this one. We may go."

Valan regarded her severely. "I beg of you, Miss Matheson, do not snort like a common tavern wench."

She hung her head. "I am sorry, sir."

"You are forgiven. Now, go with Lady Chastity and, I beg you, behave—at least until I next see you."

"I promise." She gave him a full smile before he said to Sir Stirling, "Good evening, Sir Stirling." He faced Lady Chastity. "My lady, thank you for your kindness."

Without so much as a glance at Gordon, he strode away.

* * *

Finding a governess on short notice wasn't terribly hard. Finding one who would not crumble under Miss Matheson's determined nature, proved more difficult. Valan settled for a woman of twenty-eight years, who was taller than his new ward by at least five inches. One would think her height would give her an advantage, but her light brown hair fastened in a severe chignon, combined with her quiet manner, reminded him of a sparrow.

She sat across from him in the carriage, her hands folded demurely in her lap, as befitted a paid companion. For today, she would satisfy propriety. He would hire someone more suitable post haste.

They reached Stirling's home exactly at four p.m., as Valan had promised in his note sent earlier that day. He alighted from the coach, then turned and assisted Miss Stone to the ground. They proceeded up the walkway and up the three steps to the door.

He knocked. A moment later, the door opened, and an austere butler led them down a short hallway and into a parlor, tastefully decorated in pale gold and blues.

"I shall tell his lordship you are here." He bowed and left.

Thankfully, Miss Stone remained quiet while they waited.

Minutes later, Sir Stirling and Lady Chastity entered with Miss Matheson between them. Miss Matheson flew across the room and threw herself into Valan's arms.

"I am so pleased to see you, sir."

"So I gather." He grasped her shoulders and set her at arm's length. "Our first order of business when we arrive home will be a serious discussion on your conduct with a gentleman." Valan turned and bowed to

Lady Chastity. "My lady. You are looking particularly radiant." She cast a curious glance at her husband. Valan turned to Sir Stirling. "Your lordship. May I introduce Miss Stone. Miss Stone, the Marquess and Marchioness of Roxburgh."

Miss Stone curtsied.

He nodded toward Jeanine. "This is your charge, Miss Matheson."

"I am not her charge," Miss Matheson said. "We agreed that I am not a child."

"I believe I agreed not to *call* you a child," Valan said.

Miss Matheson cast him a sideways glance, then said to Miss Stone, "You are very tall."

"That is not polite," Valan said. "I wager Miss Peddington taught you better manners."

"I did not say being tall was a bad thing. So, I wasn't being rude."

"Perhaps we do not understand one another," he said. "If you want to be my ward, you will not contradict me."

"I—"

"Do you wish to be my ward?" he cut in.

She clamped her mouth shut and nodded.

"Then we are agreed," he said.

She nodded again and looked at Miss Stone. "Truly, I meant no offense."

The young woman smiled. "It is true, I am unusually tall, but I'm certain I surprised you. His lordship is correct, however. A lady never points out another's shortcomings, no matter how obvious they are."

Miss Matheson's eyes darkened. "Being tall is not a shortcoming. Anyone who says otherwise is cruel."

"You are right, of course," Miss Stone said.

Miss Matheson's expression cleared. "We shall get along famously." She looked up at Valan and smiled. "You have chosen well, sir."

He lifted a brow. "Have I, indeed?"

"You have, and are quite pleased with yourself."

"A man takes pleasure where he can. Shall we go?"

"May I have a word with you before you leave?" Stirling said.

Valan angled his head in agreement, then said to Miss Matheson, "Will you and Miss Stone wait in the carriage, please?"

"Come along, ladies," Lady Chastity said. "We will make certain Miss Matheson's boxes are collected."

"Boxes?" Valan repeated.

"Chastity purchased a few essentials for Miss Matheson," Sir Stirling said.

"How kind of you," Valan said.

The ladies left, and Valan said, "Thank you for keeping her. Please forward me the bills for her things."

Stirling shook his head. "Chastity wanted to give her a few items. I promise you, the real expense for her wardrobe still lays with you. She's a very vivacious young lady."

Valan met his gaze squarely. "I have no designs on her, if that is your concern."

"I'm not the least bit concerned. I thought you might like to know that Lord Gordon has petitioned Chastity's father to intercede for the girl."

"Has he, now?" Valan murmured. "One wonders where Lord Gordon finds the time to crusade so determinedly. His own father's affairs have suffered these last two years."

"He has designs on her, of course," Stirling said.

Valan stared. "I had no idea you were so forthright."

Sterling laughed. "I'm not always. But I feel certain you already knew Gordon wanted her."

"Aye," Valan said. "I haven't known him to do anything out of the goodness of his heart."

"Many would say the same of you," Sterling said.

"They would be right," Valan admitted.

"Then why do this?"

"Whatever my reasons, I do not lie when I say the girl is in no danger from me."

Stirling studied him. "Those reasons are, I think, to annoy Lord Gordon."

"I'm not certain I believe you when you say you're not always so forth-right," Valan said.

Stirling smiled. "Nonetheless, it is true. Being blunt with you is necessary."

"I see," Valan said in a dry voice. "Will His Grace interfere?"

Stirling shook his head. "I doubt it. Chastity will speak with him."

"I'm surprised she isn't concerned for Miss Matheson," Valan said.

Stirling's grin widened. "Chastity married a man who carried her down the aisle over his shoulder then *encouraged* her to take her vows. She is not given to nerves, particularly around unorthodox men."

"You are a fortunate man."

"I am. If ye need further help, don't hesitate to ask," Stirling said.

Valan thanked him, took his leave, and found his ward and her chaper-one waiting in the carriage, boxes piled high on top of the vehicle.

Miss Matheson squealed with delight as he stepped into the carriage and pulled the door shut. Valan sat on the seat opposite them. "Miss Matheson, I ask that you conduct yourself as purports a lady. You will no-tice that Miss Stone remained calm as I entered the carriage. Please follow her example."

"You cannot expect all ladies to react in exactly the same fashion, sir."

Valan rapped on the roof of the carriage, which soon jolted into mo-tion. "In public, and in matters of propriety, I can, indeed, expect you to adhere to similar manners."

She tilted her head. "But in private, I may behave naturally?"

"You may speak plainly with me, Miss Matheson."

She made a face.

He sighed. "What is it now?"

"If we are to speak plainly when alone, then you must call me Jennie."

"I will not," he said. "Jeanine, will do."

"My mother and sisters call me Jennie," she said.

"That is their prerogative," he said. "In public, or when we have guests, I will call you Miss Matheson. When we are at home or alone, I will call you Jeanine."

She clapped her hands. "And I shall call you Valan."

He shook his head. "In public, you will address me as 'my lord' or 'Lord Northington,' or even 'sir.' In private, you will address me as 'sir' or 'my lord.'"

She wrinkled her nose. "It does not seem fair that you can call me by my Christian name, but I must always call you 'my lord' or 'sir.'"

"Anyone who told you life is fair, my dear, was lying."

CHAPTER FOUR

THEY ARRIVED HOME TO find tea waiting for them in the parlor.

Jeanine and Miss Matheson settled on the settee and Valan took the chair to their left. Miss Stone poured and handed out the cups.

"What does a ward do?" Jeanine asked.

Valan paused as he lifted the teacup to his lips. "I am not quite sure."

"She will continue her education as a lady," Miss Stone said. "Sewing, pianoforte, party planning, perhaps a little Latin and French. *Parlez-vous françaiss, mademoiselle?*" she said in flawless French.

"Miss Stone, you surprise me," Valan said.

"*Tu parles français comme un parisien,*" Jeanine said.

"Miss Matheson," Valan said in delight. "You, too, speak French like a Parisian. Where did you learn?"

"From Lady Peddington, of course."

"Surely, you spoke the language before you attended her school," he said.

Jeanine beamed and shook her head. "Nae. She said I was a natural. I don't speak fluently, but I would love to visit Paris and practice."

"Well, the way you and Miss Stone speak French, it would be a crime not to go." He looked at Miss Stone. "Is a trip to France permissible for a ward?"

"Very much so, sir."

"Then it's settled."

Baldwin entered, carrying a single envelope on a silver tray. "Forgive the interruption, my lord." He stopped in front of Valan. "This just arrived for you from Lady Douglas. Her man awaits a reply."

Valan set down his teacup, took the envelope and pulled the notecard from within:

An invitation from Lady Douglas for an intimate luncheon on the morrow. He looked at Baldwin. "Please have the man waiting, inform Lady Douglas that Miss Matheson and Miss Stone will be happy to attend the party."

"As you wish, sir." Baldwin bowed and left.

"A party?" Miss Matheson said.

Valan handed her the invitation.

She scanned the note, then looked up. "How did Lady Douglas learn so soon that I am to be your ward?"

"You are not 'to be' my ward," Valan corrected. "You *are* my ward. As for how she knew so quickly…" He thought of Lord Gordon. "*Society* always finds a way to spread the latest news."

"I am not particularly interested in a luncheon," Jeanine said.

"Miss Douglas has been kind enough to extend the invitation at this late date. You will attend."

"You do not mean to attend?" she demanded.

He hadn't planned to attend, then imagined her strolling in the garden and being accosted by a wolf who didn't know she was the Marquess of Northington's ward. "Of course, I will accompany you."

Mischief danced in her eyes. "You're afraid to let me go alone, aren't you?"

"I fear, whether I accompany you or not, we shall have our challenges."

"We must bring Miss Stone, of course."

"Of course. Anywhere you go, Miss Stone goes."

The lady looked startled. "Forgive me, my lord, but I do not have a gown for such grand parties."

"Hmm." He looked at Jeanine. "May I ask how many gowns you own?"

"Three ball gowns and one day dress."

"Just as I thought." Valan glanced at the mantle clock. 5:45.

He rose and crossed to the small secretary located near the hearth. He jotted a note to the modiste, then tugged the bell pull. Baldwin appeared before he'd returned to his seat.

"Baldwin, please have this note sent to Mrs. Morgan. She lives on the end of Bryant Street, a modest brick building, if I recall. Wait for a reply. If she is able to come now, please fetch her." He handed the note to the steward.

Baldwin bowed, then left.

"I don't see why you must buy new gowns," Jeanine said.

Valan returned to his chair. "Would you rob Miss Stone of the pleasure of new gowns?"

"Oh, you're right, of course."

"Of course." Valan reached for his tea, then decided something stronger was called for. He went to the sideboard, and poured a liberal dose of scotch into a glass tumbler.

"You need not trouble yourself on my account, sir," said Miss Stone.

Valan returned to his seat, swirled the liquor and took a sniff before drinking half the liquid. He looked at her and smiled politely. "As I will not sew the dresses, it is no trouble for me."

"But the expense," Miss Stone said.

Valan regarded them. "I wonder at my good fortune to find the only two women in Scotland who care nothing for new dresses."

"No one said we didn't care," Jeanine said. "But, really, how many dresses does a woman need?"

"How many, indeed?" he repeated softly.

* * *

Jeanine started to open the library door, then paused and knocked.

"Enter," the marquess called.

She opened the door. Despite the gloomy weather, the red of the wall paint and deep blues of the curtains gave the room a warm feel. To her left, French doors paned with glass stood open to reveal a quaint balcony. Opposite the balcony doors, books filled ceiling-high cherrywood shelves. A rolling ladder leaned against the shelves to the right of the marquess's desk, where he sat, a quill in hand. He'd paused his letter writing to watch her.

She smiled. "I like this room."

"I am deeply gratified." His attention returned to his letter. "To what do I owe the honor of your visit this morning?"

"Visit? We live in the same house."

"In this large house, it is conceivable that we might not see one another for weeks."

"Weeks?" She crossed to the chair opposite his desk and sat down. "That is terrible. I will see you every day."

"How fortunate for me," he said dryly.

"You do not wish to see me?"

"I am always pleased to see you," he said. "But I expect you will be busy, what with today's party and your lessons in Latin and French, sewing, shopping and dress fittings—" he spared her a glance "—I assume you have more fittings?"

"Miss Stone insisted."

He nodded and resumed writing. "Have you and Miss Stone reviewed the latest party invitations?"

She scrunched her nose in distaste. "Can't I simply pick one from the pile? They're all the same."

"Forgive me, but they're not all the same."

She waved an airy hand. "Dancing, champagne, crowded ballrooms, pheasant for dinner—they are alike."

With a sigh, he laid down his pen and leaned back in his chair. "Perhaps there are some similarities in the programming, but I can assure you, that does not mean they are all the same."

"You mean that some are more socially important than others."

He nodded. "Something you might remember, if you are to find that elderly gentleman you want."

"How long do you think it will take me to find this gentleman?"

"Are you in a hurry?" he asked.

"I will no' be young forever," she said. "I am already nineteen."

He nodded gravely, but the glint in his eyes told her he was laughing at her. "I believe you have enough time to find someone before you are on the shelf."

"Laugh all you want," she said. "There are plenty of younger women than I—and more beautiful. I cannot afford to waste time. My younger sisters are already married."

He regarded her. "You are bothered by the fact that they married before you?"

"Of course. The eldest sister is supposed to marry first."

"Surely, there was some young man you could have married?"

"There are always young men to marry. But I want a wealthy gentleman who…"

"Who is ready to move on to his reward?" he finished for her. "This has been a plan of yours for some time, I take it?"

Jeanine nodded. "Since my mother decided to remarry, two years ago. They only just married last year, which is why I knew I had to take action."

His lordships' brows shot up in surprise. "You have a father?"

"Stepfather," she corrected. "It isn't at all the same thing."

"Either way, he will have something to say about who you marry," the marquess said. "Surely, he will want you to return home and find a husband?"

"Oh no, I can never return home." Her gaze caught on the small game table to the left of the ladder. "Is that a chess board?"

"There is a chess board inside the table," he said.

"I like chess. Will you play with me sometime?"

"If you like. Why can you never return home?" he asked." His eyes shifted past Jeanine and she twisted in her chair as a light knock came to the open door. Miss Stone stood in the doorway.

"Come in," his lordship said.

Jeanine jumped to her feet as Miss Stone approached. "Doesn't she look lovely? The pale yellow fabric compliments her complexion. The needlework on the ruffled sleeves is perfect. I insisted that Mrs. Morgan sew her a day dress straight away. It arrived last night."

His eyes bore into Miss Stone. "And she agreed?" he said.

Miss Stone stopped in front of his desk. "Nae, sir, I did not. In fact, I instructed Mrs. Morgan to sew Miss Matheson's dress first. When this dress arrived yesterday, I sent her a note demanding to know why she had ignored my instructions."

The marquess's eyes shifted to Jeanine. "I have an idea why."

"Do not be angry," Jeanine said. "You must agree that Miss Stone's clothes are…oh, what is the word, outdated—yes—that's it, her clothes are outdated. Whereas, mine are only not as lavish as you would like."

"I would not have even worn the dress, my lord," Miss Stone said, "but Miss Matheson threatened to burn my clothes if I didn't."

"She is quite capable of carrying out the threat," he murmured.

Miss Stone clasped her hands at her waist." Forgive me for saying so, sir, but I believe she is."

"Perhaps that is the threat I should use against her clothes," he said.

"I doubt it would work, sir," Miss Stone said. "She would only devise a way to get even."

His lordship's brows shot up. "You surprise me, Miss Stone."

"I cannot imagine why, my lord."

"You comprehend Miss Matheson's character better than I thought you would."

"It isn't hard. She does little to hide her actions and motivations."

He looked at Jeanine and she grinned. "Nae, she does not," he said.

Miss Stone turned to Jeanine. "We must leave in half an hour, if we are to arrive at Mrs. Morgan's shop on time."

"Just as I thought." The marquess picked up his quill. "I will meet you ladies in the foyer at two-thirty."

"I won't see you until then?" Jeanine asked.

"I did say I expected that you would be busy today, Miss Matheson."

She lifted a finger. "You promised to call me Jeanine in the privacy of our home."

A corner of his mouth twitched. "In the privacy of *our* home. Aye, Jeanine."

She smiled. "Very good, Valan."

His gaze sharpened. "I also said, you would address me as either 'sir' or 'my lord.'"

"Aye, that is what you said," she replied, then turned, and left with Miss Stone.

* * *

At the luncheon, the marquess allowed Jeanine to have two glasses of wine—well, technically, one glass, for each time he filled the glass only halfway. She now watched as he played commerce with three other gentlemen near the balcony, at a table in a corner of the massive parlor. A servant appeared at the table and filled the men's glasses with sherry and brandy, then left.

"Ye might bring some scotch, lad," said the large gentleman to the marquess's right.

"The French brandy isn't good enough for you?" Mr. Phillips said.

"Brandy is well and good," he said in a thick Scottish burr, "but a man needs strong liquor when he's gambling."

"This is not a hell, MacLean," Phillips said.

The man grinned. "Depends on if ye are winning or losing."

Jeanine glanced at the refreshments table on the far side of the room.

Half a dozen people gathered around the table. Perhaps she could nip over and fill her wine glass without being missed.

"Where is Miss Stone, Miss Matheson?" his lordship asked.

Jeanine started. "Lady Douglas has taken her away."

"Away?" He glanced at her.

"Aye," she replied. "I believe Lady Douglas wanted to learn more about Miss Stone's previous employer."

In the instant before he returned his gaze to his cards, she glimpsed a strange smile. From the corner of her eye, a flash of red captured her attention. She turned slightly and recognized Lord Gordon as he entered the room. His bright burgundy coat made him stand out like a parrot amongst sparrows. He passed from sight behind a group of men.

He did not approve of her being the ward of the Marquess of Northington—which was foolish. Anyone with eyes could see the marquess hadn't taken her as ward in order to make her his lover.

"Miss Matheson," the marquess said, "sit. I will teach you how to play commerce."

"Really?" Jeanine cried. "I would love to play."

He stood and stepped around his chair. "Have my seat." She took the chair. He pushed it closer to the table, then signaled a servant to bring another chair.

The Scot sitting to her right, stood. "No need to call for another chair, Northington. You took my last hundred pounds. I'm out. Take my chair."

His lordship gave a slight bow. "Thank you, MacLean." He sat down, then scooted his chair closer to hers. "Phillips," he nodded to the dealer, who sat directly across from them, "I will sit out this round. Please deal the lady in."

"Perhaps the lady would prefer a game of vingt-et-un," the handsome gentleman to her left said.

Jeanine started to roll her eyes, then caught sight of the marquess's arched brows. She peeked at him from beneath her lashes and then looked at the gentleman and smiled sweetly. "If you are more comfortable with a game of luck, sir, I will oblige."

Chuckles sounded behind her.

"Miss Matheson may play commerce if she chooses," the marquess said. "I promised to teach her."

The man looked back at Jeanine and angled his head. "As you wish, ma'am."

"The object of the game," the marquess began.

"Oh, I know the game," Jeanine said.

"Indeed?" he said. "You didn't tell me you know how to play."

"You didn't ask," she replied as Phillips began the deal.

"She's got you there, Northington," a man said behind her.

Phillips laid three cards facedown before each of the four players, himself included, then laid three cards face up to form the widow. An ace of hearts, two of clubs, and ten of diamonds. He placed a fifty pound note in the middle of the table. The other two men did the same, and the marquess took a fifty pound note from the stack of bills in front of him and tossed it onto the pile.

Phillips took the ace, slipped it facedown at the bottom of his three cards, then took his top facedown card and turned it up beside the other two face-up cards. A murmur went up. He'd exchanged the ace of hearts for a king of hearts. He would be wanting that card back.

Jeanine lifted the corners of her three cards and looked at them. Three of spades, queen of clubs, and an ace of diamonds. The marquess leaned toward her.

Jeanine covered her cards and looked at him. "What are you doing?"

"I am not playing," he said. "It is permissible to show me your cards."

She shook her head. "I don't want your expression to give away my hand."

More chuckles from the men.

His lordship lifted a brow. "Are you saying I cannot school my expression?"

"Would you let me see your cards if you were playing?" she asked.

"It is only fair I see how you are spending my money," he countered.

Jeanine started to snort, then thought better of it. "I am not spending it," she replied. "It is simply a stake."

The blond gentleman to Phillips' left traded a four of diamonds for the king Phillips had discarded. Good. It was unlikely Phillips would be able to get the king now.

Jeanine traded her queen for the two of clubs. The handsome gentleman to her left took her queen and left the four of spades. The round had reached Phillips, and he pulled another card from the deck and laid it face up with the widow. A Jack of spades. Phillips placed another fifty-pound note in the pool. The player to his left shook his head and leaned back in his chair. Janine reached for a hundred-pound note in the stack in front of the marquess.

He placed a staying hand on hers. "Perhaps you should show me your cards, Miss Matheson."

"That would ruin the game," she said. "If you approve the bet, no one will match me, and I won't win as much money." He didn't move and she added, "If I lose, you will lose less than the cost of that waistcoat."

His expression remained impassive. "I believe you already owe me the cost of one waistcoat."

"All the more reason for me to make the bet."

He remained motionless for two heartbeats, then removed his hand. She took the hundred-pound note and added it to the pool.

The handsome gentleman to her left placed a hundred pound note on top of hers. "I pray you will not hold it against me if I am the man responsible for you owing Lord Northington the price of two waistcoats."

She shrugged. "Since I will win, that will not be an issue."

The bet returned to Phillips. His mouth thinned, but he added another fifty-pound note, then traded the jack he'd just laid down for a six of clubs. The play was now Jeanine's and, with a smile, she gave a small shake of her head. Two more rounds followed before the handsome gentleman picked up a nine and discarded a two. Her gaze snagged on the card and, as hoped, when Phillips added a new card to the widow, a three of diamonds, he exchanged a seven for the two.

Jeanine relaxed against her chair, intensely aware of his lordship's eyes on her. When her turn came, she looked at the marquess, smiled, then took another hundred-pound note from his stack and added it to the pool. Phillips visibly blanched. The handsome gentleman matched her bet, but took no cards.

Phillips' gaze locked with hers. "As you can see, Miss Matheson, I do not have the money to match your bet. I assume you will take my marker." He reached into his coat pocket.

Jeanine shook her head. "Nae, sir, I do not accept bets from men who can't afford to lose their money."

His face reddened. "You mistake the lack of money on my person for an inability to pay."

She shrugged. "Then next time, bring more money."

Phillips opened his mouth to reply, but the marquess said, "It is the other player's prerogative to decline a marker, Phillips."

"She is only declining my marker because she knows that will eliminate me from the game," he snapped.

"That is a strategy that will likely save you a great deal of money this night," his lordship replied, then said to Jeanine, "It is your turn, Miss Matheson."

She reached for the marquess's pile of money. This time, he didn't stop her when she placed five hundred-pound notes in the pool. Jeanine met the handsome gentleman's gaze.

He angled his head slightly. "I will forfeit the bet to you."

"Of course, you will." She laughed. "You do not have the money to match my bet."

"Perhaps not," he said. "Show us your cards."

She shook her head and laughed again. "You did not pay for the privilege of seeing my cards."

"True," he agreed. "But I ask it as a favor."

Jeanine shrugged, then turned over her cards.

Laughter and murmurs rose amongst the men.

"Beat by an ace, two and three," the handsome gentleman said. "You are a very good player, Miss Matheson. May I ask where you learned to play?"

"I have six cousins, all boys. They taught me."

"By all that is holy, Northington, you are letting her gamble?"

Jeanine turned slightly and looked up at Lord Gordon. The burgundy coat really was horrid.

"Why not?" the handsome gentleman said. "Such talent shouldn't go to waste."

"This is exactly what I feared," Lord Gordon said.

"I was certain it was something else you feared, my dear," the marquess drawled.

Lord Gordon pointedly ignored him. "Miss Matheson, would you care to have a glass of punch with me?"

The handsome gentleman stood. "You are too late, Gordon. The lady has agreed to take a turn around the room with me." He looked at the marquess. "With your permission, of course, my lord."

His attention shifted to the handsome gentleman. "You will not leave the parlor."

"Of course not." The handsome gentleman smiled at her.

She would have refused, but remembered the refreshments table on the other side of the room. An escort would be nice, not to mention, the marquess was likely not to let her go too far out of his sight alone. She rose, and the other men stood as the marquess pulled her chair out for her.

Jeanine faced the handsome gentleman. "Oh, dear, I don't know your name."

"That is my fault," his lordship said.

"You are going to allow Miss Matheson to-to *go off* with a man she hasn't been introduced to?" Lord Gordon cried.

"I don't think it's as bad as all that," Lord Northington said. "A turn around the room isn't 'going off' with someone. And I was about to introduce her to Mr. Westland. Mr. Westland, may I introduce my ward, Miss Matheson."

Mr. Westland grasped her hand and bent over her fingers. "An honor to meet you, Miss Matheson."

"You're not angry that I beat you at cards?" she asked. "My cousins would get so angry when I beat them, they wouldn't play with me for weeks. Eventually, they would need another player and be forced to ask me to play."

Mr. Westland smiled. "I am not at all angry."

She smiled. "Good. Otherwise, it would be awkward for us to walk together."

"Indeed," he said with a laugh, then extended an arm. Jeanine laid her hand atop his as they started away, and behind her Lord Gordon said, "I must protest."

"At least he didn't protest while pointing a pistol," Phillips mumbled.

The table went dead silent and Jeanine glanced over her shoulder.

His lordship stared at Mr. Phillips, a strange smile playing on his lips.

"Didn't mean anything by it," Phillips said.

"Oh, but you did," the marquess said.

Jeanine faced forward.

"I will be speaking with His Grace about this," she heard Lord Gordon say.

"Of course, you will," his lordship said before she passed beyond hearing.

CHAPTER FIVE

VALAN DID NOT THROW parties. But then, he'd never before had a ward.

He spent the week out and about to ensure everyone knew about the upcoming party, whether they were invited or not. The spare moments of respite away from his once quiet household were spent at his club, where no one spoke above a murmur, even on days like today, when seats were in high demand.

Valan read his newspaper in the quiet corner hear the hearth, but noted the approach of Baron Rosemund, who claimed an empty chair at the small round table to Valan's right.

"Kind of you to have brandy ready for me." Brendan reached across the intervening space, lifted Valan's decanter and filled the empty glass that sat beside Valan's full glass.

"I regret to tell you, that the brandy was not for you," Valan replied.

"I am wounded." Brendan set the decanter down, picked up the filled glass, relaxed against his chair and rested the glass on his leg. "You are making quite a stir these days. Tell me the latest gossip isn't true."

Valan perused the business section of the paper. "At the risk of sounding pompous, which latest gossip do you mean?"

Brendan gave him a sideways glance.

"Aye, it is true," Valan said.

Brendan sipped his brandy. "Is she beautiful?"

"Some would say so."

"That is a new tack for you."

"She is my ward," Valan said.

"I know you too well to believe this isn't something more," Brendan said without rancor.

Valan chuckled. "You bear quite a burden being my friend."

"A thankless task," he replied with wry humor.

Valan lowered his newspaper and looked at him. "I beg your pardon, that was a fine dinner we enjoyed last month in Inverness—at my expense."

Brendan lifted his glass in salute. "Many thanks." He took another sip. "If you don't have designs on the woman, what could possibly induce you to take her as your ward?"

Twenty years dropped away, as Valan once again fitted his booted foot to the final rung in the trestle leading to Lady Victoria's bedchamber window and grasped the window sill. He hoisted himself up and swung his feet over, then straightened in the dimly lit room. It wasn't the cool metal of the pistol pressed to the back of his neck when he stepped deeper inside the room that bothered him—if he had an underage sister and a man had climbed through her window, he would've done the same—but the pistol Gordon held when he emerged from the dressing screen across the room.

Despite prolonged efforts, Valan never learned how Gordon had discovered that Valan's father had shot himself only hours before, leaving Valan a pauper. The only thing his father hadn't lost in that card game was their ancestral castle on the Isle of Mull. Valan hadn't visited the castle since.

As if on cue, Lord Gordon entered the sitting room. Valan reached for his glass of brandy and directed his attention back to the paper. Three heartbeats later, Lord Gordon entered his peripheral view. An instant later, he stopped in front of him. Valan kept his attention on his paper.

"Rosemund," Gordon said with a curt nod to Brendan, then to Valan, "A word with you, Northington."

Valan kept his gaze on the paper. "Of course."

"In private, if you will."

"I have no secrets from Brendan. Say what you will."

A moment of silence passed, then Gordon said, "At least do me the courtesy of giving me your full attention."

Valan lifted his gaze from the paper. "Forgive me. Will you sit? I can call for a chair and another brandy glass."

"You can call for— I can have a chair brought, if I so choose," he snapped. "I do not need you to command one of your lackeys."

"I would hardly call Brummell's servants 'lackeys,' and they are not my lackey's, at any rate." He sipped his brandy, then stared, waiting.

Gordon drew himself up as if for battle. "I have appealed to Duke Roxburgh to intervene on Miss Matheson's behalf."

"I expected nothing less. Pray, sit. I am distressed that you stand while we sit."

"I am satisfied to stand," he said. "I demand you return Miss Matheson to Lady Peddington's school."

"Return her? You speak as if she is property. You credit me with far too much influence. First, Brummell's servants are my lackeys, now I own Miss Matheson. I admit that a lady has her pleasant uses, but I am enlightened enough to know that I do not own a single one." He thought of Jeanine's desire to marry a wealthy old gentleman with one foot in the grave. That young lady had no intention of ever becoming property.

"You know full well the child has no comprehension of your intentions," Lord Gordon said. "She sees you only as a generous benefactor."

Valan smiled. "An intelligent female, to be sure."

"An innocent in the clutches of a man who charms women for nefarious purposes," Lord Gordon snapped.

"I am indeed guilty of that. But perhaps not in this case."

"I am giving you the opportunity to do the right thing before it is too late," Lord Gordon said.

Valan laughed. "You never cease to amuse. You, of all people, know it is far too late for me to do the right thing."

"I warn you," Gordon said through tight lips.

"You are overset, my dear," Valan said. "A brandy would do you good. Are you sure—"

"Nae, I do not want a damned brandy," Gordon nearly shouted.

Glances came their way. Gordon sent a withering glare to a man seated at a nearby table, then whirled and stalked from the room.

"I believe you," Brendan said.

Valan looked at him. "I am gratified to have your trust, but to what do I own such an honor?"

"Your ward--what is her name...Miss Matheson--is safe from your masculine clutches."

"I have many faults," Valan said, "but lying is not one of them."

"You simply say nothing," Brendon said.

Valan shrugged.

"It's been twenty years," Brendon said. "I thought you'd forgotten."

Valan offered a wistful smile. "Then, Brendan, you don't know me as well as you thought you did."

* * *

Valan entered his library and went straight to the sideboard to pour himself a brandy.

"There you are."

He glanced right as Miss Matheson hurried into the room with Miss Stone following at a sedate pace.

He replaced the decanter's top, crossed to his desk, and sat down. "Good afternoon, Miss Matheson. Miss Stone."

Miss Stone halted before his desk, hands clasped in front of her.

Jeanine sat in the chair opposite his desk, then jumped to her feet. "We need a chair for you, Miss Stone."

"I am content to stand," she said.

Jeanine's eyes lit on the chairs that surrounded the gaming table.

Valan rose. "Sit, Jeanine. I will fetch the chair."

She smiled. "You are gallant."

"Hardly," he replied. "I fear you will topple and break your neck if you try to carry the chair." He carried the chair to the desk and set it to her left. "Miss Stone, you may sit."

She obeyed and he returned to his seat. "Do you need something?" he asked.

"We don't need anything," Jeanine said. "Well, unless you count answering a question as needing something."

"Ask the question and we shall see." He sipped his brandy.

"Are we allowed to invite guests to the party?"

"Who are the guests?"

"My friends from Lady Peddington's school."

"Aye," he replied. "You may invite them."

She beamed. "See, that wasn't so difficult, now, was it?"

"It was not."

"Have you invited everyone you wanted to invite?" she asked.

"For the most part."

"Who have you invited?"

"I doubt you know most of them." He paused in lifting the glass to his lips. "Where are you from?"

She giggled. "How funny that you made me your ward and you never asked where I lived."

"I believe I did ask you that night at Lady Peddington's ball, but you wouldn't tell me." he said, and drank half the brandy.

"You're right, of course." Jeanine regarded him. "Why did you make me your ward?"

"It is polite to answer the question you were asked before you ask one," he said.

Her eyes twinkled. "I am from Perth. Now, why did you make me your ward?"

"To aid in your quest to find a husband."

"That is silly." She looked at Miss Stone. "Isn't that silly, Miss Stone?"

"You are fortunate that his lordship has taken an interest in your well-being," she replied.

Jeanine waved a hand. "Oh, I know that. But that doesn't change the fact that he didn't have to take an interest. What kind of food will there be at the party? Please don't say pheasant. Everyone serves pheasant."

"I have no idea what is on the menu. You may speak with Mrs. McPhee, if you wish."

"Will there be dancing?"

He nodded. "Aye."

"I love to dance. You can dance with me—and Miss Stone, as well."

"There will be many young bucks anxious to dance with you and Miss Stone."

She shook her head. "Miss Stone may dance with them, of course. But you know I am not interested in a young buck."

His mouth twitched. "You would rob them of the pleasure of your company?"

She snorted. "They do not care about my company."

"Mr. Westland seemed to enjoy your company at the luncheon. Did you not find him charming?"

"He is charming." She cast a sideways glance at Miss Stone. "He would enjoy Miss Stone's company much more, however."

"I could never replace you," Miss Stone said.

"Of course, you could," Jeanine said. "Did you notice Miss Stone's hair, Grey? It is my creation. She is lovely, isn't she?"

He started. "What did you call me?"

She smiled. "Grey."

"I believe I said that you were to address me as 'sir' or 'my lord.'"

"You did, but when we are alone, that is too formal for a family."

He lifted a brow. "Family?"

She nodded enthusiastically.

"We are not alone," he pointed out. "Miss Stone is present."

"Isn't Miss Stone a part of our family?" Jeanine asked.

"I suppose she is." Valan lifted his glass to Miss Stone. "My condolences, Miss Stone." He finished the sherry and started to rise, then paused when Baldwin entered.

"Pardon the interruption, my lord, but there is a problem with a delivery."

Valan frowned. "What can that possibly have to do with me?"

"Mrs. McPhee is arguing with the deliveryman and I fear they will come to blows."

"If that happens, then we must pity the deliveryman. What is the argument?"

"Mrs. McPhee insists the delivery is too much. The deliveryman swears that this is the amount ordered for the party."

"You are the steward," Valan said. "Deal with the matter."

Mrs. MacPhee's voice rose in the hallway. A man's muffled reply followed.

Valan pinned Baldwin with a horrified stare. "Is a deliveryman actually headed for my study?"

"He is quite determined, my lord," Baldwin said.

The voices neared, and Mrs. McPhee burst into the room with a short, stalky man close on her heels. He appeared small beside her stout frame.

"There ye are, my lord." Mrs. McPhee hurried to his desk and halted near Miss Stone's chair.

The deliveryman stopped beside her.

"I have had enough of this miscreant," the housekeeper said.

"I am no miscreant," the man growled. "I only want to be paid for my delivery."

She narrowed her eyes on him. "I will not pay for something I didn't order."

The deliveryman shook a piece of paper in her face. "I cannae sell the fresh vegetables anywhere else. They will rot."

"That is *your* mistake," she said.

The man opened his mouth to rebut, but Valan stood and said, "May I ask who ordered the, er, vegetables, is it?"

The man thrust his paper toward Valan. Valan took it and scanned the list. He looked at Mrs. McPhee. "Who wrote the list?"

"That is Brenda's handwriting."

"Brenda?" Valan searched his memory. "She assists in the kitchen?"

Mrs. McPhee nodded.

"Then you did order the vegetables," he said.

She shook her head. "If ye look at the amounts, they have been scratched out and larger portions written in. This man is trying to cheat us."

"I never cheated anyone in my life," the deliveryman burst out.

Valan looked at the list again. "Is this the first order of vegetables for the party?"

"It is," replied Mrs. McPhee.

"In fact, it doesn't seem to be enough for the two hundred and fifty guests we invited," he said. "I expect at least fifty more spouses and friends to accompany the invited guests."

"I told ye that you needed more," the delivery man interjected.

"I will not buy more vegetables until I am sure we need more," Mrs. McPhee shot back. "His lordship doesn't like to waste money."

"While I appreciate your consideration, Mrs. McPhee, I do, in fact, waste money, and quite often," Valan said. "This does not seem to me an exorbitant amount to spend on vegetables."

"We cannae trust a man who tries to bilk us," she insisted.

The man swung to face her squarely and was forced to look up at her. "I willnae have my honor called into question."

"Honor?" she cried. "Thieves have no honor."

The man stepped closer. Mrs. McPhee drew back a fist and drove it into his jaw. He jerked left. Valan glimpsed Miss Stone's slippered foot shoot out right before the man tripped over her foot and flailed backwards two steps. Jeanine leapt to her feet. The deliveryman crashed into the game table. Wood splintered and game pieces flew everywhere. Valan took three steps and stopped beside him.

"He's broken your table," Jeanine cried.

"So he has."

The man sat up and gave his head a shake. He started to push to his feet.

"I suggest you stay down," Valan said. "Mrs. McPhee outweighs you by at least two stone."

The man looked up at him and blinked. "What?"

"As you may have guessed, Mrs. McPhee does not back down from a fight," Valan said.

The man's dazed eyes slipped past him. His face reddened and he struggled to his feet. "I demand my money."

"Why you scoundrel," Mrs. McPhee muttered darkly.

"Baldwin," Valan said, "pay the gentleman and see him safely out the door."

The deliveryman kept his glare fixed on Mrs. McPhee, who deigned to cast only a cursory glance at him as he passed. Valan looked at his game table and sighed before returning to his seat. Miss Stone, he noted, sat primly in her seat, hands clasped on her lap.

"Mrs. McPhee," Jeanine said a little breathless, "I have never seen anything so courageous. How did you manage to hit him so hard? Doesn't your hand hurt? I once punched Willy, my oldest cousin, and my hand hurt for days."

"I use my right hand to pound bread dough," the housekeeper replied with pride. "My right hand is stronger than the left."

"Perhaps I should start pounding bread dough," Jeanine said.

"Not if you intend to punch someone," Valan said.

Mrs. McPhee drew herself up. "The man deserved everything I gave him."

"A man almost always deserves what a woman gives him," Valan said. "However—" He broke off when a maid came skidding into the room.

"Where is Mr. Baldwin?" the girl cried.

"He just left with the deliveryman," Mrs. McPhee said. "What is wrong, Dora?"

The girl cast a nervous glance Valan's way. He raised a brow. "M-Mr. Baldwin will w-want to see what is going on in the ballroom," she stammered.

"Dare I ask what is going on in the ballroom?" Valan asked.

"They are bringing in chairs and tables for the party, but a leg has broken off one chair, an arm off another, and a table is sitting crooked," the girl answered.

"I am surrounded by people who intend to destroy all I own," Valan muttered.

The maid nodded vigorously. "I think you're right, my lord. But that is no' all."

"God help me," he said.

"They're bringing in candles. Too many, I think."

"A broken table or chair I will forgive, but I cannot allow my house to be burnt down," he said. "I am startled to realize how incompetent is my staff."

"We are not incompetent," Mrs. McPhee said. "I saved you from being bilked by that deliveryman. As for the chairs and tables, they are old."

"Old?" Valan repeated. "I had no idea I owned 'old' furniture."

"Ye havenae had a party in fifteen years," the housekeeper said. "We don't keep all those chairs and tables out. They are being brought down from the attic. Those in the ballroom, well, some of them are probably rotted."

"Has it really been fifteen years since you've thrown a party?" Jeanine asked.

He nodded slowly. "So it would seem."

Footsteps sounded in the hallway. An instant later, Baldwin entered. "The deliveryman has departed," he announced.

"Is there a reason for this announcement?" Valan asked.

"There is another delivery," Baldwin replied.

"I'll see to it." Mrs. McPhee started to turn.

"Mrs. McPhee," Valan said, "I beg you, do not beat this deliveryman. I would rather not have goods shipped in from England because all of Edinburgh's merchants are afraid of my housekeeper. Baldwin, please have my carriage brought round. I must fetch help before it is too late."

CHAPTER SIX

VALAN ARRIVED WITH MISS Matheson and Miss Stone at his cousin's home and directed the servant to escort the ladies to the garden. He then went to the drawing room where he was told his cousin rested. Legs curled up beneath her skirts on a pale yellow divan, Peigi rested her chin on her arm, which was stretched out across the divan back. She turned her gaze from the window overlooking the east lawn.

"Valan, what a surprise." She straightened and extended a hand.

He dutifully crossed the room, grasped her fingers and bowed over them. "You are looking well," he said.

She sighed. "Well, I am not well."

Valan sat on the far end of the divan. "Are you ill?"

"Don't be ridiculous. You know I am never sick. Nae, it is Richard. He is intolerable."

"Ah, what has your husband done now?" Valan asked.

She pouted. "You needn't act as if it is he who must tolerate me. I know how you men are."

"Indeed?"

"Yes, you protect one another."

"If that is true, it is only because women are such formidable foes."

"There you are," she cried. "Why must men see women as foes?"

"I doubt I could explain it to your satisfaction," he said.

"Because the notion is ridiculous," she replied.

"You are probably right. In any case, I did not come here to discuss the male mind. I need your help."

"My help?" Her brows rose. "I have never known you to ask anyone for help."

"Be that as it may, I am doing so now. I am planning a party and would like you to help."

"A party?" She frowned. "You never throw parties."

"I admit, it has been some time."

She regarded him. "What are you up to?"

"I am not 'up to' anything. I have simply taken a ward and am introducing her into society."

"Her?" Peigi stiffened. "You are mistaken, sir, if you think I will be party to your *affaire de coeur*."

"This is no affair," he replied mildly.

"No one will be fooled by the pretense—least of all Richard. You know he will never allow me to associate with one of your light o' loves. Besides, I know you too well."

"Pray tell, what do you know?"

"I know that you do not do anything that doesn't benefit you. Don't be cross," she quickly added. "We all have our faults and that is yours. I love you, nonetheless."

"I am grateful. However, despite your...accurate assessment of my character, Miss Matheson is, indeed, my ward and nothing more."

"I don't believe you."

"My dear, Peigi, have you ever noted amongst my, er, shortcomings, that I am a liar?"

Her brow furrowed. "Well, not exactly."

He lifted a brow.

She rolled her eyes. "Oh, all right. But it's not because you aren't capable of it."

He laughed. "If you are to condemn me for what I can do, instead of what I have done, you might as well sentence me to the gallows this instant."

She shuddered. "Nothing so dramatic."

He angled his head. "Thank you. Now, I expect you to accord Miss Matheson all the respect due my ward."

She narrowed her eyes. "I warn you, Valan, I will not be made a fool. If I discover she is not who you say she is—"

"Your warnings are unwarranted, my dear. You may recall that I am quite strict when it comes to your reputation."

"Well." Peigi smoothed her skirt. "That is true." She giggled. "Remember when you challenged poor Mr. Nicholson to a duel? I vow, I was sure you would kill him and be forced to flee to France—or worse, the Colonies."

"I believe it is you who is now being dramatic," he said.

"Not at all. That really was quite foolish of you. All over a kiss."

"While I am not known for bending the truth, you are. We both know it was more than a kiss."

Her eyes flashed. "Not so much to be worth a duel."

"Make no mistake, that is due only to the fact that I challenged him."

"You act as if I don't have a brain," she said.

He gave a low laugh. "You do, indeed, have a brain. That is what makes you so dangerous."

She narrowed her eyes. "I see. Women are your foes because we have a brain."

"If it were only your brains, we would be in no danger," he said with another laugh.

She lifted her chin. "You cannot blame us for being beautiful."

"Indeed, we can. But forget this silly debate. Come, I wish to show you my ward."

"You brought her here?" Peigi demanded.

"Of course." He sighed when her eyes narrowed. "Remember, Peigi, I will not compromise you. Please, have a look and you will see for yourself that she is nothing more than a child." He rose and extended a hand toward her.

"I can never really be angry with you." She laid a delicate hand in his and allowed him to pull her to her feet.

He led her from the drawing room and into a small study that over-looked the garden. To the far left, Miss Stone sat on the granite bench beside the rose bushes.

"Valan, she is twenty-five years old, if she's a day—and she is so demure. I can well believe you are not dallying with her but—" She broke off when Miss Matheson came into view. "What—" She looked up at him. "Her?"

He nodded. "Her."

Peigi returned her attention to the window. "She's quite beautiful. You can't expect me to believe—"

"I expect you to believe exactly what I've told you," he cut in.

She cast him a startled glance, then watched Miss Matheson for anoth-er moment before turning away from the window. "Why do you need my help with the party? You have servants."

"All fools," he said. "They will destroy every piece of furniture I own, then burn the house down in a funerary pyre."

"Lord, Valan, you're in a mood. What is wrong?"

"I would like this ball to go off well," he replied.

She studied him. "You are serious."

"I am," he replied. Still, she hesitated. Valan crossed to the bell pull near the door and rang for a servant.

"What are you doing?" Peigi asked.

"Introducing you to Miss Matheson."

A young maid appeared a moment later and Valan bade her bring Miss Matheson and Miss Stone to the sitting room. He returned with his cousin to the room and, a moment later, the maid brought the two women.

Jeanine's eyes met his and her face lit with a smile. "Did you see the roses, Grey? They are the most beautiful I have ever seen."

"We are not at home, Jeanine," he said. "You will address me as 'sir' or 'my lord.'"

"But this is your cousin's home. She is family." Her eyes shifted to Peigi. "Is this her? Of course, you are her," she went on before anyone could reply. Jeanine hurried across the room to the couch where Peigi sat. She gave a pretty curtsey then clapped her hands. "You are beautiful. Of course, I knew you would be. I wish I had blonde hair like yours. Mine is plain old brown. Your blue dress compliments your hair perfectly. Do you like Miss Stone's dress? Oh dear, we haven't introduced you to Miss Stone. How rude." Jeanine looked at Valan

"I was waiting for you to finish, my dear."

She wrinkled her nose. "Is that your way of saying that I talk too much?" She grinned. "You may proceed, *sir*."

He angled his head in thanks, then said, "Peigi, as you must have guessed, this is my ward Miss Jeanine Matheson, and this is her companion, Miss Stone."

Miss Stone curtsied and murmured, "My lady."

"Do you like Miss Stone's dress?" Jeanine asked. "Mrs. Morgan made it for her. I did her hair, but I think you could do better."

Peigi blinked. "I beg your pardon?"

"Your hair is so beautifully done that I know you can help Miss Stone with hers. I am only tolerably good at styling a lady's hair."

"Of course, I know how to style a lady's hair," Peigi said, "But it is Matilda who styled mine."

"But you directed her, I'm sure," Jeanine said. "And you would accept nothing less than perfection."

"That is true," Peigi demurred.

Jeanine beamed. "Would you do her hair for the party? You are coming, of course?"

Peigi looked at Valan and he lifted a brow. "Well, my dear," he said, "will you be attending?"

CHAPTER SEVEN

THE NEXT TEN DAYS flew by and Jeanine was surprised to find that the marquess was right. In his large home, she saw him but half a dozen times, and then only in passing. He had promised to attend tonight's party, but still, it was only just after breakfast, and waiting until the evening seemed an interminable amount of time not to see him. He made no appearance and Miss Stone's efforts to divert her attention were for naught.

"Perhaps we could shop for a fan to match the ivory gown you're to wear." Miss Stone finished refilling their teacups, then returned the pot to the tray and lifted her cup from the coffee table. "Mrs. Morgan suggested a fan."

Jeanine clasped the top edge of the sofa back and rested her cheek against her hand. "Do you think Grey doesn't like me anymore?"

"Of course, he likes you," Miss Stone said. "What would make you think otherwise?" She met Jeanine's gaze and sipped her tea.

"He's never around," Jeanine replied.

"He is an important man. I'm sure that business keeps him busy."

Jeanine sighed. "But it's almost as if he's avoiding me."

"I haven't noticed anything like that," Miss Stone said.

"Really? You're not trying to spare my feelings?"

"No, ma'am. I would never think of being anything less than honest with you."

Jeanine beamed. "That's what I like best about you, Miss Stone. You're not like so many others who only say what benefits them."

Miss Stone smiled serenely. "I have never been a good liar."

Jeanine laughed. "You say that as if it is a bad thing."

"There are times when it is best not to be forthcoming."

Jeanine grimaced. "You're right, of course. I often get into trouble by being too honest."

"Are you sure you don't want to go shopping? You will want to please his lordship by looking your best."

Jeanine lifted her head. "You're right."

Forty-five minutes later, they entered a small shop that sold only the finest ladies' fans. Jeanine took no more than ten minutes to choose a plain bone fan with a single hummingbird painted on it.

They left the shop and Jeanine linked arms with Miss Stone. "We are off on a special errand, Miss Stone."

Miss Stone looked at Jeanine, her expression perfect politeness, and she said, "Indeed, Miss Matheson?"

Jeanine nodded. "Indeed."

They waited for two passing couples, then started across the walk to their carriage. Their footman, seated next to Mr. Potts, the driver, spotted them and stood from the driver's seat. He leapt down and opened the coach door.

Jeanine brought herself and Miss Stone to a stop and shook her head. "We will be walking." She looked up at the driver. "Mr. Potts, can you tell me where we can find a shop that sells cravats?"

"I beg your pardon, Miss, cravats?"

She nodded.

"You want to go to a men's shop, Miss?"

"That is where they sell cravats," she said.

"Are you sure, Miss?"

"Sure that is where they sell men's cravats?" she asked. "Of course. Where else would I buy a cravat?"

"No, Miss. I mean, are you sure you want to go there? Ladies do not generally shop at a gentleman's clothing store," he said.

"How silly," she said. "If you do not know where a shop is, I'm sure I can get the direction from a passerby."

"Nae," he hurriedly replied. "In fact, I know the shop where his lordship gets his cravats."

"Perfect,' Jeanine cried. "Where is it?"

He exchanged a look with the footman, who shrugged, then said, "It isn't far. I will take you and Miss Stone."

"It's too beautiful a day to ride. We will walk. Just direct us, please."

His eyes widened in horror. "I cannae let you walk alone."

"Don't be silly," she said. "Where is the shop?"

He shook his head stubbornly. "His lordship will dismiss me if I let you walk alone—after he beat me, that is."

"Mr. Potts is right," Miss Stone said. "If you are set on walking, our footman should accompany us."

Jeanine smiled. "How clever of you."

The driver finally gave them directions, but said he would follow with the carriage so that he could take them home from the shop. They reached the shop in ten minutes and entered. To the left, two brown leather chairs resided near the window, separated by a table that held a tray containing a decanter of amber liquid and four glasses. To the right, shelves displayed cravats, hats, and other sundry man's articles in a multitude of colors.

A tall, wiry man, writing in a ledger, stood behind the long counter at the far end of the shop. He looked up and frowned. "May I help you?"

Jeanine crossed to the counter with Miss Stone alongside, and said, "We are looking for a cravat."

His frown deepened. "Are you sure you're in the right shop?"

"You do sell cravats," Jeanine said. "I see lots there on the shelves."

The man stiffened. "We sell *gentlemen's* cravats."

"I beg your pardon?" Miss Stone said. "A *gentleman's* cravat is exactly what Miss Matheson is looking for. She is shopping for the Marquess of Northington."

The man's eyes narrowed. "His lordship does buy his cravats here. But I feel certain you have the wrong shop. Ladies who purchase cravats—"

"This lady is Lord Northington's ward," Miss Stone cut in.

The man blinked in surprise, then his mouth thinned. "His lordship sends me an order when he desires more cravats. He does not send his *ward* to purchase them for him."

"You misunderstand," Jeanine said. "Gre-er, his lordship did not send me. I am buying him a gift."

"I believe I understand perfectly well, Miss."

"I am certain you do not," Miss Stone said in a chilly voice that startled Jeanine. "His lordship will not be pleased to hear that the man who sells him his cravats was so shockingly rude to his ward." She looked down her nose at him and waited.

Fifteen minutes later, they left the shop with a lovely ivory cravat, along with a dusky blue cravat, purchased at Miss Stone's suggestion. She said the color would complement Grey's dark eyes, and Jeanine was certain she was right. Their carriage sat in front of the shop with Mr. Potts in the driver seat and the footman waiting at the door. He opened the door as they approached, but Jeanine slowed at sight of another shop across the street. A sign over the door read Branby's Furniture and in the window were displayed chairs and tables.

"There's a shop across the street I would like to look at," Jeanine said, and started toward the street.

"Miss," Mr. Potts cried, "I must object. His lordship would not want you going about the city unescorted."

"Then we are in no danger of upsetting him." She waved a dismissive hand. "Miss Stone accompanies me, and you and Mr. McKinnon are only a few steps away."

Mr. Potts leapt from his perch and hurried to the curb as Jeanine and Miss Stone crossed the street. They reached the shop and entered. The room was nicely furnished with two chairs, a couch, two tables with lamps, and a sideboard that bore a crystal decanter and half a dozen tumblers.

A stalky man emerged from a curtained door behind a counter in the far left-hand corner of the room and halted. "May I help you?"

"I was hoping to purchase a table for Lord Northington," Jeanine said

The man frowned. "The Marquess of Northington?"

She nodded. "But it seems you don't have what I want."

The shopkeeper drew himself up. "My shop carries only the highest quality furniture. Perhaps something on Glenmore Street would be more to your taste."

"Miss Matheson is the Marquess of Northington's ward," Miss Stone said. "She does not shop on Glenmore Street."

The man frowned. "I hadn't heard he took a ward."

"He has," Miss Stone said in a chilly voice. "In fact, he's throwing a ball in her honor this very evening."

The man's head snapped in Jeanine's direction.

She nodded enthusiastically. "Perhaps you would like to come."

His eyes widened.

"I'm not certain his lordship would be pleased," Miss Stone said.

"He said I could invite guests," Jeanine said.

"He said you could invite friends from Lady Paddington's School for Young Ladies," Miss Stone pointed out.

Jeanine waved a dismissive hand. "Oh, pooh. It makes no difference." She smiled at the shopkeeper. "Surely, you would like to come? You know where we live, of course."

The man remained mute, but shook his head.

"Never mind," she said. "I can write it down for you. Oh, it is a shame you don't have a game table. You see, he had a game table, but it was broken, and it is my fault because Mrs. McPhee and the deliveryman got into a row."

"A row?" the man repeated.

She nodded. "Mrs. McPhee was angry with the deliveryman because she was certain he was trying to cheat Grey. I like Mrs. McPhee, but I think it was just a mistake. The deliveryman delivered too many vegetables--according to Mrs. McPhee, you understand. Gr-er, his lordship said he didn't think they were enough vegetables. They had a terrible disagreement and Mrs. McPhee punched him in the jaw."

"Punched him in the jaw?" the man mimicked.

"Exactly," Jeanine said. "Mrs. McPhee uses her right hand to knead dough, which means she is very strong. I think that is very fortunate, for a woman must be able to defend herself. Don't you agree?" She smiled before he could answer, and added, "Of course you do. When Mrs. McPhee punched the deliveryman, he crashed into the marquess's game table. So, if not for the fact that he was throwing this party in my honor, the deliveryman would never have come, and he and Mrs. McPhee would never have been fighting, and the table wouldn't have been broken. That makes it my fault. He didn't complain—the marquess, I mean—but he wouldn't, for his manners are too good." She slanted a glance at Miss Stone. "Isn't that so, Miss Stone?"

"Indeed, it is," she replied.

"There you are," Jeanine said. "The table was a very nice table, so it is only fair I should replace it." She sighed. "I do wish you had one."

The shopkeeper blinked. "But I do have one."

"You do?" she exclaimed. "Why didn't you say so in the first place?"

The man looked helplessly at Miss Stone, who shrugged. He sighed in obvious resignation and said, "If you will follow me, please," then turned.

He led them through the curtained door into a large storeroom crammed full of furniture. They weaved through the cramped rows and she spotted the game table beside a hideous green divan. When they reached the table, Jeanine knew it was exactly what she'd been looking for. The black and white checkered marble top was flawless. The dark wood, cherrywood, she guessed, perfectly complemented the marble. A drawer on the left side might hold cards and chess pieces while a lower shelf provided extra storage.

"It's beautiful," she breathed. "Do you like it, Miss Stone?"

"I believe his lordship will be very pleased," she said.

Jeanine looked at the shopkeeper. "Can you deliver it today, please?"

"Today? I would have to get a deliveryman."

Jeanine laughed. "Just be careful to bring only the table, or Mrs. McPhee is liable to punch him." The man's eyes widened, and Jeanine added, "No need to worry. I'll make sure she understands the table is to be delivered. Please say you can do it today. It would be a great favor, as the ball is this evening and I so want to surprise him beforehand. I must give you the address. That way you will know where to come to the party tonight."

"I am certain the Marquess of Northington would not include me on his guest list," the shopkeeper said.

"Why not? The party begins at eight. No one arrives at eight, I think—if they want to be fashionable, that is. But, of course, you know that." She smiled again and wondered why the shopkeeper had gone pale.

CHAPTER EIGHT

Y OU ARE SO CLEVER to suggest a walk in the park." Jeanine turned her face to the sun and slowed her walk alongside Lady Guilford. She closed her eyes and concentrated on the soft warmth that seemed to penetrate her bones. "I believe I was driving poor Miss Stone to distraction looking for something to do. She must be glad for a little time away from me."

"Walking is very good for the constitution," Lady Guilford said.

Jeanine opened her eyes in time to avoid a large bump in the path. "My mother often walks the path from our house to town," she said.

"Where is your town?" Lady Guilford asked.

"Perth."

A young couple passed them. Lady Guilford acknowledged them with a graceful cant of her head and they responded in kind. "Your mother allowed you to come to Edinburgh alone?" she asked when they'd passed the man and woman.

Jeanine shook her head. "Joshua brought me—well, he and my youngest sister and her husband. I suppose that means Rebecca and her husband are who brought me. Though it was Joshua's wagon and he drove."

"Who, pray tell, is Joshua?" asked Lady Guilford.

Jeanine spotted a butterfly hovering over a patch of lush heather, just off the path. "A lad I grew up with," she said as they approached, and the butterfly flitted away.

Lady Guilford cast her a sideways glance. "It was kind of this childhood friend to bring you all the way to Edinburgh."

"He is kind that way."

"I see. Will he take you back home?"

Jeanine looked sharply at her. "I don't plan to return. Grey promised to help me find an elderly husband."

Lady Guilford raised brow. "An elderly husband?"

Jeanine nodded. "Aye. I plan to use his money to open a school like Lady Peddington's."

Behind them, a creak of wheels approached and a phaeton passed them on a coach path to their left.

"I suppose Joshua doesn't approve of the idea of you running a ladies' school," Lady Guilford said.

Jeanine made a face. "Not in the least. He believes ladies should stay at home to cook, clean, and have their husband's children."

"He could not have been happy you preferred Edinburgh to marrying him."

"He wasn't at all pleased." Jeanine caught herself and frowned. "You tricked me. That was unkind of you."

"Not at all," Lady Guilford replied. "Is there some reason you would want to keep secret the fact that you have an admirer?"

"Nae," Jeanine hedged.

Lady Guilford gave her a penetrating stare and waited.

Jeanine relaxed. "It's just that if I don't find a gentleman to marry then I will have to return home and marry Joshua. I would be stuck in his cottage all day with a dozen of his children."

"Perhaps not a dozen," Lady Guilford said with a half-smile.

"One is too many," Jeanine said.

Lady Guilford sidestepped a rock. "Do you not want children?"

"They are a great deal of trouble," Jeanine said. "Do you have children?"

"Nae."

"There you go. You understand."

Lady Guilford nodded, but something in the slight downturn of her mouth gave Jeanine pause.

"Surely, there are men to choose from other than Joshua," Lady Guilford said. "You are young. Go home and let the young men court you."

Jeanine shook her head. "Oh, I can never return home," Jeanine replied. "My mother has remarried."

"Your mother has remarried," Lady Guilford began, then broke off when a man turned onto the path up ahead.

He neared. Something about him seemed familiar. Lady Guilford whispered unintelligible words under her breath. In the next instant, Jeanine recognized Lord Gordon. He lifted a hand and waved, then called out to them as he quickened his step.

He reached them, and they were forced to stop when he halted and bowed. "Lady Guilford, what a pleasure to see you."

"Lord Gordon," she replied in a cool voice.

He seemed not to notice, and looked at Jeanine. "A pleasure to see you, Miss Matheson. I did not know you liked to walk."

Jeanine followed Lady Guilford's example and replied in an aloof tone, "Of course, everyone likes to walk."

He smiled. "Quite right. May I have the pleasure of your company for the remainder of your stroll?" The question seemed directed at Jeanine, which struck her as rude, for he should have addressed Lady Guilford.

"We will be returning home soon," Lady Guilford said.

"It would be a pleasure to accompany you however far you go," he said, clearly oblivious to her reticence.

To Jeanine's surprise, he stepped to her right and winged an arm toward her. Jeanine looked at Lady Guilford for approval. She gave a curt nod and Jeanine wondered if she'd done something wrong, but slipped her hand into the crook of his arm.

"How is Lord Guilford, my lady?" he asked, and covered Jeanine's hand with his as they started forward.

"Quite well, thank you," she said.

Jeanine resisted the urge to pull her hand free of his as he prattled on about the weather, how lovely they both looked, and confirmed that they remained in good health.

"You must be terribly busy with plans for the ball your cousin is hosting tonight, Lady Guilford."

She gave a careless laugh. "No more than usual."

"I do believe all of Edinburgh is talking about the party," he said.

"It will likely be the ball of the season," she replied casually.

"With you at the helm, success is assured," he said. "Miss Matheson, you must be looking forward to this evening."

"Oh yes. I don't think I have ever attended a ball quite so large. Grey says at least three hundred people should attend. I'm not sure his ballroom will hold that many."

Lady Guilford shot her a warning look, and said, "Of course, it will."

A carriage rattled past followed by two men on horseback.

"It is certainly larger than any ball I have attended," Lord Gordon said.

"I cannot believe Gre—"

Lady Guilford looked sharply at her.

Jeanine realized her mistake, and amended, "—his lordship knows so many people."

"He is the Marquess of Northington and 6th Earl of Edmonds," Lord Gordon said. "He knows everyone."

"He is an earl, as well as a marquess?" Jeanine laughed. "I didn't know that."

They came to a Y in the path. Left, led to town. To the right, their carriage waited at the edge of the trees up ahead. They angled right. As they approached the carriage, the driver opened the door and stood aside.

Lord Gordon helped Lady Guilford into the carriage, then Jeanine. He grasped the door, then hesitated and said, "Forgive me for being forward, Miss Matheson, but I hope that I might call on you sometime soon at Finley Hall."

Jeanine started.

"You would have to speak with Valan about that," Lady Guilford interjected. "The ball is tonight, so he is busy, of course, and I believe he has business through next week."

His face fell, and he said in such a forlorn voice, "Of course," that Jeanine said, "We will see you at the ball?"

Hope lit his expression, and she was relieved when he looked to Lady Guilford for confirmation.

"Of course, you are coming," she said, but her words lacked warmth.

He beamed. "Most kind of you. I wouldn't think of missing it. Until tonight."

He closed the door and Lady Guilford stared out the window as the carriage rolled past the trees. They reached the street and the silence closed in on Jeanine.

"I have done something wrong, haven't I?" she said.

Lady Guilford looked at her. "I beg your pardon?"

"I know that I forget to call Grey 'his lordship' when we are in public. He told me I must do so, but his name is out of my mouth before I realize it. I am sorry. I know it's very improper."

"You must try to remember. Valan does not want any scandal associated with you."

"Why would there be scandal associated with me?"

Lady Guilford hesitated. "There won't be, so long as you conduct yourself appropriately."

Jeanine regarded her. "You don't like Lord Gordon very much. I don't think Grey likes him, either. I must admit, he can be annoying."

"He is much more than annoying," Lady Guilford said under her breath.

"Why do you think he asked to call on me?" Jeanine asked.

Lady Guilford snorted. "Because he cannot countenance Valan having something he does not."

Jeanine frowned. "You mean me."

Startlement crossed Lady Guilford's face. "Put my words out of your mind. I am talking out of place. Something Valan will not quickly forgive."

"I don't have to tell him that you said that. Not that is matters," Jeanine added. "I have no idea what you mean."

"Then there is no harm done," she replied. "Let's not mention it again."

"If you say so," Jeanine said, but she couldn't help thinking harm had been done.

* * *

Valan entered his house and paused in the foyer. The bustle of party preparations filtered throughout the mansion. The indistinct murmur of voices, the distant rattle of pots, quick footsteps. Clearly, the majority of the work had been done. Things were quiet compared to the tension and harried air that had permeated the house until yesterday.

He strode down the hallway to his library and went inside, pulling the door closed behind him. The faint noise cut off, and quiet descended. He hadn't been certain he would survive the preparations, but he had. He started for the sideboard located against the wall to the right of the hearth, then halted at sight of the game table sitting where his old game table had been.

He didn't remember buying a new table. Valan crossed to the table and stared at it. He traced a finger across the exquisite inlaid marble. The table might very well be finer than the one he had owned—even if it hadn't been in his family for three generations.

He slid open the drawer on the left-hand side and found inside the cards and game pieces that had filled the other table's drawer. Baldwin must've taken the liberty of replacing the table, which surprised him. Baldwin knew Valan's taste as well as he did himself, and the steward had not failed on this point, but Valan had never known him to take such initiative. Still, he couldn't complain.

A knock sounded on the door and Baldwin entered. "Forgive the inter-ruption, sir, but you have a visitor. Baron Rosemund."

"Show him in," Valan said. Baldwin started to turn, and Valan said, "Baldwin, I must thank you for the game table."

The steward shook his head. "I did not procure the table for you, sir. I believe that was Miss Matheson's doing."

"Indeed?" Valan replied. "Wonders never cease."

Baldwin left, and a moment later reappeared with Brendan. Baldwin bowed and closed the door as he left.

"I believe Baldwin grows more dour by the year," the baron said. "How long have you employed him?"

"Fifteen years," Valan said.

"Perhaps that explains his somber mood."

Valan gave him a dry look, then headed for the sideboard. "Have you come here simply to abuse me?"

Brendan laughed. "Forgive me. But you must admit that I am right."

Valan poured two glasses of sherry. "I must admit nothing of the sort. The party is tonight, my dear. You're very early and not dressed for the evening. Don't tell me you're here to say you cannot attend. I have plans for you tonight."

He crossed to his desk, handed Brendan one of the glasses, then mo-tioned to the chairs that faced the low-burning fire in the hearth.

"The knowledge you have plans for me is enough to have me come down with a fever and cry off," the baron said as he settled into one of the chairs. "What are these plans?"

"What would be the fun if I told you?" Valan replied.

"None for you, I imagine. I'm here to ask if you heard that Latham left Edinburgh."

Valan sipped his sherry. "I believe I did hear that bit of gossip."

"I fear it is more than gossip, Valan. He is nowhere to be found."

"One need only know where to look," Valan said.

Brandan's eyes narrowed. "You know where he is."

"I not only know where he is, I sent him there."

Brendan released a breath. "Then we need not worry on account of our investment."

"You need not," Valan said. "Though Latham will no longer be handling our business."

"What? But you said— What have you done?" Brendan asked.

"It is best you not ask," Valan answered. "Just rest easy that our investments are now in the hands of someone who won't try to steal them."

Shock registered on Brendan's face. "Embezzlement?"

"Attempted embezzlement," Valan said.

"Who's in charge now?" the baron asked.

Valan took another sip of sherry and smiled.

"Never say you are handling the shipments?" Brendan said. "Good God."

"Should I take offense?" Valan asked.

"What?" Brendan gave a distracted shake of his head. "Nae, it's just a shock. Embezzlement, and you running the company."

"Just long enough for us to receive payment," Valan said.

"Everyone will be glad to hear you took charge and saved us."

"Let us not say anything just yet," Valan said.

Brendan regarded him. "Johnston may not be too pleased."

"Nor Anthony."

Brendan nodded. "I will leave everything to you."

"Very sensible. Now, do you—"

Voices sounded outside the door and a quick knock followed, then the door opened and Jeanine and Miss Stone entered.

Jeanine clutched a flat box. When her gaze met Valan's, her face brightened. "I told you he was here." She hurried toward him. Miss Stone followed at a sedate pace.

"My God," Brendan murmured.

The ladies reached them and Valan and Brendan rose. Jeanine curtsied and looked up at Brendan. "Hello, sir."

"Brendan, this is my ward, Miss Matheson," Valan said. "Jeanine, may I present Baron Rosemund."

Brendan bowed over her hand. "A pleasure, Miss Matheson."

"How do you do, sir?" Jeanine replied, and before Valan could introduce Miss Stone, Jeanine said, "This is my friend, Miss Stone."

Brendan bowed over her hand. "Ma'am. Please, have my seat," he told Jeanine. I will fetch a chair for Miss Stone and myself."

"How very kind of you," Jeanine said. "Miss Stone, you sit. I have sat enough for today." Miss Stone took the offered chair and Jeanine then turned to Valan. "Did you see the table? Is it not beautiful? We found it today when we were shopping for this." She extended the box.

He took it. "What is this?"

She smiled. "Open it and find out, silly."

Brendan didn't successfully stifle his laughter. Valan removed the top and started at sight of two exquisite cravats lying side by side: one ivory, the other a dark blue.

He looked at Jeanine. "What are these for?"

"They're cravats. They're to wear," she said.

More low laughter from Brendan, who had placed another chair beside Miss Stone's chair.

"So, I see," Valan said. "To what do I owe the honor of this gift?"

"My mother says a man can never have too many cravats. I intended only to purchase the ivory, but Miss Stone said the blue would complement your eyes." Jeanine lifted the blue cravat and held it against his temple. She smiled. "She was right—not that I doubted her." Jeanine laid the cravat back in the box. "Do you not like them? Was my mother wrong, do you have too many cravats?"

"Never," he said. "The blue is particularly nice, and I don't believe I have one that color. Thank you."

"Shall we sit?" He pointed to his chair.

She shook her head. "We only came to give you the cravats and to see if you like the table. Do you like the table? You didn't say so. Oh dear, did we miscalculate? I was so sure you would like it."

"If you will permit me to explain," he said, "it is exquisite."

She beamed. "I knew you would like it. Well, we must go. Lady Guilford was very specific in saying that we must begin preparation for the party no later than six." Jeanine leaned close to him and said in a conspiratorial whisper, "She is a little frightening."

He laughed. "Indeed, she is."

"I plan to cheat just a little and go to the kitchen first and beg some chocolate and pastries from Mrs. McPhee," Jeanine said. "But we must be certain there is no chocolate left on our mouths when Lady Guilford arrives."

"Heaven forbid," he agreed with all seriousness.

"If you are ready, Miss Stone," Jeanine said.

Miss Stone stood. She nodded to Valan and Brendan, and murmured, "My lords," then started toward the door alongside Jeanine.

Jeanine halted and looked over her shoulder at Valan. "You will be at the ball?"

"Of course."

She nodded, and they left.

Valan reclaimed his seat beside Brendan.

"I don't believe it," Brendan said.

"Believe what, my dear?"

"She is not at all what I expected."

Valan looked at him. "What did you expect?"

"Well...a femme fatale, I suppose."

"Goodness, why would you expect that?"

Branden lifted a brow and grinned. "Because, my friend, that is the only kind of woman I've ever seen you with."

"Ah, I see your error." Valan finished off his sherry. "I am not 'with' Miss Matheson."

Brendan laughed. "Does she know that?"

CHAPTER NINE

JEANINE SCANNED THE CROWDED ballroom. "I don't see Grey anywhere. Do you, Miss Stone? Your superior height gives you an advantage."

"I am afraid I don't. It would seem everyone who received an invitation is here. I have never seen such a crowded ballroom."

"Oh, I see him," Jeanine said. "Is that him in the far left corner talking to that redheaded woman?"

"I believe you're right," Miss Stone said.

"We better hurry before we lose him," Jeanine said, and started forward.

Miss Stone kept up with her, oftentimes parting the way when people didn't see Jeanine.

"You're so fortunate to be tall," Jeanine said.

"If you say so, Miss Matheson."

They skirted a large crowd of women and Jeanine spotted the marquess with the woman.

"She's standing too close to him. Don't you agree, Miss Stone?" Jeanine said in a whisper.

"The ladies today are too fast," Miss Stone said in a prim voice.

The woman leaned even closer to him and laughed at something he said. Jeanine and Miss Stone neared him and he looked past the woman at Jeanine. She came to a stop in front of him with Miss Stone beside her.

His lordship smiled. "Good evening, Miss Matheson."

"Good evening, *sir*," she said.

Amusement tugged at his mouth. "Lady Claire, may I introduce my ward, Miss Matheson. Jeanine, this is Lady Claire."

Jeanine curtsied. "My lady."

Lady Claire gave a slight nod.

"And this is her companion, Miss Stone," the marquess said. "Miss Stone, I present Lady Claire."

Miss Stone curtsied. "My lady."

Lady Claire angled her head in a graceful nod.

"Are you enjoying the party?" he asked Jeanine.

She nodded. "It's very exciting. Miss Stone has already danced with two gentlemen."

The marquess smiled politely. "How very fortunate for the gentlemen."

"Lady Guilford made introductions," Miss Stone said. "The gentlemen could do no less than ask me to dance."

"That is not so." Jeanine looked at the marquess. "I am correct, am I not?"

"Quite correct," he agreed. "Rest assured, Miss Stone, my cousin simply knows how to pair up good dancers."

Miss Stone angled her head in acquiescence. "As you say, my lord."

Jeanine caught sight of a tall, wiry man standing just beyond the dance floor, scanning the large ballroom. "How grand. Look, Miss Stone, it is Mr. Craig." She nodded in his direction.

"Mr. Craig?" the marquess asked.

"I must fetch him," Jeanine said.

"Allow me," Miss Stone said, and started away.

"May I ask, who is Mr. Craig?" his lordship asked.

"Of course. You will not be surprised," Jeanine said.

"I pray not, but I am curious to know how you made the acquaintance of a gentleman I am unaware of."

Jeanine laughed. "You're not unaware of him—not really. He is the gentleman who owns the shop where I purchased the game table."

"Game table?' Lady Claire repeated.

"Aye," Jeanine said. "I had to replace it because—"

"I think we can forego the telling of that tedious story," Grey interrupted.

Jeanine's heart fell. "Aye."

Miss Stone arrived with Mr. Craig. She made introductions and Mr. Craig bowed stiffly. "My lord, I hope I am not intruding. Miss Matheson was quite adamant that I attend. If this is an intrusion, I understand."

"Not in the least," the marquess said. "Miss Matheson may invite any-one she likes. You are welcome at Finley Hall."

Jeanine caught the look of surprise that Lady Claire couldn't quite hide.

The marquess introduced Mr. Craig to Lady Claire. The man bowed low again and Jeanine wondered if he might break in half.

The orchestra struck up a waltz. "A waltz," she cried. "How enlight-ened of you to have the orchestra play a waltz, sir. This is perfect. You promised me a dance."

His lordship lifted a brow. "I don't remember that promise."

"Oh yes, you did—and you cannot say you have forgotten because you are old, because you are not."

"But if I have forgotten, then it must be from age."

She grinned. "Then you admit you promised."

"Very clever, my dear, but I admit nothing of the kind."

She shrugged. "I suppose if you cannot remember, I will have to settle for dancing with Lord Pomeroy."

"Lord Pomeroy is not the sort of man you should dance with, partic-ularly the waltz."

"But I promised. I cannot break my promise."

His eyes narrowed slightly, then he addressed Lady Claire. "You'll have to excuse me, Lady Claire."

She gave him a pretty pout, and Jeanine repressed a roll of her eyes when the pout leaked into her voice, "But you promised me a walk, my lord." She looked at him through her lashes. "I feel certain you have not forgotten *that* promise."

He caught her hand and brushed his lips across her fingers. "I have not forgotten. But that will have to wait." He released her hand, and turned. "Sir," he said to Mr. Craig, and then to Miss Stone, "Miss Stone."

Jeanine glimpsed the startlement on Lady Claire's face before the woman's eyes narrowed. Then his lordship cupped Jeanine's elbow and turned her toward the dance floor.

At the edge of the dance floor, he swung her into his arms, his right hand pressed lightly against her back, his left clasping her right hand. He stepped back to arm's length, then pulled her into the music with flawless rhythm. He steered them around a couple who nearly collided with them, then turned her in a tight circle that took her breath. Jeanine laughed, and when she looked up at him, he was smiling down at her. She smiled back and slid right as the press of his hand on her back cued her.

"You are an excellent dancer," she said. "Not at all too old."

"I never said I couldn't dance." His express turned serious. "I would prefer you didn't dance with Lord Pomeroy."

"Is he a rake?" she asked.

"He is."

"You are afraid my reputation will be tarnished."

"Something like that," he said.

She shrugged. "I don't really like him."

"But you would have danced with him, despite my request that you not."

"I will not dance with him, if you prefer I don't."

"That's very generous of you, considering you coerced me into dancing with you."

She gave him a bright smile.

An answering smile tugged at the corners of his mouth before he said in mock sternness, "Perhaps it isn't you I need worry about, but the gentlemen you bewitch."

She laughed again and said no more.

Three dances later, Mr. Westland escorted Jeanine from the dance floor and she had to admit she was fatigued.

"You look as though you could use some refreshment," he said.

They approached a large alcove, but Jeanine stopped when it seemed he might continue inside. Lady Guilford had been very specific in her instructions that Jeanine was, under no condition, to enter an alcove alone with any gentleman.

She looked up at Mr. Westland. "I am thirsty."

He smiled. "Let me fetch you some punch."

She gave him a grateful smile before he left. Jeanine looked for a place to sit, but there was no place, save the alcove. She considered. After all, she wasn't with a gentleman, so she wouldn't be disobeying Lady Guilford. Jeanine sighed. Mr. Westland would return and then she would be alone with him in the alcove. The open balcony doors, thirty feet to her right, beckoned. She could cool off outside for a moment or two, then return before Mr. Westland made it back.

She wound her way through the crowd and out onto the balcony, which she was surprised to find deserted save for a couple who occupied a bench in the shadows of the far corner. At her appearance, they rose and hurried down the half dozen steps onto the lawn. She sat on the bench in the shadows to the left of the door, near the railing, and watched until the couple were silhouettes beyond the ballroom lights, and then disappeared amongst the darker shadows of trees and bushes.

Lady Claire had said that Grey promised her a walk in the gardens. Jeanine hadn't seen him since their dance. Had he taken Lady Claire for that walk? Maybe they still lingered in the gardens. She breathed deep of the fresh air. The night was warm, but cooler than the stuffy ballroom. Maybe Grey would take her for a walk.

So far, she hadn't met a single gentleman who suited her purposes. How long could she remain Grey's ward if she didn't find a proper husband soon? He said he would help her. That had to mean he would send her home until he found her a suitable husband, as he'd promised. Had he an elderly gentleman in mind? When she thought about it, it wasn't surprising that an elderly gentleman wasn't at the ball. How could a gentleman that old attend a ball? Well, perhaps he could, if he remained seated. But that would be no fun at all.

Tomorrow, she would ask Grey about his plans. Jeanine thought about Miss Stone. What would happen to her once she married? Jeanine would have to bring her to her new household. She couldn't allow her to leave without a good position, because too many employers mistreated companions.

A man and woman emerged from the ballroom. Jeanine's gaze lingered on the lady's dark blue satin dress. She planned to ask Mrs. Morgan if she could make a dress of that color for Miss Stone.

The couple slowed, and the woman said, "Did you see them on the dance floor—and after the way he was carrying on with Lady Claire?"

Jeanine's mind snapped to attention.

"The Morning Star is a master of deceit," she said. "That girl cannot be an innocent."

Jeanine jumped to her feet. "How dare you say such a thing."

The man and woman whirled.

Jeanine stalked to where they stood. "His lordship was perfectly proper with me."

The woman's eyes widened and she glanced at the man, who said, "You misunderstand, my dear."

"I didn't misunderstand anything. G-Grey has been very proper, he even held me at arm's length on the dance floor—which you would have noticed if you weren't so spiteful."

The woman gasped. "How dare you?"

"How can you tell such horrid lies?" Jeanine demanded.

"They aren't lies," the woman spat. "Everyone knows the Morning Star is the worst sort of man."

"D-don't call him that, you mean woman."

The woman's eyes shifted past Jeanine and a male voice drawled, "How very pleasant it is to find you here on the balcony, Lord Fletcher." The marquess halted beside Jeanine. "You're looking lovely, Lady Fletcher. I have been hoping for the opportunity to thank you both for attending tonight's little party."

"It is an honor," Lord Fletcher said. "Thank you for the invitation. However, I believe it is getting late. I must get Margaret home."

The marquess gave a bland smile. "I quite agree."

Lord Fletcher cupped his wife's elbow. "Good night, my lord." He bowed. "Miss Matheson."

They started away. Jeanine turned and watched them reenter the ballroom. "She is a mean and s-spiteful woman," Jeanine said.

"There is no need to excite yourself, my dear," the marquess said.

"But she said awful things about you."

"If I got upset every time someone said awful things about me, I would be upset all the time. "

"Sometimes I d-despise people," she said.

"You are a better person than me," he said. "I despise them all the time. Come, let us sit." He urged her back to the bench where she'd been sitting and lowered himself onto the seat as she sat.

"Why are people so cruel?" she asked.

"The reasons are far too numerous to name and not worth our time," he replied. "Lady Fletcher has a love of gossip and isn't above creating a juicy story if no real tale exists."

"I know," Jeanine said. "She lied outright about you."

"It isn't the first time someone lied about me, and will not be the last. In fairness, Lady Fletcher is not wholly to blame. I invite gossip by living as I please without regard for *Society*."

"That only means you are courageous," she said.

His brows shot up. "How, may I ask, came you to this conclusion?"

She waved a dismissive hand toward the open doors. "They are sheep who follow what *Society* dictates because they do not have the courage— or intelligence—to think for themselves. They are jealous that you do as you please, so they lie to salve their egos."

He stared at her, a strange light in his eyes. "Just the other day, I was told you aren't a grown woman."

"Who said that?" she demanded.

He laughed. "My dear, you are contrary."

Lady Guilford emerged from the ballroom and glanced around the balcony. When her gaze landed on them, she hurried to the bench. "There you are, Jeanine. You are to dance with Mr. Ross soon."

Jeanine shook her head. "I don't want to dance anymore tonight."

"You promised him a dance."

His lordship stood. "If you promised Mr. Ross a dance, then you must dance with him."

"I don't feel like dancing."

His gaze locked with hers. "A lady does not break her promise without good reason."

"I have a good reason. I am angry."

That is *not* a good reason." His expression hardened. "Lady Guilford has worked hard to make this soiree a success. You will not disgrace her *or* me."

Jeanine jumped to her feet. "I would never do that."

"I'm relieved to hear you say so."

"I will not give those scorpions a reason to say anything bad about you on my account." Jeanine grasped his hand. "You believe me, don't you?"

Startlement flickered through his eyes before he gave a gentle smile. "Aye, lass. I believe you. Now, go with my cousin and do as she asks. She knows best what to do at parties like this. An old bachelor like me, I am too out of practice."

She released his hand and snorted. "You may say that all you like, but I am not fooled. You danced with me better than anyone else I danced with tonight."

He laughed. "Go, before I decide that my ward deserves a beating."

She grinned. "You would never do that. But I will go."

CHAPTER TEN

JEANINE REENTERED THE BALLROOM with Lady Guilford and realized the orchestra was playing a country dance. A good stroke of luck that. At least the dance she would share with Mr. Ross would not be a shorter dance. Lady Guilford slipped along the wall and halted at the corner of the ballroom near the hallway leading to the refreshments table, and scanned the still crowded room.

"We may not find him in time for the next dance," she said more to herself than Jeanine.

Jeanine watched the dancers, suddenly irritated by the loud murmur of voices. She'd never attended a party this large back home. A party with more than a hundred people would have been considered a huge success.

The marquess reentered the ballroom and Jeanine wished that she could dance with him again. He really was a much better dancer than any other partner she'd danced with. She forgot to ask if he had found an elderly gentleman for her.

Lady Claire stepped up behind him and touched his arm. He turned and Jeanine glimpsed his smile when he saw the lady. She leaned close—too close for propriety—and said something. Jeanine couldn't discern his expression, but he leaned a little closer.

"Does Grey know Lady Claire well?" she asked Lady Guilford.

Lady Guilford looked in the direction Jeanine stared. "Well enough," she replied. "Lady Claire's brother is in negotiations with Valan for her hand in marriage."

Jeanine looked sharply at her. "They are to be married?"

Lady Guilford again scanned the ballroom. "Where is Mr. Ross?"

"I didn't know that Grey was to marry," Jeanine said.

"He wouldn't say anything. He is an intensely private man." She laughed. "Despite the fact that he constantly flaunts his improprieties to society. But there is a method to that madness."

"What do you mean?" Jeanine said

Lady Guilford cast her a side glance. "Never mind."

"When will they marry?" Jeanine asked.

"No contract has been signed, and if Valan doesn't take care for his reputation, her brother will retract the offer."

"But he is a marquess—and an earl—not to mention, he is very wealthy. Why would her brother do that?"

"Even a title and money does not save a man from closed doors, if he goes too far. Three years ago, Lord Ingers married a bastard girl barely out of the schoolroom. He found all doors closed to him. He moved to the country and, three years later, his young wife ran off with a navy captain. He never returned to *Town*."

"That could never happen to Grey," Jeanine said. "He is too... too intelligent to let that happen."

"Lady Claire's family does not need a title or money. An alliance must be without reproach," Lady Guilford said. "In truth, I am surprised the family is interested in the connection. Though, ours is a very old family."

Janine started to ask if Grey wanted to marry her, but stopped when he smiled down at Lady Claire. He certainly acted like a man who might consider marriage. What would happen if they married before Jeanine found an elderly gentleman to marry? Would Grey send her away? If his new wife wanted it, yes.

Two dances later, Jeanine decided she really had danced enough for one evening. The gentlemen were polite enough, but they were too young—they would live at least twenty years, maybe thirty—and she'd heard more than enough about new jackets, new horses, and how pretty her eyes were to last a lifetime. She hadn't seen Miss Stone in over an hour. Perhaps she had been smart enough to slip away. Jeanine scanned the ballroom as best as her diminished height would allow, but found no sign of Miss Stone. Perhaps she could slip away too. But she discarded the idea as quickly as it formed, for she knew that Grey would not be pleased, as the party was held in her honor.

She turned to the right to find Miss Stone two steps away. "Miss Stone," she said when her companion reached her, "I've never been so happy to see anyone in my life."

"I am flattered, Miss Matheson. But, surely, you have spoken with many people far more interesting than me tonight."

Jeanine shook her head. "You couldn't be more wrong. Most of the people I spoke with are very dull."

"I find that hard to believe," Miss Stone whispered. "Tonight's guests are among *Society's* most elite. They are highly educated."

"Educated about pretty clothes and horses." Jeanine snorted. "Oh, and food. I have never met so many people obsessed with food."

"One must know good food in order to entertain," Miss Stone pointed out.

Jeanine sent her a deprecating look. "You're being too kind. I think—" She broke off when two young ladies bypassed a nearby group of men, their eyes on Jeanine.

They stopped in front of her. She had met the girls earlier in the evening, but couldn't recall their names. A frantic search of memory failed to provide any trace of their names.

"Miss Smith." Miss Stone angled her head toward the girl on their left. "Lady Bethany." Miss Stone looked at the other girl then curtsied, and Jeanine could have kissed her.

The two girls acknowledged Miss Stone with a bare nod, then looked at Jeanine as Miss Smith said, "Bethany is hosting a card party tomorrow afternoon. You simply must come."

"Tomorrow afternoon?" Jeanine repeated, and Lady Bethany nodded.

"Do say you will come," Bethany said.

Their eyes remained fixed on Jeanine, as if Miss Stone didn't exist.

"I *adore* cards," Jeanine adopted the same exaggerated, cultured tones the girls used. "We would be delighted to come."

They blinked in surprise.

"We?" Lady Bethany repeated.

Jeanine nodded with exaggerated enthusiasm. "Oh yes, Miss Stone is a wonderful Pharo player."

"Pharo?" the girls said in unison, then exchanged a glance.

"Lord Northington will be pleased to hear that I'm getting out," Jeanine went on as if not noticing their discomfort. "Just yesterday, he commented that Miss Stone and I must accept more invitations."

"Of course," Lady Bethany quickly agreed, and Jeanine had to force back a disgusted roll of her eyes. "I am so pleased you can come," Lady Bethany went on with the same sickening fervor.

Jeanine curtsied. "We are pleased to accept, my lady."

Irritation flicked in the girl's eyes, but she smiled brightly. "Wonderful. I will send round my direction in the morning."

Lady Bethany turned, and Miss Smith followed like an obedient lap dog. They halted as a group of elderly matrons strolled past and Miss Smith said to Lady Bethany in a loud whisper, "Of all the nerve, inviting *her.*"

"It was all I could do to remain civil," replied Lady Bethany.

Jeanine looked sharply at Miss Stone, who seemed oblivious to the insults. That was impossible, however. Miss Stone was too intelligent not to know the malicious creatures were referring to her. Jeanine took a step toward them, then halted when Miss Stone grasped her arm.

"I cannot allow you to get into trouble on my account," Miss Stone whispered.

"They deserve to be lashed," Jeanine hissed back.

"Perhaps," Miss Stone replied, "but you mustn't allow them to goad you into doing something that will embarrass you."

"You can't expect culture from a country girl," Lady Bethany said.

Miss Stone took two quick steps to where the girls stood, backs to them. Her slippered toe appeared from beneath her skirt and tamped down on the hem of Miss Smith's satin dress.

"There you are, Miss Stone."

Jeanine whirled to the left at the soft drawl of the marquess's voice. He smiled at her, then turned his attention to Miss Stone, who now faced him, hands clasped before her.

The elderly ladies passed, and the two girls began walking, oblivious to the near ruin of Miss Smith's dress.

"I must compliment you on your pink slippers, Miss Stone," his lordship said.

Miss Stone smiled serenely. "Thank you, sir, but Mrs. Morgan sewed them. All credit must go to her."

"I see. Perhaps I will ask Mrs. Morgan to sew another pair."

"That is too kind of you, my lord, and unnecessary. These are sufficient."

"Aye," he replied. "But you need a pair that doesn't have a mind of their own."

Jeanine seriously pondered escape. Surely, in these wee hours of the morning, Grey could not fault her for going to bed. Thankfully, some guests had left, but two-thirds remained. One might think they vied for the right to boast that they were the last to leave the Marquess of Northington's party.

"I was hoping to have a moment alone with you."

Jeanine turned at the sound of Lord Gordon's voice.

"You are looking well," he said. "How clever of you to keep up such a brave face."

If ever there was a reason to escape, Lord Gordon provided that reason.

He smiled down at her. "Soon, this will all be over, and I will have you safely out of his reach."

She must be very tired. The man was speaking gibberish. "What will be over?"

He gave her a pitying look. "You are such a sweet innocent." He cupped her elbow and urged her back toward the wall, away from a cluster of nearby ladies. "You may put your faith in me," he whispered. "I have set a plan into motion that will cast him out of *Society* for good."

Her mind snapped to attention. "I beg your pardon?"

"This is not the first time I have saved an innocent from his clutches," he went on.

Her heart began to pound. "What do you mean?"

He hesitated, though she sensed his hesitation was intended to achieve dramatic effect. It took all her willpower not to seize his shoulders and shake the words from him.

"Of course, you wouldn't have heard," he said. "You were not yet born when *The Morning Star* cast his spell upon the first of his notable victims. Since then, he has made a career of ruining innocents like yourself."

A righteous fervor lit his eyes, and Jeanine refrained from shrinking away.

"At least I was able to save that young woman from a life of ruin." He gave a bitter laugh. "He actually told the poor girl that he wanted to marry her. Can you imagine? The Morning Star in love?"

"What did you do?" Jeanine whispered.

The light in his eyes vanished and he blinked as if startled by her presence. "I have frightened you." He grasped her hand and squeezed. "Forgive me. Let us not speak of this again. Rest easy that he shall not have you." He released her hand and started to turn away, then hesitated as if caught in some terrible inner battle. He looked at her. "I will save you. I only pray that when all is revealed, you will understand why I had to take such drastic measures."

"What drastic measures?" she demanded, but he hurried past the group of ladies.

Jeanine froze for an instant, heart pounding, then started after him. She had to know what he intended. She skirted the ladies, then passed another, smaller group of younger ladies and slowed. He was nowhere in sight.

"Look, she's even chasing after him," a woman whispered behind her.

Jeanine slowed.

"I have it on good authority that she and the marquess were caught together in his library with her kneeling between his legs."

Titters went up.

"That is scandalous, even for the marquess," said another girl.

Jeanine started to face them, then caught herself. She could not make a scene in the ballroom. Grey had been very specific in saying she was not to disgrace him.

Her heart twisted. She could think of only one way to ensure she didn't disgrace him.

CHAPTER ELEVEN

VALAN ENTERED THE BREAKFAST room the following morning to find Jeanine staring at her ham and eggs.

She looked up. "Good morning, sir."

Valan lifted a brow as he took his place at the head of the table. "Sir? I have never known you to be so formal at home." He picked up the pot of coffee and filled his cup. "Are you ill?"

Jeanine frowned. "What? Oh, nae. I just—" She hesitated. "I suppose I am still in the mindset of last night's party, surrounded by so many strangers."

Valan forked a slice of ham from the platter and spooned eggs onto his plate. "Did you enjoy the party?"

She nodded. "Of course. It was very gay, was it not?"

"I suppose it was," he said. "But you don't sound enthused."

She smiled, though the smile didn't reach her eyes. "I am just a little tired. It was a great deal of excitement."

"That it was," he agreed. "What plans have you for today?" He took a sip of coffee, then nodded toward the tray of invitations sitting near the edge of the table between them. "It looks as though you and Miss Stone have become much sought after."

Her eyes snapped onto the tray and her expression darkened. "We were invited to a card party. By Lady Bethany. Today."

Valan buttered a triangle of toast. "I assume you will attend?"

"Yes, I would like to attend very much—with Miss Stone, of course."

Valan angled his head in agreement. "Of course. It would be quite rude to leave Miss Stone at home while you attended a party."

Relief flooded her expression. "That is exactly what I thought."

"Is Miss Stone amenable to going?"

"She wasn't, at first. I told her it was only fair that she go with me. You said it would be rude to leave her home," Jeanine added. "But that is the same thing, don't you agree?"

"I agree wholeheartedly," he said. "Miss Stone must surely accompany you." He would give five hundred pounds to see Lady Bethany's face when Jeanine arrived with Miss Stone.

Jeanine gave him a real smile. "I am so glad you agree. Now, Miss Stone cannot refuse to go with me."

"Do you think she would have refused?"

She nodded, then quickly added, "But not because she is stubborn, you understand. She is very aware of propriety—too much so, if you ask me—and she did not want to attend a party where she might be intruding."

"Miss Stone could never intrude," he said, and sipped more coffee.

"That's exactly what I told her. Anyone who thinks differently, well, they deserve what they get."

Valan cut his ham. "What might they get?"

Her gaze sharpened. "I don't know, exactly. But I'm sure it would be unpleasant."

"Just remember, my dear, that the unpleasantness that happens to people who deserve those things, should be dished out by unpleasant people. Not young ladies."

Her eyes widened in surprise, then a twinkle animated the blue orbs, and he was oddly relieved. "Must you take the fun out of everything, Grey?"

He should have been insulted. Instead, he experienced relief that she called him by name. "Forgive me, my dear, but I feel I must. If only to keep my own neck out of the noose."

The twinkle abruptly vanished and her expression clouded over. "You are right, of course." She returned her attention to her food and seemed to consider, then said, "I believe I have changed my mind, I do no' want to attend the card party."

"Really?" he said. "Only a moment ago, you were excited at the prospect. What has changed in so short a time?" He forked eggs into his mouth and chewed.

She stabbed a bit of ham, moved it to the opposite side of her plate, and used a knife to free it from the tines. "Playing cards is a bore, don't you think?"

"I didn't think so when you won at commerce two weeks ago."

"That is very different. Playing cards, gambling with gentlemen, is far more interesting than playing piquet with ladies who don't truly understand the game."

He would have trouble arguing with that logic. "Perhaps, but there will be a luncheon, maybe a walk in the garden, and even gossip. You cannot tell me that you do not like gossip."

Her head snapped up, and he was startled at the fear in her eyes. "I detest gossip." She laid down her fork. "I am finished with breakfast." She pushed back her chair and rose.

Valan opened his mouth to remind her that a lady always excused herself before leaving a room, but stopped short when he glimpsed a shimmer of moisture in her eyes an instant before she turned and hurried from the room. He leaned back in his chair, staring at the doorway, his mind on last night.

* * *

The carriage approached the home and Jeanine was surprised at the size of the mansion. "Lord Gordon's home is larger than Grey's," she said to Miss Stone. "I imagined that Grey had more money than him."

"The size of a man's house does not necessarily indicate his true wealth," Miss Stone said. "His lordship is a man of genteel taste. He will not flaunt his wealth. I am not certain the same can be said of Lord Gordon."

"I suppose you are right," Jeanine said. Lord Gordon certainly didn't have Grey's manners.

The carriage stopped, then tilted to the right as the footman left the perch beside Mr. Potts and descended to the cobblestone. He opened the door and helped them down. Half a dozen other carriages lined the street.

"We will wait here for you, Miss," Mr. Potts said.

"Jeanine smiled up at him. "Thank you, Mr. Potts."

She and Miss Stone started up the walk.

"I must advise against your course of action once more, Miss Matheson," Miss Stone murmured. "I feel certain his lordship can deal with Mr. Gordon."

Jeanine shook her head. "He will advise us to ignore Lord Gordon. I cannot allow Grey's reputation to be blemished on my account. If he wishes to marry Lady Claire, then we must help him."

"I find it difficult to believe he wants to marry her," Miss Stone said.

"Lady Guilford said they discussed marriage negotiations. Men don't enter into marriage negotiations if they don't want to be married."

They reached the door and it opened before they could knock. A somber butler led them down the hallway and upstairs to the first floor. Jeanine spotted servants' stairs to her left as they passed. Two doors down, they reached a parlor and entered.

Jeanine blinked against the glare of the room's bright purples and blues. "My goodness," she blurted, then looked at Miss Stone, whose expression remained bland. Only the hint of disdain in her dark eyes gave away her true feelings. Miss Stone was right. Lord Gordon's taste was not as refined as Grey's.

Two dozen people occupied the room, some at cards tables, some sitting on divans and chairs drinking tea, chatting.

"Miss Matheson." Lord Gordon approached from her right.

Jeanine smiled, and hoped her shock at seeing a bright yellow waistcoat beneath his jacket wasn't obvious. She forced her eyes to meet his and not linger on the ridiculously complex cravat that hung halfway down his chest. He reached them and grasped her hand, then pressed his lips to the back of her hand.

She froze the smile on her face and said, "You remember Miss Stone?"

He bowed, but didn't take Miss Stone's hand. "Of course. A pleasure to see you again, Miss Stone." The words were proper, but Jeanine caught frustration in his voice.

He led them to a table, ordered a maid to bring tea and cake, then launched into inane chatter about the weather, food, and upcoming parties, until Jeanine wanted to scream. She had to break free of him and have a look around the house.

"The ball last night was quite fantastic," he said.

Jeanine nibbled on cake and nodded. "Lady Guilford's efforts made the party an enormous success."

"Indeed," he said. "Indeed. Do you play cards, Miss Stone?"

"No more than passably, sir. Miss Matheson is the expert card player."

"Lady Melanie has despaired of being able to find players. Perhaps you would oblige and play with her."

"As I said, sir, I play only a passable game. I doubt I would offer any challenge."

"But you would," he said. "Lady Melanie is a new player, so could use a patient player like yourself to lend guidance."

"I regret that I must decline," Miss Stone said. "I must remain with my charge."

"Nonsense," Jeanine said. "You have nothing to fear by leaving me to play cards. I will be nearby with Lord Gordon."

Lord Gordon puffed out his chest like a ridiculous peacock. "There you have it, Miss Stone." He rose. "Let me introduce you to Lady Melanie."

Miss Stone glanced at Jeanine, and Jeanine noted genuine concern in her expression. This was the first time she and Miss Stone had disagreed. Shame wormed its way through her. Miss Stone's concerns were founded.

"I must remind you, Miss Matheson, that his lordship instructed us to return after one hour."

A total lie, and one Jeanine hadn't prepared for.

Miss Stone looked at Lord Gordon. "You will forgive us if we don't stay long. His lordship has dinner plans, and allowed us to leave only after extracting the promise that we would not be late."

Irritation flashed in his eyes and he said in a too-genial voice, "Of course, Miss Stone. I shall make it my mission to escort you to your carriage within the allotted hour."

Miss Stone rose, albeit, Jeanine knew, with reluctance, and accompanied Lord Gordon to a table in the far corner of the room near the balcony. The young lady at the table looked to be barely out of the schoolroom. As soon as Lord Gordon turned his back, Jeanine rose and hurried to the door through which they had entered. She slipped from the room, found the hallway empty, and sprinted in the direction they'd come. A second later, she reached the servants' stairs and bounded up the winding staircase.

Light spilled around a curve up ahead. Heart pounding, Jeanine raced up the final stairs and burst into a well-lit hallway. She halted, breathing hard, and strained to hear above the rush of blood in her ears. She saw no one. Not surprising. This had to be Lord Gordon's private chambers. At this time of day, servants might not be allowed on this floor, and most were likely busy with the party.

She tried three doors, found a bedchamber she assumed was Lord Gordon's, but nothing to indicate what he'd meant when he told her he had a plan to cast Grey out of *Society* for good. The next door opened to a private study. She headed for the large mahogany desk at the far end of the room. She had been away from the card room fifteen, maybe twenty minutes. By now, Lord Gordon would believe she had left—or perhaps gone to the garden, if he had one. Miss Stone would have joined the search for her. It was unlikely he would think she'd come upstairs, but anxiety knotted her stomach, nonetheless.

She sat down at the desk and began searching through drawers, but found only paper, pen, personal correspondences that seemed meaningless, and business papers concerning properties he held in the north of Scotland. She opened the bottom right drawer and found several envelopes bound together by a ribbon. Jeanine slid aside the bow that covered the center of the top envelope and started at sight of Grey's first name on the envelope.

With shaking fingers, she tugged the bow free, then untied the ribbon and withdrew the top letter from its envelope.

My dearest Valan,

As usual, I find it easier to put down on paper the words I cannot say. Since becoming your ward, my life had taken on new meaning. It matters not to me what the future holds, so long as we are together. I care nothing for what Society says. I am yours as long as you will have me.

Yours,

Jeanine

Her heart pounded so fiercely, she became lightheaded. She opened a second letter written in a different hand.

My darling Jeanine,

Forget Society. They have never been a friend of mine. I will take you away from here where no one will know us. Never fear, I will not allow harm to come to you or the child you carry... Our child.

Yours forever, Valan

Our child?

Anger twisted through her. She hadn't written these letters. Since she hadn't written these letters, it only made sense that Grey hadn't written the others. And the child that she carried? There was no child. They had never...

Lies. Terrible, vicious lies.

She remembered Lady Fletcher and the girls who had spoken so ill of her and Grey. How many lies were being told about Grey? Now this? But why this?

Then she understood. Lord Gordon had created these terrible lies with the intention of ruining Grey. But why? No one would believe them. Miss Stone lived with them. She could attest to how proper their household ran.

She was not with child. That would prove these were lies. But Grey's reputation would be destroyed before anybody knew they were lies. A mixture of rage and fear brought tears to her eyes. She would not let Lord Gordon do this.

Jeanine quickly gathered the letters and retied the bow. Grey would know what to do. She stood, then hesitated. She couldn't give him the letters. He would be furious. Not because Lord Gordon tried to ruin him, but because Lord Gordon's plan would have ruined her. She didn't know him well, but that much she did know.

The letters had to be destroyed. But that wouldn't be enough, she realized with rising panic. Lord Gordon would only write more. How could she stop him?

She swiped at a tear.

She couldn't. Jeanine thought of Lady Claire. Grey wanted a respectable marriage. She couldn't allow anything to get in his way, even her.

She hurried toward the door. Two steps from the door, it opened. Jeanine came to an abrupt halt. Lord Gordon stood in the doorway. His eyes dropped to the letters she held.

He stepped inside the room and closed the door. "The entire household is searching for you. It never occurred to me you might be here." He took a step toward her and she retreated. He stopped. "There is no need to be afraid. Remember what I told you, that I hoped you would understand why I had to do what I did?"

Jeanine said nothing.

"I will care for you. You will never want for anything. I will marry you."

"M-Marry me?" Jeanine shook the letters in front of her. "I will b-be ruined."

He frowned. "Do you have a speech impediment?"

"Aye. You cannot want a woman who s-stutters."

His frown deepened. "We can deal with that later."

Her mind raced. "I will be ruined. Surely, you c-cannot want to marry a woman whose reputation was ruined by the Marquess of Northington."

"Northington will be blamed," he said. "He is not called *The Morning Star* for nothing. People will understand, and they will draw you into their hearts once you have married me."

"I will no' m-marry you," she spat.

He smiled in what she knew was meant to be comforting, but the effect was undone by the anger that blazed in his eyes. "You do not understand. I know what's best."

Jeanine straightened. "I wish to leave."

He went to a small table beside the door, opened the drawer and withdrew a key. Jeanine watched in horror as he closed the drawer, then locked the door and slipped the key into the front pocket of his waistcoat.

He faced her. "This is for your own good."

He advanced. Jeanine backed up. The back of her leg bumped something. She leapt aside and glanced at the table she'd bumped. She'd retreated nearly to the hearth. From the corner of her eye, she glimpsed the poker resting against the brick. Her heart leapt into her throat. She yanked her gaze back on to Lord Gordon. He stood a foot away.

"Miss Matheson—Jeanine—you need not fear me." He halted. "I understand. Forgive me, dearest. Northington has mistreated you and now you fear all man. I promise, I will be gentle. Come," he grasped her arm.

She started to pull away, then another plan struck. Jeanine tripped and collided with Lord Gordon. She seized his cravat in an effort not to fall—he wasn't quick as Grey had been in catching her—and slipped her fingers into the front pocket of his waistcoat. She fisted the key as he grasped her shoulders.

She thought he would set her back from him, but his hold tightened, and she realized he intended to kiss her. Revulsion turned her stomach. Could she pretend to like the kiss? Wait, he believed she was afraid of Grey. His mouth neared hers. She whimpered.

He froze. "He really has hurt you." The dangerous light of fanatical righteousness flared in his eyes. But, to her relief, he released her. "Sit down." He indicated the nearby chairs. "I will fetch you a sherry. It will be good for your nerves."

He turned, and Jeanine gauged the distance to the door. It was too far. She could never reach it and unlock the door before he set upon her. She would not allow him to trap her. If she didn't escape, then his plans to ruin Grey would succeed. She looked at the poker leaning against the brick of the hearth. Dare she?

"We can live in France, until the worst of the scandal dies down," he went on. "Have you ever been to France? You will love it."

Jeanine edged to the poker and snatched it up. He filled the first sherry glass, then a second. She had little time. He replaced the lid on the decanter. Jeanine took three steps and lifted the poker with her right hand, while clutching the letters and the key in the other. She swung at his head. He cried out and dropped the sherry glasses. They shattered against the sideboard.

Jeanine dropped the poker and stumbled back two paces. He grabbed the side of his head and swung toward her. She whirled and lunged for the door. Hard fingers seized her arm. She cried out. His fingers dug deeper. He yanked her toward him and she brought her fisted hand up. He grabbed for her and caught the letters. She yanked them free from his grasp. The key struck the carpet.

She stumbled backward as he fell against a chair. Jeanine dove for the key, scooped it up, then raced for the door. Her hands shook so badly she feared she couldn't fit the key into the lock. A moan behind her caused her to glance over her shoulder. He was struggling to his feet. She faced forward, commanded calm, thrust the key into the lock, then turned. The lock clicked. She threw the door open and raced down the hall to the servants' stairs.

She forced herself to slow enough not to fall headlong down the corkscrew stairs. At the bottom, she raced toward the parlor. A shout went up in that direction. Jeanine whirled in the opposite direction and pumped her legs faster. She reached the stairs they had ascended when the butler had shown them in and descended as quickly as she could.

At the bottom, she spun left, toward the front door. Pounding footfalls on the front steps sent her into a panic. She turned right, ran down another hallway that twisted around, and burst into a storage room. Folded linens lined the high shelves. Sacks of fruit and barrels of oats, or maybe flour, encircled the room. She hurried through the small room and nearly cried aloud at sight of a side door. She found the door unlocked, and raced outside into an enclosed garden. Jeanine kept going toward the wooden door on the left side of the stone wall.

Please do not be locked, she prayed. She reached the door, drew the latch, and raced into the alley.

CHAPTER TWELVE

ONE LEG CROSSED OVER the other and an arm stretched along the top edge of the divan, Valan stared at the emerald ring he wore as he listened to Peigi ramble on about last night's party.

"I had no opportunity to tell you that she invited Lord Gordon," she said. "Of course, with so many last-minute preparations, I then forgot until I saw him enter the ballroom. He had her cornered. I vow, Valan, he all but made violent love to her."

Valan lifted an eyebrow. "I suggest, my dear, that, if you think Jeanine would allow Lord Gordon to make violent love to her in public, that it has been some time since Richard has made violent love to you."

She stiffened. "I beg your pardon. Richard makes violent love to me on a regular basis. I tell you, Lord Gordon was unacceptably fervent."

"Lord Gordon is often fervent," Valan reminded her.

"I don't like it by half," she said. "I wouldn't be one bit surprised to discover that he is trying to talk her into running off with him."

Valan noticed a scuff on one boot. He would have to have a talk with Baldwin.

"Are you listening, Valan?"

He straightened and picked up his teacup from the table. "Of course. I don't think we have to worry about Jeanine running off with Gordon." He sipped his tea, then rested the cup on his leg and leaned back against the cushion.

"What if he attempts to force her?"

He laughed. "I doubt he has the courage."

"That meeting in the park was no accident," Peigi said. "He asked if he could call on her."

Valan chuckled, the imagined scene vivid in his mind's eye. "What was my ward's response to his advance?"

"She didn't respond. I informed him that he must speak with you."

Valan looked sharply at her. "I appreciate your concern, Peigi, but you might allow Jeanine to speak for herself next time."

She frowned. "Next time? You think he will ask again?"

"I think he cannot help himself."

"You would let him court her?" Peigi demanded. Then before he could answer, she added, "So that's your game. This is low, even for you, Valan."

"What is low even for me?" he asked.

"Using the girl to get even with Gordon. That pistol incident happened twenty years ago. Even you should have forgotten it by now."

"Do you think so?" he asked. "I feel certain Gordon has not forgotten."

Peigi regarded him in that way women do when they are puzzling something out about a man, which that man would rather they didn't know. "Perhaps the girl is using *you*."

"Do you really think so?" He considered. "That would be a novel experience."

Peigi shrugged. "You bought her a whole new wardrobe. She lives here, in one of the most luxurious homes in Edinburgh. She travels in the highest of style. Servants cater to her every whim. Women have used men for far less."

"I cannot contradict you on that matter," he said. "In Jeanine's case, however, she asked for none of it."

Peigi snorted. "Lord, but I wouldn't have guessed in a million years that you could be so naïve."

"Naïve?" he said. "Today is truly a singular day. First, I am being used by a woman, now I am naïve."

"What woman wouldn't love living the lifestyle you've provided?" she asked.

"Why shouldn't she love it?" He sipped more tea, then returned the cup to his leg.

Her gaze sharpened. "I have never seen you like this with anyone."

"Like what?" He laughed.

"What if she develops true feelings for Lord Gordon?"

"Jeanine is far too sensible for that. Besides, she wants an elderly gentleman who is facing his next reward."

"So that she can use his money to open a school for young ladies," Peigi said.

He stared at the teacup, remembering the night in the garden when Jeanine revealed her plan to him. "Quite a plan, don't you agree?" he asked.

"I wish she could return home and marry the young man who's in love with her."

Valan looked up. "What young man?"

"Joshua. He drove her here in his wagon—with her younger sister and brother-in-law as chaperones."

Valan nodded slowly. "Today truly is a singular day. That is an eventuality I hadn't considered. It is, of course, only natural that some young swain back home would have fallen prey to her charms. What do you know of this young man?"

"I gather he is a local farmer. She spoke of life in his cottage, raising his children."

"Most women of her rank aspire to such a life," he murmured. "But not Jeanine."

"Are you certain?" his cousin asked.

"She was very clear on that point," he said.

Peigi shrugged. "I suppose it is of no consequence. I suspect she can't return home."

Valan frowned. "What do you mean?"

"She told me she couldn't return home because her mother has just remarried."

Memory slammed into him of their conversation that night in the garden. "...*my mother decided to remarry, two years ago*," she'd said. "*They only just married last year, which is why I knew I had to take action.*"

"*Did your mother teach you not to trust strange men?*" he'd asked.

She replied, "*Oh, I learned that on my own—and you usually can't trust those you know, either.*"

"Her stepfather," he whispered. If the man had— His teacup shattered. The remaining tea spotted his breeches. He straightened.

"Valan!" Peigi cried. "What in the world?" She snapped her eyes up to his face as he picked up the pieces of the cup. "Are you hurt?" she demanded.

"Nae." He set the pieces of china on the tray, snatched up a napkin, and dabbed at the wet spot on his breeches.

She picked up two pieces of broken china from the floor and set them on the tray beside the others. "I see the idea disturbs you as much as it does me."

He didn't have to ask what she meant. "Aye."

"Do you plan to find her a match?" Peigi asked. "The notion of an elderly gentleman is out of the question."

"I am ashamed to admit that I have given the matter little thought." He tossed the napkin onto the table, then crossed his legs.

"So, you intend to have your revenge on Lord Gordon, then send her on her merry way?" Peigi asked with uncharacteristic perceptiveness.

He hadn't thought about that, either. It would seem he hadn't quite considered this plan as well as he thought he had. Aye, a truly singular day in more ways than he cared to admit.

"It is best you make her a match before it's too late. Do you not agree?" Peigi asked.

"Too late?" he repeated. "Peigi, her reputation is as safe with me as it would be with you."

She gave a frustrated *humph*. "It isn't that. I heard the whispers behind her back at the party."

He stilled. "What sorts of whispers?"

"You cannot be surprised, Valan. She is a country girl. The ladies in town are not kind to girls of her ilk."

"If, by 'her ilk,' you mean girls who are not obsessed with wearing a new dress to every party and throwing themselves into the path of any eligible man, then, aye, you are right."

Her gaze sharpened on him. "Hmm," she hummed.

The door abruptly swung open and Miss Stone hurried in. Strands of hair had fallen loose of her chignon, making her look younger, and a shadow troubled her usually tranquil eyes. She scanned the room, then stilled when her gaze fell on them. Valan had never seen Miss Stone look anything but serene and well-maintained.

"You have returned from the card party, Miss Stone," he said. "Where is Miss Matheson?"

She hesitated. He'd never seen her hesitate. "I must speak with you, my lord—alone."

"You may speak freely in front of Lady Guilford," he said.

"As you wish, sir. I fear you will turn me out without a reference. I only ask that, once you find Miss Matheson, that you let me know that she is safe."

Valan dropped both feet to the floor and leaned forward. "You alarm me, Miss Stone. What do you mean by 'once you find her'? Is she lost?"

"Not lost, sir. Kidnapped."

When Miss Stone finished her story, Valan again stared at the emerald ring he wore. "When I said today was a singular day, little did I know how right I was."

"We must go at once to Lord Gordon's home and demand that he return Jeanine to us," Peigi exclaimed.

"That is exactly what he would expect us to do," Valan said grimly.

"You don't mean to leave her with him?" Peigi cried.

"I do not." Valan looked at Miss Stone, who sat on the chair to his left, her hands clasped on her lap more tightly than usual. "You searched for half an hour with no sign of her?" he asked. "Gordon was with you that entire time?"

She nodded. "At least for that time, he could not have been aware of her whereabouts."

Valan nodded. "I wonder that my carriage has not returned. You instructed them to stay there until they saw Jeanine?"

"Aye, my lord." She met his gaze squarely. "Despite her command not to tell you, I should have come directly to you."

"On that point, we are in agreement," he said. "We will leave that for later. First, I would like to know if my carriage is still there. If it is, then Gordon will expect a visit from me." He rose and crossed to the door, then pulled the bell pull.

A moment later, Baldwin appeared. "Please have my bay saddled immediately," Valan instructed. "I shall be ready to leave in fifteen minutes."

Baldwin bowed and left.

"You cannot go alone," Peigi said. "Lord Gordon would love nothing better than to finish what he started twenty years ago."

Valan lifted a brow. "Only an hour ago, you told me that I should have forgotten that incident."

She tsked. "An hour ago, he hadn't kidnapped Jeanine. Oh, how I would like to shoot him myself."

He looked at her in surprise. "Peigi, I have never seen you roused to such passions."

Her brow knit in a deep frown. "You're awfully blasé for a man whose ward has been kidnapped."

"Quite the contrary," he said. "But I plan to save my passions for Gordon."

"Do hurry, sir," Miss Stone said. "I am very afraid that he will hurt her."

"That is unlikely," Valan said. "It is me he wants to hurt."

"Would he go so far as to try and force her to marry him?" Peigi asked, but before he could answer, she added, "I am going with you. My presence will hamper him."

"You surprise me, Peigi."

She gave him a haughty look. "Why? You think I don't have a brain."

"Nae, my dear. I simply seldom see you use it." He started toward the door.

"Should I come, as well, sir?" Miss Stone asked.

"If Peigi comes, you come."

A commotion sounded in the hallway and he reached the door as it was flung open. Jeanine entered, accompanied by Mr. Potts and Baldwin.

"I am sorry, sir," Baldwin said. "Mr. Potts insisted on escorting Miss Matheson to you."

"Begging your pardon, sir," Mr. Potts said, "but the young miss was not agreeable to returning home. Miss Stone was very clear that we should see her home if she came out of Lord Gordon's mansion."

Valan took in the hair that had come loose from Jeanine's soft chignon, her torn sleeve, and a handful of envelopes wrapped in a bow that she gripped. Her mouth was set in a mutinous line.

"When she came out of the alley behind Lord Gordon's house we hurried to pick her up, but she didn't want to come with us," Mr. Potts went on. "We had to force her into the carriage."

Valan looked sharply at him. "Is that when her dress was torn?"

Mr. Potts drew himself up. "We would never harm a hair on the lass' head. She came out of Lord Gordon's home looking like this."

Valan looked at Jeanine. "Is that so?"

"Mr. Potts kidnapped me," she said.

"I was under the impression it was Gordon who kidnapped you," Valan said.

Her lower lip trembled, then fury flashed in her eyes. "He tried to kidnap me. But I brained him with a poker and escaped."

"Brained him with a poker?" Valan repeated in shock.

She nodded.

"Am I to assume you killed him?"

"Unfortunately, his head was too hard for me to kill him that easily."

"I must admit, I am much relieved," Valan said.

"He deserved to be killed," she said with heat.

"I quite agree," Valan said. "Only, you shouldn't be the one to kill him."

Her eyes lit. "Will you kill him, Grey?"

He frowned. Your love of violence concerns me, my dear." He looked at Baldwin and said, "I will not need my bay, Baldwin." Then, to the driver, "I owe you a great debt, Mr. Potts".

"Harry deserves as much credit as I do, my lord."

"Harry?" Valan asked.

"Aye, sir, Harry MacLean, the footman who was with me."

Valan nodded. "It seems I am in both your debts."

"Think nothing of it, my lord." The man bowed and left with Baldwin.

Valan turned to Miss Stone. "I owe you thanks as well, Miss Stone."

"I cannot see how, sir, as it is my fault that Miss Matheson was kidnapped."

"I wouldn't go that far," he said. "I will ask, however, that the next time you two decide upon a scheme, that you speak with me first."

"It isn't her fault," Jeanine said. "I told her not to tell you."

Valan nodded. "The blame lays at your feet, never fear, my dear. But we will discuss that later. For now, I would like you and Miss Stone to go upstairs and rest. We shall have dinner, then go to the opera."

"I don't want to go to the opera," she said.

"I understand you've had trying day," he said. "But I ask that you do me this favor." He looked at Miss Stone. "I would like you to accompany us—and Peigi, if Richard can spare you, I require your presence, as well."

Miss Stone rose and walked to where Jeanine stood. "You are unharmed, Miss Matheson?"

"Aye, he didn't hurt me at all."

Valan's attention caught on the envelopes she held. "What are those?"

She looked down at them as if having forgotten them. "You will no' like it."

"Does that mean they have something to do with Gordon's plot to ostracize me from *Society*?"

Jeanine looked at Miss Stone, hurt in her eyes. "You told."

"Don't blame her," Valan said. "She believed you had been kidnapped. May I have them, please?"

She hesitated. "On one condition."

He waited.

"You will promise not to take action."

"Only a moment ago you wanted me to commit murder."

She looked at the floor. "Aye, but if you did that it would be calculated. After reading these letters, you will be so angry that you might make a mistake." She lifted her eyes to his face. "You...cannot be killed and you cannot be involved in another scandal, if you are to marry Lady Claire."

"Marry Lady Claire?" he blurted. "Where did you get that idea?"

Her eyes widened. "I heard it."

"I have no intention of marrying Lady Claire," he said.

"Her brother isn't in negotiations with you for marriage with her?"

"Her brother has been trying to talk me into marrying her for two years," Valan said.

"You see," Miss Stone said, "I told you he didn't want to marry her."

"But I—"

"Up to your rooms," he cut off Jeanine. She sighed, then started to turn toward the door. "Jeanine." She stopped. "The letters, please."

Fear flickered in her eyes, but she handed them to him and left the room like a woman walking the gallows.

The door clicked closed behind them and Valan returned to his seat on the divan. He pulled the ribbon from the envelopes. "Peigi, I prefer you do not discuss my personal affairs with anyone, Jeanine in particular."

"I am sorry," she said. "It is true, the earl did send you a contract."

"Which I promptly returned unopened—for the third time."

"She cares for you, Valan."

He laughed as he pulled a paper from the first envelope. "Lady Claire cares for herself only."

"I meant Jeanine.

He looked up at her.

"She is protecting *your* reputation."

"Can you imagine?" he said. "An innocent wants to protect *The Morning Star*. I will likely never experience another day like today."

He withdrew the letter from within the first envelope and began reading.

CHAPTER THIRTEEN

WHEN THEY ENTERED THE opera house, the furtive glances and low murmurs told Valan the gossip that Jeanine had rejected Lord Gordon's suit had spread through Edinburgh more quickly and thoroughly than he'd hoped. He would have to thank Peigi. Her network of gossipmongers was impressive.

He kept Jeanine close. Between himself, Miss Stone and Peigi, she would remain safe. Valan had to admit, he'd never enjoyed the opera more, and intermission came all too soon. He ordered refreshments and stood. He was getting to old to sit for so long without stretching. A knock came to the box door. The women all looked at him.

He started toward the door.

"Please do not get angry," Jeanine begged.

"What have I to be angry about, my dear?" He opened the door.

Young Martin Hayes stood outside their box in the dimly lit walkway. Valan had a good idea what the lad wanted. An unexpected sadness stabbed.

"My lord," Martin began.

Valan held up a hand, palm out, and looked over his shoulder at the women. His attention caught on Jeanine's midnight blue satin dress. The fabric hugged her curves and almost gleamed in the candlelight. Her met her gaze. Fear shone in her eyes.

He smiled gently. "Ladies, excuse me. I will be just outside the door, speaking with Mr. Hayes." He stepped from the room and closed the door.

"My lord, forgive the intrusion," Martin began, then waited as a man and woman passed. When they were out of earshot, he said, "What is this nonsense about my grandfather wedding a young woman?"

"Perhaps you should speak with your grandfather," Valan said.

"I have, but he refuses to give me any details other than you know the lady. Is that true?"

"It is," Valan said.

"Sir, surely you realize my grandfather is quite elderly. What can he possibly want with any wife, much less a young one?"

"Perhaps when you are an old man you will understand," Valan said.

The lad stiffened. "I am a man of the world, and not ignorant of a lady's charms. But my grandfather—bloody hell, sir, she can be of no good use to him, and he certainly cannot be of any use to her."

"You might underestimate your grandfather," he replied mildly, and was startled to realize the thought bothered him.

Martin frowned as if Valan were insane. "I demand that you cease interfering in my grandfather's affairs."

"I would say it is you who are interfering."

"The young lady will not be welcome in our house," Martin snapped.

Valan looked at him through shuttered eyes. "Do you refer to Whitmore House or perhaps Howton Castle?"

The lad's mouth fell open. "Are you saying *we*, his family, would not be welcome in our grandfather's home?"

"I believe that is what you are saying."

A manservant arrived with the refreshments Valan had ordered. He stepped aside and allowed the man entrance, then said to Martin, "You will excuse me. I hope you enjoy the remainder of the opera." Valan angled his head in a slight bow, then returned to the opera box and closed the door.

* * *

When they finally arrived home, Jeanine wasn't surprised when Grey insisted that Peigi stay the night, as her home was nearly an hour away. She took the Gold guest chambers.

Despite Miss Stone's insistence that she needed to help Jeanine with her evening toilet, Jeanine sent Miss Stone to her chambers. Jeanine sat on the bench at her vanity, her heart filled with a mixture of relief and apprehension. The half dozen prayers she'd sent up during the opera had been answered. Lord Gordon hadn't made an appearance. But she knew too well he wasn't finished with the marquess. Grey said he wasn't to marry Lady Claire, but what if that had been a lie so that she wouldn't feel responsible for the trouble she'd caused?

Either way, Lord Gordon could—and would—ruin him on account of her. Not to mention, Grey was certain to exact revenge for the awful letters Lord Gordon had written. Grey hadn't said a word to her about the letters, but he wouldn't. Lady Guildford was right; Grey was an intensely private man.

Her heart squeezed. She had to leave Finley Hall.

Tomorrow morning, before Grey and Miss Stone arose, she would slip away. Tears pricked. Grey could find some respectable lady to marry. Maybe even Lady Claire. Lady Claire certainly would not want to marry a man who had a full-grown woman as his ward. Jeanine's heart began to beat fast. This meant that when she'd bid Grey good night ten minutes ago, that would be the last time she would see him. Had she known that would be their final goodbye, she would have lingered a moment longer. Would have memorized his face a little better, the cool look in his eyes. She might even have squeezed his hand to feel the warmth of his touch one final time.

Jeanine jumped to her feet and began pacing. Could she really leave without seeing him at least once more? She shook her head. She was simply trying to talk herself out of leaving tomorrow. She had to leave before Lord Gordon had the opportunity to put another plan into action. She swiped at tears and crossed to the small secretary near the bay window. She sat down, pulled out a pen and paper, and penned a short note explaining to Grey that she had returned home and he need not worry.

She hesitated over the signature. Should she say 'Yours, Jeanine?' Or 'Your Friend, Jeanine?' Maybe that was too personal. Maybe she should sign, 'Miss Matheson.' She glanced at her salutation. *Dear Grey.* She couldn't call him Grey then sign as 'Miss Matheson.' She had to sign her Christian name. She considered for another moment, then wrote, *Your Friend, Jeanine.* She folded the note, then stared at it. All that remained was for her to slip away tomorrow morning.

But tomorrow morning was hours away.

Jeanine jumped to her feet. She opened the door and stepped into the hallway, then came to an abrupt halt when Miss Stone rose from the chair on the opposite wall.

"Miss Stone, what are you doing here?"

"Forgive me, Miss Matheson, but I feared you would try to run away. You shouldn't, you know. Lord Northington will deal with Lord Gordon."

Tears pressed the backs of Jeanine's eyes. Where would she ever find a truer friend? Never. But she couldn't tell her good friend the truth.

Jeanine smiled. "I am still in my gown. I would never run away dressed in an evening gown."

"I am not so certain."

Jeanine laughed. "I cannot sleep. I am just going downstairs to see if Grey is still up. You go to bed and I will see you in the morning." Jeanine started to turn.

"Miss Matheson."

Jeanine stopped.

"I am sorry I deserted you at Lord Gordon's."

"What—you didn't desert me." Guilt assailed her.

Jeanine pulled her into a hug. She thought for an instant she detected a tremble in Miss Stone, but Miss Stone stepped back and stared with her usual composed expression.

"I will see you in the morning," Jeanine said.

"Do you promise?"

She smiled. "I promise."

Miss Stone nodded, and Jeanine went downstairs to Grey's library. She couldn't allow herself to think of Miss Stone, for Grey would guess in an instant that something was wrong. Soft light fanned out beneath the library door. Her pulse jumped. He hadn't gone to bed yet.

She knocked. He called "enter," and she opened the door.

The marquess looked up in surprise. Aside from the modest light from the hallway, the room was lit by only a single candelabra located on the desk where he sat. One of Lord Gordon's letters lay open before him, the others in a stack to his right.

He folded the letter and rose. He had taken off his coat and cravat. The top buttons on his shirt were undone, revealing tanned skin and his sleeves were rolled up to his forearms. A strange tremor rippled through her.

"Is something wrong?" he asked.

Jeanine started to close the door, then remembered that he had told her she was never to close the door when they were in a room alone together.

She crossed to his desk and said, "I couldn't sleep."

He smiled gently. "So, I see. You're still in your ballgown. It is past time we go to sleep, though, don't you agree."

Her heart fell.

He smiled. "Perhaps a sherry will relax us both."

She smiled in return. "Yes, please."

He poured two sherries, then faced her, glasses in hand. "Shall we sit?"

An idea struck. "Can we play a game of chess?"

He lifted a brow. "You play?"

She nodded. "My father loved to play, but none of my cousins played with him, so he taught me."

Grey approached and handed her one of the glasses of sherry. "Your father sounds like an enlightened man."

She laughed. "It's more likely he was just desperate for someone to play with. I am a fair player."

Grey canted his head. "We can start a game and finish tomorrow, if necessary."

They sat at the game table and set up the pieces. Jeanine felt as if they existed in their own private world with the candlelight enveloping them in soft light while the rest of the room lay in shadow. Grey took the black pieces, of course, and she the white. Jeanine went first, and took her time deciding on the first move. Grey decided his first move more quickly than she did, but she intended to draw the game out as long as possible. Her head slightly bent as if her attention was on the board, she lifted her eyes and studied his serious expression when it came his turn to move.

Twenty minutes into the game, he leaned back in his chair and sipped his sherry, his eyes on her face. "I can see why your father liked playing with you. Was he a good player?"

"Oh yes, much better than me."

"Then he was quite good."

Jeanine moved her knight. "Your turn."

She sipped her sherry. "What are your plans for tomorrow?"

"I have no particular plans. I seldom do."

"Really? But you always seem to be busy," she said

His mouth lifted in a tiny smile. "Do I?"

"What do you do all day?"

"Nothing that would interest you."

She leaned forward. "But it would interest me."

He studied the board a little longer this time.

"Did it please you to take me as your ward?" she asked.

"It did."

"Despite all the trouble I've been?"

He smiled, but kept his attention on the board. "Despite all the trouble you've been." He moved his queen.

"I'm very sorry about the trouble with Lord Gordon."

He looked sharply at her. "That was not your fault."

"But I went to his house and I shouldn't have."

The marquess picked up his sherry glass again and leaned back his seat. "True, you shouldn't have. But Lord Gordon was troublesome long before you came along."

She frowned. "He said something about saving another innocent from your clutches."

Grey's expression darkened. He downed the last of his sherry in one swallow, then rose and crossed to the sideboard. "Did he say anything more?"

"Nae. I asked what he meant, but he was very cryptic. I knew he was lying. He is a terrible person." The memory of his words fired her blood. "I almost wish I had killed him when I hit him with the poker. I wanted to."

Valan returned to his seat. "Be glad you didn't. We might very well have been forced to flee to France or, worse, the Colonies."

She thought of her and Grey in France, attending dances and drinking coffee every morning. "Would that have been so terrible?"

"Indeed, it would," he said with such conviction that her heart hurt. He must have read her expression, for he said, "Not because I don't enjoy your company, but I would not have you a wanted criminal."

"Really?" she asked. "My company is not so terrible?"

A strange light entered his eyes. "Not so terrible, at all."

"I promise, I will not be any more trouble," she said.

She thought his gaze had shifted to her mouth, then he dazzled her with a bright smile and said, "I can't imagine how you will manage that," and she decided she'd been wrong.

Her heart twisted. This would be the last time she would see that sparkle in his eyes. She ducked her head and looked at the chess pieces. "Thank you for making me your ward. I have been very happy."

"Then I am happy, as well," he murmured in a strange voice.

Jeanine nodded and dared not look at him for fear she would cry. She moved her rook. He reached for his rook, and her gaze fixed on his long fingers as he moved his chess piece across the board in line with her queen.

"Really, Grey," she said with disdain. "That move is too obvious. If I didn't see that I would be a real ninny."

"And you are no ninny."

She pinned him with a stare. "You're planning a trap."

His eyes widened in mock innocence. "Me? Never."

Jeanine studied the board. If her calculations were correct—

A shadow fell across the carpet to her right and she looked up and gasped. Lord Gordon stood in the doorway.

"How very cozy the two of you are," he said with mock sweetness.

The word 'cozy' sounded more like 'coshy.' Was he drunk?

"It seems I was closer to the mark with you two than even I realized," he said.

'Seems' came out 'sheems'

Valan rose. "The hour is late, Gordon. Why are you here?"

Lord Gordon stepped into the room and listed a little to the right. "You know full well why I'm here." The words were more of a drunken growl than English.

"I am distressed that the footman who should've shown you in didn't announce you," Valan said.

"Never mind him," Lord Gordon snapped. "How dare you tell everyone that she rejected *my* suit. You can't stand that I bested you twenty years ago. *The Morning Star*," he sneered the name. "You flout *Society*, yet they welcome you with open arms." His eyes snagged on the letters sitting on the desk. He took two steps to the desk and snatched up the envelopes. "So, your little whore came straight to you." He threw them onto the carpet. "All the better. Servants will whisper about how they saw the letters in your library." His bloodshot eyes swung onto Jeanine. "I thought you were different."

Anger swept through her. She leapt to her feet. "Different from what?"

"I believe he is referring to an old friend of mine," Grey said.

"Old friend, that's rich," Lord Gordon said. "She was just another one of your whores."

"Being drunk is no excuse for being a liar," Grey said in a voice so cold that it sent a shiver down Jeanine's back.

Grey started toward him. Lord Gordon jammed a hand into his coat pocket and whipped out a pistol. Grey froze. Jeanine drew a sharp breath.

Grey stepped in front of her. "Your quarrel is with me, Gordon."

He gave a vicious laugh. "You believe you are so superior to the rest of us." His eyes glittered. "I was there, you know."

"There?" Grey repeated as if they were discussing nothing more than afternoon tea.

"When they found your father."

Jeanine's attention caught on the flex of Grey's hands into fists.

"His death should have finished you," Gordon said with such spite that Jeanine wished she had another poker so that she could brain him again. This time, she would kill him. His mouth twisted upward in a malicious smile. "How does it feel being guilty of the same crime your father's murderer was guilty of? He is a murderer, you know. When Lord Graves won your father's fortune, he might as well have pulled the trigger of the pistol your father used to shoot himself. Did the man whose fortune you won shoot himself, as well?" Lord Gordon stepped toward them. "You've guarded that secret jealously. Who was he?"

"A Frenchman," Grey replied. "You wouldn't know him."

Cold fingers inched up Jeanine's spine. She had the strangest feeling he was lying.

"What do you want?" Grey asked.

"I plan to marry her." He motioned with the pistol in Jeanine's direction.

"I won't marry you," Jeanine exclaimed.

"I imagine you intend to shoot me first," Grey said in a level voice.

He kept the pistol pointed at Grey. "Come here, Miss Matheson, or I *will* shoot him."

"Stay where you are, Jeanine," Grey said. "I am sorry, Gordon, but I cannot allow you to take her."

"How will you stop me? You don't keep a pistol in your house. Can't stomach the sight of them, I understand. The night you climbed into Lady Victoria's bedchambers, you didn't put up even the slightest bit of a fight. The pistols her brother and I pointed at you rendered you helpless as a little girl."

"You won," Grey said. "That isn't enough?"

"She never stopped talking of you," he snarled. "Her brother had to send her away."

"She was fifteen," Grey said. "Girls that age are prone to lovesickness. She married a viscount and has three children."

"She should have been mine," Lord Gordon snapped. "She would have been, but you ruined her."

"I never touched her," Grey said.

"Liar," he hissed. Eyes on Grey, he said, "Come here, Miss Matheson. Defy me, and I'll shoot him."

"You can't possibly get away with this," Grey said.

"On the contrary. You put it about that Miss Matheson rejected me, but when they learn that we married, they'll know that was just spiteful gossip spun by you. *Society* will have to acknowledge that a simple country girl preferred me to *The Morning Star*."

"I will tell everyone the truth," Jeanine spat.

He gave her a harsh smile. "When we return from France with you heavy with my child, you will be glad for my protection. Unless you really are carrying his child already."

Jeanine lifted her chin. "Grey has been nothing but a gentleman."

"How noble."

Movement in the hallway caught her attention.

Grey took a step toward Gordon.

"Nae," Jeanine cried. "He will shoot you."

Miss Stone lunged through the doorway. Grey dove for Gordon. The gun fired with a deafening roar. Jeanine screamed when Grey stumbled.

She sprang forward as Miss Stone collided with Lord Gordon, but felt as if she was struggling through quicksand.

The marquess caught himself and stumbled toward Lord Gordon. Miss Stone raked her nails down Lord Gordon's cheek. He howled and shoved her aside. She hit the carpet and the marquess crashed into him. They fell to the rug with a thud as Jeanine reached them. She leapt aside as the two men rolled across the rug in a death grip.

Miss Stone shoved into a sitting position. Jeanine looked wildly about the room for something to hit Lord Gordon with. Her ears rang. Two men appeared in the doorway. She yanked her gaze up and saw the gentleman she'd met in Grey's library two days ago, Baron Rosemund, along with another tall, dark-haired man.

"What in God's name—" Baron Rosemund rushed to Grey and Lord Gordon.

He dealt a hard kick to the side of Lord Gordon's head with his boot heel. The man went limp. Jeanine rushed to Grey's side and fell to her knees beside him. Blood spotted the sleeve of his left shoulder.

Baron Rosemund nodded toward Lord Gordon. "I assume he is the reason your door is open and a footman is lying unconscious in your foyer?"

The marquess looked sharply at him. "Is the footman dead?"

Brendan shook his head. "Nae. But I'll wager he has a devil of a headache tomorrow."

"What are you doing here?" Grey actually sounded peeved.

"We had a meeting," the baron said.

Grey grunted. "I sent a note, cancelling."

"Anthony insisted on ignoring that," Rosemund said. "You should be grateful he did."

"What the devil is all this about?" the other man demanded.

Jeanine gingerly fingered Grey's wound. "You are bleeding." She dropped onto her backside and pinned him with a hard stare. "I specifically instructed you not to be hurt on my account."

His brows rose. "The bullet barely grazed me." He looked up at the baron. "Brendan, if you would." He extended a hand.

The baron clasped his hand and hauled him to his feet. Grey reached for Jeanine, but she scrambled to her feet and grabbed his arm.

"You must sit down." Jeanine looked over her shoulder. "Miss Stone, please wake Mr. Baldwin and have him call for a doctor."

Lady Guilford burst into the room with Mr. Baldwin and Mrs. McPhee close behind.

Lady Guilford skidded to a halt, her sleeping cap askew on her head. Her eyes widened and her hand flew to her heart. "What happened? Valan, you're bleeding."

"A mere flesh wound," he said with exasperation.

"Mr. Baldwin," Jeanine said, "please call for a doctor."

Mr. Baldwin glanced at Grey, who sighed and said, "She will not be satisfied until a doctor confirms that I am not dying."

The steward disappeared.

"Mrs. McPhee, will you bring tea for everyone?" Jeanine asked.

The housekeeper looked at Grey. He nodded, and she hurried from the room.

"Very clever of you, my dear," Grey said to Jeanine. "They will stay busy for some time."

"Will someone tell me what is going on?" Lady Guilford demanded. Lord Gordon moaned and she jumped. "Good lord, is that—" Her eyes snapped onto the marquess. "I told you he would go too far."

"As usual, you were right, Peigi."

"We should call for a constable," she said.

"Aye." Grey looked at Baron Rosemund. "Brendan, I would greatly appreciate—"

The baron held up a hand. "Say no more—well, until we return. I will want to hear this story in full."

Grey canted his head. "I would prefer to tell the story but once. When the constable comes, you and Anthony may hear everything in full."

"Come along, Anthony."

Baron Rosemund grabbed Lord Gordon by his left arm and the other man grabbed his right arm, and they hauled him to his feet. He moaned as they dragged him out the door.

"You must sit down." Jeanine pulled him to the couch and pushed him onto the cushion. "Miss Stone." Jeanine whirled. Miss Stone stood near the desk, hair askew. "Are you unharmed?"

"I am perfectly fine."

"What in the world were you doing in the hall?" Jeanine demanded.

"I feared you weren't being truthful when you said you would see me in the morning."

Jeanine flushed, but said, "Well, I am immensely glad you were there. Will you fetch water and some fresh cloths, please?"

She nodded and hurried from the room. Only Lady Guilford remained.

"Peigi, if you are to hear the story, I suggest you dress," said his lordship. "Brendan and Anthony will no doubt return within an hour accompanied by a constable."

She nodded and left.

Then Grey looked at Jeanine.

CHAPTER FOURTEEN

VALAN WAS LOATH TO admit that even a flesh wound could ache. He was getting too old for such nonsense. Despite the fact he had bled only enough to ruin his crisp white shirt, Jeanine was still applying pressure to the 'wound.'

Valan regarded her with a stern eye. "That was foolish of you."

"Me?" She dropped onto the couch beside him, her fingers *still* pressed against the wound. "You are the one who ran straight into the barrel of a pistol."

He grunted. "Gordon has always been a bad shot."

Jeanine's eyes widened, then she burst into tears and buried her head in his chest.

He grimaced when she squeezed his wound. Valan grasped her hand and held it. "Shh, sweet. All is well. I am not really hurt."

"You could have been killed," she wailed.

"I am not so easily killed."

"You would have been better off to have never known me."

His life had been far less complicated before her, quieter, colder...without love.

"Now the scandal will ruin you," she sobbed into his shirt. "You won't be able to marry Lady Claire."

He frowned. "I believe I told you that I had no intention of marrying Lady Claire."

"You just said that to make me feel better."

"I never say things just to make anyone feel better. I have never had any desire to marry Lady Claire."

"You wanted to walk with her in the gardens," Jeanine blubbered.

He laughed. "That is a far cry from wanting to marry someone."

She drew back and turned her tearstained face up to him. "What is wanting to marry someone?"

With the pad of this thumb, he gently wiped tears from her cheek. "Wanting to marry someone is being unable to imagine a day without them."

She straightened. "Oh dear."

He tensed. "What is amiss?"

She looked at her lap and shook her head. With a finger beneath her chin, he tipped her face up toward him. He lifted a brow and waited.

She stared back for a long moment, then sighed. "If wanting to marry someone is not being able to imagine a day without them, then I want to marry you."

Longing twisted through him. "Perhaps there is a bit more to it than that," he said.

"Such as liking to play chess with them? Or..." Her gaze dropped to his mouth and lingered there for two heartbeats, then lifted again to meet his eyes. "Or wanting to kiss them?"

He tweaked a lock of her hair that had come loose of the chignon. "You want to kiss a young man. I am too old for you, my dear."

"That is silly. I said from the start that I wanted an older man."

"You said that you wanted a man with one foot in the grave. I am, I hope, too many years away from that to qualify."

"I do not want you to die," she blurted. "I want—" She looked up at him through her lashes and nibbled on her bottom lip. "I want you to marry me."

He smiled gently. "I do not think that's what you really want."

"It is. You *must* marry me."

He lifted a brow. "Indeed?"

She nodded. "It's the only way to save you from scandal. You know that what happened here tonight will be all over Edinburgh by breakfast."

She was right about that.

"And the story will be twisted to paint you in a very poor light."

She was right about that, as well. "It won't be the first time, and not the last," he replied.

"People marry all the time to save themselves from scandal," she said.

"Perhaps, but I am too far gone to be saved."

She continued to nibble her bottom lip. "Then marry me to save *me* from scandal." He started to reply, but she added, "I cannot return home. My mother's new husband would never allow it."

He wouldn't allow that, anyway. "What of Joshua?" he asked gently.

Surprise flickered in her eyes. "Joshua is kind, but if rumors reach him that I am pregnant with your child..." She shrugged.

Valan pictured Gordon slumped between Brendan and Anthony when they dragged him from the room and was glad he was gone. If the two men hadn't take him away, Valan would kill him. Still...Gordon wasn't wholly to blame.

He looked at Jeanine. "There is no need for you to sacrifice yourself. I have found an elderly gentleman for you to marry."

"You did?" she exclaimed, then frowned. "I do no' care. It's marry you or be ruined."

He laughed. "More experienced women than you have tried to coerce me into marriage."

"I think you mean 'tricked.' I am not tricking you. I am telling you directly that it's marriage or ruin."

Sadness squeezed his heart. "Why would you want to marry me, love?"

She looked at him in surprise. "Because I love you, silly."

Peigi and Miss Stone entered. Peigi wore a soft yellow day dress, and Miss Stone carried a basin and pitcher, and had clean cloths slung over her shoulder. They stopped inside the doorway.

"Marry the elderly gentleman, Jeanine," he urged. "Your comfort will be assured."

She stared up at him, eyes shimmering. "Don't you love me just a little?"

He smiled sadly. "I love you far too much to marry you. I don't deserve you."

"Yes, you do—and I deserve you." She threw her arms around his neck. "Say yes. I promise I will not be one bit of trouble anymore and I will do everything just as you tell me to."

"I don't think you can," he said with a laugh.

She pulled back and looked up at him, her expression serious. "Marry me and I will make certain you are never sorry."

"It isn't me who will be sorry, love."

She tilted her head to one side. "Will you be sorry if you don't marry me?"

"Yes, but that is my penance."

Jeanine stood. "Do you want me to be happy?"

He sighed. "With all my heart."

She held out her hand.

He clasped it and stood.

She looked up into his face. "I cannot imagine life without you."

"It's insanity," he whispered.

Tears glistened in her eyes. "Insanity?" she repeated. "It is insanity to be apart."

He wondered how he would face tomorrow without her bursting into his study with some new gift or a story about Miss Stone.

"You are certain?" he asked. "If we wed, I will not let you go." He wondered if he could let her go if she refused.

Jeanine frowned. "Where would I go?"

Valan crushed her to him and closed his eyes. Something primal twisted in his chest. She loved him. The urge to protect her nearly suffocated him. She didn't need his money, his house...his body.

Him. She wanted him.

He released a deep breath, then loosened his hold on her and looked over her head at his cousin. "Peigi, if you are available, we require your presence three days hence for a wedding."

Peigi clapped her hands. "We must start planning immediately." She turned and frowned at Miss Stone. "Stop gawking, Miss Stone, and see to his lordship's arm before he feigns death in order to escape his own wedding."

Miss Stone started toward him, but Valan dipped his head and kissed his future wife.

A MARRIAGE OF NECESSITY

THE MARRIAGE MAKER
BOOK EIGHT RULES OF REFINEMENT

TARAH SCOTT

CHAPTER ONE

ANNE ANGLED AWAY FROM her best friend, Jeanine, drew back the edge of her glove, and glanced at the face of the silver gilded watch pinned to the inside of the fabric. 11:57. If her watch was correct, and the time piece had kept perfect time for three generations, the third ball of the season would end in three minutes when the minuet concluded. Then Lady Peddington's famed Midnight Ball would begin.

A year of her life, along with funds her family could ill afford to lose, gone. All for nothing, if she didn't find a wealthy husband by the next ball, which was one short week away. Her heart constricted. *Oh, papa, why didn't you tell us?*

She knew why. Her father had been a Weber male through and through. They were stubborn to a fault, determined to care for their own at all costs, and slaves to the gambling halls. In the end, he had the presence of mind to lay down his cards before he lost the castle on Loch Lomond, and the estate and land north of Perth. Her father, however, feared he couldn't resist the temptation to gamble away their remaining holdings and drank himself to death.

The need to cry rushed to the surface.

Nae, the time for despair was long past. She had to—

A tall, dark, good-looking gentleman approached. Anne's mind snapped to attention. Two minutes remained of the respectable ball. It was impossible to join in the dance so late in the set, but would this gentleman engage her in conversation? He continued toward them. Anne turned her attention to Jeanine. It wouldn't do for her to appear too eager.

"I am so glad this ball is almost over," Jeanine said. "I met an interesting gentleman earlier. He's older—though not old enough for my purposes." She sighed. "It is so hot and stuffy in here. I think there are more guests tonight than last week. I wonder if there will be even more for the final ball of the season next week."

From the corner of her eye, Anne watched the man's approach. He brushed past a group of men.

"Aye, it is warm tonight," Anne said to Jeanine. "We can go back to our rooms together, if ye like."

The man reached them, and she and Jeanine faced him. He looked at Anne. Her pulse jumped. Finally, a gentleman was going to speak with her. He would be the first of the evening.

Then his attention shifted to Jeanine. "Would ye honor me with a turn around the ballroom?"

Tears stung Anne's eyes. She ducked her head as Jeanine said, "I am tired. But Lady Anne is free. Why don't you walk with her?"

Anne snapped her head up in time to see the man stiffen. "I beg your pardon, but it is getting late," he said. "I must be going. Have a good evening." He started to turn.

"Wait," Jeanine cried. The man stopped, interest lighting his eyes. "Why won't you walk with Anne?" Jeanine demanded.

"Jeanine," Anne hissed under her breath, and she glanced at a group of nearby ladies who were frowning in their direction. But Jeanine ignored her.

"Do you know that she's the heir to a title?" Jeanine asked.

"I have no need of a title," he said, and before they could reply, he spun and strode away.

Jeanine faced her. "I am certain of it. Linda and Dorothy are speaking badly about you. Fiona, too, I wager," she added in a dark tone.

"Why would they?" Anne said. "What can they possibly say that would alienate these gentlemen? And why say anything at all? There are plenty of gentlemen seeking ladies."

"Because the gentlemen fawned all over you that first night," Jeanine said. "You're more beautiful than any other lady here."

That, Anne knew, was untrue. There were some very beautiful girls here. Jeanine was one. But leave it to Jeanine to be loyal to a fault. Still, something was wrong, and Anne couldn't escape the feeling that the girls Jeanine had named did have something to do with it.

The lights began to dim. Her heart fell. The respectable ball had ended. Anne spotted half a dozen servants weaving throughout the ballroom and snuffing out candles. They would extinguish more than half the candles, leaving the massive room with many shadows.

"It's time to leave," Jeanine said.

Anxiety knotted Anne's stomach. Once she left the party, she would have to wait another week for the opportunity to find a suitable match. There had to be some way to prepare for the next week. She couldn't sit passively in Lady Peddington's parlor and sew, sip tea, and talk about the final upcoming ball. Even if she met a gentleman tonight or next week, what guarantee was there she would make a match? She couldn't wait to the last minute and simply hope to find a husband. The candles on the table behind them were snuffed, leaving them standing in soft shadows.

Jeanine tugged on her arm. "Come along, Anne."

Dare she stay? Anne scanned the ballroom. At least one hundred and fifty guests, including Lady Peddington's girls, had attended the night's ball. Half of those had left. Anne counted ten graduates of Lady Peddington's School for Young ladies amongst the guests. Some had even removed their gloves. Three girls stood far too close to gentlemen, and the orchestra struck up a waltz. The Midnight Ball had officially begun.

Two gentlemen looked their way.

"Oh dear," Jeanine whispered. "Two gentlemen are headed our way. If we hurry, we can avoid them."

Anne faced Jeanine. "Quickly, you go on. I'll be up later."

"Nae, you need a husband with money," Jeanine's whisper grew urgent. "These men can offer you nothing."

Jeanine might not be correct. Some courtesans received very expensive gifts. Might she receive enough expensive gifts to support her estate for the next three years? Her mother had a good head for business. She could manage the tenants while Anne earned the money it would take to plant and harvest three years of crops. After that, Dover Hall could support itself *and* Castle Dòmnallach.

But that required substantial money...

The two gentlemen reached them and stopped closer than propriety allowed. But then, this was the Midnight Ball. Propriety had exited along with all the proper ladies.

The gentleman who stopped in front of Jeanine gave a slight bow. "May I have the honor of this dance?"

Jeanine glanced at Anne.

"Go on up to your room," Anne said. "I will be up later." She glimpsed the satisfied gleam in the eyes of the man standing near her.

"Just one dance, my dear," Jeanine's admirer urged.

Jeanine narrowed her eyes on Anne. "If you're staying, then I am staying." She looked at the gentleman. "I am happy to dance with you."

Before Anne could object, Jeanine slipped her hand into the crook of the man's arm and allowed him to lead her toward the dance floor.

Anne hesitated. She should go after her. Oh, this was a terrible mess.

"Would you care for a walk in the garden, love?"

Anne looked sharply at the man standing uncomfortably close. She had no experience with men who were seeking mistresses, but she had been the object of male attention since the age of fourteen. Six years was long enough to gain some understanding of male passions. Only twice before had a gentleman referred to her with a personal endearment—outside of her father, of course. The first, was the boy she fell in love with at sixteen. They fell out of love a year later, but remained friends to this day. The other time mirrored tonight. The intimacy hadn't been earned, and evoked a sense of uneasiness that made her skin crawl.

Was this how a courtesan felt? Could she give the most private part of herself to a man who viewed her as nothing more than an object to serve his pleasure? Memories rose of her mother sitting before the hearth at Dover Hall, sewing on a cool autumn evening and her sister, Louisa, racing into the room with a drawing to show them or a passage from a favorite book she wanted to share, and the answer was a resounding yes.

But did that mean a walk in the garden?

Once they reached the cover of darkness, what would stop this man from taking what he wanted and then not paying for her charms? She flushed hot at her thoughts, but shoved aside the shame. How did a courtesan go about getting a man to offer a contract? The answer came more easily than she liked. She must tease just enough to entice him to offer a contract—a good contract.

Anne slanted her head and looked up at the man through her lashes. "Perhaps, sir, it would be better if we began with a dance. A walk in the gardens might be something for people who are on more...intimate terms."

A corner of his mouth lifted, and dread seeped through her. "My dear, I have no qualms about counting myself among the fortunate number of your lovers, but I have no intention of being the man who finances them."

Anne blinked. "I-I beg your pardon?" Her thoughts whirled. Finances *them*? She drew a sharp breath. "You think that I am looking for a protector and want to take lovers at his expense?"

He leaned closer and she stiffened when he traced a finger up her arm. "After we have enjoyed ourselves, I *might* introduce ye to a man who will look the other way when you take lovers while under his protection."

Her mind cleared. "You believe I will trade my-my—for a—" Words failed as fury clouded her thinking. She arched a brow. "A walk in the garden, you say? You like the dark, sir?"

"Like it?" he said with a growl. "I prefer it."

Men were fools.

This time, she met his gaze squarely. "In my experience, a man who prefers the cover of darkness to make love to a woman is a man who is lacking in the proper—" she gave him a cool smile "—*tools* to please a lady."

He blinked, then his mouth thinned. "The gentlemen you draw into your web are most fortunate."

She lifted her chin. "You will not count yourself amongst their ranks."

It seemed he would say more, but he spun on his heel and strode away.

Anne released a deep breath, then realized a nearby group of men were staring. God help her, by tomorrow, word will have spread through Edinburgh that one of Lady Peddington's graduates was available for the taking.

"You can't fully blame him, you know," drawled a deep male voice behind her.

Anne whirled to face the speaker, a tall man leaning against the wall. Good heavens, he was handsome. The blue eyes that started at her were made all the more blue by his raven dark hair.

"I beg your pardon?" she said.

"There is no denying that Niall is uncouth," he said. "But you can't fault him for speaking the truth."

The temper that had got her into far too much trouble over the course of her life—including just a moment ago—reared its ugly head once again. "You know nothing of the situation."

"Unlike Niall, I respect a woman who knows what she wants and isn't afraid to pursue it," he said without rancor.

She frowned. "What the devil are you talking about?"

"A woman has just as much right to pursue her pleasure as does a man," he said.

Then she understood. "Where did you get the idea that I'm seeking lovers?" She should have known better than to stay for the Midnight Ball.

"Are ye saying it isn't true?" he asked, but before she could answer, he added. "It seems to be a well-known fact."

"Something can be a fact only if it's true," she said with exasperation.

He laughed. "You just rejected Niall's advances by telling him that you won't add him to your list of lovers."

She gave a frustrated shake of her head. "I was angry."

He laughed. "There is no need to be coy. I meant what I said, I respect a woman who isn't afraid to go after what she wants."

Anne exhaled a breath in an effort to control her temper. "But you insist that what I want is a string of lovers. What in heaven would I do with them?"

He pushed away from the wall. "Perhaps I can be of help in demonstrating the benefits of having at least one lover."

She rolled her eyes. "That would completely undermine my plans."

"What might those plans be?"

"I fail to see how that is any of your business," she said.

He shrugged. "If I'm to help, I must know your plans."

"Help?" Anne narrowed her eyes. "If you intend to help in the same fashion as that other gentleman, no thank you."

"I would never be so uncouth," he said.

A twinge of hope surfaced.

"Niall should never have asked you to trade your charms for the possibility of introducing you to a man who might be interested in becoming your protector."

"What should he have done?" she asked cautiously.

The man took two steps closer and grasped her hand. The warmth of his fingers caught her off guard. Eyes locked with hers, he lifted her hand and brushed his lips across her fingers, then released her.

"A lady should always know what to expect from a gentleman."

Anne agreed completely.

"A woman as beautiful as you should expect nothing less than a diamond bracelet after an intimate evening."

She stiffened. He didn't intend to make her his mistress. He intended to have her for one night, then send her home. *With a diamond bracelet*, her mind whispered. The situation had grown far more desperate than she could have imagined. Not only had she failed to capture the interest of a suitable prospect for a husband, she couldn't even interest a man in making her his mistress.

It made no sense. Men had vied for her attention—many, for her hand in marriage—since she'd turned sixteen. Now that she *needed* to marry, she was avoided. Quite a few men had approached her at Lady Peddington's first ball—or, at least the first half of the ball, now that she thought about it.

"Good heavens," she said under her breath. Jeanine was right. Someone had spread rumors about her. She regarded the gentleman. "Where did ye hear these things about me?"

"Men talk—just as women do, I wager."

"How dare they," she muttered.

"I beg your pardon?"

"They've ruined my chances of finding the right man."

"Perhaps I am the right man," he said.

She surveyed him, his raven hair, blue eyes, broad shoulders and long legs, then shook her head. "Nae, you are too handsome."

He blinked. "I had no idea being 'too handsome' was a drawback."

"It is for my purposes."

"I promise you, my dear, it isn't."

She gave a frustrated shake of her head. "A man like you has no need of a mistress, much less a wife."

His expression remained impassive. "Are those the only choices?"

She narrowed her eyes. "There you have it. I am correct. You are looking for a woman who will entertain you for an evening and then leave her with some silly trinket."

"I assure you, I never give 'silly trinkets' to ladies."

Nervous laughter emanated from somewhere in the shadows to Anne's right, but she kept her attention on the man. "How expensive is the jewelry that you would give?"

He lifted a brow. "Are we negotiating?"

Anne suddenly felt certain the conversation was going all wrong for a courtesan searching for a protector. Still, she said, "Call it curiosity."

Amusement appeared in his eyes. "Just the other day, I happened to see a particularly lovely gold bracelet and was saddened by the fact that I had no one to give it to. The bracelet would cost me two hundred pounds."

That meant she might sell it for one hundred pounds, if she were lucky. Her stomach knotted tighter. A man and woman glided past them.

Anne shook her head. "Such a small gift would do me no good."

His gaze sharpened. "What would do you some good?"

She waved him off. "I have no time to waste when you are offering me a bauble for my trouble."

"Trouble?" he repeated, then laughed again, this time full, rich and with amusement.

To her horror, warmth rippled through her. He stepped closer. So close, she caught a whiff of the sandlewood soap he'd used to bathe. But unlike Niall, he made no move to touch her, and her desire to step back wasn't out of revulsion, but a desire to hide the blush that warmed her cheeks. Good Lord, the man was charming.

"I promise ye, my lady, that you will not consider a night with me 'trouble.'"

The spell broke. Anne narrowed her eyes. "I see, I am to consider myself fortunate to have a night with you, and grateful for the bonus of a gold bracelet."

"I don't think that's quite what I said."

"It is exactly what you said," she retorted. "It's the height of arrogance for a man to think that a woman should thank him for bedding her."

His expression cooled. "I believe it is you who *asked* me to thank you with a gold bracelet."

She drew a sharp breath. He was right. Still... "Aye, but you act as if some of that payment should come in the form of gratitude for being fortunate enough to be chosen for your one night of-of..." she was at a loss for words.

"*Affaire d'amour?*" he drawled.

She snorted. "One night can hardly be called an affair and has nothing whatsoever to do with love."

"Is that what you want, my lady, love?"

"A woman always wants love. Well, love doesn't put food on the table." She read the surprise in his eyes and realized she'd lost control of the situation. "Take yourself off to some other woman who is willing to sell herself for a gold bracelet," she said. "I have business to attend to."

* * *

Kennedy Douglas, Viscount Buchanan, entered his study and the erotic fantasy of the ravishing beauty at Lady Peddington's ball lying on his sheets beneath him vanished at sight of his stepmother seated on the divan near the window. She sat straight—the proper wife—her honey-brown hair swept off her shoulders in a carefully coiffured mound atop her head. Her ivory evening dress, befitting a thirty-year-old woman, hugged her trim, perfect curves. Too bad her husband had one foot in the grave.

"What fresh hell has brought you here at this time of night, Jacqueline?"

"I realize it is after one in the morning," she said, "but I have been waiting since nine."

He had indulged a little too much in the free-flowing champagne at the ball, but the presence of his father's wife in his study at one forty-five in the morning dictated that he have something stronger than champagne to drink. He crossed to the sideboard where sat half a dozen decanters filled with various liquors, and poured himself a liberal dose of scotch. He put the top back on the decanter, picked up the glass, and turned.

He leaned against the sideboard. "Short of forcibly throwing you out, I suppose I can't stop you from telling me what the earl wants. Unless, that is, I simply retire to my bedchambers." Kennedy sipped his scotch and watched her over the edge of the glass. "Would you be bold enough to follow me, if I did?"

"I am here on an errand for your father, nothing more," she replied.

"Of course. You won't risk him questioning your faithlessness with his death so close at hand."

"Really, Kennedy. Must you always be so cruel?"

He gave her a cold smile. "With you, my sweet, I am afraid so. I know I'll regret asking, but what is so important that you waited nearly five hours to tell me? I know it isn't that my father is dead, for you would have hazarded the gates of hell to find me, if that were the case." He took another drink of whisky. The pleasant burn comforted. "Not to mention, you're not smiling."

"It really is unkind of you to continue to imply that I will be happy when your father dies."

"As I said, with you, there is no other way. What do you want?"

She reached into her reticule, withdrew a piece of paper, and looked up at him. "This is from your father."

He gave a mirthless laugh. "You could've left that on my desk. Better yet, you could have sent it by messenger. Why are you here?"

"Since you refuse to see your father, he sent me with this message, and instructed me to wait for a reply."

Kennedy finished the scotch and turned to refill the glass. "As I have no desire to see my father, what could induce me to read his letter?"

She sighed, then the rustling of a paper followed, and she said, "Kennedy, I imagine you will not deign to touch a paper that I have touched. No matter. If you force Jaqueline to read this, it will be all the worse for you. I am dying. But you know that."

Kennedy poured a double dose of liquor.

"I have commanded you to marry," Jacqueline went on, "but you go about your business as if you have no responsibility to me, the title, or our position in society. I believe that you have not married—will not marry—just to spite me. But I cannot allow your vendetta to bring an end to our line. I know threats of cutting you off from my money are meaningless. You would rather live in squalor than do a single thing I ask. Therefore, you leave me no choice."

Kennedy slowed in sliding the decanter top back on the decanter.

"You will marry within the week" –Kennedy released the decanter top as she finished the sentence— "or I will marry your sister to Lord Granbury ten days from now on her sixteenth birthday."

Kennedy whirled. "What the bloody hell?"

Jacqueline said, "There is more. 'You might think to make off with your sister and hide her somewhere, which is why I have already sent her away. No one save myself knows where she is. If I die tomorrow, no one will know where to look for her.'"

Kennedy stared. "This is insanity."

Jacqueline didn't shift her eyes from the letter, but continued, "I will not settle for a betrothal. You must marry and produce an heir within a year. Do so, and I will allow you to choose your sister's husband when the time comes. Defy me, and I will not only marry her and Granbury, but they shall not return home until she has produced an heir for him."

Kennedy dashed his glass against the hearth and took two steps toward Jacqueline. "This reeks of your handiwork."

She shook her head. "You underestimate your father, and overestimate my influence."

"I know you both too well to mistake either of you," he snarled.

"What possible reason could I have for wanting to see you married?" She dropped her gaze. "I had always hoped..." She raised her head, eyes shimmering with moisture.

"By God," he exploded, "you missed your calling. You should have been an actress. Pray, do not pretend you have any tender feelings for me. Those illusions were shattered the day you rose from my bed and announced your engagement to my father." He snorted in derision. "I suppose I should thank him for marrying you. Though had he any idea that he was saving me from making the greatest mistake of my life, I'm sure he wouldn't have done it."

A tear slipped down her cheek.

Rage rammed through him. He crossed the room, seized her wrist and yanked her to her feet. "Where is Rose?"

She shrank back and shook her head. "I don't know. As the letter states, only he knows. He wouldn't chance my telling you." More tears slid down her cheeks. "He knows that you and I are close."

Kennedy released her and staggered back two paces. "Of course, he knows. That's why he married you."

She shook her head. "Nae, he does not know that we were—" She broke off

"Lovers?" he sneered.

"We were much more than that." She took a step toward him.

He turned away, his steps faltering, and reached his desk in time to brace himself, his back to her. "Leave, Jacqueline."

"Please, Kennedy, we cannot leave things like this between us."

"There is no *us*," he said.

Her skirts rustled and he realized she was walking toward him. He whirled to find her three steps away. He had to get away from her. Kennedy strode to the door. Hand on the knob, he looked back at her. "I suggest you not return home to your husband for at least an hour."

Half an hour later, Kennedy banged on the door of his father's mansion. The door opened in two seconds. Somewhere in the recesses of his mind, he realized the footman had been waiting for him. He pushed past the man and raced up the stairs to his father's bedchamber. The door stood open. Aye, his father expected him. He continued inside and found his father propped up in bed. A fission of alarm shot through him at sight of his father's yellow pallor. He looked far worse than when Kennedy had last seen him a year ago. Cruel fate. Only an hour ago, he would have rejoiced in seeing his father's decline. Now, until Rose was safely home, his father's illness frightened him more than anything ever had in his life.

The earl laid aside the book he'd been reading and met Kennedy's gaze.

"Where is she?" Kennedy demanded.

"Once you are married—to a proper lady, mind you, no peasant from the country—and once you produce an heir, I will bring her home," he replied in a strong voice that belied his appearance.

Kennedy's hands worked into fists at his sides. "I will kill you for this."

"Then you will never find your sister."

"She is not a child. She can find her way home." But she was a child. Only fifteen.

His father's gaze remained locked with his. "Do you really think I would make it that easy?"

Rage threatened to overwhelm him. His thoughts jumbled. His sister, only fifteen years old, being held prisoner somewhere. Would her jailers safeguard her?

Kennedy swayed. "How do I know she is safe?"

"She will always be safe under my care," his father replied.

"Your threat to marry her to Granbury proves otherwise," he snarled. "You know full well he beat his first wife to death."

"You are intelligent enough to know that gossip rarely resembles true events," the earl replied.

"I'm intelligent enough to know that most gossip has some grain of truth to it. If one hair on her head is harmed, I will kill you."

"You're threatening a dying man, Kennedy. I have made peace with my imminent death."

"You could live another year, to three or four. I can end you before that. I can end you tonight."

"Then you would never see your sister again."

"What happens if you die before I can produce an heir?" His heart thundered.

"I suggest you pray that doesn't happen."

Kennedy stared. His father was a bastard, but this went beyond anything Kennedy could have imagined the old man capable of. "You cannot keep her prisoner forever. She will escape. She will return home. Your threat is unreasonable." The last, he said more for himself than his father.

"Your sister isn't in Scotland. Escape is nigh to impossible. Even if she did manage by some miracle to escape, she would have to journey home. She has no friends, no money, no escort." The last words were said with an emphasis that told Kennedy his father knew the exact picture that had arisen in Kennedy's mind at the thought of his young sister trying to return home on her own. And she would try just that.

"You would sacrifice your daughter?" he whispered. "Risk her losing everything, possibly even her life, just to force me to marry?"

"You see my actions as those of a man bent on hurting you. I see my actions as those of a desperate man trying to preserve his legacy."

"Legacy?" Kennedy sneered. "I should have known. This has nothing to do with me. You don't give a damn if I marry or even carry on the title. This is about you wanting to be *remembered*." Kennedy released a harsh breath. "If you wanted to extract revenge because I had Jacqueline before you did, I would have more respect for you. But this—" He shook his head. "You are right. These are the actions of a desperate man. You're a liar, Father. You do fear death." His father's eyes narrowed, but Kennedy gave him no chance to reply. "I will marry within a week. But on one condition."

His father waited.

"Once you confirm my wife is with child, you will bring Rose home."

His father shook his head. "Your wife could lose the child, and the child might not be a male. I know you well enough to know that you wouldn't touch her again just to spite me."

Kennedy stared. "I would agree to the terms, if I were you. Keep in mind, I have considerable resources at my disposal. You know, of course, the moment I leave this house, I will begin my own search for Rose. If fortune favors me—and she often does—and I find my sister before you die, I will divorce my wife and immediately set about siring a string of bastards, none of whom can claim your title." Kennedy gave him a cold smile. "Then I will seduce your wife and sire a child on her that cannot possibly inherit your title."

His father's eyes widened. "You're not capable of such dastardly actions."

Kennedy gave him a cold smile. "I am capable of far worse. After all, I am your son."

CHAPTER TWO

THE FOLLOWING MORNING, KENNEDY had just called for his carriage when a footman announced the arrival of a guest, Sir Stirling James. Kennedy frowned. What was the marquess doing here so early, and without an appointment?

"Show him in," he said.

Moments later, the footman reappeared and announced Sir Stirling James. Kennedy rose, circled his desk and extended a hand toward Sir Stirling. They clasped hands.

"Forgive the intrusion," Sir Stirling said, and released him.

Kennedy indicated the chairs and divan hear the window. Stirling took the seat and Kennedy sat on the divan.

"It's no intrusion," Kennedy said. "What can I do for you this morning."

"I believe it is what I can do for you," Sir Stirling replied. "I understand you need a wife—immediately."

Kennedy blinked. "How the devil do you know that?"

Stirling flashed white teeth. "The news appeared in this morning's gossip sheets."

"I wouldn't take you for a man to read gossip sheets," Kennedy said.

Stirling's smile didn't falter. "A man needn't read the gossip sheets for news of this magnitude to reach him."

"How the bloody hell did the news get out so quickly?" Kennedy muttered. Then instantly knew the answer. Not only had his father known that he would show up in his home last night, he had known Kennedy would capitulate.

That made no difference.

Kennedy refocused on Stirling. "Forgive me, but I have important business this morning. I was on my way out when you arrived."

"No doubt on your way to propose to whichever lady it is you've chosen to marry."

The man was uncannily perceptive. But, then, perhaps it wasn't that hard to guess. Or was it? Kennedy regarded him. "The fact that I'm on the hunt for a wife in no way indicates that I'm racing to the altar. Yet, I get the impression that's what you think."

"You must marry within one week, if I understand correctly."

Kennedy started. "Surely that wasn't in the gossip sheets?" That would ruin him.

Sir Stirling shook his head. "Forgive me, nae. *Society* only believes that you have decided to marry. However, I understand that your father gave you a week to marry."

Anger surged through him. "My lord, you and I are not well acquainted. Forgive me, but how the hell do you know that?"

"The best I can say, is that servants talk."

Kennedy cursed. "What has any of this to do with you?" His mind raced. He knew Sir Stirling only casually. He wouldn't have pegged the man for someone who engaged in idle gossip, or who took advantage of those in a vulnerable position. But he'd been wrong about men—and women—before.

"It is well known that you have no interest in marriage," Sir Stirling said. "To my knowledge, there is no one particular lady that you favor."

"What of it?" Kennedy demanded.

"I assume, that you would choose a lady among your acquaintances to fulfill your father's demands. However, I know a lady who I believe will suit your purposes quite well."

Kennedy was at a loss as to how to reply. Of all the things this man might say, this had never entered his mind. He sat down. "How is it you know someone who will suit my needs?"

"Pure luck, I assure you. This is a lady who is in need of a husband with money."

Kennedy barked a laugh. "That is a qualification that could include half the women in Edinburgh."

Stirling nodded. "True. However, this is a lady who is sure to satisfy your father in a way most other ladies cannot. It's an obvious conclusion to say that your father would like you to carry on the title. However, the earl strikes me as the sort of man who would like to leave behind, shall we say, a legacy."

Kennedy gave a slow nod. "Your information is uncannily accurate."

A smile tugged at Sir Stirling's mouth. "This is more of an impression than information I have gleaned. I don't know your father well. In fact, I've met him but twice, and the last time I saw him was five years ago at a soirée in London. He is a man who is certain of his place in the world, and the impression he will leave behind."

"You almost make him sound noble."

"He's your father, and I would not speak ill of—"

"I have no illusions as to what sort of man my father is," Kennedy cut in.

Stirling gave a slow nod. "He cares a great deal about how he is viewed by the world. By you and your son carrying on his title, he believes part of him will live on. That is not an unnatural feeling. However, he might consider your successes and even your son's successes to be a result of his actions."

"It's more than that," Kennedy said more to himself than Stirling. "Even now, with one foot in the grave, he can't stand to have *Society* view him as weak. He must be the ever-constant force that keeps the world in motion."

Stirling smiled, and Kennedy was surprised at the compassion he read in the man's eyes. "What a shame that he's wasted his life on meaningless pursuits, instead of caring for the one person whose world did revolve around him, if only for a little while."

Kennedy felt as if he'd been punched in the gut. What tiny bit of love that had remained after his father tore him from his mother's deathbed and sent him to university a year ahead of schedule, he'd killed when he'd married Jacqueline. Kennedy barely remembered the days when he'd worshiped his father. Yet those feelings cut like a knife.

"Of course, your father assumes you will choose from the pool of ladies with whom you are acquainted."

Kennedy realized Stirling was speaking. "What? Oh, yes, I must marry a woman of breeding. He was very clear on that point."

"This lady will fulfill that qualification. She is, in fact, Viscountess Kinsely, heir to the title. Her father died with no male heir."

"A second title in the bargain," Kennedy murmured. "You are correct, that would please my father."

"It would please him even more if he thought the idea was his," Stirling said.

Kennedy frowned. "What do you mean?"

"I mean, if your father decided who you should marry..." His words trailed off and he shrugged.

In truth, Kennedy was surprised his father hadn't chosen his bride. "How will my father come to this conclusion?" he asked.

Stirling grinned. "Leave that to me."

"I can take no chances," Kennedy said.

"Of course not." Stirling rose. "I would guess that you'll hear from your father by tomorrow."

Kennedy stood. "How do you plan on making him think this was his idea?"

Stirling shrugged. "Very simple, really. All that must happen is for him to learn of the lady's existence. He will be unable to refrain from interfering."

* * *

The carriage slowed, and Anne caught sight of a massive stone mansion through the window. She had to be dreaming. The last two nights she'd lain awake searching for a plan that would save her home and her family. Nothing short of ten thousand pounds would ensure they had a chance at survival. Two hours ago, she'd received a note. A summons, really. The Earl of Buchanan requested—commanded—her appearance at his home at three for the purpose of... Despite the presence of the maid sitting across from her, Anne couldn't help pulling the note from her reticule and reading it for the hundredth time. *...arrange a betrothal between you and my son, Viscount Buchanan.*

A hundred questions swirled inside her head. Why couldn't his son find a wife? Why did the Earl want to marry *her* to his son? How had the Earl heard of her? She was the daughter of an impoverished viscount who didn't move in *Society*. She couldn't remember the last time her father had visited Edinburgh. Had the Earl not heard the terrible rumors about her? Maybe he had, but his son couldn't get anyone better than an unfaithful woman. Her head felt near to bursting with questions.

The coach tipped slightly and in the next instance, the door opened. Anne extended her hand and allowed the footman to help her to the ground, then he helped her companion. Lady Peddington had insisted the maid accompany her. In truth, Anne was glad for her presence, even if her companion couldn't offer any advice.

The footman closed the coach door and Anne nodded her thanks, then walked with the maid up the walkway to the door. She knocked. A moment later, the door opened and a footman led them to a large parlor where they settled on a divan. Anne's heart began to pound and her hands sweated inside her gloves. She had not the slightest idea what to expect. How she wished Lady Peddington had come with her, but other duties prohibited her from accompanying Anne.

The door opened and a short, thin man entered. Anne rose and Molly followed her example.

"I am Mr. Spector, my lady." He bowed. "His lordship's solicitor."

Anne looked past him at the open door.

"His lordship will not be here," he said. "He is very ill. I represent his interests."

Anne nodded. "Oh, forgive me. This is Molly, my companion," she said.

Mr. Spector bowed again, and said, "Please, be seated."

They resumed their seats on the divan and Mr. Spector took the chair to Anne's left.

"As I said, his lordship is ill. He wishes his son to marry post haste." The man gave what, Anne assumed, was meant to be a comforting smile, but it looked more pained than comforting. "He is willing to offer you a generous settlement."

Anne's heart pounded. She had known this topic would arise, but had assumed that by the time it did, she would be on intimate enough terms with her prospective husband for him to understand that her title would be her dowry. But a man in line for an earldom had no need of a title as viscount.

"Sir, perhaps his lordship is unaware that I have no dowry to offer, other than the title that will pass to my future husband."

Again, the man offered a smile, this one almost a grimace. "Indeed, my lady, the earl is well aware you have no dowry. He is pleased that his son will carry your title. If you will take a moment and review the contract." He pulled a document from an inside jacket pocket, unfolded it, and handed it to her.

Anne angled her head in thanks, and began reading. When she'd finished, she was more than certain she was dreaming. The earl would settle five thousand pounds on her on the day they married—which would be two days hence—and another ten thousand pounds the day she bore his son an heir. On top of that, she would receive a thousand pounds a year to do with as she pleased. The five thousand pounds was enough to get them through the first harvest season.

Her thoughts threatened to churn into chaos, but she forced order and concentrated on one thing: the money. There was no guarantee she would bear a son the first year. A thousand pounds a year wouldn't support the estate, but another fifteen hundred would get them by. As the wife of a wealthy viscount who was heir to an earldom, there had to be a way for her to get more money. But how? Never mind. She would figure that out along the way. She couldn't possibly get a better offer than this one.

She looked at Mr. Spector. "I own property north of Perth as well as in the Highlands. That property will remain in my possession."

"I believe that will be acceptable, my lady. So long as the property falls to your son at your death."

She nodded. "My mother and sister live at Dover Hall. They will remain there as long as they wish."

He nodded. "You will reside here in Edinburgh until you bear an heir. After that, you may retire to the country, if you wish. Of course, your son will remain here in Edinburgh."

A chill swept through her. Leave her son? She hadn't considered that. But then, she hadn't considered children beyond the knowledge that children were an obvious result of marriage.

"Are you saying, I will be banished to the country while my children remain here in Edinburgh?"

"Nae, my lady. I am saying that you would not be allowed to leave your husband and take them to the country."

"Not even for a visit?"

"Of course, you and your husband may decide to visit anywhere you like. But the children will be raised here in Edinburgh."

Her heart sank. She hadn't given a thought to where her children might be raised, but upon reflection, she couldn't imagine them being raised anywhere but at Dover Hall. This was far more complicated than she'd considered. But then, like now, she had considered only the money. What a fool she'd been to think she could simply marry a man and live life as she chose. She had to marry, of that there was no question. But her life would no longer be her own. She could visit Dover Hall and Marr Castle, but even that was dependent upon her husband's goodwill.

What choice had she? At best, she her sister and their mother would last one more year before the creditors swooped down upon them. If that happened, none of them would have a home.

CHAPTER THREE

ANNE HALF WISHED SHE'D insisted upon meeting her future husband at the church rather than agree to wait at Lady Peddington's for his carriage. Whether he picked up her and her family from Lady Peddington's and rode with them to the church, or met them at the church, there was no turning back.

Her sister fidgeted beside her on the couch in the parlor, and her mother sat in the chair to their right, gripping a handkerchief, as they awaited the viscount's carriage.

"You look so terribly pale," Anne's sister said.

Anne gave Louisa a smile. "Nerves, nothing more. Once the ceremony is over and we're all settled into our new life, things will be just fine."

"I know it makes no difference, but I still want to say once more that I wish you hadn't done this," Louisa said. "We would have found another way. That nice Mr. Allen has been courting Mama. A marriage proposal is sure to come any day."

"Mr. Allen is a nice man," their mother said, "but he has no money to speak of."

"Between us three and him, we could have found a way," Louisa insisted.

Anne smiled. The determination and hope of youth. Only a year ago, she had been full of that same optimism.

"I've made a good match," Anne said. "He's the heir to an earldom—a very wealthy earldom. We need never again worry about money."

"Only if he gives ye enough money to help us keep Dover Hall running,"

Louisa said. "Not to mention, Castle Dòmnallach."

"Two years from now, the estates will be self-sufficient," Anne said. She would see to that. "You and Mama need never worry about having a home. You will have time to make a good match, Louisa, and Mama can marry whomever she likes, whether or not he has the skills necessary to run the estates. We shall stay in control of our property."

"Dover Hall will go to your son," Louisa said.

"Only upon my death," Anne said. But Castle Dòmnallach will remain yours."

At the thump of boot falls in the corridor, Anne snapped her attention toward the parlor door. Her heart began to pound.

Steady, she told herself. *Mama and Louisa are here. You do not want them to see you frightened.*

The boot falls came closer. Her mother's and sister's attentions were also fixed on the open door. Closer. He would be here any second.

Anne tore her gaze from the doorway, reached for Louisa's hand and squeezed gently. Louisa's head snapped in her direction.

"Remember," Anne whispered, "this man will be your new brother. We must not make him uncomfortable."

Louisa nodded, but worry furrowed her brow. From the corner of her eye, Anne glimpsed movement in the doorway.

"Viscount Buchanan is here to see you, my lady," the butler announced.

Louisa's eyes widened. Their mother started to rise. Anne, still holding her sister's hand, pushed to her feet, pulling her sister up with her, and faced her future husband.

The butler stepped aside and Anne stared. In all her wildest dreams, she wouldn't have guessed that the man she was betrothed to was— "You," she whispered.

"Bloody hell," he muttered.

Their mother dropped into a courtesy. Louisa curtsied, pulling Anne down into a curtsy with her.

Anne straightened and extended her hand toward him. "It is a pleasure to meet you at last, my Lord."

Something flickered in his eyes. She realized she'd miscalculated, but didn't know how. He approached, grasped her hand with long fingers, and brushed his lips against her knuckles.

"I cannot tell ye how pleased I am to meet you, my lady."

He still gripped her hand. She tugged harder than she should've had to in order to free herself. She turned slightly. "May I present my sister, Lady Louisa, and my mother, the dowager viscountess."

The viscount bowed over both their hands, then said, "It is a pleasure to meet you."

"It was very kind of you to fetch us yourself, my lord," her mother said.

He gave her a polite smile. "It is my pleasure, and, please, ma'am, call me Kennedy."

Her mother angled her head in acquiescence and started to reply, when Dorothy and Fiona entered the room. They stopped short as if in surprise, and Dorothy's hand flew to her mouth.

"Oh my," Dorothy exclaimed. "We didn't realize this room was in use. Forgive the intrusion."

They realized it quite well, Anne wagered. The girls were not typically in this part of the house at this time of day. But all the better.

Anne smiled. "It's no intrusion, Dorothy. Ladies, may I introduce Viscount Buchanan. My lord, this is Miss Williams and Miss Evans."

The girls curtsied and the viscount gave a slight bow.

"How wonderful to finally meet you, my lord," Linda said. "We didn't have the chance to meet you when you attended Lady Peddington's ball last week."

Anne stiffened. The little vipers thought they would expose her to her mother.

"Which ball would that be again?" the viscount said.

"Lady Peddington's ball, last Saturday evening," Dorothy said.

The viscount frowned as if in thought. "Ah, yes, I believe I did drop by, but arrived later than intended, during Lady Peddington's Midnight Ball."

Anne stared. Was he giving them a set down for trying to embarrass her?

The girl's faces turned ashen.

"Sir, you must be mistaken," Linda quickly said. "We did not attend the Midnight Ball."

His frown deepened. "Then perhaps it wasn't me you saw." He faced Anne and her family. "Forgive me, but we should leave if we are to reach the church on time." His gaze shifted to Anne. "Have you any trunks, my lady?"

"Nothing to take with us to the church, sir," she replied.

"And you are dressed for the ceremony?"

Her cheeks warmed. "Aye, sir. The lace is the finest in all of Scotland and the pink satin," she smiled, "pink is a favorite of mine."

"It is a stunning color on you," he said. "Shall we go?"

They nodded and he stood aside as they walked past Dorothy and Linda and proceeded him out of the room. He caught up to Anne and her heart thundered with the fear that he would mention their meeting at Lady Peddington's. He didn't, however, and he helped them into the carriage, and they started forward with a creak of the carriage wheels. Anne was all too aware of the heat from his body. He remained a perfect gentleman, but made no effort to sit far away from her on their side of the carriage. Was he was taunting her? Was he one of those men who needed a woman to stay close at his side?

"Do you live in Edinburgh?"

Anne started at the sound of Louisa's voice. To her surprise, the viscount smiled gently at Louisa. "A great deal of the time, aye. We have a castle in Inverness, which I used to visit every year."

"Not anymore?" she asked.

"Not as much as I'd like," he said. "Perhaps you will like to visit."

Louisa smiled. "Indeed, sir, I would."

He looked at Anne and her face heated. "Do you like Inverness, my lady?"

"I have never been."

"It's quite beautiful."

Had that been a wistful note in his voice?

"You and your family are welcome to spend as much time there as you like."

Anne's stomach knotted. Was he going to send them away? Mr. Spector said otherwise, but…

They reached the church and entered the foyer. Anne glimpsed only four people sitting in the pews before a young woman ushered her mother and sister into the chapel, leaving Anne alone in the foyer with the viscount.

"Very clever," he said in a low voice once they were out of earshot.

He didn't have to explain, she knew exactly what he meant. "I had no idea you were the man I met at Lady Peddington's ball," she said.

He gave a mirthless laugh. "The coincidence is too much of a, well, coincidence. I do no' believe you."

She let out a frustrated breath. "How could I possibly have arranged this? Your father contacted me. I never met him."

Doubt flickered in his eyes. "Do you know Sir Stirling James?" he demanded.

She frowned. "Who?"

"Never mind," he said. "I supposed it doesn't matter."

His tone said it did matter. The murmur of voices echoed back to them from the chapel. "When I saw you at the ball, you did not appear to be a man desperate to marry," she said.

"How does a man act who is desperate to marry?" he asked. "Any desire to marry had little to do with me being at that ball."

She snorted again. "That, I believe."

He gave her a critical look. "Your actions were not those of a woman interested in marriage."

"You're basing that on vicious gossip."

"Hardly. I am basing that on the fact that you negotiated with me for a night in your bed."

She lifted her brows. "I thought it was a night in *your* bed."

His mouth twitched in what she realized was amusement, but the mood vanished almost as quickly as it came. "Let me be very clear on one important point. You will take no lovers until I have an heir and a spare."

Fury whipped through her. "I assume the same rule does not apply to you?"

A cool smile spread across his face. "A man's by blows will never be mistaken for his heirs."

"Then the vows we are about to take mean nothing to you."

"On the contrary, they mean a great deal to me. You and our children will have my protection and my support."

"But not your loyalty," she retorted.

"Make no mistake, my lady, real loyalty takes place outside the bedroom."

* * *

The priest entered the foyer, and Kennedy turned to face him.

"If you are ready, my lord, my lady," he said.

Kennedy nodded and the priest returned to the chapel.

Kennedy looked at his wife-to-be. "Shall we? He winged his arm toward her.

She slipped her hand into the crook of his arm, then he led her into the sanctuary and up to the altar. Only half a dozen people sat in the pews, including Anne's sister and mother. His father's solicitor sat beside Jacqueline in the left front pew. Kennedy wouldn't be surprised to find her outside their bed chambers with her ear pressed against the door, so that she could confirm the consummation of the marriage. One other man sat in the third pew. Sir Stirling James. Stirling gave him an almost imperceptible nod as they passed. After the ceremony, Kennedy would speak with him. He wanted to know how Stirling knew of Anne—and got word to his father about her existence.

They reached the altar. Anne pulled her hand free and turned to face him.

Christ, he was about to marry a woman who only last week had bartered with him for her charms. She was lovely, there was no doubt about that, but he would have his father's head for this.

Kennedy weaved through the ceremony like a man in a dream. When the priest asked for the rings, Kennedy slipped onto her finger the diamond and ruby ring that had been his mother's. She put on his finger a simple gold band. That, he was surprised to admit, suited him well. The priest pronounced them man and wife and bade Kennedy kiss his wife. He slipped an arm around her slim waist and pulled her closer than intended. She clasped his shoulders and he glimpsed her closed eyes in the instant before his mouth touched hers.

As he knew they would be, her full lips were soft and warm. The embrace lasted by three heartbeats. She pulled back before he did, and the priest led them to the registry. They signed, but Kennedy felt no relief despite the fact he'd taken the first step toward fulfilling his father's demands. Unless his search for his sister succeeded, at least three months of hell lay before him, and that was only if he was able to impregnate his wife right away. What would he do if it turned out she was barren, or worse, he was unable to sire a child?

He couldn't help a rueful mental laugh. All these years, he'd been careful not to father a by-blow. If he had been careless—or lucky, depending on how one viewed the matter—and had sired a bastard, at least he would know he was able to father a child.

Suddenly, his wife was being hugged by her mother and sister. He was forced to allow Jacqueline to kiss his cheek, and she did the same to Anne, her sister and mother. Mr. Spector shook hands with Kennedy. Kennedy looked back at the pews, but Sir Stirling was gone.

Forty-five minutes later, they sat at the dining table at his townhouse, partaking of the wedding feast. Kennedy would have gladly sent Jacqueline home, but here she sat to his left, while his wife sat to his right. He wasn't likely to forget this day for the rest of his life.

"Will you visit us at Dover Hall, my lord?" Lady Louisa asked him.

He looked up from his plate and smiled at her. "I beg you, call me Kennedy. We are family now, I am your brother."

She beamed. "Then ye must call me Louisa."

He nodded. "Thank you, Louisa. As to your question, we will plan a time to visit Dover Hall. For the moment, I have business that keeps me in Edinburgh. Of course, you and your mother are welcome to stay with us as long as you like."

"That is most kind of you," the dowager viscountess said. "Unfortunately, we must return home tomorrow." She smiled. "Like you, business beckons."

He wondered what business the dowager viscountess might have, but he would save that question for another day. "Of course, I understand."

"Perhaps we will be fortunate enough for your business to conclude in the not-too-distant future, so that you might come visit us," she said.

Kennedy had no intention of going anywhere until his son was born. But he smiled and said, "Perhaps."

"Anne can always come and visit us, as well," Louisa said.

Kennedy had no intention of allowing her to go anywhere until they had a son, but, again, he said, "Perhaps, though I may want to keep her to myself for just a little while."

That comment earned him a startled look from his wife. He didn't know her well—in truth, he didn't know her at all—but he had a suspicion that silence wasn't her normal state, and he wondered if he should be worried.

"Do you spend much time in Edinburgh, my lady?" Jacqueline asked the dowager viscountess.

"Nae, the running of Dover Hall demands most of my time."

Kennedy forked pheasant into this mouth. Was this the business she spoke of? The running of an estate could monopolize one's time.

"Surely you will spend more time here now that Anne and Kennedy are married. Are you certain you cannot stay another two days? We are planning a ball in their honor tomorrow evening."

Kennedy snapped his gaze onto Jacqueline. "I know nothing of this."

"Your father wanted it to be a surprise, and we had to be sure the preparations were in order before we said anything. I'm pleased to say that we have sent out two hundred invitations."

Kennedy thinned his lips. "It didn't occur to my father that we might have plans?"

She gave a gentle smile, a mother's smile, that would have fooled anyone except him. "Your father is not long for this world, Kennedy. Would you deny him something so simple?"

"It seems I cannot deny him anything."

Anne gave him a startled look and Kennedy realized she hadn't spoken a single word the entire breakfast.

Jacqueline laid a hand on his arm. "Kennedy, your father wanted me to tell you that he will be sending a wedding gift."

Anne's gaze flicked to Jacqueline's hand on his arm. Kennedy cursed inwardly. He had intended to keep his life separate from his marriage. Jacqueline, however, clearly had other ideas.

CHAPTER FOUR

ANNE PULLED HER SHAWL closer about her shoulders and paced the carpet in front of her bedchamber's low burning hearth. She was a virgin, but she wasn't without knowledge of what transpired between a man and a woman. It wasn't that which had her on edge, however. Well, not totally, at any rate. Part of the problem—a large part of the problem—was that she found her husband attractive. It would be far easier for their marriage of convenience to remain a convenience and nothing more. To make matters worse, he believed she was a loose woman. But was that truly the worst part? She hadn't missed the way his stepmother laid her hand on his arm. The gesture was intimate, that of lovers. Surely her husband wasn't having an affair with his father's wife?

She stopped and plopped down on the chair in front of the hearth. Why hadn't she been fortunate enough to simply marry a short, pudgy man with bad breath? Instead, she married a man who could rival the gods. He clearly had no intention of being faithful to her—not that she'd ever given that much thought. But she would rather not be embroiled in a family drama that would land them in the gossip sheets. Had she married that short, pudgy man with bad breath, in all likelihood, he would have had little opportunity to be unfaithful.

She braced her elbows on her knees and rested her chin in her hands. She was an idiot. Any man with money could find a woman who would spread her legs for him. Why in God's name did she care? She had yet to consummate her marriage and already she worried about her husband taking a lover. No doubt, the viscount would have a string of women over the course of their marriage. She would save herself a great deal of grief by giving the matter no more thought. She only hoped his stepmother wasn't among those lovers.

What mattered now was the money she would receive upon producing an heir. That attempt would begin tonight. She wished she had a little time to become comfortable in her marriage before having a child. Even a marriage of convenience would take some time to grow accustomed to. But she had no more the luxury of time now than she had a week ago.

A knock sounded on the side door and she jumped. Good Lord, what was that? The door connecting her rooms to the master's chamber, she realized. Her heart began to beat fast. Another knock.

She stood. "Come in."

The door open and the viscount entered. He wore a silk robe cinched at the waist. Tanned flesh was visible in the V at his neck. He was even barefoot. Was he naked beneath the robe? She'd never been alone with a man in such a state of undress.

"Are your mother and sister settled in?" he said.

Anne nodded. "Yes, thank you. And thank you for having them here."

"This is now your home," he said. "They are welcome anytime."

She nodded, he said nothing, and she had the sense that he simply wanted to get the night over with. She recalled their conversation at Lady Peddington's ball—his implication that a night with him would be well spent. Oddly, he seemed to have lost that bravado.

"Why did your father choose me to marry you?" she asked.

He hesitated, then said, "He wanted your title."

Anne frowned. "Why would he want my title? He is an earl. My title is meaningless."

"But it isn't meaningless. It's another feather in his cap. He made a match for me that brought with it an elevated status in society."

"Your father is ill. Why would he possibly care about such things?"

He gave a mirthless laugh. "My father will care about such things from the grave. He has an insatiable desire for power and status."

"He would have you marry an impoverished woman just because you could take on the title of viscount?"

"My current title as Viscount Buchanen is courtesy, because I am his son. That is no longer the case. I am now Viscount Kinsley, and with that comes all the privilege and status, along with the property you own."

She tensed. "I informed your father's solicitor that the property that my father owned would remain mine. Dover Hall will go to our son, but Castle Dòmnallach will remain with my sister."

He nodded. "I have no intention of taking possession of your property. I'm only explaining to you my father's motivation. When my father dies, I will be the sixth Earl of Buchanen and Viscount Kinsley." He lifted a brow. "Very impressive, do you not agree?"

Anne noted sarcasm in his voice.

His expression grew speculative. "I explained why my father chose you. Now, explain why you agreed to marry me."

She shrugged. "I would think that should be obvious. I need money."

"That's why a two-hundred-pound bracelet wasn't worth the night with me," he said.

She nodded. There was no use pretending otherwise. "Your father is very anxious to have a grandson."

"So anxious, he would offer you five thousand pounds once one is born. That's a king's ransom compared to a paltry two-hundred-pound bracelet."

He almost sounded offended. "Our marriage is a business agreement," she said. "Would you prefer I wanted love?"

He grimaced and said, "God forbid," with such fervor that she wondered if she should be offended.

But she said, "Then you are in luck," with more emphasis than intended, and cursed her temper. "I have a family to care for. That is why I married you. You needed an heir—and your father wanted another title. A perfect match." She regarded him. "Why did you allow your father to choose your bride?"

"He wanted me married immediately and I had no preference."

"How sad," she murmured.

"Do you think so?" he said. "Should a man always be in love?"

Anne shook her head. This time she had offended him. "A man needn't be in love to have at least one friend he might be able to choose as a wife."

"Perhaps I take more seriously the task of choosing a wife than you did a husband."

"On the contrary, I put a great deal of thought into the sort of husband I need."

"Your only requirement is that he have enough money to support your ancestral homes."

Was he trying to make her angry? For once in her life, she couldn't be riled so easily. She gave a slow nod. "Aye, I had but one requirement: he must have money. But it seems you had no requirements."

"That is where you are mistaken, my sweet. My one requirement was that my father approved."

"Perhaps you and I are not so different," she said. "A man of your rank and wealth, would allow his father to choose his wife for only one reason. Did he threaten to cut you off?" She couldn't help but smile. "Have no fear, my lord. I admire a man who knows what he wants and isn't afraid to pursue it."

* * *

Kennedy stared at his wife for a moment in surprise, then threw back his head and laughed. "At least I will no' be bored with you, my dear." His amusement vanished. "Perhaps my father did me more of a good turn that I realized."

Her brows shot up. "Never say that is a complement, sir."

He chuckled. "A man must give due were due is deserved. I believe I might keep that to myself, however. My father need not know."

"When will I meet him?" she asked.

"Good God, never, if I have anything to say about it."

"Surely, he will want to meet me," she said.

"If he were a normal father, aye. But he isn't. He will want to see our son when he is born."

Her cheeks pinked prettily, and he realized they'd better get on with the business of the evening. She dark hair tumbled past her shoulders. He took the two steps to her side, then gently removed the shawl from her shoulders and tossed it aside. She wore a practical linen nightshift that didn't quite hide the rose-colored tips of her breasts. His cock began to rise. Aye, he would have no trouble bedding this woman. When he slipped an arm around her waist and pulled her close, she leaned away from him.

He looked down at her. "Husbands are often known to show their gratitude with jewelry."

Her mouth parted in surprise, then her eyes narrowed, and he realized his mistake. "How very kind of you to show your gratitude to your *wife* with jewelry. Do you mind if I show mine by selling it?"

He blinked in surprise, expected anger, but had to laugh again. "Are you always so delightfully honest?"

"Aye," she said without hesitation, and he laughed harder.

Kennedy was forced to release her or laugh in her face. Perhaps the laughter was a delayed response of hysteria. Or perhaps she was simply funny.

How was he supposed to make love to a woman who kept him laughing? There was only one answer. He stepped, closer yanked her against him, and kissed her. She gave a squeak of surprise. He thought for an instant he would laugh again, then she melted against him and the laughter vanished. She grasped his shoulders as she had when he kissed her at the ceremony, but this time, the heat of her fingers penetrated the thin fabric of his silk robe. When she squeezed the hard muscle, he wondered what her fingers would feel like around his hard length.

He flicked his tongue against her lips. She hesitated, then opened for him. Kennedy slipped his tongue inside her mouth and her tongue cautiously touched his. A jolt of desire tightened his bollocks. The woman could easily bring a man to his knees. A thought struck. She said that her desperation to marry stemmed from a need to care for her family, but what if it was something more? What if she was carrying another man's child?"

He wanted to laugh again, only this time the humor was dark. It would serve his father right for Kennedy's heir to be another man's offspring. Kennedy, however, wasn't so certain he liked the idea. He brushed off the thought. If she was already pregnant, that only meant Rose would return home soon.

Kennedy slid his hand down her back and over the curve of her firm buttocks. She drew a sharp breath as he gently undulated his erection against her belly. He broke the kiss and slid his mouth along her cheek to her ear. When he took her lobe into his mouth and nibbled, she wiggled in his grasp, and he realized he wanted her—badly.

He swept her into his arms and crossed to the bed. When he laid her on the mattress, her hair fanned around her face just as he'd imagined that first night. She really was lovely. He couldn't blame her if she carried another man's child. Hadn't he told her that a woman had just as much right as a man to see to her pleasures? A woman in her position, however, might find it prudent to bear her husband an heir first. For all he knew, that had been her plan. Perhaps she'd been engaged, and the man jilted her. Whatever the case, he could have done far worse.

With a flourish, he yanked the tie free on his robe and sloughed it from his back, then came down on top of her. Her soft curves molded to his body as if made for him. He cupped her face between his hands and kissed her gently. Slowly, she slid her hands up his shoulders and wrapped her arms around his neck.

He broke the kiss and slid his mouth downward along her jaw, her neck, to the rise of her breasts and finally to the nipple that now pressed like a pebble against the fabric of her night shift. He took one bud in his mouth and suckled. She drew a sharp breath. Desire swept through him.

When was the last time a woman had excited him so quickly? Jacqueline? He thrust his cock against her abdomen. She fisted his hair. He gave a low laugh then switched to her other breast. There was something to be said about marrying a woman who knew what she wanted.

He really had to get that damned shift off her.

Kenney levered up on his arms and looked down at her. "What do you say, love? Are you ready to take off that shift?" Her cheeks colored and Kennedy laughed, then rolled onto the mattress beside her. He stuffed his hands beneath his head. "Go ahead, I will watch."

Her mouth fell open. "You want to watch while I undress?"

He shrugged. "Why not? I let you watch while I took off my robe."

Her blush deepened. "Aye, but you are-are, and I am—" She broke off.

"There is no need to be shy with me, love," he said. "I told you. I don't mind that you're a woman who has already sought her pleasures."

She blinked, then fury played across her features, and he realized his mistake. Kennedy set upright ad reached for her, but too late.

She scrambled off the bed and backed up two paces. "If you believe I am a loose woman, why did you marry me?" Before he could answer, she said. "Oh, yes, of course. I forgot. Your father commanded you to marry, and that is all that matters."

An answering fury whipped through him and Kennedy shoved from the bed to his feet. Her wide-eyed gaze flicked to his erection, which jutted upward like a steel rod.

"Aye, madam, producing an heir is *all* that matters. Just as you needing money is all that matters to you."

"Thank heavens for that," she retorted. "Otherwise, I would be disappointed."

"Then you *are* one of those women who expect love," he said.

"Ha!" She burst out. "Thankfully, I do not suffer that malady."

An odd pain stabbed at his heart. "Then you won't mind if I carry on as I always have."

"As will I." She arched a brow. "You did say that you admired a woman who knew what she wanted and wasn't afraid to pursue it."

"You will not pursue your pleasure until I have an heir."

"That is not a point stipulated in the marriage contract."

He knew she was angry, knew the argument had gotten out of hand, but he couldn't stop himself from saying. "Test me on this, my dear, and you will find your lovers meeting me at a dawn appointment." With that, he quit the room.

* * *

Anne gave thanks when she entered the breakfast room the following morning to find Kennedy absent. Her mother and sister were having coffee, and she slipped into the chair opposite her mother.

"Good morning, Mama. Louisa. How did you sleep?"

"Very well," her mother replied.

Anne kept her eyes on her cup as she poured coffee.

"I slept with Mama," Louisa said. "This house has noises that ours doesn't."

Anne smiled. "I think it's more accurate to say that Dover Hall has noises, while his lordship's townhouse is too quiet."

"His lordship?" her mother said.

Anne sighed inwardly. Leave it to her mother to notice the smallest slip. "It will take some time for me to grow accustomed to calling him by his Christian name," Anne said.

"Hmm," her mother intoned as she raised her cup.

Anne took a hearty drink of her coffee and didn't respond to her mother.

"We have decided to stay for two more days," her mother said.

Anne looked up. "Why?"

"It sounds as if you are disappointed we are staying," Louisa said.

Anne shook her head. "Not at all. I was just surprised, is all." She wasn't certain if that was the truth, however. She felt oddly self-conscious with her mother and sister here.

"We received a personal invitation from Kennedy's father to attend the ball tonight," her mother said.

"That was very kind of him," Anne replied, but she wondered if her husband would feel the same.

"I have only the one dress I brought with me," Louisa said.

Anne heard the hope in her sister's voice. At fourteen, Louisa wouldn't typically attend parties. But this party was held in honor of her sister's wedding. Of course, she would accompany them. Her presence would be a good excuse for Anne to leave early.

"There is no time to have anything sewn," Anne said.

Louisa nodded, but the enthusiasm in her eyes dimmed, and guilt stabbed when Louisa said, "Of course. The dress I have will do quite well."

Here she was newly married to a wealthy viscount and worried about spending money on dresses for her sister. Dared she spend his money?

Anne rose and went to the door and pulled the bell pull. She sat back down, and a moment later the maid entered.

"What is your name?" Anne asked.

The girl glanced nervously around the room. "Emma, my lady," she said, and curtsied.

Anne smiled reassuringly. "Emma, can you please tell the housekeeper that I would like to see her?"

The girl's eyes widened and she bobbed a curtsy, and said, "Aye, my lady." She whirled and hurried from the room.

Anne's mother gave her a curious look, but said nothing. Anne filled her plate with eggs and ham and began to eat.

A few minutes later, a short, thin woman of about fifty-five years entered. "You asked to see me, my lady?"

Anne smiled. "May I ask your name, ma'am?"

The woman looked startled, but said, "Mrs. Hampshire."

"It is a pleasure to meet you, Mrs. Hampshire. This is my mother, Lady Kinsley, and my sister, Lady Louisa."

Mrs. Hampshire curtsied, then looked at Anne expectantly.

"Mrs. Hampshire, do ye by chance know a dress shop where my sister can purchase a dress for the ball we are to attend tonight?"

"Why, yes, my lady, I know of several very nice dress shops downtown."

Anne beamed. "When you have a moment, if you could please write down the addresses, I would appreciate that."

Of course, my lady. Is there anything else?"

"Aye, now that you mention it. Can you tell me what would be the best time to go to one of the dress shops?"

"Not before one o'clock, my lady. You might begin at Mrs. Gerard's shop. She is known for opening earlier than many of the other shops and I have heard ladies say that they like her work."

"That is perfect, thank you very much, Mrs. Hampshire," Anne said. "Who do I speak to about having the carriage ready at one o'clock?"

"That would be the butler, Mr. Bingham," she said. "I can direct him to have the carriage ready for ye, ma'am."

"Thank you very much, Mrs. Hampshire."

The housekeeper curtsied, and Anne said, "Mrs. Hampshire, there is no need to be so formal. You will wear yourself out."

Mrs. Hampshire smiled. "Thank you, my lady. If there is nothing else…"

"You have been most helpful, thank you. That will be all," Anne said.

The housekeeper left, and Anne looked at Louisa. "Do you think you can be ready at one o'clock to go shopping?"

Louisa jumped up from her seat, raced around the table, and threw herself into Anne's arms.

Tears pricked her eyes.

This is why I married a stranger.

CHAPTER FIVE

KENNEDY STOPPED AT THE office door and knocked.

"Enter," the man inside called.

Kennedy open the door and entered. A large man who sat behind the desk looked up and smiled. "You're early." He rose and shook Kennedy's hand when he reached the desk.

"This is important, John."

John nodded toward the chair opposite his desk. Kennedy sat down while John resumed his seat.

"It's been nine days, Kennedy. A lifetime for you, I know. But a mere pittance for me."

Kennedy's chest constricted. "No clues as to her whereabouts, then, I take it?"

John's brows rose. "I didnae say that."

Kennedy sat forward in his chair. "You have something?"

John rested his arms on his desk and clasped his hands. "Your sister and her maid, Sarah, left your father's estate at eight p.m., the evening before you contacted me."

"What? You mean my father had only just sent her away? Had I been home instead of out at a damned ball, I would've gone to see him much earlier and perhaps—"

"Perhaps nothing," John cut in. "Whether an hour or day, unless your carriage crossed hers on the street, you simply couldn't have known."

John was right, of course. But it was still too bitter a pill to swallow. She'd been gone no more than an hour when Jacqueline came to his home.

He refocused on John. "Is there anything else, anything at all? How did you discover this?"

John leaned back in his chair and flashed a wide smile. "No matter how hard you nobles try, you can never really hide anything from servants. Have you ever considered the possibility that by making your servants invisible to the world, you yourself stop seeing them?"

"Enough of the philosophical rantings," Kennedy said. "You are well aware that I don't hold with treating my servants as if they aren't human. So, you questioned the servants. What else did you learn?"

"It looks as though your father was telling the truth when he said Rose is no longer in Scotland. She took three large trunks, the sorts of trunks that one might take on a ship."

"France," Kennedy whispered.

"Let's hope so. If it were the Colonies…" his voice trailed off.

Kennedy shook his head. "We know no one in America. Despite my father's bravado, he clings to life like a man hanging from a cliff by his fingernails. Somewhere in the recesses of his diseased mind, he believes he will cheat death for a time. If I do produce an heir in the next nine months, and Rose does not return home safely, he knows I will kill him."

"Have you friends, associations, of any sort in France?" John asked.

Kennedy nodded. "Aye, many, even some distant relatives. But he knows better than to send my sister to any of them. However, he would make certain there was someone nearby who could help with any problems. He would also want to know if any problems arose."

John gave a slow nod. "My thoughts exactly. Which is why I have a man watching Chesterfield at all times.

Kennedy left John with this office, certain he'd hired the right man to help find his sister. It was John's logic—along with the fact he had barred the door when Kennedy had decided to begin the search for Rose himself. John was one of the few men he knew big enough to stop him. He was also one of the few men Kennedy knew who made sense when he argued a case. He'd been right, of course. Kennedy's first order of business was marrying a woman and getting her with child. In all likelihood, once he succeeded, his father really would bring Rose home. Kennedy still wasn't certain he would bring her home before a child was born, despite Kennedy's demands. However, once Anne was pregnant, Kennedy could join the search for his sister.

Kennedy returned home that afternoon to find his wife, her mother and sister out. When he questioned the staff, he learned they had gone dress shopping. For a woman in such need of money, she certainly didn't mind spending it on frivolous things at the first opportunity.

He headed to his office and threw himself into work, hoping to forget his inability to help his sister. He hadn't even bedded his wife yet. He winced at memory of last night's argument. He'd been completely in the wrong. Once his anger abated, he recognized the wide-eyed shock on her face when she'd caught sight of his erection. That look belonged to a woman who'd never seen a man's arousal.

He hadn't meant to insult her, but he meant what he said. The antiquated idea that a man could seek pleasure whenever and wherever he chose, while a woman was obligated to remain chaste, was ridiculous. Jacqueline hadn't been a virgin, and he hadn't cared. But Anne wasn't Jacqueline. She clearly considered any attack on her chastity an attack on her honor.

A commotion in the hallway jarred Kennedy from his work on the labor contracts he reviewed. He glanced at the clock. Four P.M. He had been working for over two hours. The voices in the hallway grew louder, and he recognized Louisa's laugh. Warmth rippled through him. Rose had often complained that she wanted a little sister. Louisa may not be exactly what she had in mind, but the two girls would get along famously.

The voices grew closer and he braced himself when the door burst open and Louisa rushed in with a dress box under her arm. She spotted him and broke into a bright smile. Anne and her mother entered the room. Anne's cheeks were flushed and her eyes were bright with laughter. She was breathtaking.

Kennedy rose and walked around his desk toward them.

"Kennedy, I am so glad you are home," Louisa cried.

He laughed. "Then I am glad, as well."

"Kennedy," the viscountess said as she removed her gloves.

"My lady." He gave a slight bow, then addressed his wife, "Anne."

"Good afternoon, my lord," she replied.

He saw none of the anger from the night before and prayed that she'd forgiven him.

Louisa hurried to the divan near the window and dropped the box she carried onto the cushion. "You must see this dress I have just purchased for the ball tonight."

Kennedy halted next to Anne. "The ball tonight?"

"Aye," Louisa said. "Mama has agreed to allow me to come." She tore the top off the box, but Kennedy was no longer looking at her.

"We are no' attending the ball tonight," he told Anne.

She frowned. "But your father and stepmother are hosting the party in honor of our marriage. We must attend."

He gave a harsh laugh. "Nae, we do not have to attend."

"We are not attending the ball?" Louisa asked.

Kennedy glanced at her. She stood, holding a pink velvet evening gown up against her body.

"My lord," Anne said, "is it not better to stay on good terms with your father?"

He snapped his gaze onto her. "I am on as good terms with him as is possible," he said in a level voice.

"Oh dear," Louisa said. "You are angry that we charged my dress and shoes to you, aren't you?"

He looked at the girl in surprise. "You charged the dress to me?" The moment the words left his mouth, he realized his mistake.

Tears appeared in the girl's eyes and she plopped down on the divan. The viscountess hurried to her daughter and sat beside her.

"Ye need not worry, my lord, I will pay for the dress," Anne said in a tight voice. She started toward her sister.

Kennedy grasped her arm. "Wait."

He released her and took the three steps to the couch and squatted eye level with Louisa. She wasn't crying—yet—but the sadness in her eyes tore at his heart. He placed a finger beneath her chin and gently tilted her head upward so that she has forced to meet his gaze.

"I don't at all mind paying for your dress," he said. "I simply hadn't planned on going to the party, so you caught me off guard." He smiled. "You know that ladies oftentimes catch gentlemen off guard."

Her expression cleared. "I have noticed that. I have a friend Robert. We've known each other since we were four. Of late, however, he sometimes says the strangest things. It's very silly and I've asked him if he has some sort of brain disease. That only seemed to upset him, though, and he gets tongue-tied. Is that what you mean?"

He laughed. "Well, I suspect that Robert's malady has more to do with the fact that you are a very pretty young lady, rather than a brother who wasn't planning to go to a party. But you have the general idea."

"If you do not want to go to the party tonight, that is quite all right. I do not mind returning the dress and the shoes and..." she gave him a sheepish smile, "the gloves."

He stood. "Not at all. Anne is correct. We should stay on good terms with my father. We shall all go."

Louisa leapt to her feet and threw her arms around him. "I wasn't at all happy about Anne marrying some stranger. But now I'm very glad she married you."

Kennedy felt his wife's eyes bore into the back of his head. He wasn't at all sure she was happy she had married him.

* * *

Anne entered the ballroom of her father-in-law's mansion on Kennedy's arm and took a deep breath as they paused in the doorway. Her mother and sister halted beside them. Dancers slid across the dancefloor in a rousing country dance and guests filled the rest of the space in the massive room.

"Oh my," Louisa breathed. "I have never seen a ballroom this large."

"Remember, you are to remain with me or Anne," their mother said.

"What of Kennedy?" Louisa smiled at him. "Surely, it is safe for me to stay with him if you and Anne are busy."

"I am sure Kennedy will be very busy," she replied.

He smiled down at her. "Louisa is welcome to remain with me, if she likes."

Louisa smiled back, adoration beaming in her eyes, and Anne realized Louisa had taken her words to heart and had embraced Kennedy as her new brother. Her heart tugged. It hadn't occurred to her that Louisa might benefit from the addition of a man into their family.

Their mother angled her head toward Kennedy. "As you wish, Kennedy." Uncharacteristic amusement shown in her eyes. "You may regret that invitation."

"There are so many people. Where do we begin?" Louisa asked.

"If ye like, I can introduce you to some ladies who might share some of your interests," Kennedy said.

Anne wondered how he might know what their interests were, but she nodded and thanked him.

The next hour was spent with Kennedy making introductions. Her head buzzed with names and music and the din of voices, but Anne had to admit that a couple of the ladies did appear quite interesting. Lady Hanna knew a great deal about agriculture, and the next lady they met, Miss Watson, clearly had a head for astronomy.

"I am surprised you associate with bluestockings," Anne said, when Miss Watson was whisked to the dance floor by a handsome gentleman.

Kennedy met her gaze. "I believe I told you that I respect a woman who knows what she wants and isn't afraid to pursue it." He lifted a brow. "Did you think I was lying?"

She narrowed her eyes. "I thought you were pursuing something that you wanted at that moment."

He laughed, then introduced them to two more ladies who talked of nothing but sewing, parties and dresses.

"Is that more to your liking, my lady? he asked when they finally left the ladies.

"It wasn't to my liking," Louisa said. "Forgive me for saying so, Kennedy, but they were excessively dull."

"Louisa," their mother hissed in a low voice when two ladies glanced their way.

"Don't reprimand her for speaking the truth," Kennedy said. "I happen to agree." He looked at Louisa. "Still, I am surprised. I know you like dresses and parties, so why did you find them dull?"

"Of course, I like dresses and parties," she said as if talking to a child. "They are great fun. But I wouldn't go on about them and talk of nothing else. Have they no other interests?"

Kennedy chuckled. "Not that I know of."

Louisa made a face. "Must we be friends with them?"

"For heaven's sake, Louisa," her mother said. "Keep your voice down."

Louisa hung her head. "Of course, Mama."

Kennedy leaned close to Louisa and whispered, "Never fear, you need not be friends with anyone you don't like."

She beamed. "Thank you. I'm thirsty, Mama. May I have champagne?"

"You may not," she replied. "You may have lemonade."

Louisa slanted a look up at Kennedy. "Kennedy, don't you think that fourteen is old enough to have just a little champagne?"

Their mother stiffened.

He tweaked one of Louisa's curls. "I think that fourteen is old enough to know better than to ask her brother to countermand her mother's instructions."

Louisa blinked and Anne thought she would pout. Instead, she shrugged and said, "I suppose I have much to learn about having a brother."

He laughed again and Anne noted a tinge of sadness this time.

The orchestra struck up a waltz.

"You and Anne haven't dance," Louisa said. "The waltz is so romantic. You must dance."

Kennedy looked at her. "Shall we, my lady?"

The last thing she wanted was to dance with him, but how could she refuse? She nodded, and he grasped her hand, tucked it into the crook of his arm, and led her toward the dance floor.

Once they were out of earshot of her mother and sister, she said, "You need not dance with me."

He looked at her. "There is nothing strange in a man dancing with his wife."

She wasn't his wife—not truly. Not yet.

"True, but Louisa forced you to ask me."

"Never fear, few people can force me to do anything."

They reached the dance floor. He pulled her close and stepped into the music. She wasn't surprised to find he was an excellent dancer.

"Who are the few people who can force you to do anything?" she asked.

His gaze snapped onto her. "What?"

"You said few people can force you to do anything. Who are those few people?"

"I suppose there is only one person in truth," he said, as if speaking to himself.

"Who?"

He seemed lost in thought, and only shook his head. "It is of no consequence."

"Your father?" she asked.

His full mouth thinned and he looked at her. "Why ask questions you already know the answers to?"

She considered. "I am sorry you were forced to marry me."

He released a breath and guided them past a couple, then sidestepped another couple who nearly rammed them.

"It isn't your fault, Anne."

"True," she replied. "But you're clearly unhappy with marriage."

Interest lit his eyes. "Are you saying that because we didn't consummate our marriage last night?"

Embarrassment warmed her cheeks. "I-I didn't mean that, at all."

The interest turned to amusement. "We are not the first married couple not to consummate their marriage on their wedding night."

Anne nibbled on her lip. "There is always tonight."

"Have you plans for me, my sweet?"

What plans did she have? "We are not truly married until…"

His amusement vanished. "You want to earn that five thousand pounds as quickly as possible. I am a fool."

Anne gasped. Then anger whipped through her. "Why not? This is a business arrangement after all—nothing more."

His eyes darkened. "Then I shall be at your service tonight, madam."

"If you are certain that you are up to it, my lord? I don't want to inconvenience you."

"Too late," he shot back. "You have inconvenienced me a great deal."

He yanked her against him and turned her in a tight whirl that made her dizzy—and aware of his hard length.

"I must now devise a way not to embarrass myself in front of Edinburgh's elite," he said.

Then she found herself being whirled off the dance floor and out the balcony doors.

* * *

Kennedy brought Anne to a halt. She tried to shove away from him, but he tightened his grip and kissed her. Then released her. She took two faltering steps backward.

"Just a preview of things to come," he said.

"How very fortunate for me," she said.

"Oh, it will be, that I promise."

She released a frustrated breath, then turned and hurried back into the ballroom.

Kennedy started after her, then thought better of it and pivoted, headed for the gardens. He crossed the balcony, took the three steps down to the lawn, and slowed to a stroll. Anne didn't deserve his disdain. She was right. Their marriage was a business arrangement. Oddly, the thought bothered him. She was also correct in that he wasn't happy being married. He'd known he would someday marry, but it galled him that his father had forced the issue and had even chosen his bride.

Underneath it all, though, he feared for Rose. He couldn't allow himself to dwell on her. For the moment, he felt certain she was safe. The longer she was away, however, the greater the chances that her keepers would grow careless. And he couldn't consider what would happen if his father died.

He needed Anne to bear him a son just as much as she wanted to. He couldn't fault her for that. Tonight, he would consummate their marriage. A small sense of satisfaction arose. If his father had any idea that he hadn't consummated the marriage last night, he'd be furious. Now that he thought of it, he should have married long ago and simply never consummated the marriage. That would've driven his father mad, and he would have had no recourse to kidnap Rose. He was wrong. His father would have secreted her away and demanded Kennedy bed is wife and bear a child.

Why hadn't it occurred to him that his father would use Rose? Because, despite everything, Kennedy simply had never believed his father would put his own daughter in jeopardy. He wouldn't underestimate the old man again.

"Kennedy."

Kennedy halted. Bloody hell. He turned to face Jacqueline. "What are you doing here?"

"I saw you and Anne leave the ballroom, but she returned immediately. Is something amiss?"

"What is amiss, Jacqueline, is that my father has kidnapped my sister and blackmailed me into marriage."

She stepped closer and laid a hand on his arm. "You know your father will never allow any harm to come to Rose."

"He threatened to marry her to Granbury. There is no worse harm that can come to her."

She shook her head. "I don't believe he would do it."

"Then you are a fool."

She stepped closer. "Does she please you?"

He didn't have to ask who the 'she' was. "Very much so," he said.

"Does she please you as much as I used to?"

Kennedy stared down at her. Even in the pale moonlight she was beautiful. "Aye, she pleases me very much."

Jacqueline laid her palms on his chest. "Perhaps you have forgotten how much I please you."

He grasped her hands and removed them from his chest. "You should remember that you're married to my father."

"You know how ill he is, Kennedy. He hasn't been able to..." She looked up at him through her lashes. "I am very lonely."

He gave her a cold smile. "Perhaps there is a stable hand who will oblige. I understand you like stable hands."

"You know that is a vicious lie."

"I know nothing of the sort. In fact, I would be surprised if it wasn't true."

She slapped him. His cheek stung. He wanted to shake her, demand to know why she'd chosen his father. But he knew why.

She whirled toward the mansion and hurried away. He watched until she disappeared from view. Had she always been so cold and calculating? He thought back. She was driven. That was something he'd always admired about her. What he hadn't understood was the motivation behind that drive. She would have what she wanted at all costs. Were all women like that?

He thought of Anne. Aye, she was determined, as well. Unlike Jacqueline, however, she never pretended to love him. Of course, he'd known her for less than two days. There was still time for her to pretend many things. He recalled her ire moments ago, and wondered if she were capable of doing anything but showing what was in her heart. He sighed. Time would tell.

CHAPTER SIX

ANNE REENTERED THE BALLROOM and scanned the room for her mother and Louisa, but found no sign of them. She stopped a passing waiter and took a glass of champagne from his tray, then glanced back in the direction of the open balcony doors. The man really was impossible. She took two deep gulps of champagne. He had better get her with child soon, because she was liable to murder him. Her stomach performed a somersault at the memory of his promise, *"I will be at your service tonight, madam."*

The words were spoken in anger, but she hadn't missed the deep timbre of his voice and the intensity of his gaze when he'd said them. Anne took another gulp of champagne. She'd never known a more insufferable man. Perhaps she should ask her mother how to deal with him. Nae. Her mother would be aghast to learn they hadn't consummated their marriage. A lady always submitted to her husband's commands in the bedchambers.

Anne lifted the champagne glass to her lips and found only a small mouthful remained. Where was another waiter? She scanned the room and caught sight of Jacqueline entering the ballroom from the balcony. Anne hadn't seen her outside. Had she spoken with Kennedy?

Had Kennedy returned to the ballroom? She searched the room again, but there were so many people, she might have overlooked him. Jacqueline turned, and their eyes met. Anne read something there. Guilt? Jacqueline started toward her. Oh Lord, she was in no mood to speak to the woman. She didn't like her. But she couldn't ignore her. Jacqueline knew that she had seen her.

"There she is, Mama," Louisa said behind her.

Anne turned as her mother and sister neared her. "I'm so relieved to see you," she blurted.

Her mother's eyes sharpened and Anne realized her mistake. She thought her mother would say something, but her eyes shifted past Anne and Jacqueline appeared beside them an instant later.

"Good evening, Lady Kinsley," she said. "Lady Louisa, you look lovely."

"Thank you," Louisa bubbled over. "This is a special dress I wore just for this party."

"It's absolutely perfect," Jacqueline said, then she turned to Anne. "I am so glad to find you. I have been looking for you for the last hour." Anne had the feeling she was lying. "The earl would like to meet you," Jacqueline said.

The earl wanted to meet her? She recalled Kennedy saying that she wouldn't meet his father if he had his way. She glanced toward the balcony doors, but saw no sign of him.

"I hope he hasn't fallen asleep," Jacqueline said. "He now sleeps far more than he is awake." She smiled at Anne's mother. "It is so difficult." She sighed, then looked at Anne. "Come, let's go up to his chambers."

"Perhaps I should wait for Kennedy," Anne said.

"Do you know where he is?" Jacqueline asked.

"I left them out on the balcony," Anne replied.

"I just came from the gardens," Jacqueline said. "He was taking a walk."

Shock reverberated through Anne. "You saw him in the gardens?"

"Oh, yes, walking in the gardens is a favorite activity of ours."

Anne caught the startled look on her mother's face.

"Kennedy has been so wonderful during his father's illness," Jacqueline said. "I don't know what I would have done without him."

Her tone was intimate. But why wouldn't it be? They were family.

Anne was being ridiculous. But it had been disturbing the way Jacqueline rested her hand on Kennedy's arm yesterday morning at the wedding feast. Anne was no fool. She'd watched her friends flirt and bat their eyes to gain a young man's attention. A woman didn't touch a man's arm like that unless they were close.

Jacqueline smiled sweetly. "Please, Joseph has expressly asked to see you." She angled her head toward Anne's mother." You will excuse us, Lady Kinsley. Come along, Anne."

Anne hesitated, then nodded. "I will return soon, Mama. Please let Kennedy know where I am. I am sure he will return from his walk in the garden soon."

Her mother nodded, then Anne followed Jacqueline through the crowd to a hallway, but she wished mightily she was in the gardens with her husband.

* * *

Kennedy reentered the ballroom with the intention of finding Anne and Louisa and returning home. They had stayed long enough for Louisa to have gotten her fill of the party. He caught sight of them near the left hand wall and started toward them. He brushed past a group of men, and waited for three ladies to pass when he heard his name called. Kennedy cursed, and turned to face his uncle as the older man reached him.

"Can we speak?" Ranald asked.

"Can it wait?" Kennedy asked. "I am meeting my wife's mother and sister."

Ranald's expression brightened. "I had hoped to meet your wife."

"Come along, then." Kennedy turned and dodged two passing gentlemen, then pushed through the throng that seemed to have grown during his walk in the garden.

They reached the two women, and the viscountess said, "Kennedy I am relieved to see you," then broke off when Ranald stepped up beside him.

"My lady, this is my uncle, Lord Ranald," Kennedy said. "Ranald, Lady Kinsley and her daughter Lady Louisa."

"Ma'am." Ranald bowed over the older woman's hand. Louisa curtsied and he bowed in return.

"What is amiss?" Kennedy demanded, then realized he had spoken too loudly when a group of nearby man looked their way. "What has happened? he said in a low voice.

She hesitated, and Kennedy said, "You may speak freely in front of my uncle."

She glanced at the older man, then said in a low voice, "Your stepmother took Anne up to meet your father."

"Bloody hell," he cursed. "I instructed her not to leave the ballroom," he said.

The dowager viscountess's brows rose. "You clearly do not know your wife, if you expected that command to be followed."

"My wife will learn to heed my commands," he said.

Amusement flickered in her eyes. "It may be you who learns a few lessons," she murmured.

"I take it you believe a wife has the right to ignore her husband's wishes?"

"Not at all. I am simply experienced enough to know that a marriage—a happy marriage—is not built on obedience to commands."

"She has a point," Ranald said.

Kennedy gave his uncle a narrow-eyed look. "I can see an interesting road lies ahead for me."

"Of that you may be assured," the viscountess said. "First, however, you might want to rescue your stepmother from Anne."

He blinked. "I beg your pardon? It is Anne who will need rescuing."

She gave him a polite smile. "You have not yet had cause to learn this, but Anne has a temper."

He barked a laugh. "Indeed, I have learned that, madam." He excused himself and headed for his father's chambers to rescue someone, though he knew not who.

* * *

Anne's heart squeezed at sight of the elderly man who sat propped up in bed reading a book. He was more than just ill. The paleness of his skin and the tremble in his hands told her he was dying. Still, a keen intelligence stared back at her through the pale blue eyes that watched their approach.

Jacqueline hurried to his bed, then pressed a kiss to his cheek, and said, "My dear, this is Anne."

Anne stopped a few feet away.

"Come closer." He beckoned with a gnarled hand.

Anne did as instructed and stopped beside Jacqueline, then curtsied.

"You are very beautiful," he said.

"Thank you, my lord," Anne said.

"What do you think of my son? Will he give you a son?"

Anne started at the question. How did she know the answer to such a question?

"I am sure he will do his best, my lord."

The man's eyes sharpened. "*Will do his best?* By now, I expect you to have been working hard to produce an heir."

Anne blinked. She and Kennedy had been married but a day. How hard could they be 'working' to have a child? "Forgive me, sir, but it is not proper for a wife to speak of such things, especially to her husband's father."

"She is right, my dear," Jacqueline said. "Anne is a new bride."

"Bah! We have no time to stand on such ceremony." His gaze locked with hers. "I know you need the five thousand pounds I promised once you produce an heir. I will pay you an extra five thousand pounds if you remain in Kennedy's bed every night between now and when you get pregnant."

Anne stared. The man was mad. But it was more than that, she realized.

Here was the reason Kennedy hadn't wanted her to meet his father. The man was trying to control his life right down to how many times they...

"Forgive me, my lord, but I cannot see how you could possibly confirm I was deserving of the extra five thousand pounds." She lifted her brows. "Unless, that is, you intend to be in the bed with us."

To her shock, the earl didn't so much as bad an eye at her sarcasm, but said, "If you get pregnant soon, then I will be satisfied that you lived up to your end of the bargain."

Kennedy might be insufferable, but this man was cruel. "There was always the chance that I might get pregnant the first or second night we are together," she said with sickeningly sweet sarcasm.

"Are you willing to take the risk that you will not receive the extra money if you don't get pregnant right away?" he countered.

"Ah, I see. If I don't get pregnant immediately, you will assume that Kennedy and I are not sharing a bed. What happens if we share a bed every night, and I do not get pregnant?"

"I am certain Kennedy is skilled enough to make his time in your bed worthwhile."

"My God, you have bollocks. Whether I get pregnant right away, a year from now, or five years from now, it will have nothing to do with you."

"But it has a great deal to do with Kennedy," he replied. "My son will see to it that you have a child within a year."

The conversation was insane. "Then why offer me more money?" she asked.

"I take no chances when it comes to the heir of my title."

"In case you have forgotten, you have an heir: my husband. And by-the-by it isn't just your title. There is mine, as well."

He nodded. "Aye, my grandson will be the eighth Earl of Buchanan, as well as Viscount Kinsley. That is why I chose you as Kennedy's bride."

She'd had enough. "Was there anything else you wanted, my lord, besides ensuring that my husband and I were spending enough time in bed together?"

He regarded her. "You will suit Kennedy well."

That, Anne hadn't expected.

"What has he told you about me?"

She hadn't expected that either. What was she supposed to say? She gave him a cool smile. "Nothing, really. I'm sure you understand we haven't spent our time talking."

Satisfaction lit his gaze. He nodded. "Good, very good. It hadn't occurred to me you might be beautiful, but the fact that you are will hold Kennedy's interest for a while."

For a while? Her heart felt as if it had been pierced with a knife.

"I expect you to name your son after me," he said.

"After you?" It wasn't uncommon for a father to name his son after his own father. Somehow, Anne doubted that Kennedy would want to follow that tradition. "I will discuss it with Kennedy, of course."

He waved his hand dismissively, and she wanted to knock the gnarled thing aside. "He will do as you ask."

Then she understood. "If you suggest that we name our child after you, he will defy you," she said more to herself than him. "But you expect me to manipulate him for your own ends."

"It is my right," he said as if that was sufficient.

Anne laughed. "Not quite. What of my father? Perhaps I would like to name our child after him."

At last, she saw ire in his eyes. Satisfaction shot through her.

"I will give you another five thousand pounds, if you talk Kennedy into naming your son after me," he said.

She couldn't believe her ears. "Keep your five thousand pounds. Keep all your money." Anne whirled and stopped short at sight of Kennedy standing in the doorway.

CHAPTER SEVEN

KENNEDY COULDN'T TAKE HIS eyes off his wife as he entered the room. She had just told his father to keep all his money. Kennedy reached her side, grasped her hand and brought it to his lips.

She frowned, her expression turning suspicious when he said, "I missed you, my dear." He released her and looked at his father. "I didn't realize you intended to meet Anne tonight, sir."

"If you had known, you wouldn't have brought her," his father replied.

Kennedy smiled coolly. "You have Anne's sister to thank for our being here. I hadn't planned on coming, but she had her heart set on attending the party and I couldn't disappoint her."

Frustration flickered across his father's face, and Kennedy cursed his own tongue. Normally, he would have pressed any advantage once he'd broken down his father's façade. But his father wasn't above changing the terms of an agreement if pushed hard enough, and Kennedy needed to assure that Rose returned home as soon as possible.

"I believe we have been here long enough to satisfy her," Anne said. "If you don't mind, I would like to go home."

Kennedy smiled at her. "Of course, my dear."

"It was a pleasure to meet you, my lord," Anne said. "I hope you feel better soon." She shifted her attention to Jacqueline and said in a cool tone, "My lady, thank you for a lovely party."

"Of course," Jaqueline said. "We are so very happy for you and Kennedy."

"Remember what I said," his father said to Anne.

She smiled. "Never fear, sir, I shall be giving everything you said a great deal of thought." Her gaze shifted onto Kennedy. "Shall we go?"

He angled his head in acknowledgement. "If you are ready, my dear." Without a backwards glance, they left.

To his wife's credit she remained quiet until they were halfway down the first flight of stairs. "Forgive me, sir, but I must tell you that your father is an abominable man."

Kennedy couldn't help himself. He laughed so hard his eyes watered.

They reached the next floor and she shot him a hard frown as they continued down the dim hallway. "I fail to see the humor in the situation. He had the gall to offer me another five thousand pounds if I spend every night in your bed until I am certain I am pregnant."

Kennedy looked sharply at her. He hadn't heard that. "I will speak to him."

She threw up her hands. "Why bother? He is clearly insane—and there is no talking to an insane person." Her expression turned sheepish. "I do not think he likes me very much."

They turned a corner in the hallway.

"He doesn't like anyone very much," Kennedy said.

"I can well believe that, but most people aren't his daughter-in-law."

"That does go too far, even for him," Kennedy said. "How does he think he will verify that you have kept your end of the bargain?"

They reached another set of stairs and he gestured for her to precede him.

"I asked that very thing," she said. "The only way he could be certain is if he were in the room with us."

Kennedy blinked. "Never say you said that to him."

"Of course, I did."

They reached the next level and sounds of the orchestra wafted up to them.

"He had the temerity to say that as long as I got pregnant right away, he would take my word that I had kept up my end of the bargain," she went on. "It would serve him right, if I didn't get pregnant anytime soon."

Alarm shot through him. "Did you tell him we hadn't consummated the marriage?"

A blush crept up her cheeks. "Nae. It is none of his business. About that, sir—"

"My fault altogether," he cut in.

She looked up at him in surprise, then smiled. His heart jumped.

"Thank you," she said.

How different she was from Jacqueline. They seldom fought—well, they seldom fought when they were lovers. But on the rare occasion they did, she made him feel as if her acceptance of his apology was a boon from on high.

Kennedy gave Anne a sideways glance. "Are you against having a child immediately?"

She shook her head. "Of course not. I expected to have children once I married." She looked up at him, a wry grin on her face. "I told him he could keep all his money. So, it seems I've talked myself out of the five thousand pounds he was going to give me once we have a son."

He'd heard that. Had she known he'd been outside the room? Her responses to his father had been so different than Jacqueline's. So... unaffected.

"Never mind," he said. "What matters is in the contract. I will ensure that he pays you the money."

She released a sigh. "The birth of our child is reduced to a business transaction. I am not certain I like that."

"Isn't that why you married me, for money?" His heart unexpectedly accelerated.

She slowed as they turned another corner and the music from the orchestra grew louder. "It's a common enough reason to marry," she said. "But I'm liking less and less the idea of taking money for bearing a child, whether it is a day from now, a year from now or five years from now."

"If it is a day from now, I will consider that most miraculous," he said with a grin.

She laughed, and he found he liked the sound. "I promise you, that will not happen," she said. "Still, I think I will refuse the money."

"You could always put it into a trust for our son." Our son. His chest tightened at the vision of her cradling their son before the hearth in their private chambers.

"I will have to think of another way to pay for the upkeep at Dover Hall." She looked up at him, again, with mischief in her eyes. "You may begin giving me expensive pieces of jewelry anytime you like."

Again, he laughed so hard his eyes watered.

* * *

Halfway home, a large crack sounded outside the carriage. Kennedy yanked Anne to him as the coach listed hard to the right. He slammed into the carriage wall. The ladies screamed. Louisa crashed into him. He hugged both women close as the carriage came to a jolting halt. The interior lamp went out and they were plunged into darkness.

"Mamma," Louisa cried, and clung to Kennedy.

"It's all right, Louisa," he murmured, then said, "Lady Kinsley, are you unharmed?"

"Aye. Louisa—" she began.

"I have her," Kennedy said. "She is unharmed. Anne, as well."

The carriage rocked, then the door to Kennedy's right was wrenched open and moonlight illuminated the interior of the carriage.

The driver stuck his head inside the carriage. "Is anyone hurt?" he demanded.

Kenney spotted Anne's mother, leaning against the carriage wall on the other side of the door. "The viscountess, James."

The footman helped her from the coach. Kennedy handed out Louisa, then Anne, and leapt from the carriage onto the sidewalk of the quiet street.

The right rear wheel broke, my lord."

"So I gathered," Kennedy said. "My lady." He took a step to the viscountess. The sleeve of her left shoulder was torn and a gash in her arm oozed blood. Kennedy gently turned her toward the streetlight and examined her. "You must have fallen against the lamp."

She nodded. "It is nothing."

"We will have a doctor attend to the wound once we reach home."

A carriage turned onto the street and slowed as they neared, then stopped. The door opened, and Kennedy's uncle stepped to the ground.

He strode to where they stood. "Is everyone unharmed?"

Kennedy nodded. "Fortunately, we weren't going fast."

"Let me take you home," Ranald said.

"Thank you." Kennedy turned to the driver. "James, I will send Matthew back with a new wheel. You and Michael remain here until they arrive."

James nodded. "Aye, my lord."

Kennedy got the ladies into the carriage, then he and Ranald stepped inside and they started away.

At home, they gathered in the drawing room while Ranald sent his carriage for the doctor. Kennedy roused Matthew and instructed him to take men to deliver the wheel and repair the carriage.

The doctor arrived half an hour later. Despite Lady Kinsley's insistence that she was fine, the doctor insisted on six stitches, then sent her to bed with a small dose of laudanum. The doctor left, and Anne sent Kennedy a grateful look, then went upstairs with her mother and sister.

"Would you like a drink?" Kennedy asked Ranald when the ladies had gone.

"Scotch, if you please," he said. "I'm glad for this opportunity to speak with you, Kennedy. Congratulations on your marriage, by-the-by. I'm sorry I missed the ceremony. I had no idea you were to marry."

Kennedy poured two scotches, then turned and motioned to the two hearth chairs. His uncle took the chair to the left. Kennedy handed him a glass of scotch and sat in the chair to the right.

"We had a very small ceremony by special license," Kennedy said.

Ranald nodded. "So I gathered. I feel certain your father had something to do with the marriage. I saw him the day before yesterday. He isn't looking well."

Kennedy took a hefty drink of scotch. He shook his head. "Nae, he isn't at all looking well."

Ranald regarded him. "I should think that you would be rejoicing."

"I will not be sorry when he is gone," Kennedy said.

"What the devil is going on?" his uncle demanded.

Kennedy took another drink of his whisky. "What do you mean?"

"There's too many strange things afoot. Pray, do not tell me you suddenly fell in love. Marriage was not on your agenda. And where is Rose? I didn't see her at Chesterfield when I visited your father. When I inquired, he said she was away. What does that mean?"

Ranald was as different from his brother as Kennedy was from his father. Kennedy had always liked his uncle, who was far too intelligent for his own good. "The earl sent her away and won't tell me where," Kennedy said. "He forced my marriage to Anne by threatening to marry Rose to Granbury if I didn't comply."

"By God, that goes too far, even for him," Ranald growled.

Kennedy nodded. "We both have underestimated my father for a long time."

Ranald nodded slowly. "Now that you're married, will Rose return home?"

Kennedy gave a harsh laugh. "Nae, there is more to the blackmail. I must produce an heir in the next year."

A rare flush of anger darkened Ranald's normally tranquil eyes. "By God, what is wrong with the man?"

"He is dying," Kennedy said with more calm than he felt. "This is a desperate attempt at eternal life."

"We all die," the older man said with heat. "A moment ago, I would've said, in his own way, he loves Rose. Now, I'm no' sure if even that is true. How long has she been gone?"

"Seven days."

"It's unlikely she'll come to any harm." His mouth thinned. "As long as he doesn't die. Have ye any idea where she is?"

"The earl said she wasn't in Scotland. Based on information I received from his servants, I'm inclined to think that's true."

Ranald nodded slowly. "France."

Kennedy nodded. "France is a big country, however. I could search Paris for years and never find her."

"Surely you plan to try?"

Kennedy grunted. "I have already begun. The only thing stopping me from going myself is the fact that I must immediately sire an heir."

Ranald frowned. "Does Joseph intend to keep Rose hidden until your first child is born?"

"Kennedy nodded. "That is exactly what he intends. I demanded that he bring Rose home once it is confirmed that my wife is pregnant. In truth, he could just as easily not comply."

Ranald leaned forward, elbows resting on his knees. "Tell me how I can help."

CHAPTER EIGHT

THE FOLLOWING MORNING, ANNE found her way into the conservatory. The building was set off from the house in a secluded corner of the gardens. The paned glass structure rested on a foundation of waist-high stones. She entered the building and knew she was home. A light rain began to patter on the glass. Anne looked up at the gray clouds that inched across the sky. Even on an overcast day like today, she could remain here for hours. She strolled through the aisles, marveling at the variety of flowers, ferns and dwarfed trees. She found roses, thistle, and even heather. Anne paused to brush her finger against the petals of a lavender sweet pea and caught sight of a chaise lounge, table and chairs in the far corner. This was even better than she'd expected.

She stepped around a fig tree, then an apricot and plum, and continued to the chaise. A modest hearth was located nearby. Too bad she hadn't brought a book. Rain pattered a little harder on the glass. She looked up at the sky. The clouds had darkened. Next time she would bring a book. For now, she would start a fire and spend a little time with her thoughts.

With a sigh, Anne knelt at the hearth. She got a low fire burning, then sat on the chaise and stared up at the black clouds. What kind of family had she married into? The earl was clearly a bitter and power-hungry man. His wife. Anne shuddered. Lady Buchanen was far too familiar with her stepson. Were she and Kennedy having an affair? Kennedy seemed to want to avoid her, and Anne had detected no affinity on his part for her. Had she made advances toward him? Anne could well believe it.

Kennedy didn't fit with them. Yesterday, when he told Louisa that he didn't mind buying dresses for her, and that he would gladly take them to the ball, he'd spoken like a real brother. The way he had hugged Anne to him and grabbed Louisa when the carriage wheel broke had caught her off guard. He was a man of action, and he cared about them—in some way, at any rate.

She wasn't certain what to make of the fact that he hadn't come to her room last night. True, the night had been more eventful than expected. Still, shouldn't a husband want to bed his wife? Despite his father's demands that they have a child immediately, perhaps Kennedy didn't want her. She recalled their wedding night. He had seemed... enthusiastic, until, that is, she'd learned he thought she was loose. Would the man never get it through his head that she cared about her honor? Whatever the case, she had to demand her wifely rights. It simply wasn't right that a marriage wasn't consummated. Her mother would be aghast if she learned they were not yet truly married.

She started from her thoughts at a sudden gust of air that swept through the conservatory. She straightened and realized the door had been opened. The door slammed closed and she jumped to her feet. An instant later, she glimpsed Kennedy amongst the foliage. He neared and his gaze met hers. He wore a dark coat with no tie and his collar lay open, revealing tanned flesh.

He neared her and said, "What the devil are you doing out here?" Then he saw the fire and nodded. "I can see this is already a favorite spot of yours."

Anne smiled. "Even on a day like today, it's a very pleasant room to be in."

He took off his dripping coat and shook the water from it. "My mother used to spend a lot of time here." He hung the coat over the back of a chair. "It's raining hard. I imagine we can wait just a little while to see if the rain will let up before returning to the house."

A tremor rippled through her. Stuck alone with him in a room with nowhere to go?

"If you have work to do, you needn't worry about keeping me company," she said. "I don't mind being alone."

He pinned her with his gaze. "Is my company so terrible that you can't bear to be alone with me for a short while?"

"Oh no, that is not at all what I meant." She blew out a frustrated breath. "I don't know what it is about you, but I always end up saying the wrong thing."

Amusement glittered in his eyes. "You wouldn't, per chance, be speaking of a similar effect to that which Louisa mentioned yesterday about her friend Robert always saying the wrong thing about her?"

She narrowed her eyes. "Hardly. That would imply some sort of affection, and I know how much you abhor such feelings from your wife."

To her surprise, he laughed. "You prove my point. You have some, if only a little, affection for me."

"Affection? How can I have affection for you? I hardly know you."

He grinned. "I'm a charming fellow."

Damn his soul, he was. But she wasn't about to admit that. "I feel certain you have charmed many a lady, my lord."

"The only lady I'm interested in charming is you."

She blinked. "I beg your pardon?"

"I believe you understand me," he said.

"Well, of course, I understand you. That is, I know what you said. As to your meaning, that could be anything."

"Come now, Anne, my meaning really can't be just *anything*."

The way he said 'anything' left little doubt as to what he meant. Heaven help her, it had gotten awfully warm in the room.

"They will probably begin to worry about us back at the house," she said. "Perhaps we should return."

He crossed to where she stood and stopped inches away. "I don't think they will worry about us overly much." He wrapped an arm around her waist and tugged her against him.

She immediately detected his hard length against her abdomen. "Oh dear," she breathed."

"Oh dear, indeed," he said, and covered her mouth with his.

Her knees weakened and she grasped his shoulders to keep herself upright. He laughed low and deep, then gently thrust his tongue between her lips and into her mouth. He tasted of scotch. His hold tightened around her waist, pulling her impossibly close. Her head swam. He broke the kiss and pressed warm kisses along her cheek to her neck. She shivered.

"Perhaps we should go to your bed chambers, my lord."

"We would never make it there without being waylaid by a family member," he murmured against her flesh, "and I have no desire to be interrupted."

She cried out when he swung her into his arms. He laid her on the chaise lounge and came down on top of her. For an instant, he felt too heavy, though she found she liked the feeling. Then he levered up on his elbows and kissed her neck. He tugged her sleeve down and kissed her shoulder. An intense ache thrummed between her legs in rhythm with her heartbeat. She started at the realization that they were surrounded by glass.

"My lord, anyone can see inside the conservatory. Perhaps we really should return to the house."

"At the very least, while I am making love to you, you could try calling me by my Christian name," he said.

She blinked. Was he reprimanding her—now? "As you wish, *Kennedy*," she retorted.

He froze, then slowly lifted his head and met her gaze. "Have I peeved you again, my sweet?"

"You seem to make a habit of it," she said.

"This time, you may be as peeved with me as you like," he said. "But we shall consummate our marriage."

She should have been ashamed, but, in truth, that was exactly what she wanted.

Eyes locked with hers, he began inching up her skirt. She didn't flinch, didn't move. At last, his fingers made contact with her outer thigh. He flattened his palm against her flesh and slid his hand upward. His hand was so warm. No man had ever touched her so intimately. He slid off her onto the chaise beside her and continued his hand's upward climb. When he neared the apex between her legs, she tensed. He gently kissed her cheek then nibbled her ear. She twisted slightly at the tickle. Then realized his fingers were brushing the intimate curls. Gently, he slipped a finger between her moist folds. She jammed her eyes shut and gripped his arm.

"Relax, love," he said. "I won't hurt you."

She wasn't afraid of being hurt, it's just, she had never imagined a man would touch her there. However, to her surprise when his fingers brushed the sensitive nub, a tingle of pleasure rippled through her. She drew a breath. He began nibbling her ear again and the tingle traveled from her ear to the place where he brushed her sex. He applied a little more pressure and began massaging her.

"Good heavens," she breathed.

The ache intensified. He flicked his tongue against her ear. The sensation was almost sinful. She started when he slid a finger inside her.

"My goodness, Kennedy, do you think you should be doing that?"

He laughed. "That and much more, if you will allow me."

Much more? She couldn't imagine anything more--then he began to slide his finger in and out of her. A strange sense of pleasure rippled deep within her. He swirled his tongue. Heaven help her, how could something so innocent illicit such a decedent response?

"You set me on fire," he whispered, and her insides turned to jelly.

He quickened his movements inside her. She should be ashamed. But she liked the sensation, liked the slide of his warm digit in and out of her. Was she supposed to like this? Her mother had explained what took place between a man and a woman, but she hadn't told Anne about *this*, about the need that made her want to close her legs around Kennedy's hand and beg him to end the torture.

She became aware of his kisses moving down along her neck. His tongue flicked the sensitive flesh, then he gently sucked.

"Let go," he whispered. "Give in to the pleasure."

He nipped at her neck. A string of pleasure shot from her neck to the nub he massaged. She cried out with a pleasure that caused spots to race across her vision. Anne seized his arm and squeezed as the spasm rolled over her a second time.

Gently, he stroked her until the pleasure dissipated into a soft echo. She was still breathing hard as he unfastened the falls on his breeches. She didn't look down at his manhood—she'd seen that and didn't need to be reminded that it was much larger than his finger. When he levered over her, she knew a moment of panic. Was she supposed to look him in the eye—how could she—or was she supposed to close her eyes?

He smiled down at her. "Trust me, Anne."

She nodded and kept her eyes open as he settled between her legs. The warmth of his thighs against hers was far more compelling than the warmth of just his hand. His length bumped her opening. He reached between them and slipped the head of his manhood just inside her folds and she tensed. He lowered his head and brushed his mouth against hers. When he breathed deep, she grasped his arms. Hard muscle flexed beneath her fingers and a thrill shot through her. His hips shifted—then he surged into her. A deep pinch came and went.

Kennedy lifted his mouth from hers and looked down at her. "Are you well?"

Anne nodded, though she wasn't certain. He felt so strange inside her.

He drew back and she gripped his arms tighter in readiness for another pinch when he thrust into her again. None came. He pulled back, then thrust. Kennedy lowered himself onto her and kissed her again, then drove deeper. Pleasure mixed with a smidgen of pain startled her. His tongue slipped inside her mouth. Her head whirled as his thrusts increased speed. Pleasure rippled through her. He drove deeper and the pain increased a little. Still, she was shocked to find she wanted more.

His kiss became insistent. With his next thrust, she lifted her hips. When their bodies collided, he groaned. The sound reverberated through her. Her mother hadn't told her about *any* of this. She also hadn't told her about the pleasure that exploded inside her when her husband drove so deep she thought he'd touched her soul.

* * *

Kennedy had read the paragraph in the report half a dozen times and still wasn't certain what it said. His focus kept returning to yesterday afternoon—and last night—with Anne. There was something about her. She excited him. He found he was looking forward to getting to know her in the years that lay ahead. Even with Jacqueline, he'd never considered such a thing. He never thought of being without Jacqueline, but he hadn't thought past what they had, either. With Anne, he found himself looking forward to more afternoons in the conservatory. With Jacqueline, he wanted her, felt he couldn't get enough of her, but he also never felt…satisfied. Anne satisfied him in a way he'd never known possible.

Was this love? He had believed himself to be in love with Jacqueline. The emotions had been intense, but somehow different. He couldn't quite put his finger on it.

A knock came to the door and he started from his thoughts as a footman entered.

"Mr. John Weston to see ye, sir," he said.

John? "Show him in, immediately," Kennedy said, but he didn't have to wait, for John stepped into the room.

Kennedy rose and hurried around his desk toward his friend. John strode toward him and the footman closed the door behind him. They met, clasped hands, and Kennedy said. "What happened? You have learned something."

Surprise shone on John's face.

"What is it?" Kennedy demanded.

"You don't know?"

Kennedy's heart began to pound. "Know what? Tell me, man."

"Your father is in a coma."

The words didn't register. "What? What do you mean?"

"I have a servant in your father's household in my employ," John said. "He just reported that the doctor visited Chesterfield two hours ago because your father wouldn't wake up."

A coma? A dozen thoughts bounced off the inside of his skull, but one word resounded: Rose. What would happen to Rose?

Kennedy looked at his friend. "What if he dies?"

"Sit down, Kennedy."

"What?" Kennedy couldn't focus on his friend's words.

"Sit." John grasped his arm, urged him over to the chair near the window and pushed him onto the seat. John sat on the divan to his right.

"Think, Kennedy. Your sister is safe, at least for now. She has only been away from home for nine days. The situation cannot have degraded in so short a time."

Kennedy nodded. He was right. But how quickly could things degrade now that the earl couldn't send instructions for her safekeeping? He prayed Ranald had luck in finding her in France.

As if reading his mind, John said, "Your father is not a complete fool. He knew you would kill him if anything happened to her. He will have made provisions. She is safe for, at least, some time."

Kennedy nodded. He was right. He had to be right.

"There is more," John said. "I didn't want to say anything until I was certain, but there is no time now to confirm. I suspect that the person your father was using to keep in contact with your sister is a servant within his household."

"What do you mean?"

"As you know, I have had the house watched at all times. Only the usual activity has taken place: food deliveries, supplies, the comings and goings of servants. I doubt any of the deliverymen are anything but what they appear to be. Therefore, it is easy to strike them off the list of potential contacts. That leaves only the servants. I have jested before about how servants know everything, but it is the truth. Someone in your father's household knows something about your sister's whereabouts. My guess is that servant is a man."

Kennedy grunted. "Of that, you can be assured. My father believes women to be weak in all things."

John chuckled. "In that he is very mistaken."

Kennedy nodded. "Have you any idea who the man might be?"

"Your father employs twenty-nine servants. Half of those are women. Half of the men are likely not intelligent enough or reliable enough to be trusted with the passage of information. I have a list of the remaining seven men. I would like you to take a look at the names." He reached inside his pocket and pulled out a folded paper, then handed it to Kennedy.

Kennedy took it and opened it. He scanned the list. "I know three of these men. David Henderson has been my father's stable master for twenty years. He is a possibility. Jason is his valet. He is loyal to my father; however, he would not be my first choice."

"Why?" John asked.

Kennedy shrugged. "My father believes in a strong separation between nobility and servants. To confide in Jason would be to elevate his station as valet."

John nodded. "What about the others?"

"The last name on the list." Kennedy pointed out the name Henry McKinley. "He has worked for my father for two years. In truth, I was surprised my father kept him on. He does not take orders well."

"Interesting," John murmured. "What about the third name on the list, Milton Hayes? He has worked for your father for only two months as a groomsman."

Kennedy shrugged. "I know nothing of him. Are any of these other men new on his staff?"

John nodded. "Aye, the fourth name on the list, Dawson. He has worked as a groomsman for two weeks."

Kennedy leaned back in his chair. "I do not know him. As he is new to my father's staff, perhaps my father hired him specifically to help keep track of Rose." Kennedy looked up at John. "What about his man of affairs, or his solicitor, Mr. Spector?"

"One of them would be an obvious choice," John said. "And your father might fear that you would approach them and try to beat the information out of them."

Kennedy thinned his lips. "He is right."

"However, they could have information without realizing it," John said. "There has to be bills relating to your sister's living expenses."

Kennedy had considered that. "Aye." His heart began to thud. "With my father in a coma, I can demand to see all his financial records."

John nodded. "My thoughts exactly. Ye may also question his servants without fear of repercussions."

CHAPTER NINE

BY THAT EVENING, KENNEDY had taken possession of all the records he could locate in Mr. Spector's office, as well as the records kept by Mr. Cummins, his father's man of affairs. Mr. Spector had refused to cooperate, but John held a pistol to his head while Kennedy confiscated everything he could find. Mr. Cummins was more cooperative, and handed over two ledgers and a box of receipts.

Kennedy didn't return home, but went to John's office, for he knew that Jacqueline would be waiting for him at home. He was confident that Anne could deal with her. He would make it up to his wife tomorrow. For now, he had to find Rose.

The afternoon turned into evening as he and John poured over files, ledgers and receipts.

"Kennedy."

Kennedy looked up from the ledger he was reading.

"I have never been inside Chesterfield, but it is large," John said.

Kennedy nodded. "Mammoth, in fact."

"Could someone be locked in a room there without the servants knowing?"

Kennedy started. "What are you saying?

John handed him a receipt. Kennedy read the receipt. A lock had been installed on a fourth floor suite in Chesterfield's west wing. Kennedy stared for a long moment before accepting what his eyes told him.

He looked at John. "It's too simple."

"That's the beauty," John said.

"She never left Chesterfield? It can't be."

"Why?"

Kennedy shook his head, unable to focus. "I could find her too easily. The west wing isn't in use. For the most part, it's reserved for guests. My mother spent a year there when she and my father were estranged."

"Then it wouldn't be difficult to lock someone in a room there without the rest of the household knowing," John said.

Kennedy shook his head. "Rose's screams would be heard. My father might trust one or two servants, but, as you said, servants see everything. They would notice."

"Would they notice someone who lived there if that someone didn't mingle with the rest of the household?" John asked.

Kennedy started to answer, then stopped. There were two entrances on that side of the house. Perhaps it could be done if someone were careful. Still… "Once Rose realized she was being held prisoner, she would scream for help," he said.

John's expression softened. "Not if she were incapacitated."

An image flashed of his sweet, dark-haired sister lying in bed, dosed with laudanum. Shock reverberated through him. He'd feared that if he couldn't comply with his father's demands that his father would make good on the threat to marry her to Granbury. He feared the earl would die and Rose would be stranded somewhere in a foreign land with no resources to reach home safely. He had hated not knowing where she was, being uncertain of her future for even a day. But he had believed that, for the moment, she was safe. Had he been wrong?

"I believed everything he said," Kennedy whispered.

"Why wouldn't you?" John said. "This is more fiendish than sending her away."

Kennedy surged to his feet. "I'm going to Chesterfield."

John stood. "Let's be off."

Kennedy shook his head. "This is not your fight, John."

John clapped him on the back. "I owe you for saving my life in Glasgow." He grinned. "Ye know how much I hate being in debt."

* * *

For an hour, Anne sat on the divan in Kennedy's study trying to read before she began to wonder if she was being foolish for waiting. After their encounter in the conservatory yesterday afternoon, he had appeared in her bedchambers later that night and made love to her a second time. But she'd woken to find him gone. After a day shopping with Louisa and her mother, she returned home to find that Kennedy had come and gone. That had been three hours ago. Her mother and Louisa were leaving tomorrow, and Louisa had begged for one last night in town. Mama, had taken her to the opera.

Anne had hoped for time alone with Kennedy, again. Her cheeks warmed at the thought. Would he think her loose now? Was a wife supposed to enjoy her husband so much? He certainly seemed to enjoy his time with her. Was this what she had to look forward to for the rest of her life? "

What had his father said? "*It hadn't occurred to me you might be beautiful, but the fact that you are will hold Kennedy's interest for a while.*" If his father spoke the truth, how long before Kennedy tired of her? What would she do when he took other lovers? I thought struck. Did he have a mistress? Her heart sank. Of course, he did. A man like him always had a mistress.

She was a fool. He bore no particular affection for her. He only married because his father commanded that he sire an heir as quickly as possible. Perhaps he was enjoying himself in the process. Perhaps once their son was born, he would lose interest in her altogether.

He wasn't home because he had no interest in seeing her, and here she was waiting for him in his study. Thank God, he hadn't come home and found her waiting. Not only would she feel like a fool, she would look like

412

a fool. She closed her book and rose. A knock sounded on the door, then the door opened and the butler entered.

"Forgive me, my lady, but there is a boy here who insists upon seeing his lordship."

"Kennedy isn't here," she said.

"I am aware he is no' at home," Mr. Bingham said. "But the boy insists that he will not leave until he has seen Lord Buchanan."

"What does he want with the viscount?" she asked.

Mr. Bingham shook his head. "He refuses to say. "

"Perhaps he will tell me. Show him in, please."

He bowed and left. Anne sat back down on the divan and, a moment later, Mr. Bingham returned with a tall lad of about fourteen years of age, dressed in britches and a rough woolen coat. He reminded her of a stable hand.

Anne remain seated as the boy approached. "I am Lady Anne," she said. "What is this message you have for my husband?"

The boy stopped near the table in front of the divan. "It's from his sister," he said.

"His sister?" Anne snapped her gaze onto the butler, who was closing the door. "Mr. Bingham, wait, please."

He paused. "Yes, ma'am?"

"Does his lordship have a sister?"

"Aye, my lady. Lady Rose. She lives with the earl."

Why hadn't Kennedy mentioned her? Why hadn't she attended their wedding? Why hadn't they met her at the ball? She hesitated. She needed to hear what the boy had to say, but she felt completely lost.

"Mr. Bingham, will you wait outside the door, please?"

"Of course, my lady." He stepped into the hallway, pulling the door closed behind him.

Anne returned her attention to the boy. "What is your name?"

"Matthew, my lady."

She smiled. "Matthew, what is the message?"

The boy stubbornly shook his head. "Lady Rose specifically instructed me to tell no one but her brother."

Anne pinned him with a hard stare. "I assume the message is important or you wouldn't be here refusing to leave."

"Aye, ma'am, very important.

"Too important to delay in delivering?" she pressed.

His brows knit in uncertainty. "It's devilish important—begging your pardon, my lady."

"Never mind that," she said. "I'm sure Lady Rose thought his lordship would be home. But he isn't, and we can't say when he will return. If it's important, perhaps ye had better tell me. I am his wife, so there is little difference between telling him and telling me." Normally, she wasn't nosy, but intense curiosity—and more than a little frustration—made her want to hear the message.

The young man considered. "I suppose ye might be right. Lady Rose sounded very desperate." His expression grew serious. "But if I tell you, I must still tell his lordship." He stood straighter. "I promised, and a gentleman never breaks his word to a lady."

Anne smiled. "Of course, you are absolutely correct. Please tell me the message, then I will have Mr. Bingham take you to the kitchen where Mrs. Hampshire will fix you tea and something to eat. You may wait until his lordship arrives, then repeat to him the message, as well."

His eyes brightened. "I am hungry, ma'am."

"Then you shall have a fine dinner. Will that do?"

He gave a concise nod. "Yes, ma'am. The young lady asked me to tell his lordship that she is being held prisoner in Chesterfield Hall."

Anne blinked. "Being held prisoner? Surely, there must be some mistake?"

He shook his head. "I said the same thing. How can anyone be a prisoner in their own home? I didn't want to call a lady a liar, but I did accuse her of making fun of me. Then she showed me bruises on her cheek and arm. She is telling the truth. I'm sure if it."

"She is being beat?" Anne asked. It was simply too fantastical.

"Aye, so you can see how I would have to believe her."

Anne nodded. "That is serious proof." But could she believe him?

"Lady Rose was very specific," he went on. "She said his lordship was to come to her by way of the west entrance, and she begged him to hurry."

"If she's being held captive, how is it you came to speak with her?"

"My father has the best milk and butter in all of Edinburgh. The earl buys our butter and milk. I was making the delivery when I passed by the window and she called to me. I must tell you the truth, though. Lady Rose told me that I must be honest. She promised that I would not get into trouble."

"If Lady Rose promised you would not get into trouble, then you shall not get into trouble." Anne studied him. "Did she promise you money for delivering the message?"

His chin lifted. "She did, but a gentleman never takes money for helping a lady in distress."

"You are right again," Anne murmured. "What is this truth you must tell me?"

"Normally, I go around the side to the servants' entrances on the east. But that's a longer walk, and I was in a hurry. So I climbed the wall and cut through on that side of the estate."

"I have seen that wall," Anne said. "It's very high."

He gave her a disparaging look. "I can easily climb it. It would be difficult if I was delivering milk because milk spills. But this time I was only delivering butter, and butter doesn't spill. It was very fortunate I took that route, according to Lady Rose, for she said no one ever came across the estate on that side."

"Did Lady Rose say why she was being held captive?"

He shook his head. "Eight days maybe. She wasn't certain."

Since last Saturday or Sunday, Anne thought. One or two days before she received the summons from the earl. That was odd.

"She said the lady who watches her is evil," Matthew said.

"Evil?" Anne repeated. "Is it she who beats Lady Rose?"

"I don't know. She did say the woman gave her laudanum to keep her quiet, but Lady Rose promised not to scream, so she didn't give her as much."

The story was too preposterous. Oh, how she wished Kennedy were here, or even her mother. "When his lordship returns home, you can repeat the story for him," Anne said.

Matthew nodded. "I hope he returns soon. Lady Rose overheard the evil woman speaking with the man who brings them their food. He said that the earl was very ill and they thought he might die soon."

That Anne knew to be true. The earl didn't look at all well.

"He has fallen into a coma," the boy said.

"A coma?" she blurted. She had heard no such thing. Surely, Kennedy would tell her if that were true. Might that be why he'd been gone all afternoon?

"I did not know anything else," he said. "Except Lady Rose is very afraid they will send her away now that the earl is dying."

"Send her away where?"

"She didn't say, she only said that she must be away for nine months or more. They said something about his lordship having a child."

Anne stared. The boy would have absolutely no reason to make up something like that.

CHAPTER TEN

ANNE HAD MR. BINGHAM take Matthew to the kitchen for a good dinner, where he would wait until Kennedy returned home. A messenger was sent to the boy's home that explained where he was—Anne swore Matthew to secrecy in regards to 'the lady's message' as he now referred to his mission. Then she asked Mr. Bingham about Lady Rose and learned that Kennedy's sister was fifteen years old, and she and Kennedy were very close. Though Mr. Bingham stated that it wasn't his place to comment, he did admit that he was surprised that Lady Rose hadn't joined them for the wedding and the bridal feast that followed, or that she hadn't been to visit in over a week. He didn't know where Kennedy had gone, and Kennedy hadn't left word when he might return. It was eight twenty, and her mother would not return for another two hours, at least.

She waited another hour, but when Kennedy didn't arrive home, she spoke once again with Matthew and learned which window he had seen Lady Rose in. Then she ordered the carriage brought around, and changed into a plain dress and cloak. As she clasped the footman's hand in preparation to enter the carriage, someone called her name. She paused and looked back to find Matthew bounding down the stairs toward her.

He reached the carriage and said between breaths, "You are going to rescue her, aren't ye, my lady?"

"I am going to see what I can learn about the situation," she said in a quiet voice.

The boy cast the footman a glance, then said, "I will come with you."

"Nae," she said. "Someone must wait here to speak with my husband when he returns. That is your job, Matthew."

He shook his head stubbornly. "That is a baby's job. I am a man. Ye can leave word with Mr. Bingham. But I am going with you, my lady. It is not right that you should go without a man to protect you."

Heaven save her from the men who wanted to protect her. "You will stay here, Matthew."

But before she could say more, he shrugged. "I can get there on my own, just as I came here."

"How did you come here?" she asked.

"I have a horse. I took her to your stables. But I can have her saddled in two minutes. A horse is much faster than a carriage, and I know a shortcut."

Anne sighed. "Then I suppose you will come with me. However, you will do exactly as I say."

He shrugged. The footman helped her into the carriage, then Matthew leapt inside and settled on the seat opposite her.

When the carriage was two blocks from the earl's estate, she had the driver stop. Of course, despite her commands, Matthew insisted on coming. James, also, refused to allow her to walk alone in the dark, and they left the footman with the carriage while they set out.

They reached the east wall that Matthew had climbed over to cut across Chesterfield's lawn. When they turned the street corner, Anne said, "James, I know this is an odd request, but I'm asking that you wait outside the gate while I continue on. I'll be safe enough once we're on the earl's estate."

He nodded, but she knew he wondered what she was up to. At least, with Matthew present, James wouldn't think she was meeting another gentleman.

They reached the wrought iron gate, which stood open. James remained at the entrance. Anne pulled her cloak tighter about her as she and

Matthew kept walking. A dim light shown in a ground floor window at the front of the house, which Anne guessed to be a parlor. Another light flickered in a third-floor window. That, she estimated to be the earl's bed chambers. Thankfully, the curtains were drawn. More soft line shone in two windows on the top floor where the servants would be.

They hurried around the drive on the right side of the house, then slowed. This side of the house was completely dark, except for a meager light that flickered against closed drapes in a fourth story window.

"That's the window," James whispered.

Anne's heart began to pound. Was his story really true? On the carriage ride, she'd considered half a dozen explanations for his story, not the least of which, that he knew just enough of current events to have fabricated the tale. She had to admit, his story contained some strange coincidences. Rose claimed to have been kidnapped just about the time she met Kennedy. But what could her meeting and marriage to Kennedy have to do with his sister? And how could someone claim to be kidnapped while still living in their home? It wouldn't really be called kidnapping. But a woman could be held prisoner in her own home.

Now that they were here, she had no idea how she would go about proving the truth, one way or the other. She scanned the wall for a door. There would be some sort of entrance on the side of the house. Of course, that door would be locked. She spotted a door farther down the side of the building, and hurried forward. As expected, it was locked.

It was only ten-thirty. Despite the light in the earl's room, he would likely be asleep. Jacqueline, too, was probably abed. Most of the servants would take advantage of the quiet and would retire to their rooms or go to bed, for they would have to rise early to complete their morning duties. Still, a few servants might be in the kitchen working or socializing.

When they turned the corner of the building she saw another door, this one smaller than the last. The other door they'd seen, while a side entrance, was clearly for visitors. This door, however, was a rear servants' entrance. She tried the knob and was surprised when it turned. Slowly, she inched the door open. Enough moonlight illuminated the room for her to recognize some sort of pantry. On a shelf to the left, sat several tapers and a tinder box. This entrance was in use.

Anne entered and lit a candle, then faced Matthew and whispered, "Remain here."

"I cannae let you go alone, my lady. I am responsible for you."

"Do you disobey your mother like this?" she asked in frustration.

"I never knew my mother," he said. "She died when I was little. It's just me and my father."

That explained much. She should have had the footman carry Matthew back to the house and tie him to a chair, but she hadn't thought of it. Anne turned and he followed as she crept forward and entered a modest kitchen. This section of the mansion clearly was intended for someone who might want to live away from the main part of the house. She located service stairs immediately to the right and they climbed to the fourth floor. Anne halted at sight of the tiny sliver of light shining into the pitch black hallway from beneath a door up ahead.

Her heart began to pound. What should she do? If Lady Rose was in the room—and if her warden was with her—how would she help the girl? Should she return home and wait for Kennedy? Should she rouse someone in the house, the earl or his wife?

She looked at Matthew, who nodded toward the light. Anne nodded acknowledgement and they crept to the door. She knocked lightly. Silence followed. With a deep breath, she grasped the knob and slowly twisted it. To her surprise, the knob turned. Why would they leave the door unlocked if they were keeping the girl prisoner? If Rose had lied—or if Matthew had lied—then she was making a huge mistake by being here.

Her hand shook, but she forced calm and eased the door open. First, she caught sight of a table and two chairs that sat before a hearth wherein a low fire burned. A tea pot and two cups sat on the table, along with a sugar bowl and cream. No one cried out, and Anne stepped into the room. To the left, sat a fourposter bed. A young woman lay in the bed, the blankets pulled up beneath her arms.

"Excuse me," Anne called, but the girl didn't reply.

Anne whispered to Matthew, "This is a lady's room. You remain here while I wake her."

Thankfully, he nodded agreement this time. She crossed to the bed and drew a sharp breath at sight of the bruise on the girl's cheek. Matthew hadn't lied. Anne set her taper on the nightstand, then grasped the girl's shoulder and gently shook her.

The girl's eyes fluttered open and her brow knit. "Rebecca?" The word was slurred, as if she had ingested laudanum.

Anger shot through Anne. Here was the reason they hadn't locked the door. The girl couldn't stand, much less escape.

"I am Kennedy's wife," Anne said.

Her frown deepened. "Kennedy? Is he here?" A tear slid down the side of her face.

Anne's heart constricted. "Can you tell me what has happened?"

Rose squeezed her eyes closed and more tears fell.

"Are you being held against your will?"

Her eyes shot open. "Rebecca will return and she will be angry."

"Shh, I am here," Anne soothed. "You have nothing to fear." Anne wasn't at all certain that was true.

Rose began to whimper.

"Matthew," Anne called, "bring me a cup of that tea on the table."

While he did as she ordered, Anne pulled the covers back, swung Rose's legs off the side of the bed and pulled her into a sitting position. Matthew appeared with the tea.

"I'll hold her upright while you get her to drink the tea," Anne said.

He complied, and they forced half the tea down her throat before Rose twisted her head aside.

"Come on, love," Anne coaxed, "drink more."

They got another couple of good swallows into her with the rest drib-bling down her chin. Anne had no idea how much laudanum this Rebecca had given her, but she gave thanks that wasn't enough for the girl to be unconscious. She had seen people given enough laudanum that they didn't wake for twelve hours.

Anne grasped Rose's chin, forcing the girl to look at her. "Can you walk?"

Her brow knit as if she were trying to understand Anne's words.

"Do you want to leave this place?" Anne asked.

Understanding lit her clouded eyes and she nodded.

"Good." Anne whipped off her cloak and swung it around Rose's shoulders, then fastened the clasp. "Come on, let's see if you can stand."

Anne pulled her to her feet. Rose swayed. Anne feared she would top-ple back onto the bed. Matthew grasped her arm and steadied her. The lad had been more right than Anne realized. She needed his help—Rose need-ed him. She was thankful when he slipped an arm around Rose's waist and took most of her weight. Anne picked up the taper and they walked with her across the room and out into the hall. How would they get her down the stairs without all of them falling and breaking their necks?

Anne came to an abrupt halt at the sound of approaching footfalls behind them. She twisted and looked over her shoulder. Light flickered around the bend up ahead and a woman rounded the corner in the next instant. She took three steps before seeing them, then shrieked and tossed her candle aside as she raced toward them.

Anne faced forward. They were too far from the stairs to have any chance of outrunning her. "Matthew, can you get Rose safely down the stairs?"

"Aye, my lady. I am very strong."

Anne prayed he was. "Get her down the stairs and out to James—quick.

"I cannot leave you, my lady," he said.

Anne released Rose and Matthew hugged her closer. "You must save the lady," she hissed. "I can take care of myself. She is just a woman." Anne whirled.

Their attacker might be just a woman, but she was a woman racing toward them as if the devil nipped at her heels—a women who stood a head taller than her.

Candle in hand, Anne walked quickly toward her. An instant later, she was within ten feet of the woman and stopped in the middle of the hallway. "Halt, madam. I am Viscountess Buchanan, the Earl of Buchanan's daughter-in-law."

The woman stopped so quickly she stumbled forward two paces before catching herself.

"What are you doing with my husband's sister?" Anne demanded.

The woman's eyes flicked past her and came back her face. "You are not supposed to be here." She started forward as if to hurry past Anne's left side, but Anne slid into her path.

The woman halted. "Out of my way," she growled.

"My husband will not be pleased that you mistreated his sister, Rebecca," Anne said.

Fear flickered in her eyes, then was followed by fury. Anne noted the subtle change in her stance and realized the woman was about to charge. Rebecca lunged. Anne whipped aside and stuck out her foot as she hurtled past. Rebecca stumbled, hands out, and crashed into the wall. She dropped to the carpet and lay motionless.

Anne retreated two paces, heart pounding, knees so weak she feared they would give out. Bootfalls echoed from the direction Rebecca had come. Anne whirled and raced down the hallway in the opposite direction. She reached the stairs and was forced to slow in the pitch darkness. A hand on each wall of the narrow staircase, she forced herself to slow, and prayed her legs wouldn't give out.

At the bottom, she gave thanks that Matthew and Rose were nowhere to be seen, then hurried through the kitchen pantry and out into the cool night. She pumped her legs faster and reached the front of the house in seconds. She nearly cried, at sight of Matthew and Rose passing through the wrought-iron gate where James stood.

A moment later, Anne reached the wrought-iron gate then turned and nearly collided with Matthew. "Dear Lord," she burst out. "What are you doing here?"

"James is assisting Lady Rose," Matthew said. "I couldnae leave you there alone."

She grabbed his arm and pulled him into a run.

A shout went up somewhere near the house. They sprinted around the corner. Anne thought her lungs would burst, but she kept going. They reached the carriage. She didn't wait for help, but grasped the door and jumped inside and onto the seat beside Rose.

"Hurry, James, we must go *now*."

Matthew leapt inside, pulling the door closed behind him.

Anne pulled Rose close as the carriage tilted left, then jolted into motion hard enough for to have to grab onto the handle. Rose cried into Anne's bodice and Anne willed herself not to burst into tears herself.

CHAPTER ELEVEN

KENNEDY GUIDED HIS HORSE up the drive to Chesterfield, with John riding alongside. They continued around the east side of the house to the rear, and Kennedy brought the animal to a halt at sight of the open servants' entrance. He leapt from the saddle and raced inside. He knew this part of the house like the back of his hand. When his mother had been alive, they often entertained guests here. After her death, Kennedy spent many a day in the deserted rooms.

Kennedy spotted the tapers and tinderbox on the pantry shelf, and cursed.

A shadow filled the doorway. "Someone is using this entrance," John said.

Kennedy's gut clenched. *Rose is here.*

He forced back the compulsion to race up the darkened stairs. He was no longer fifteen. The narrow staircase was pitch black at night and he was sure to break his fool neck.

He lit a candle, and said to John, "Come on," then hurried from the pantry into the kitchen and took the stairs to the right.

They reached the fourth floor. Light spilled from an open door halfway down the hallway. He blew out the candle, tossed it aside, and raced toward the open door. He and John burst inside the room to find a man sitting on the mattress beside a woman.

"*Rose*," Kennedy growled, and took two steps toward the man before strong fingers seized his arm and yanked him back.

"That is not Rose," John said.

For an instant, Kennedy didn't understand, then he whipped his head around and looked at the couple. The man stood, staring at them. The woman was not Rose.

Not Rose. Where was his sister?

Kennedy yanked free of John and said to the man, "Where is my sister?"

He shook his head. "I dinnae know. I returned to find Rebecca unconscious in the hallway."

Kennedy rounded the bed, then took the woman by the shoulders. Her head lolled to the side. He shook her.

"Leave her be!" the man shouted.

Kennedy yanked his gaze onto the man and he backed up two steps. Kennedy looked back at the woman and she shook her again.

John appeared at his side. "Here, maybe this will help." He tossed water from a pitcher onto the woman's face.

She sputtered and shook her head. Her eyes snapped open. Her gaze met Kennedy's and her eyes widened.

"Where is my sister?" he demanded.

She looked at the man.

Kennedy gave her a hard shake. "Where is Lady Rose?"

"A woman took her."

Panic muddled his thoughts. "A woman? What woman? Where did she take her?"

"She-she said she was Lady Buchanan."

"Lady Buchanan?" he repeated. "Jacqueline?"

"N-nae," the woman stuttered. "Viscountess Buchanan, Lady Rose's sister-in-law."

"Anne?" Had he heard correctly? "My wife was here?"

The woman's eyes widened. "You are Viscount Buchanan?" She shrank away from him.

He released her and straightened. "You are certain it was Viscountess Buchanan who was here?"

She nodded vigorously. "She had a lad with her. She tripped me and I hit the wall." The woman turned her head to the side and showed him the bruise forming on her forehead.

Kennedy could hardly credit it. He looked at John. "What the bloody hell was my wife doing here?"

John shook his head. "I can't imagine."

Kennedy looked at the man. "Who are you?"

"Angus Dunning. I bring food to Rebecca while she is tending to the young lady."

"What you mean 'tending to the young lady'?"

"Her father didn't want to put her into an insane asylum," Rebecca said. "So, he paid me to care for her here. He said it was better than the insane asylum," she quickly added. "He is very kind."

"Kind?" Kennedy snarled. "We shall see if that defense holds up in court." He looked at John. "I must return home. Will you keep them here until I return?"

"Here, now," Angus said. "There's no call to treat us like criminals. We were paid to take care of the young lady for her father. Rebecca and I can leave anytime we like."

John flashed white teeth. "You are free to try, lad."

Kennedy glimpsed the man's wide eyes an instant before he whirled and strode from the room.

Kennedy reached home half an hour later and leapt off his horse almost before the beast stopped. He bounded up the steps and banged the knocker until the door was yanked open.

"Whoever you are—" Bingham broke off. "I beg your pardon, my lord. I didn't realize—"

Kennedy pushed past him. "Where is my wife?"

"In the Burgundy guest chamber, sir, with Lady Rose."

"My sister is here?" he said in a harsh whisper.

Bingham nodded. "Aye," he replied, but Kennedy was already racing up the stairs.

He burst into the Burgundy guest chambers to find Anne standing with her mother and sister while the doctor sat on the bed, blocking view of his patient.

Kennedy took a step forward. "Rose?"

The doctor stood, and Rose cried, "Kennedy!"

Kennedy drew a sharp breath. His sister sat propped up in bed, her left cheek, yellowed with a bruise. He strode across the room to the bed, fell to his knees and pulled her to him. She threw her arms around his neck and he buried his face in her neck and wept.

* * *

Anne felt Kennedy's eyes on her for the dozenth time as she and Matthew related their tale, but she kept her gaze on her hands clasped in her lap. Louisa sat between her and her mother on the divan in the drawing room, for Louisa refused to be sent to bed. Kennedy sat in the chair to the left, as Matthew continued his story.

"Her ladyship refused to leave with Lady Rose and I," Matthew said, and Anne winced.

"What did she do?" her husband asked.

"She stayed to fight the evil woman while Lady Rose and I escaped."

From the corner of her eye, she saw Kennedy stare at her again.

"Was that when you tripped her?" Kennedy asked.

Anne looked sharply at him. "How do you know that?"

"I had a talk with Rebecca."

"Oh," she said, and fell silent again.

"I got Lady Rose outside to James," Matthew went on. "Then her ladyship came, and we were able to escape." Matthew stood straighter, as if waiting for further instructions.

Kennedy rose and extended his hand to the lad. "I owe you more than I can ever repay."

The boy looked up at him in surprise then clasped Kennedy's hand and they shook.

"Name any price," Kennedy said, "and it is yours."

Anne hid a smile when Matthew said, "A gentleman never takes money for rescuing a lady."

Kennedy stared, as if uncertain what to say, then nodded. "When Rose is better, we would consider it an honor if you would join us for dinner. She will want to thank you personally."

Startlement flashed across the boy's face, then he said in a solemn voice, "It would be my honor."

A knock came to the door and Mr. Bingham entered." A message has arrived for you, my lord." He crossed to Kennedy and handed him a note, then waited.

Kennedy scanned the note, which was from John, stating that the constable Kennedy had sent for had arrived at Chesterfield. He had Rebecca and Angus in custody, and Kennedy was to appear in the morning to make formal charges.

Kennedy looked at Bingham. "Bingham, please send a note to John with my thanks, and tell him I will visit him tomorrow."

Bingham bowed, then left.

"Matthew," Kennedy said, "my carriage will take you home."

"There is no need for that. I have a horse."

Kennedy shook his head. "Indulge me in this, lad. I would rest easier if my coach takes you. I will direct the driver to pick you up tomorrow so that you may retrieve your horse in daylight hours."

"If that is what you wish, my lord."

"You didn't obey me so easily," Anne said under her breath.

The boy looked at her in surprise. "Of course not, my lady. What you asked me to do was impossible."

"Ahh," she intoned. "I forget myself. You were supposed to protect me...and Lady Rose." She smiled. "I don't know what I would've done without you." It wasn't a lie. "Thank you."

He bowed, and Kennedy directed him to tell Mr. Bingham to have a carriage brought around. Matthew left, then her mother stood and said, "Come along, Louisa. It's late."

"But, Mama."

"No arguments," their mother cut in. "Come along." She looked at Kennedy. "We are very happy your sister is home, Kennedy."

He nodded, and said in a hoarse voice, "Thank you, my lady."

She smiled gently and said, "Perhaps you should call me, Christina." Then she and Louisa left Anne alone with her husband.

Anne didn't know why, but she was suddenly terrified.

Kennedy stared at her. "What sort of woman are you?"

She looked at him. "I don't understand."

"You hardly know me. You don't know Rose, at all. Yet you put yourself in jeopardy to save her."

Anne shrugged. "When I saw her, the situation she was in, it was clear she was being held against her will. I couldn't leave her there."

"You could've come to me. You could have not gone at all and let Matthew tell me his story when I returned home."

"Matthew said Lady Rose feared that they were going to take her away. In truth, my lord, I couldn't credit that the story was true. But there were enough truths that I couldn't ignore the possibility that the tale might be true." She hesitated, and said, "Why did your father have her locked up?"

His mouth thinned. "Are you sure you want to know the answer? You won't like it."

"Of course, I won't like it. There is nothing that justifies locking someone up, much less one's own child." Her blood boiled at the memory of finding the girl half out of her mind with the laudanum, and clearly physically abused.

"That isn't what I mean," Kennedy said. "The reason concerns you— our marriage."

She frowned, then comprehension dawned. "You mean your father used her to force you to marry me? How— I-I don't understand."

"My father told me that he had Rose taken away. I believed he had taken her from Scotland. Sent her to France, perhaps. Had I the slightest idea she was still in Edinburgh, in her own home—" His hands worked into fists at his sides.

Anne could well understand his anger and panic. She couldn't imagine anything happening to Louisa.

"He demanded I marry immediately and produce an heir," Kennedy said.

Anne nodded. He'd been right. She didn't want to know. She'd known the earl had instigated the marriage. Yet, somehow, this knowledge tainted their union in a way she couldn't describe.

She looked at her hands, still clasped in her lap. "I am so sorry." Tears pressed at the backs of her eyes. "Of course, we cannot remain married."

"What?" he said sharply.

She snapped her head up.

He crossed to her and stopped beside the divan. "We've been married three days. I need time to learn how to be a husband. Surely, you will give me more time."

She looked at him in confusion. "We married because your father held your sister captive. I-I cannot imagine how you can even stand to look at me."

"Quite the contrary. I cannot bear the thought of not seeing your face every day for the rest of my life."

She blinked. "What? I don't understand. Our marriage—"

He grasped her arm and pulled her to her feet. "Is the best thing that ever happened to me. I am sorry, my dear, but I have no intention of letting you go."

Before she could reply, he kissed her until she couldn't think straight.

EPILOGUE

KENNEDY'S FATHER DIED THE following evening. Three days later, Kennedy gave Jacqueline his townhouse and moved his new family into Chesterfield Hall. It would take a month for all their belongings to be brought over. But he cared not. He had grown up in this house. His mother had died in this house. His sister had been imprisoned and then rescued in this house. Lastly, he would never forget that even his father had died in this house. This was where they belonged.

The dowager viscountess returned to Dover Hall, and left Louisa with them. Two months had passed. In another week, they would go to Dover Hall for the summer. By the time they returned home, Anne would be entering her sixth month of pregnancy and they would settle in until the birth of their child.

Light footfalls sounded outside his study, then the door burst open and Louisa and Rose rushed in.

Rose waved a note card. "We have been invited to a lawn party this afternoon. Please say we may go."

"It's up to Anne," he said.

"Where is she?" Louisa asked.

Kennedy stood. He would guess, in the conservatory. "I will find her."

He left the girls and went to the conservatory. This conservatory was twice the size of the one in his townhouse. He entered and ambled to the rear of the room where, as expected, he found his wife lying on the chaise that he had put there in front of the hearth, where only embers burned. A book lay open across her stomach, which had yet to show signs of the life growing inside of her. But she was napping. Something she did a little more often now than she used to—at least, according to her.

He put another log on the fire, then stood and turned to find her staring at him.

"This is my favorite room in the house," she said.

He lifted a brow. "Your favorite room?"

She shrugged. "Perhaps my second favorite."

He went to the chaise and sat beside her. "Perhaps you would like to spend a little time in your favorite room with me."

She released a contented sigh. "Why move when this is such a comfortable chaise?"

He smoothed back a lock that had escaped her chignon. "Our sisters want to attend a lawn party this afternoon."

She scooted over and patted the empty place beside her. He stretched out and pulled her against his chest.

She snuggled close and his heart constricted. "How is it I came to be so fortunate as to find you?" he asked.

"You're a very lucky person, I suppose," she murmured."

He supposed that was true. He closed his eyes and drew in a deep breath. "I imagine we should let the girls go to the party."

She nodded against his chest. "We shall never hear the end of it if we don't."

"Do we have to tell them now?"

Anne shifted and pulled his mouth down to hers. "Only if you really want to," she said against his lips.

The only thing he wanted to do was make love to his wife. "Have I told you that I love you?" he said.

She nibbled on his bottom lip. "Only three other times today."

He tightened his arms around her. "I am falling behind. I love you."

She bit a little harder and he suddenly wanted her badly.

"Good," she said. "Because I love you, too."

Be sure to look for the next Marriage Maker collection
The Marriage Maker Goes Undercover
The most dangerous weapons are those of the heart...

Lady Elana Gallaway, known as master spy The Raven, has made a career of navigating enemy territory and risking her life in situations and places no gentlewoman should know exist. She possesses all the social graces, and is adept at sweeping into glittering royal courts on the Continent, then vanishing without a trace after she's ferreted out the treacherous secrets that drew her there in the name of duty. She's equally accomplished in London and Edinburgh, or wherever the British King requires her service. But never has a mission struck so close to her heart—or proved so daunting—as finding love for four retired spies.

These operatives have helped her many times, once or twice, even saving her from certain death at risk to their own lives.

Now, they live solitary lives, lonely lives while surrounded by throngs. Luckily, Elana hasn't forgotten them. Her career has introduced her to more than enemies. Among her close friends is Sir Stirling James, the famous Inverness marriage maker. He's just the man she needs.

A Scoundrel in the Making
Tarah Scott

My Lady of Danger
Summer Hanford

Her Wicked Highland Spy
Erin Rye

The Marriage Obligation
Susana Ellis
www.scarsdalepublishing.com

www.ingramcontent.com/pod-product-compliance
Lightning Source LLC
Chambersburg PA
CBHW051539250626
47157CB00001B/114